BRON, DAUGHTER OF PROPHECY

The Story of Bron
Part I

Iris Lloyd

Pen Press Publishers Ltd

First published in Great Britain by
Pen Press Publishers Ltd
25, Eastern Place
Brighton
BN2 1GJ

ISBN 978-1-905621-99-6

Printed and bound in the UK

A catalogue record of this book is available from
the British Library

Cover design Jacqueline Abromeit

Born in Clapham, London, before the war, at the age of five Iris Lloyd moved out to a new estate in Queensbury, Middlesex, with her parents and her brother. They were caught at her grandmother's in Clapham on the first night of the Blitz, and soon were all evacuated by her father's employers to Chesham, Buckinghamshire, returning to Queensbury when she was 14 years old. Her sister was born during the post-war baby boom.

When 17, she joined a superb church youth club, and wrote eight annual pantomimes for them to perform (usually directing and choreographing as well, as she has been dancing since the age of three), then nine more scripts co-written with a friend for his drama group. Three have been published by Cambridge Publishing Services Ltd. and are performed regularly by amateur companies.

In the 1950's, Iris also wrote the script of a romantic musical set in 1730, which was performed by a church group. Recently, she entered two full-length plays for competitions at her local professional theatre, the Watermill, in Newbury.

Two years (1959-61) were enjoyed as secretary to the Editor of Children's Books at Macmillan's publishers in London, where she met author Ray Bethers, and later she line edited for him five of his short children's books.

In recent years, she wrote and performed, one Sunday morning on Radio Oxford/Berkshire, a dramatic monologue and (with a friend) a two-hander between Barabbas and the mother of the thief on the Cross. She has written sketches and plays for stage, church and parties. Two of her poems have been published in anthologies.

A correspondent for many years for the Newbury Weekly News, her local independent newspaper, she had several half-page and full-page articles on various topics published. And in her last parish, she was chief editor of the church magazine and of a prestigious village book which was produced for the millennium. Having moved to Hungerford, Berkshire, eighteen months ago, she has now taken on sole editorship of their monthly parish magazine.

Having been married to Denis, who for 27 years was self-employed in the construction industry, and widowed 19 years ago, Iris is the proud mother of two daughters and grandmother to three lively grandchildren.

For exercise, she still teaches tap dancing to adults.

ACKNOWLEDGEMENTS

Victor Pocock, who introduced me to the site at Beedon and who is always willing to give information, lend books and display artefacts, and who inspires many by his hard physical labour, dedication and passion for his 'dig'.

For advice and encouragement: Maureen Freely, ex-tutor of many writing courses for Oxford University Department for Continuing Education; many other tutors at Oxford; also at the Winchester Writers' Conference; and all the enthusiastic and greatly talented students I have enjoyed meeting on these courses and in various writing groups.

Doug Watts at Jacqui Bennett Writers' Bureau, for his editing skills, his unfailing encouragement and faith in the MSS so that I was able to take publishers' rejections in my stride.

Friends who have been eager to read the MSS and who have given so much encouragement and made sensible and pertinent comments and suggestions.

Finally, to Lindsay Allason-Jones for her book, *Women in Roman Britain* (ISBN 0-7141-1392-1), which was my constant companion during my research.

To all these – many thanks.

Iris Lloyd

DEDICATION

To dear, funny Jo – my friend, who was the first to hear the beginning
of this book, and kept me reading for three hours until she had
listened to all that had been written, but who left us before the
manuscript was completed.

CONTENTS

Roman Towns, Villages and Rivers mentioned in the story

Byden – Beedon, north of Newbury, Berkshire
Calleva Atrebatum – Silchester
Camulodunum – Colchester
Durnovaria – Dorchester
Eboracum – York
Lambburnan – Lambourn
Londinium – London
River Chenet – River Kennet
Spinis – Speen, Newbury
Stan stream – no longer flowing
Stanmere – Stanmore, Beedon, Berkshire
Venta Belgarum – Winchester
Verulamium – St. Albans

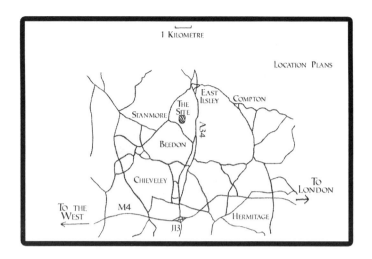

EAST ILSLEY

COMPTON

STANMORE

THE SITE

A34

BEEDON

CHIEVELEY

M4

J13

HERMITAGE

TO LONDON

TO THE WEST

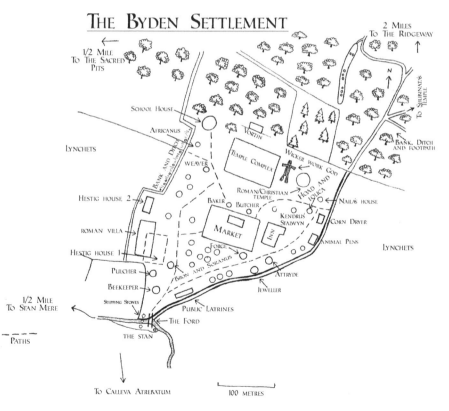

THE BYDEN SETTLEMENT

2 MILES TO THE RIDGEWAY

1/2 MILE TO THE SACRED PITS

SCHOOL HOUSE

AFRICANUS

LYNCHETS

BANK AND DITCH

VORTIN

TEMPLE COMPLEX

WICKER WORK GOD

WEAVER

N

TO SHURINATA'S TEMPLE

BANK, DITCH AND FOOTPATH

HESTIG HOUSE 2

BAKER

BUTCHER

ROMAN/CHRISTIAN TEMPLE

HOAD AND LOUCA

NAILA'S HOUSE

ROMAN VILLA

MARKET

KENDRUS STALWYN

INN

CORN DRYER

LYNCHETS

HESTIG HOUSE 1

FORGE

BRON AND SORANUS

ANIMAL PENS

PULCHER

ATTRYDE

BEEKEEPER

JEWELLER

1/2 MILE TO STAN MERE

STEPPING STONES

PUBLIC LATRINES

THE FORD

THE STAN

PATHS

TO CALLEVA ATREBATUM

100 METRES

Reminder List of Characters

Bron's Family

Bron	
Hestig	Bron's Father
Trifena	Bron's Mother
Hestigys	Bron's brother
Trifosa	Bron's sister
Aelia	Bron's baby sister
Bettina	Household slave
Skeel	Their dog

Temple

Vortin	High Priest
Iraina	High Priestess
Nobilianus	Their son
Sharma	Priest
Selvid	Priest
Jeetuna	Priestess
Veneta	Priestess
Brocchus	Eunuch

Reminder List of Characters (Cont'd)

Temple Children

Vitius	Priest-in-training
Sorin }	
Naila }	Bron's friends
Edreda }	

Villagers

Pulcher	Neighbour, a dwarf
Selena	Weaver's wife
Dagvald	Weaver
Campania	Selena's daughter-in-law
Soranus	Campania's son, Selena's grandson
Africanus	Schoolteacher, of African origins
Severus	Leader of village council
Stalwyn	Midwife and nurse
Kendrus	Doctor, husband of Stalwyn
Hoad	Shepherd
Louca	Hoad's wife
Septima	Prostitute at inn
Attryde	Blacksmith's wife/widow/ employer of Soranus

Reminder List of Characters (Cont'd)

Romans

Julius Gaius	Roman official
Lucilla	His wife
Flavia	Their daughter
Adrianus Maximus	Ex-governor of Eboracum
Aurelius Catus	Junior Roman officer

At Calleva Atrebatum

Asher	A Christian pilgrim
Chrystella	A woman of Christian faith

In the Wood

Umbella	Clairvoyant, herbalist, abortionist

Prologue

AD 385 – An April Evening

Alone in the deep gloom of her woodland hut, Umbella took breath then tilted back her head and gulped down the contents of the glass phial. She waited, licking the blue stain from her cracked lips.

As always, the evil-smelling liquid burnt fire into her tongue and toothless gums. Sitting hunched on the dirty mattress against the mud wall, she loosened the black woollen cloak that was wound round her scrawny old body and tattered clothing, disturbing the cockroaches, which scuttled off across the floor in all directions.

Then came sensuous pleasure as the liquid flowed down the back of her throat, as cold and slippery as silk. She hardly breathed, anticipating the familiar heaviness of limbs as she lay back on the mattress, one high note singing in her ears, her muscles gradually relaxing as she let her mind recede down the long, dark tunnel.

But tonight was different. Perhaps she had mixed too strong a concoction, perhaps drunk too much of it. Suddenly icy cold, she pulled the cloak round her again. Then she was sweating, the perspiration gathering in the wrinkles on her forehead or spilling over into her eyes. Her straggly, grey hair clung to her scalp and her bony hands began to rattle uncontrollably.

She dragged herself to her knees on the mattress, then to her feet on the beaten earth, and stood, her body bent and shaking.

"I'm not ready," she gasped, "not yet! I'm ill!"

But the spirit she had summoned was impatient, would not wait, and sent her crashing to the floor.

As she lay there, her ribs digging painfully into the earth, seeing nothing, she heard the familiar disembodied voice above her, but strident, raised in anger.

"*I* choose when you are ready, not *you*!"

She closed her eyes in submission.

"That's better." The voice was now as soft and silky as the liquid that had lubricated the back of her throat. "Listen, and listen well. I will show you what is, and what is to be."

Umbella listened long into the moonless night, appalled as she walked through the carnage wreaked in the Byden settlement, screaming in terror when engulfed in the flames. It took a full hour (or it might have been two or three) before she was able to speak again.

"Can one baby destroy a whole community?" she challenged.

"This baby can, by dredging up the evil in others."

"Will no one prevent it? What if I warned someone – High Priest, Vortin – anyone? They'll take notice of old Umbella. That whelp should not live!" There was no answer. "Then why show me these things?"

"We are in the realms of divining the future, you and I, not changing it. Is it not enough that those in fear pay more than you deserve for the foresight I give you?"

Now it was Umbella's turn to remain silent as she pondered her hidden hoard of treasure. With such golden radiance glittering nightly beneath her torch's flame, what need had she of sunlight?

"Exactly." The spirit, as always, had read her thoughts.

"But I will not live to see the destruction?" she asked, relief evident in her voice.

"You will not live to see it."

"And the manner of my death? You hid that vision in mist."

She lay very still, waiting for the answer.

At last the spirit spoke again.

"It is better that you do not know how or when. I have spared you that."

Umbella felt a cold tide from the floor creeping up through her body. It was the damp night air, she convinced herself, and not her terror.

"Will I die alone?"

"Far from it."

"So there will be someone to tell others of my passing?"

"The birds shall bear news to the settlement. Now no more questions! I have shown you all there is. I am leaving and it is time for you to sleep."

Umbella was not surprised to find she was lying on her mattress again. Except for the busy cockroaches, the hut was empty and silent and she knew the spirit had left her.

She would sleep well now but determined to wake early, as curiosity would impel her to take the several hours' walk to Byden wood to confront the mother of this abhorrent baby.

Her dreams were invaded by flocks of starlings winging their way up through the canopy, through branches and leaves that kept the sunlight out of her clearing.

In reality, only a solitary black bat circled the roof of her hut.

Section I

TRIFENA

CHAPTER I (1)

I'm going home! Happily, Trifena had been trying to keep pace with Hestig, her new husband, but finally had to give up and tugged, panting, at his sleeve.

"Sorry," he apologised, smiling down at her, slackening his pace. "I should have realised…"

He reached across and took one of the woollen bundles from her. All they possessed was carried in those bundles and the leather pouch slung round her waist.

Trifena smiled her thanks. About to step out again, she shivered suddenly.

"Cold?" Hestig asked, concern in his voice. Trifena shook her head. "What then?"

"I've the strangest feeling we're being watched."

Hestig looked around. They had been walking in the warm April sunshine for almost two hours since leaving the great Ridgeway to the north, and were now following a well-worn path beneath a canopy of spring foliage.

"Can't see anyone."

Trifena's eyes searched the trees and undergrowth.

"Neither can I, but there's somebody there."

"You don't usually get spooked. Perhaps it's your… Perhaps you need a rest?"

He was facing her, his back to the direction they were taking, so did not see the dark, shapeless apparition eerily materialising ahead of them. When Trifena gasped in fright, he swung round, one arm pulling her protectively towards himself. Both stood quite still, not at all sure whether it was spirit or human. They could not have passed whatever it was without separating and walking on each side of it – something neither was prepared to do.

They were aware of two ominous dark eyes peering out at them – the only part of a face they could see. The malodour of unwashed body and soiled clothes now offended their nostrils. It was obviously human.

Eventually, Hestig said uncertainly, "We would like to pass."

"Does old Umbella frighten you?" The voice was low, and crackled like pork rind on a spit.

"Of course not. Should we be frightened?"

"Maybe, maybe not."

The piercing eyes shifted to Trifena's face. "Pale skin, hazel hair, hazel eyes. Yes, you are Trifosa's daughter right enough!"

Trifena nodded warily, alarmed that the apparition knew so much about her.

"You were only a baby when your mother took you away."

"I was three," Trifena corrected her.

"And now you return to Byden to birth your own baby."

Trifena's free hand flew to her stomach, as if to protect the new life developing inside her from this unexpected threat. But she was comforted to reflect that here was little need for clairvoyance, as her seven-month pregnancy was obvious for all to see.

"May we pass now?" Hestig asked again, impatiently.

The old woman moved on to the path running off to their left, leaving the way clear. However, as the young couple started forward, she stretched a bony finger towards Trifena, who shivered again, then halted, transfixed, staring at the dirty fingernail pointed in her direction.

The old voice spoke again from the depths of the rags, clearing and gaining strength. "Folk will curse the day you returned to Byden," she declared, "bearing your mongrel child and unleashing sword, fire and total destruction!"

"What utter nonsense!" Hestig declared. "You're frightening my wife. Let us pass, old woman!"

"I'm not stopping you!" The finger was withdrawn and hidden again in the folds of black cloth. "But on the day you run to old Umbella for help, you will not stand so proud."

"What help can that old hag possibly offer *us*?" muttered Trifena, when out of earshot. Then she thought she heard low laughter and turned, but Umbella was nowhere to be seen. The path was clear and there was not even a shadow among the crowding silver birch and hazel. Only a faint malodour, tainting the breeze, hinted at where she had stood.

Hestig put his arm round his wife's shoulders. "Forget her," he said. "She's just a mad old woman."

As they continued in silence, Trifena attempted to concentrate on the reason for their being here, her mother's words as she lay dying: "Never deny who you are. You are not Roman. You are of the southern tribe of the Atrebates and your ancestral home is Byden."

Trifena was too young to understand, but had been made to repeat the words over and over again so that she would not forget. She reflected that there were times when she had forgotten – almost – but not any more. By returning to the settlement she was keeping faith with her mother and her ancestors who lay in their sacred graves half a mile away to the west.

A few moments later, their sandals were scuffing the chalky soil of the shallow defence ditch before they passed through the gap in the high grassy bank.

Trifena smiled up at her husband. "Welcome to Byden," she said.

CHAPTER II (2)

The path led them past a wooden corn dryer and clusters of round, thatched houses directly to the market place, a scene of busy morning activity. Some traders had taken advantage of the covered market at one side of the square, but most had set up stalls and awnings in the open area, or were laying out wares on the flattened earth.

The inn, the young couple's destination, dominated the eastern boundary. Hestig held open the heavy oak door for Trifena to pass into the reception hall, where dark green floor tiles reflected the vibrant flames of a charcoal fire heaped against the opposite wall.

He led her across to a couch, settled her comfortably, then went in search of the innkeeper. She had fallen asleep by the time the two men returned and woke to find Hestig's hand on her shoulder.

"We're in luck," he said, "there's an unoccupied room. They have a bathhouse and the women are bathing now, so you may like to join them – it's through the blue door there. Then he'll bring us something to eat and you can sleep while I join the men this afternoon."

The innkeeper whispered in Hestig's ear. "By the way," the young man added with some embarrassment, "there's no access through that door."

The door indicated was clearly marked, "No entry". Trifena blushed.

"I'm hardly likely to be mistaken for one of the inn's ladies," she said, smiling and stroking her stomach to quieten the baby kicking inside her.

Their room was small and furnished with a wooden table, chairs and chests. A bathe was just what Trifena needed to soothe away her aches, so she retrieved her leather toilet bag and left Hestig to take his ease on the mattress.

On opening the blue door, she found herself in a short corridor, also painted blue, which led to a warm changing room where the colours had blended into green. As she undressed, she could hear the animated babble of women's voices on the other side of an archway.

Leaving her outer clothes in a tidy heap on a bench, and wearing only her white linen shift, Trifena passed through the archway into a small square room with a high window.

The room was occupied by women of all ages, some sitting on stone benches round the walls, others standing in groups, chatting and laughing. One middle-aged woman, who said she was the mother-in-law of the blacksmith, moved along the bench to make room for Trifena to sit down. Above her head swam representations of strange fish and sea monsters. It was very warm in there and she began to perspire.

She followed the women to the caldarium and alveus, the hot room and hot plunge bath. By this time she had also met the butcher's wife, the baker's wife, the shoemaker's mother, several smallholders' and traders' daughters and a couple of grandmothers.

She said simply that she was "Trifena, Hestig's wife, from Eboracum".

One of the grandmothers, who had introduced herself as Selena, the weaver's wife, was first to enquire. She was sitting at the side of the bath, feet dangling, her ample body modestly enveloped in a capacious linen towel. Trifena was still relaxing in the pleasantly hot water and massaging oil of roses into her distended stomach beneath her shift, watching with interest as a slave tried to add colour to the matron's white hair by rubbing in a blend of beech ash and goat's fat.

"Excuse me for asking, my dear, but one or two of us feel we've met you before."

Trifena smiled. "You may remember me. I'm Trifosa's daughter."

Selena looked down at her intently. "Yes, of course – Trifosa. That's it, ladies!" She turned jubilantly to her companions, juice dripping from her chin. There was a general murmur as the younger members of the group nudged the older ones, who took no notice, all clamouring for information.

"How is your mother?"

"Well, I hope?"

"We heard nothing once you'd left."

"We got as far as Eboracum," Trifena told them. "My mother died a year later." The women said how sorry they were to hear it. Trifena said she thought her mother had died of a broken heart.

"My father had gone to fight the Picts and Scots on the Great Wall," she reminded them. "My mother received word that he had been killed." The older women nodded and said they remembered the arrival of the messenger. "Not long afterwards we left Byden and went north."

She paused. For a few moments the only sound between them was the *scrape, scrape* of the bronze strigils as slaves removed ingrained dirt from soft bodies.

Finally, she asked, "What happened here that made my mother leave her home, her people, and take me on that long journey north?"

One of them said, "She couldn't believe your father had been killed."

"It was something more than that," persisted Trifena. She climbed the steps out of the bath and sat next to Selena.

"It's not a memory we're proud of," the older woman confessed, "and I feel especially embarrassed because my husband took over your mother's business after you left. It was because of the High Priest at the time. He wouldn't leave your mother alone. As soon as he heard that your father had been killed, he began calling on her, waylaying her as she went to and from the stream, always being out and about when she was shopping. It really used to upset her, especially as she was still mourning your father. When she would have nothing to do with him, he turned his eyes on you."

"On me?" Trifena breathed in sharply as a shiver of revulsion shot through her. No one else spoke. All pampering ceased and everyone waited, their full attention on the speaker.

"And none of us was allowed to help," continued Selena, clearly distressed at the memory. "The Temple started commissioning vestments from traders in Calleva instead of from her, and people stopped ordering her garments. If she had encouraged him, you could have lived in luxury for the rest of your lives, but as it was, she finished up with no money, no help – no one. So one day she left everything and took you away. It was very brave of her. I liked your mother – she was a hard worker. She could have made a good living here if it hadn't been for that old devil."

Trifena followed the women into the tepidarium, the warm room, where they spread themselves about on the stone platforms.

The room was already occupied. A tall, graceful girl was lying naked on the raised stone. As the women came in, she sat up, and her long hair, the colour of ripening wheat, fell round her shoulders almost to her waist.

The women exchanged greetings then turned their attention to Trifena, wanting to hear the rest of her story. She told them how her mother had become slave woman to Adrianus Maximus, the handsome provincial governor of Eboracum.

"After she died, he took me into his household as a playmate for his daughter. When she grew up, I became her slave. Then last year she married and left the praetorium, and I lost my job. I didn't know what would happen to me."

She paused and lowered her eyes then took breath, looking again at her listeners, who were quietly waiting for her to continue.

"Adrianus Maximus has been nothing but kindness to us, Hestig and me. When I became pregnant, he freed us both, and we were married before the altar of Juno. I wanted to come home and Hestig agreed – so here we are – for good, I hope."

"You didn't walk all the way, surely not, in your condition?" asked the naked girl. A slave was manicuring her nails while another gently worked with a pumice stone, shaving her long legs.

"Adrianus Maximus lent us his carriage as far as the Ridgeway – four days' journey – so we only had to walk for a couple of hours," explained Trifena.

"Generous," commented her inquisitor.

Trifena was taking a dislike to this beautiful but supercilious young woman, whom no one had thought of introducing. Her tone made Trifena defensive.

"He said it was his way of thanking us both for long and loyal service, and because of the baby. We travelled safely under the protection of Juno."

The young woman snorted. "Juno? Those Roman gods have no power here, and you'd do well to remember it!"

"Yes, of course."

"We have only one god and that's Ashuba, and his goddess wife, Shubinata. She may be gracious enough to overlook your blasphemy if you make her an offering. You'd be wise to arrange that soon if you want your baby born alive and whole."

Trifena was alarmed by this threat and stammered that she would do so.

A cold plunge in the frigidarium was welcome following the heat, and after a rub down with oil to keep out any chills, the women dressed and began to leave the baths by an outside door.

The last to leave was the girl with manicured nails, who stayed behind to make up her face. Fascinated, Trifena watched as she rouged her lips and cheeks with a paste of cochineal and blackened her eyebrows, eyelashes and eyelids with charcoal, which dramatically emphasised the rich autumn gold of her hair.

Men turned in admiration as she walked through the market, her fine black woollen cloak billowing behind her, and a chatelaine of toiletry tools jingling from a chain round her waist.

"They look, but they daren't touch," whispered Selena as she and Trifena followed.

"Who is she?" asked Trifena.

"Jeetuna – a priestess at the Temple, and Vortin's property."

"Vortin?"

"He's High Priest now. It was his father who bothered your mother. If he feels generous, he'll pass Jeetuna down to his assistant priests. The men of the settlement have to make do with the Temple prostitutes, if they can afford them, or the cheaper girls at the inn."

She smoothed her now patchy blonde-tinted hair. "Jeetuna's duties include taking care of the prostitutes at the Temple. Now, if you don't want your baby, she's the one to consult, before or after the birth. She's very experienced in these matters."

Trifena was shocked at the thought, but couldn't resist asking mischievously, "With those long nails?"

Selena laughed. "She never does what's required herself, but can arrange it. She uses the services of an old harridan who lives in the wood to the south."

"*Umbella!*" thought Trifena silently, and was on the verge of telling Selena about their strange meeting, but decided against it. If people learned about Umbella's warning – what was it she'd prophesied, "Sword, fire and total destruction"? – and believed it, they might reject her and Hestig and their baby.

Instead, she shook her head. "There's no question of that. This one's wanted, and we intend to bring him up in Byden. Jeetuna said I must make an offering to your goddess."

"Shubinata's altar is in the wood – you must have crossed the path on your way through."

Trifena nodded. It was where they had met Umbella.

"Ask at the Temple for either of the priestesses – Jeetuna you know now, but Veneta is more approachable – and she'll ask the High Priestess to arrange the sacrifice. They'll expect whatever they think you can afford, so be warned and don't go gossiping about how much you're worth."

Trifena looked towards the Temple, glimmering white in the spring sunshine and dominating the crown of the hill.

As they parted company, the older woman warned her, "You really do need to watch Jeetuna. Everything you say will get straight back to Vortin."

"Thank you for all your advice."

"You just can't be too careful. If you do things right, you'll get on. Come and see me if you have any problems. We live by the Temple portico – it's your old house. Come any time, I'm usually there. If not, I'll be at my daughter-in-law's, looking after my grandson."

Trifena accepted the invitation with eagerness. She couldn't resist the thought of stepping through that doorway once again and meeting the shadowy half-memory of her mother sitting weaving in the gloom.

Later that evening, lying on their woollen mattress, with a background of men's voices and women's laughter coming from the bathhouse, she and Hestig talked of the son they were about to bring into the world, the home they hoped to build and the pottery Hestig wanted to establish.

"Selena says we must do things right," Trifena told him, "and that means making an offering to the goddess."

"Of course." She was always reassured by Hestig's easy smile.

"Hestig," she ventured, "that meeting with Umbella –"

"Forget it," he advised her. "You're worrying about nothing."

He turned towards her and raised himself on one elbow. His northern blue eyes looked down at her and an unruly strand of hair, whose rich brown always reminded Trifena of field mice, fell over his forehead and tickled her nose.

"Trifena, I've loved you so much for so long. I never, ever thought we'd be together – and free, at that. We've a lot to thank Adrianus Maximus for."

"Everything," Trifena agreed softly, but her eyes faltered beneath that clear blue gaze. Then, answering his unspoken invitation, she kissed him lovingly on the cheek and blew out the candle.

"Sleep," she said. "We've both got a busy day tomorrow."

CHAPTER III (3)

It was still dark when Trifena awoke. For a while she lay listening to the crowing of the fighting cockerels, then crept out of bed and wrapped a coverlet about her. Hestig could use the broken amphora left in the room for the purpose, but Trifena needed to use the latrine in the bathhouse.

The slaves had obviously been up for some time, as all signs of the previous night's activities had been cleared away and the fire in the stoke hole had been well tended. Two men, left over from the night before, were lolling in the hot water, but they didn't notice her and she was able to freshen up in the cold room without attracting any attention.

When she returned to their room, Hestig was already washed and dressed. The slave who brought his hot water had invited them to a bread-and-cheese breakfast in the reception hall.

Trifena dressed carefully, mindful of her visit to the Temple, then announced herself ready for breakfast.

As they left the inn after they'd eaten, to go their separate ways, the settlement was coming to life. Trifena chose to walk through the market, passing among the traders, who were shouting ribald greetings to each other.

While avoiding scattered barrels, sacks and woven baskets of goods and produce, she almost trod on a line of escaping ducks. A mother duck was noisily coaxing her ducklings into line as they waddled in the general direction of the Stan stream, only narrowly avoiding the careless feet of children, who were darting between the legs of harassed stallholders.

The Temple, preserver and stern guardian of the village's religious beliefs and ritual practices, rose solidly above her to the right. Her mother had told her that it was built long before the Romans came, but no one knew for certain how old it was. Some said it had been designed by Ashuba himself when he walked the earth, so the people could worship him as befitted his divinity, and his wife Shubinata had gone off in a huff and founded her own altar in the wood.

Trifena was wondering whether it was too early to call on Selena, but was reassured when she saw her in the curved, stonewalled pathway that protected their doorway from the wind. She was helping her husband load bales of cloth on to a cart. He greeted her kindly when they were introduced.

"Dagvald's embarrassed, of course, knowing who you are," Selena confided. "Come in, and welcome!"

Trifena stepped across the threshold. The circular room was just as she remembered it, but smaller. A fire burned in a hearth in the centre of the beaten floor, the smoke escaping as best it could through the twisted branches and turfs of the roof.

Against the circular base stone wall, on the earth platform where her parents had slept, a mattress was covered with a rich red and blue tapestry. There were plenty of rugs and wall hangings, and loose covers thrown over the couch. Selena's basket chair and footstool, a couple of wooden storage chests, cupboards, a table, more stools and a stone sideboard completed the furniture in the room.

Trifena's father had added a kitchen and small workroom, away from the smoke of the fire, and Selena showed her that these were still in use.

Tears filled Trifena's eyes. For the first three years of her life, this had been her home. Selena patted her on the arm and said she would go with her to the Temple.

Trifena followed her up the shallow steps and on to the high platform on which the Temple was built. Pausing beneath the stone canopy by the two pairs of massive pillars at the entrance, Selena removed her sandals and indicated that Trifena should do the same. They left their footwear in the small vestibule before entering the holy place.

Trifena looked round with interest. Compared with the temples in Eboracum, this was very small and dark. There were windows high up in the plastered walls, but of thick green glass, and most of the illumination came from torches fixed in iron brackets along the walls. The ceiling was hidden in shadow.

Ahead stood the impressive stone altar, covered with a white linen cloth and fronted by a brightly-coloured tapestry shot through with glittering gold thread and dripping with loops of brightly-coloured beads. On the cloth lay a clay cylinder painted red, blue and gold, which Trifena guessed contained holy writings on rolled sheets of parchment.

Behind and above the altar towered the great, nude, yellow-stone god Ashuba. Eunuchs were replacing and rekindling a hundred scented candles around his huge, parted feet. Trifena had difficulty in controlling a fit of dry coughing as she breathed in the ill-ventilated, perfumed atmosphere and was embarrassed to be drawing attention to herself.

When she recovered, her gaze was drawn upwards past Ashuba's strong, shapeless legs, like tree trunks, to his swollen and exaggerated male organs and onwards past his flat stomach to muscular arms folded across his chest.

Light flickered up into his stone face and through the haze of smoke and incense, above jutting jaw, wide firm mouth that never smiled, and thin nose, she was greatly alarmed to find glowing red eyes meeting hers. The base of her spine tingled uncomfortably but she couldn't look away. Ashuba's eyes held hers as a fox transfixes the eyes of a trapped hare before he leaps in for the kill.

What do you want from me?

The question forced from her was silently asked, and received no reply, but Trifena felt sure that Ashuba would reply, in his own time.

The candle flames danced aside in a current of air, the light left his face and he released her.

"Trifena, are you all right? Do you need a drink of water?" enquired Selena, anxiously.

Trifena forced herself to turn away from the altar and said that she was fine.

Selena led her across the tiled floor to where a group of children of various ages sat cross-legged. As she drew close, Trifena saw that they were sitting round a colourful mosaic. One of their number, a boy of about fourteen years, had a long stick in his hand and was pointing out features of the design.

"The sun," said the boy, "is Ashuba, who gives us light and

warmth. And here you see the wife of our lord, Shubinata, whose beautiful spirit moved across the face of the seas at the world's creation. She sparkles in our stream, the Stan. Who would you say is more powerful?"

Some of the children answered, "The Sun, of course," while others insisted, "No, Water – it must be Water."

"Here is a great mystery," confided the boy. "The Sun can make Water vanish, but Water can kill a fire, so you could say that one is as powerful as the other. However, consider – the Sun has never dried up the streams and rivers, but neither have they killed the Sun, so you could say they are as powerless as each other. Yes, this is a great mystery and only our lord Ashuba knows the answer."

The two women were about to learn the mysteries of the other elements of the design – the flowers, insects and animals – when a voice that reminded Trifena of a warm summer afternoon spoke to them.

"Are you enjoying the lesson?"

Trifena turned and met a pair of brown eyes above a gently smiling mouth. "Good morning, Selena. Will you introduce me to your friend?"

Selena made the introductions. "This is Trifena, wife of Hestig, who arrived from Eboracum yesterday. Trifena, this is Veneta, priestess and a dear friend."

Veneta nodded. "Ah yes, I've heard your story from Jeetuna. Welcome to Byden Temple. You've worshipped Juno in the past, I hear, but she has no authority in Byden."

"That's why we've come, Veneta. You can see that Trifena is heavily pregnant and she wants to make an offering to Shubinata as soon as possible, before the baby arrives. I hoped you would advise her how to do everything properly as laid down in the great Book of the Altar."

"Readily," agreed the priestess. "Selena, you can listen to Vitius as he teaches the children, while Trifena and I take a stroll and get to know each other."

Trifena took an immediate liking to this young priestess, who she judged was a few years older than herself. Avoiding a crate of candles that had been left near the altar, they walked together round the circumference of the walls, their shadows keeping them company as they passed from light to gloom beneath the flaming torches. The deep red of the painted wall panels threw Trifena's green dress and Veneta's blue robes into sharp relief.

"When is your baby due?"

"About the end of June. I'm rather nervous," Trifena confessed, "as it's my first and I've had little advice. It's now I miss my mother."

"Advice? Oh, you'll get plenty of that," said Veneta with a chuckle, "probably too much. You'll be told what to do by the women at the baths, by the stallholders' wives in the market, by Selena, by us – in fact, every woman in the settlement will be your teacher. And why not? They've had many children between them, and most have survived. The others are buried in their postholes and storage pits and by their thresholds, to bring good fortune and more babies.

"The first person you should visit, however, is Stalwyn, the midwife. She organises the wet nurses, too. They have saved many a life threatened with extinction almost before it began. So have no fear, you'll have plenty of assistance when the time comes."

Trifena felt relieved. "And the sacrifice I have to make?"

They had made a full circuit of the Temple walls and were back where they started, by the altar. Turning away from anyone who might be watching, Trifena took hold of the leather pouch hanging from her girdle, widened its mouth, then slipped her hand inside. When she carefully withdrew it, the contents were wound round her fingers. Veneta gasped.

"They're beautiful," was all she could say.

Trifena placed the amber and pearl necklace in the priestess's hands. Veneta caressed the smooth round gems, each unique, transparent to opaque.

"They're so beautiful," she repeated. Then she took hold of Trifena's right hand and placed the necklace in the palm, her fingers closing Trifena's tightly round the stones. "It's too much," she remonstrated.

"But I'm told they have all been gathered from the sea," insisted Trifena. "There are Sun stones – see how the amber reflects the Sun from inside – and Water stones – each pearl a drop of the sea's night fluorescence. What could be a better offering to the gods of sun and water for the gift of my healthy baby?"

"It's too much," Veneta said again.

"Too much?" asked a voice. "Too much for what?"

Veneta spun round, shielding her visitor, whether purposefully or not, Trifena could not be sure. They had been so engrossed in the necklace that neither had heard the approach of Jeetuna, who now stood in front of them, looking suspiciously from one to the other, waiting for an answer.

Trifena was again unnerved by the beautiful priestess and was angry with herself for being so. Her fingers tightened round the necklace, though she did wonder whether she should hand it over. Fortunately, instinct prevented her from doing so.

"We were discussing what thank-offering she should make to the goddess," Veneta explained.

"Nothing is *too much* to give to Shubinata," countered Jeetuna. "What had you in mind?"

"I – I –" stammered Trifena.

"She doesn't know," Veneta interrupted. She was still standing between them.

On impulse, Trifena backed up against the nearby crate of candles and slowly moved the hand holding the necklace behind her. Gently uncurling her fingers, she let the necklace slip, hoping it wouldn't make a noise as it fell among the candles. There was the slightest clatter, which was covered by Veneta's explanation.

"I was just saying that we didn't expect her to bring anything of great value, being just slaves as she and her husband were. I was going to suggest a length of cloth or a hand-made woven or embroidered wall hanging, or some home-cooked sweetmeats."

"Any of those gifts would be most pleasing to the goddess, I'm sure," commented Jeetuna in a voice of honey sweetness, "though perhaps she could think of something more original?"

For a moment, Trifena thought the priestess must be aware of the necklace, then decided that was not possible.

"We'll think of something," promised Veneta.

"Good. I'll tell the High Priestess to expect something special."

She turned and walked towards the sanctuary, Veneta's eyes on her back. Trifena's eyes were on the crate of candles, which at that moment was being carried by two eunuchs towards the altar rail. She watched as they entered the sanctuary and put the crate down on the tiles.

"*They're going to find it*!" Trifena agonised, now watching Jeetuna as she too reached the rail.

"Veneta," she whispered, "I dropped the necklace into the crate! She'll guess whose it is – or perhaps pretend she doesn't know. Either way, she'll claim it for your goddess and I will lose it!"

There was nothing either could do but watch. Jeetuna stopped momentarily, then entered the sanctuary.

"What's this?" the priestess demanded, seemingly looking right into the crate. Trifena held her breath. The eunuchs stopped what they were doing and looked where her elegantly sandaled foot with its painted toe nails was digging at something on the tiles. They were flustered and stammering their answers.

"It – it's candle grease, Jeetuna."

"I can see that, stupid! What's it doing there?"

"Sorry, Jeetuna, sorry! We'll – I'll clear it up immediately! Straight away!"

"Then what are you waiting for?" she bellowed. "You are defiling Ashuba's sanctuary with your incompetence! Vortin will hear about this!"

One of the young men scurried off to find a scraper to clear up the mess, while the other was still apologising profusely as he moved the crate out of the way of the dripped wax. Another, who had been lighting candles before placing them in the empty holders on the altar, became so flustered beneath Jeetuna's scowl that he fumbled the two he held in his hands and dropped one on her foot.

She let out such a yell of surprise and pain, then of fear as the flame began to lick at her robe, that the eunuch dropped the second lit candle as he started towards her. It fell into the crate. A sudden flare showed that it had caught another of the candles alight.

Veneta and Trifena sped towards the altar. Trifena had to stop at the rail but Veneta continued into the sanctuary and began to beat out Jeetuna's singeing hem with her bare hands. While doing that, she had the presence of mind to order the eunuchs to take the burning crate out of the sanctuary, which they did.

They ran back to the two priestesses after Trifena helpfully offered to blow out the lighted candles in the crate. That done, glad of her long sleeves, she was able to scrabble among the candles until she found her necklace, then thankfully hid it beneath one of the turned-back cuffs.

Order was eventually restored. Jeetuna gathered her dignity about her and, with a toss of her long hair and a flounce of her shoulders, marched off, intending to find Vortin in his office behind the altar so that she could report the matter.

The young men returned nervously to their work, muttering among themselves, while Veneta came back to Trifena, dabbing ruefully with the hem of her robe at the red patches on her hands.

"I must put some cream on these burns," she grimaced.

"Won't Shubinata be angry if I don't give her the necklace after all that?" Trifena asked anxiously, as she returned it to the pouch.

"More to the point, Jeetuna would be angry if she knew about our deception, and she would certainly tell Iraina, our High Priestess. Do yourself a favour, Trifena – don't let anyone know you have it. Think of something else."

The first day of May was arranged for the sacrificial offering. Veneta said she would ask the High Priestess to officiate. That settled, they returned to Selena and the children, who had remained quite oblivious of the drama at the altar, and shortly afterwards the two women left the Temple.

Trifena was aware that Veneta had not voiced the one question she must be longing to ask. *How was it that she, one-time slave, possessed such a valuable piece of jewellery?* Trifena reflected that Hestig, her husband, knew the answer, and that was all that mattered.

CHAPTER IV (4)

Meanwhile, Hestig was asking around for Severus who, he had discovered, was leader of the council. He found the old man in the council chamber above the covered market.

Severus fingered his long, white, wispy hair as he listened attentively to Hestig's request and said there would be no problem in buying a plot of land for a house, but the matter would have to be discussed in full council. What price did Hestig have in mind? The figure obviously surprised him, and he offered to accompany Hestig straight away to show him the choice plots.

The young man enjoyed his tour of the settlement with Severus. Their stroll was continually interrupted by greetings, introductions, complaints, appeals and expressions of gratitude that met the old man as they passed through the market. Hestig thought he must have been introduced to the entire population of Byden by the time they reached the western bank and ditch, having inspected various vacant sites on the way.

There Severus pointed out a good-sized plot that would accommodate a house suitable for a family of three, with room for extensions, and land enough to keep a cow, a couple of sheep, chickens and a pig. Beyond the bank and ditch were the lynchets, low earthen barriers that divided the fields into strips for planting with cereals, fruit and vegetables, so that each family could be self-sufficient.

"Your nearest neighbour would be the bee-keeper down the hill – not counting Pulcher, of course."

Hestig was curious. "Pulcher? That's Latin for 'beautiful'."

Severus laughed. "Beautiful? That was his mother's warped sense of humour! He's a freak – a dwarf. And only fifteen – lives on his own."

"Is that why he doesn't count, because he's a dwarf?" asked Hestig.

Severus nodded. "His parents crept away one night when he was eight years old and left him behind in the house. Fortunately for him, the people took him under their wing. They say he brings good luck to the settlement – a lot of superstitious rubbish, of course. You can't miss him – he's not much taller than a child, and bandy legged."

When Hestig arrived back at the inn he found Trifena waiting for him.

"I've found just the plot for our house," he said excitedly. "I'm sure you'll love it. It's high on the west side of the settlement and looks south across the stream and the valley. If it's designed well, we could have sunshine in one or other of the rooms all day. I'll take you to see it this afternoon."

"And the price?" queried Trifena.

"A little more than we discussed – but that's all right. We can afford it. Our offer now has to go before the full council. I've also asked about hiring a stall in the market so I can get back to work and earn some money. Now, how was *your* meeting?"

Trifena recounted the morning's happenings. She said she was undecided about what to take to Shubinata as a thank-offering.

"We'll think of something," promised her husband.

That afternoon Hestig stood again on the plot of land he had chosen for their first home, his arm around Trifena's waist. He looked down at her to catch her reaction, and was relieved to see that she was as enchanted as he was.

Suddenly they both became aware of watching eyes and turned towards the round house a little lower down the hill. They were just in time to see a small figure disappearing inside.

"That must be Pulcher," Hestig said, and repeated what Severus had told him about their new neighbour.

"I hope he'll be safe – with our baby, I mean." Trifena sounded anxious.

"Severus said he's harmless," her husband reassured her.

He was summoned to a meeting in the council chamber two days later and was granted permission to start building. Trifena was overjoyed, and they spent many hours in the hall of the inn, planning and replanning their first home.

Hestig paid for a ride to Calleva Atrebatum in one of the farmer's carts, a journey of about five hours, to meet architects, surveyors and builders who were used to constructing in the Roman style, and a week later there was great excitement as three strangers arrived in Byden, each with a small metal abacus in hand, to inspect the site and draw up plans and specifications.

The young couple recruited local building labourers and took them up to the Temple to ask Ashuba's seal of approval on the whole operation.

As the site was cleared, the foundations dug and building work commenced, people in the settlement were curious. *How could two freed slaves, however long and loyal their service to their Roman master, afford such luxury?*

CHAPTER V (5)

Early on the first day of May, traditionally the beginning of summer, Trifena and her new friend, Selena, set off towards the wood. Both were clad in white, as was the custom on May Day. Hestig had solved the problem of the offering, and Trifena had her gift, safely wrapped in cloth, clutched tightly in her hand.

The pair left the main path at the intersection where Umbella had made herself known and struck off to the right, through the bluebells, in the direction of Shubinata's temple. Their walk was accompanied by the rich, high piping notes of a nightingale, which had been singing since they left the settlement. Occasionally, they caught sight of the little brown bird with chestnut-coloured tail in his flight above the trees.

They had not gone far when they heard young girls' voices, chattering and giggling. On following the path as it curved round an ancient oak tree, they saw running towards them a group of girls aged about thirteen or fourteen, dressed all in white, their faces still wet with May dew, carrying hooped garlands of fresh leaves, wild flowers and brightly-coloured ribbons.

At that moment such a cacophony of sound broke out among the trees that it stopped Trifena and Selena in their tracks and silenced the nightingale.

"Whatever's that terrible noise?" shouted Trifena.

"It's the May Day cow horns! The boys have been waiting for the girls to come back from Shubinata's temple," explained the older woman.

A band of young men came crashing through the trees on each side of the path and gave chase to the girls who, squealing in mock terror, lifted their tunics round their knees and began to run. The boys leapt past the women, calling and laughing to them and the girls, still blowing their horns.

It was not until they had all disappeared through the trees that the women noticed a small, moaning figure curled up and rolling about on the ground. His hands were flattened over his ears, his eyes tightly shut, and all his unusual facial features were crumpled into as small a space as possible.

"It's Pulcher!" Selena exclaimed, hurrying towards him, with Trifena following.

The older woman bent over and dragged the dwarf to his feet, against his will.

"It's all right, Pulcher," she reassured him, "they've gone now." She tried to pull his hands away from his ears, without succeeding.

Trifena laid her hands over his and at her soft touch he stopped moaning, opened his eyes, and allowed her to take his hands from his ears and place them at his sides.

"They've all gone," she said gently. He stared at her. "I'm your new neighbour – or I will be, when the house is built."

He continued to stare, then reached out a deformed hand and laid it gently on her stomach, before turning and hobbling off along the path towards the settlement.

"A strange one, that one," commented Selena as they resumed their walk, "but he's never been any trouble. I think he hears and understands things the rest of us don't. One can never be quite sure about these afflicted creatures, but it seems you've made a friend."

It was not long before they reached their destination. Beneath the embroidery of spreading beech tree branches stood a small round temple with roof of woven brush. On the ground in front of the doorway lay a leather mantle. Small pools of water had gathered in its soft folds.

"It's the May dew," explained Selena. "You don't need it, Trifena, but do you want to bathe your face in it? It will give your baby an unblemished complexion, as well as yourself, and make sure you have good luck in the coming year."

Trifena laughed. "I could probably get down there, but I don't think I could get up again."

"And I'm not sure about my knees," confessed Selena reluctantly.

"Then let me help you both," offered the voice of summer behind them, and there was Veneta. She disappeared into the dark interior of the temple and reappeared with a large pottery bowl, a scoop, and a towel draped over one arm. With a smile she crouched and ladled some of the dewy water into the bowl then stood and offered it to each in turn.

The cold, clear freshness of the water splashing over her face made Trifena gasp, but then she laughed with pleasure and scooped up several more handfuls, and had to pat face and neck dry with the towel.

Selena did the same, but one cupped handful was enough for her.

"There was more point to this when I was young," she commented ruefully.

"High Priestess Iraina is not here yet," Veneta told them, indicating that they should sit on a rough bench, "but she has asked me to instruct you."

For half-an-hour Veneta talked about the birth rituals that Ashuba had decreed long ago when the gods walked the earth. Trifena noticed that Selena paid scant attention and guessed it was because she had taken part in the ceremonies so many times, the most recent being before and after the birth of her grandson.

"If your baby is a girl, you must bring her here for purification and naming when she is eight days old," Veneta instructed.

"It's a boy," Trifena insisted. "Stalwyn, the midwife, dangled a ring above my stomach."

"Then you must take him to Ashuba's Temple on the ninth day."

The instruction over, Veneta invited them both into the presence of the goddess, Shubinata.

Trifena picked up her offering from where she had laid it on the ground and the two women removed their shoes and followed the bare-foot priestess into the simple temple.

It took a while for their eyes to adjust to the darkness inside, but once adjusted there was sufficient light fingering through the new green boughs of the roof, aided by a large candle on a pedestal, to see most of what the interior held.

From the doorway, a red carpet laid on beaten earth led to a carved wooden altar, on this occasion strewn with sprays of white hawthorn. In the curtained shadows behind the altar, on a pedestal, stood the naked stone figure of the goddess. Her hair flowed around her like waves, covering her shoulders but leaving bare her ample breasts and distended belly. Her blatant fertility offered hope to the childless women who came to her with their tears and gifts.

Veneta and Selena stayed by the door as Trifena approached the goddess along the red carpet, eyes downcast. She knelt on the long low stool upholstered in white to honour the season. A movement in the shadows caused Trifena to jump and the deep voice of the High Priestess began chanting the words of humble access.

Trifena had not noticed Iraina enter the temple. Was there a private door behind the curtains? She joined in the responses, prompted by Veneta and Selena in the doorway:

"Loi, loi, vani ecta. Ista vanum, ista vector. Loi, loi."

The prayers continued – for purity, for comfort from the mother goddess during labour, for a live delivery and healthy baby, the mother's blood staunched but her milk flowing.

The moment came for the gift offering and Iraina materialised from the shadows. Trifena gazed in awe at the figure towering above her. A sleeveless white robe enveloped her slender body, a golden girdle tied at the waist. Long slender arms were encased to the elbows in golden bracelets. Confident and beautiful, her violet eyes met Trifena's, but there was no warmth in them.

Trifena handed her the gift. The two women at the door craned their necks to watch as Iraina carefully unfolded the cloth, revealing the small, incised clay pot Hestig had so carefully moulded and sealed with beeswax. Her hands caressed the smooth plump outline.

"Honey?" enquired the High Priestess, but Trifena shook her head. Iraina inverted the pot and heard the coins chinking inside. Her violet eyes gleamed and she turned to the altar, cleared a space among the hawthorn, and after raising the pot high towards the goddess, laid it on the wooden surface. A short blessing and the ritual came to an end.

Iraina stood motionless and watched as Trifena backed towards the door before following her companions through it.

CHAPTER VI (6)

Preparations for the great Midsummer Festival began several weeks in advance. Trifena became aware of its approach one morning at the end of May when she found Jeetuna in Selena's workroom. Selena's husband, Dagvald, was showing her new weaves he had created.

Selena was sweating in the steam rising from her stone vat as, with a short wooden pole held in fingers dyed red, she stirred a length of material in a liquid that Trifena guessed had been obtained by boiling bedstraw. Surrounding the vat were untidy piles of raspberry and carrot leaves, onion skins and strips of silver birch bark, which would later produce dyes of varying shades of green and yellow.

Trifena apologised for interrupting.

"Don't leave on my account," Jeetuna said quickly. "You can help me choose. What are they wearing in Eboracum?"

Trifena considered. "Purple is very popular."

"Then I shall choose that for Iraina. She has stopped dyeing her hair with saffron and is experimenting with chalk and lime water, so the purple should suit her – and set Vortin alight. What do you suggest I wear?"

Trifena looked at the weaves again. "How about the acorn green twill?" Jeetuna nodded in agreement. "And for Veneta –" continued Trifena.

Jeetuna shrugged. "This brown will do for Veneta – she's not fussy."

Trifena pictured the priestess, her thick, light brown hair combed back and tied at the nape of her neck, her high forehead above brown eyes and smiling mouth.

"Mixed with gold," she suggested.

When the priestess had left with samples to show Iraina, Trifena asked what happened at the Midsummer Festival.

"I have work to do and you ladies are cluttering up my workroom," complained Dagvald hurriedly.

Selena left the vat, dried her hands, and guided Trifena into the family room.

"You'll find out," was all she would say.

Trifena was about to press her friend for more information when they were interrupted by the arrival of a toddler, unsteady on his feet, closely followed by his mother. Selena swept him up in her arms and covered his face with kisses, which he rubbed off with the back of his hand. Selena chuckled.

"Trifena, I don't think you've met my daughter-in-law, Campania. And this is our little godsend, Soranus."

"Not always such a godsend," laughed his mother.

"No one would have guessed," smiled Trifena. "I hope Soranus and my son will be good friends, in time."

The women chatted together for a few minutes before Trifena took her leave of them.

Passing through the market, she headed for the spot where Hestig had set up his potter's wheel and kiln. On all sides, traders shouted their wares, persuading the men to buy all sorts of festive knick-knacks for their wives, toys and board games for their children, or statuettes of Ashuba and Shubinata for household shrines.

Trifena stopped by a stall displaying buckled belts.

"Buying a Festival present for your man?" The male voice too close to her ear was insolent, and Trifena shivered involuntarily. "There obviously *is* a man in your life!"

The speaker laughed and, as she turned towards him, threw back the hood of his black robe, revealing a shaven head. He looked only a few years older than herself.

"Are yer buying today, Brocchus?" the stallholder asked him.

Trifena was glad that the man called Brocchus turned to inspect a black leather armlet, as she was unable to disguise her urge to retch at the heavy smell of incense that impregnated his robe.

"I might be, if the price is right," insinuated Brocchus. The stallholder reduced the price and made a sale.

Brocchus turned again and inspected Trifena, his eyes resting on her bulging stomach.

"You don't need to be with us this Midsummer Eve," he commented, "but send your man up to the Temple – he'll be welcome!"

He winked knowingly at the stallholder, laughed again at Trifena and moved off into the crowd.

"Ignore 'im," advised the stallholder kindly. " 'E's got a mind more putrid than the sewer from the public latrines."

"Who is he?" she asked, watching the tall black figure climbing the rise towards the Temple.

"One of the eunuchs – no use to man or woman, though you wouldn't think it, the way 'e talks – it's all talk, though."

Suddenly she was not in the mood to buy anything and, telling the tradesman she would be back, continued on her way to Hestig's stall. His smile at her approach was not returned.

"What's wrong?" he asked and Trifena told him.

"Ignore it," advised her husband. "They're strange creatures – neither one thing nor the other."

"Hestig, do you know what happens at the Festival?" asked Trifena.

"I have heard the men on the building site talking," he replied awkwardly. "It's likely to be a rowdy night, but that needn't affect us. I hope we'll be in our own house by then. Why don't you take a walk over there and see how it's progressing? Then you can go back to the inn and plan a house blessing."

The weather had been dry for weeks and the men were conscientious workers, but even so, Trifena was surprised to see how high the walls had grown since she last visited. The foreman offered to show her round after he had organised the unloading of a cartful of bricks that had been delivered from the kiln on Byden Hill. The men were surprisingly caring, making sure she avoided the rough places and stepped safely over broken bricks and piles of sand.

"We'll have you in before your littl'un's born," promised the foreman.

Next morning, after a light breakfast in the inn and a stroll along the bank of the Stan, Trifena's curiosity overcame her and she collected her leather toilet bag and again paid a visit to the bathhouse. As usual, it was very busy. Trifena knew that Selena wouldn't be there, as she was looking after Soranus while his mother visited a friend in Calleva.

The slave who massaged her neck and shoulders told all she knew about Brocchus.

"He took a Roman name because it was a Roman soldier who raped his mother – at least, she said it was rape. The women say she tried everything to get rid of him – hot bread poultices and baths in linseed, and she even went to some old hag in the wood, which nearly killed her, but none of it worked, so she abandoned him when he was born and went back into the wood and committed suicide. When he was sixteen he castrated himself to get a job in the Temple. That's a job for life if you keep your head down and get on with it. It worked in his case because he's Sharma's favourite."

Trifena asked who Sharma was. "He's assistant priest to Vortin, the High Priest. They all wield a lot of power. It's best to keep out of the way of all of them up there, except perhaps Selvid. There, does that feel any better?"

"Bliss," Trifena said, as she was helped out of the chair. "Who's Selvid?"

"Vortin's other assistant priest. He's different – as gentle as Sharma is a bully – ask Veneta."

Trifena joined the group of women in the caldarium. Several were sewing or braiding headbands as they gossiped, the sweat running in trickles down faces and necks above their towels.

Their main topic of conversation was the state of mind of four-year-old Nobilianus, son of High Priest and Priestess, Vortin and Iraina, who had been seen torching a chicken and gloating over the poor creature's squawks of agony.

Trifena went straight to the point. "Would someone please tell me what happens at the Midsummer Festival?"

The chatter stopped in mid-flow and there was a momentary silence. Then a woman who was seated at a table, selling grain and pulses to the bathers, replied hesitantly, "It celebrates the longest day, when Ashuba, our sun god, is most powerful." Trifena said she already knew that.

The jeweller's wife said that it was good for business as husbands bought sun-coloured glass trinkets for their wives.

"But jasper for the Temple prostitutes," wryly commented the blacksmith's young wife, rubbing a sticky bean flower gently on to her black eye.

"Those girls are too expensive for the family budget," stated the shoemaker's wife grimly. "I make sure my husband spends the night at the inn rather than the Temple."

"If you get him drunk early in the evening, like I do my husband, he doesn't go anywhere," the butcher's wife advised. "It's for his own good – he's getting too old. The girls talk too much and it saves him a lot of embarrassment next day."

She looked pointedly at a very young, dark-haired girl with a sallow complexion. Trifena recognised her as Septima, said to be the seventh daughter of a seventh daughter, and one of the young women she had seen emerge from the door in the inn marked "No entry".

"I don't have any trouble, either." Trifena knew the speaker was the wife of the man who cleaned out the latrines and sewers. "I just make sure he does a full day's work that day, and no one will go near him!"

The women were still laughing as they slipped into the welcoming embrace of the hot bath.

"Hestig won't want to go out that night," Trifena stated confidently. "He has no need."

"Looking at the size of you, I would think he has every need," commented Septima spitefully.

Trifena flushed. Once or twice at the inn she had caught this girl looking at Hestig in a way that made her decidedly uncomfortable. Hestig appeared not to notice.

"Wash out your mouth, Septima!" The command came from a woman sitting in a corner, cutting leather and making purses and bags for sale. "They're newly married and, anyway, not all the men go out on Midsummer's Eve."

"There are not many who don't," persisted the girl, with the confidence of one who knew.

"And not only the men," commented the baker's wife. "There are few paths you can walk without tripping over writhing bodies."

"And how would you know? Unless of course you're out there with them!" sneered Septima. Not waiting for an answer, she continued with great relish, "But no one's told Trifena what Vortin has especially planned this year."

"But you're going to, obviously," said the pulse seller.

"An hour before dawn, everyone gathers in front of the Temple. It's ablaze with thousands of candles – looks almost like daylight."

"How would you know what daylight looks like?" muttered the baker's wife under her breath, getting her own back. The other women's faces were grim and tight-lipped.

"Half an hour later –" continued Septima, building up to full flow, but she was interrupted by the arrival of the innkeeper's wife.

"Sorry, ladies, but you'll have to get dressed and leave immediately. We've had word from Jeetuna that Iraina's coming to bathe. She'll be here at any minute and my slaves need time to mop up first."

Grumbling at having to leave in such haste without a dip in the cold bath to close the pores of their skin, and discussing the probability of catching chills, the women hurriedly dressed and went out by the back door.

"You'll find out," hissed Septima in Trifena's ear.

So Trifena returned to her room at the inn, little the wiser.

CHAPTER VII (7)

True to his word, the foreman had the house finished before the birth of their baby. A delighted Hestig invited him and his men to the house blessing a week later.

The day they left the inn with their bundles and took possession of their new home was a very happy one for the young couple. Trifena felt like a queen as Hestig picked her up, with some difficulty, and carried her across the threshold. He closed the wooden door behind them.

They were standing in a small covered courtyard. On a plinth in the centre stood a stone lion with crystal water pouring from its wide-open mouth into a shell-shaped basin.

Around the courtyard were small rooms – three bedrooms, a bathroom, reception room and kitchen. Trifena referred to the reception room as the "triclinium", in Roman fashion.

As yet there was not much furniture, just the basics: three couches round the u-shaped central dining table that gave the room its Latin name, a mattress in their bedroom, pots and pans in the kitchen. However, both of them considered it great luxury in which to raise their son.

Standing in the triclinium, Trifena gazed with delight at the beautiful mosaic that covered most of the floor, cleverly designed by her young husband and executed by a specialist from Calleva. It displayed wreaths of wheat and wild flowers, birds and insects – similar to the one in the Temple. Hestig had wanted a geometric pattern but had given way to his wife's more traditional taste. Trifena decided that, in time, she would have the plastered walls and ceiling painted, as befitted such a splendid house.

Beneath their feet was the hypocaust – an underfloor cavity, into which hot air from the stoke hole was directed, to keep the room warm in winter.

Trifena knew that Hestig worried about the work involved for her in stocking cupboards and shelves, but she was blooming like a flower and had suddenly found a lot of energy.

The house blessing was arranged for the evening before the great Midsummer Festival. Trifena had carefully prepared the house shrine in a niche in the triclinium. Flowers covered the semicircular red-tiled base, and ten red candles stood in their holders along the back edge of the altar, ready for lighting, leaving room for festive offerings in front. A red curtain could be pulled across, to ensure privacy for the god and goddess, currently absent, at times when they were not being worshipped.

In the late afternoon, a procession left the Temple on foot and made its way down the steps and through the market place in the direction of the new house. Leading the way was the slim, erect figure of Selvid, assistant to the High Priest. Behind him walked two of the eunuchs, reverently carrying a stone statuette of Ashuba – a replica of the one in the Temple.

Veneta walked behind them, and following her, two Temple prostitutes, carrying Shubinata. The statuette was fully robed, her hair piled high but with bunches of ringlets falling to each shoulder.

The procession was attended by six of the older children who served in the Temple, led by the boy Vitius. All except Veneta were dressed in green. She wore her new robe of brown and gold weave. Joining them along the way were about thirty guests invited by the young couple: Selena and Dagvald and their daughter-in-law Campania, a very excited Pulcher, the builders and craftsmen who had worked on the house, Severus as leader of the council, and the women Trifena had met in the bathhouse, with their husbands.

The procession stopped outside the new house and Selvid knocked on the door, three times for Ashuba, followed by Veneta's three knocks for Shubinata. Hestig came to the door, Trifena standing behind him in the courtyard, and responded to the ritual greeting.

"The great god Ashuba desires to know whether he is welcome in this house."

"He is welcome."

Veneta enquired, "Shubinata desires to know whether she is welcome in this house."

Trifena replied, "She is welcome."

"Then Ashuba and his goddess wife seek entrance."

Hestig flung open the door and the priest and priestess and company entered the courtyard.

"May no misfortune fall upon this house," intoned Selvid and Veneta in unison. They led the hosts and their guests from room to room, holding the statuettes high and praying, "Blessings on this room and may misfortune never fall upon those within."

The people responded, "Blessings and never misfortune," as they strewed scabious over the floor, with cow parsley, campion and white nettle.

Finally, the company reached the triclinium. Hestig pulled back the red curtain that protected the shrine.

"Ashuba and Shubinata have come to take possession of their own," declared Selvid and Veneta as the statuettes were placed on the plinths prepared for them. Young Vitius lit the candles.

"The gods greet the family of Hestig and Trifena and welcome them to their shrine," intoned Selvid and Veneta.

"We are welcome," responded the young couple.

"Cursed be those who plan evil against this house," recited the priest and priestess.

"*Uni diva, uni tatum* – So be it, let it be so," chorused the company.

Selvid and Veneta took two steps backwards and bowed to the gods, then the people bowed. The candles were blown out and the curtain pulled across.

"Now I feel we are safe from all harm," smiled Trifena.

When the official party had returned to the Temple, the guests moved out into the courtyard. Hestig called for the Spanish wine he had bought in Calleva and, when all were holding full goblets, Severus, as father of the council, toasted the young couple and their unborn baby.

It was then that Trifena felt the first twinge, but said nothing. Only Stalwyn, physician's wife and Trifena's midwife, noticed her screw up her face and clutch her stomach, but the moment passed and Trifena relaxed. Stalwyn doubted that either of them would manage a full night's sleep that night.

Severus had lent his slaves for the evening to assist Bettina, a young woman from Gaul, newly acquired by Hestig in Calleva, and they made sure that the wine and locally-brewed beer flowed as freely as the chatter, and the dishes of snacks were replenished time and again.

Trifena thought that only Selena and Dagvald appeared not to be enjoying the occasion. She looked closely at her friend and was sure that she had been crying.

"Are you all right, Selena?" she asked anxiously. "Is something upsetting you?"

"No, nothing, dear," Selena answered quickly.

Trifena was unconvinced but could not think what the problem might be, if indeed there was a problem. She had observed that Selena and Dagvald seemed very happily married, and as their daughter-in-law, Campania, was in the corner, wine in hand, laughing at a joke made by the shoemaker, there could be nothing amiss in the family.

She was puzzling over this when Pulcher accidentally knocked his goblet into the fountain then gleefully splashed himself and the lion all over with the now pink liquid. No one minded, and the more they laughed, the more he splashed.

The house lamps had been lit for a full hour before the first guests said they must leave. All the women had preparations to make for the Midsummer Festival and the men had a morning's work to do before packing up for the public holiday.

Pulcher was reluctant to go home and would not do so until Trifena promised to visit him next day.

"Hestig," said Trifena when they finally got to bed, "What did you think of Selvid?"

"I liked him," Hestig replied. "When I was talking to him I was able to forget he was a priest."

"I thought Veneta looked lovely. Did you notice the way Selvid looked at her?"

"No, how did he look at her?" Hestig kissed Trifena on the forehead and pulled her bulk towards him, preparing to settle down to sleep.

"I'm not sure – not like a priest is supposed to look at a priestess, though."

"Lust?" asked Hestig.

"No – that would be nothing strange. He looked at her as if – as if – he was in love with her."

"Priests don't fall in love with priestesses, Trifena – it's just not allowed. They make love, but *in* love? No, it's not what they're about."

"I know that, but even so –"

"Women! Always looking for liaisons and intrigues! You're imagining things, dear heart. Now go to sleep – I thought you were looking tired towards the end of the evening."

"It was such a happy house blessing. Thank you for my lovely new home."

She suddenly sat up in bed.

"What now?" asked Hestig with resignation.

"I forgot to pull the curtain back. I want the shrine open during the night."

Trifena pushed the bed covers aside and with some difficulty stood up. She really was feeling very heavy tonight.

Having entered the triclinium and crossed the mosaic, she reached out and pulled back the curtain protecting the altar. Her gasp in the dark was audible as her gaze met that of Ashuba, his eyes luminous red although there was no light in the room. She tried to take a step backwards but his eyes would not release her. She screamed for Hestig.

He came immediately and found her semi-conscious and lying in her own blood.

CHAPTER VIII (8)

Wild-eyed and wearing only his nightshirt, Hestig pounded loudly on Pulcher's front door. The dwarf opened it, peering out blearily into the darkness.

"It's Trifena," Hestig gasped. "Please go and fetch Stalwyn. Tell her the baby's coming and Trifena's bleeding!"

Pulcher did not need to be asked twice. He flung a cloak round his shoulders and waddled off in the direction of the physician's house, while Hestig ran back to Trifena. He had picked her up off the floor and laid her gently on the mattress, which was now soaked with blood beneath her, although the flow seemed to have staunched.

Trifena was clearly very frightened and her mind was rambling. Most of the time Hestig couldn't understand what she was saying, although she was repeating the name of Ashuba over and over again.

He brought a basin of cold water and a cloth and dabbed her face, trying to calm her, though he was panicking inside.

"Hush, Trifena, hush," he kept repeating, holding her hand tightly and kissing her face. "Help is on the way. Pulcher's gone to fetch Stalwyn. She'll be here any minute. Try to keep still."

It seemed forever till the tall, reassuring figure of Stalwyn appeared in the doorway, Pulcher looking tiny beside her. The dwarf's eyes filled with apprehension as he waited at the foot of the bed. Stalwyn signalled that he should leave the room but Trifena saw him and held out her hand.

"Thank you," she said as he reached her side. "When the baby's born, Pulcher, will you be one of his fathers in god? Hestig and I would be so honoured if you would say yes."

Pulcher drew back his shoulders with evident pride and seemed to grow in stature. He nodded happily.

"I guard your son – my life," he promised. "I pray now to Shubinata – baby perfect, not like me!"

Stalwyn opened the door then and ushered him out.

Hestig watched Trifena closely as she lay pale against the pillow. Stalwyn had been counting the length of time the contractions lasted and the interval between each. They were slowing down and Trifena was now taking the occasional mild pain in her stride. The initial panic was over.

"Nothing's going to happen for a long time," Stalwyn told Hestig, who was wiping perspiration from his forehead with the back of his hand. "Try to keep her calm – the rest will do her most good. Encourage her to eat something light and drink as much water as she can, to stimulate the milk flow. I'll call in again later in the day to see how she is."

Hestig was terrified at the thought of being left alone with Trifena in labour, but Stalwyn reassured him that all was well, and nature would take her own course in her own time.

"I'll ask Pulcher to fetch Selena during the morning, to keep her company," suggested Hestig, the anxiety receding from his voice. "She'll sit with her."

Stalwyn hesitated. "I'm not sure that Selena will be able to come. She has a few problems of her own at the moment."

"Oh? She didn't mention anything at the house blessing. I'll try, anyway."

Stalwyn opened her mouth to say something more but seemed to think better of it and left the house quietly.

Hestig wanted to turn the mattress over but Trifena had dozed off so he sat in the birthing chair by her side and also took the opportunity to sleep away the remaining hours of darkness.

He was woken in the morning by Pulcher knocking anxiously at the front door. Hestig was glad to see him, and asked if he would tell Selena that Trifena would like her to visit. Pulcher looked uncomfortable at being asked to call at the weaver's house but said nothing and set off to climb up the slope to the Temple area.

A little later, Trifena woke up, and Hestig was surprised to learn that the contractions had stopped altogether. He gave her a piece of bread and a drink of water, which was all she wanted, and wished he was not so ignorant about the idiosyncrasies of childbirth. They were both hoping Selena would not delay calling.

"I'm sure she won't be long," he said encouragingly, as he plumped up the pillows to make Trifena more comfortable.

When Pulcher returned, Hestig could tell at once that he was reluctant to deliver his message.

"Well," asked Hestig, "is she coming?"

Pulcher shook his head, visibly upset. "Sends love, but something important – visit soon."

Hestig wondered what could be more important than the imminent arrival of their baby. He recognised that some mystery existed here that he couldn't comprehend so he nodded and went to break the news to Trifena as gently as he was able.

She lay there for the remainder of the day, uncomfortable and miserable, still hoping Selena would call – not that she lacked anything with Hestig taking care of her every need.

The contractions began again as soon as it became dark, then Trifena's waters broke. It was Midsummer Eve.

Pulcher was despatched to fetch Stalwyn at about midnight. She came with him immediately.

Their way was well lit as they passed the inn, candlelight fluttering through the translucent green window glass from almost every room, and raucous laughter and noise gushing out from the bathhouse.

The Temple was ablaze with candlelight and some men, their purses jingling, were confidently entering through the vestibule, presumably to climb the well-worn spiral iron staircase to the floor above.

Crowds jostled along the walkways, meeting by arrangement and by chance, shouting greetings, seeking introductions, laughing at corny ribald jokes, prior to choosing partners for the night.

As the couple left the brightly lit area, the paths became dark, and they had to weave their way between the young and not so young who were taking advantage of the licence permitted that night, as it had been permitted for generations before.

Accidentally tripping over a man, Pulcher was cursed for his clumsiness by the thick voice of the blacksmith. Stalwyn confided that she feared, before the Festival was over, her doctor husband would be called out to the blacksmith's abused young wife, who was no doubt being made to wait at home for her man.

Ignoring the giggles and gasps coming from the darkness, they hurried on to Hestig's house.

He was waiting at the entrance. "The pains have started again," he said, practically dragging Stalwyn inside, "but are much worse. Whatever is going on out there?" He closed the door, forgetting Pulcher standing outside.

"Nothing that need concern us. We've more important matters in hand," she replied. "I've attended too many confinements to take the birth process for granted."

Before attending Trifena, she knelt at the house shrine and prayed to Shubinata.

"On this night of all nights, mother goddess, please deliver this mother and baby safe and well. And have pity on the shepherd's family who live by the eastern ditch. Mother goddess, have pity on us all this terrible night."

Hestig heard her prayer, which he thought rather strange, but forgot his puzzlement when Trifena called out to him that the pain was building again.

Then there was nothing to do but wait.

"Babies come in their own good time," Stalwyn told him, "and we just have to be patient. Why don't you go and sit with Pulcher for an hour or so? Trifena will be safe with me."

But he would not leave her, and did all he could to support her through each wave of pain. After three hours, he felt he could not bear to see her suffering any longer. Trifena must have seen the helplessness in his face because she was quick to reassure him.

"Just be here, dearest Hestig," she said, "that's all I want."

Another half an hour passed and the mood in the settlement changed. The frenzy in the darkness climaxed and dissipated and the voices quietened. Young men and girls, matrons and old men, dishevelled and dusty, some not bothering to hide torn clothing, began to emerge from the side paths and back walkways, making their way up to the Temple, eyes blinking in the sudden blaze of light, faces expectant. They gathered in groups or pushed their way to the front, determined not to miss the spectacle paraded before them, as it had been paraded on Midsummer Night for countless generations.

Except that this night there was a difference. Some thought with relish of the rituals to come, others hung back, some decided to go home. The majority were curious, awaiting events. But many more than usual had stayed indoors this night.

CHAPTER IX (9)

For an hour past, silent figures had been making their way through the wood towards Shubinata's temple.

Three rings of lit candles encircled the perimeter, leaving only a gap wide enough to enter and leave. There were seven thick round candles burning on pedestals inside the temple. The red carpet was strewn with white roses, as was the wooden altar, and Shubinata wore a crown of red and white roses.

Iraina knelt before the altar, feet bare, head bowed, murmuring the words of a very private prayer. Having given instructions not to be disturbed, she was able to give full vent to her frustration, and was now prostrating her beautiful body seven times before the goddess she had worshipped all her life and served for the past nine years as High Priestess.

On this night, Midsummer Eve, she would go to Vortin and perform the centuries-old ritual on the high altar. High Priest and Priestess would become one flesh, symbolising the spiritual unity between Ashuba and Shubinata, and thereby producing the unblemished sacred babies, future high priest and priestess. Thus continuity would be ensured, allowing no alien impure blood to corrupt the sacred succession of priesthood.

But there had been no unblemished sacred baby, only Nobilianus, their son – four years old and already showing signs of imbalance and dysfunction. Iraina thought with disgust that even Pulcher would have been preferable to Nobilianus. She loathed the child her body had produced with such pain and effort, the child who would have killed her had it not been for the skill of midwife Stalwyn. She loathed him vehemently, but for Vortin's sake cherished the boy as if he were the answer to her prayers, and made sure he had everything he needed and many things he did not.

And Vortin was getting old and had little strength left in him when it came to sexual prowess, but she must go through this age-old ritual tonight because the people expected it, relished it in their crazed and drunken midsummer night stupor, shared the experience in their imaginations – all those men reacting to their thoughts about her body, so that they all reached climax together.

Except that there had been no climax last year and she had had to fake it to save Vortin's reputation. This year she had arranged for priest and priestess, Sharma and Jeetuna, on her signal, to cover them with a specially woven and richly embroidered coverlet, just in case.

And what of this other business? In his disappointment at not producing heirs to the priestly line, Vortin had reintroduced an ancient custom, which his grandfather had abolished. Vortin was her lord and master, earthly representative of the great Ashuba, to be revered and obeyed, and she had always revered and obeyed him since she was a little girl, but this –!

Iraina rose from her knees and turned towards the doorway. She clapped her hands twice and her priestesses, Jeetuna and Veneta, hurried in. At a signal from the High Priestess, they encircled her waist with a daisy chain the young Temple girls had been making all day, and, one holding each end, brought her out through the three rings of candles into the warm, summer-fragrant air.

There they crowned her head with red and white roses, draped a white mantle about her shoulders, and helped her into a chariot drawn by two white oxen. She stood tall, reins clasped in her hands. Jeetuna and Veneta clambered in and stood behind her. Guarding each side of the chariot were the six Temple prostitutes. All were bare-footed.

Leading the procession was a small group of women musicians, strident brass supported by percussion and reed pipes. Behind them, young Temple flower girls, holding bunches of red and white roses, stood ready to walk in front of the chariot. Their instruction was to throw the roses before the feet of the oxen once they had cleared the wood and were entering the village. Surrounding them all was a circle of older girls carrying flaring torches.

All were dressed in white with plentiful red adornments of flowers, ribbons and jewellery. White for innocence and purity, red for blood.

At a signal from Iraina, the trumpeters sounded the first clear notes, proclaiming that the great Midsummer Festival had begun. It was an hour before daybreak. The people in the square heard the opening crescendo and their cheers reached the procession as it moved forward.

At a pace set by the oxen, whose cloven feet plodded along in their iron shoes, it wound its way along the path through the wood, with much laughter and song and chatter from the young girls. The adults were silent. As they approached the edge of the wood, they could see lights in the distance, slowly coming towards them. Iraina reined in the oxen and ordered the procession to stop. The musicians ceased playing and lowered their heads.

There was no room on the path for the two processions to pass each other. Unexpectedly, the High Priestess ordered her retinue to move to one side, into the trees, to allow the other passage.

On it came, the wooden, closed carriage pulled by two black horses, black-plumed heads nodding in unison with the measured tread of hooves that were muffled in sacking. The priestly escort trudged along silently on each side of the carriage, shapeless in their flowing black capes, arms folded inside wide sleeves and heads bowed within capacious hoods.

Most of the waiting adults lowered their eyes as the cortege passed. The younger children, uncomprehending, hid their faces in the skirts of the nearest woman, or watched fearfully. The interior of the carriage was too dark to see the two black-hooded figures who sat there with the tiny black bundle in the arms of one of them.

Iraina waited until the procession had passed on its way to Shubinata's temple and had disappeared round a bend, before ordering her people back on to the path and on towards the village.

As they left the wood, traversed the wide ditch and passed through the gap in the bank, the children began to strew the red and white roses in front of the oxen's feet, while those trained by Veneta in the art of singing began humming softly a melody she had written especially for the occasion.

The crowd in the square was waiting quietly, but as soon as they saw the cavalcade approaching, all let out a great shout that drowned the children's voices.

"Welcome to Iraina, High Priestess of Shubinata, wife of the great god! Ashuba welcomes you! Vortin waits for you!"

The procession drew to a halt in front of the Temple steps. Vitius and a group of boys joined the girls to form a guard of honour lining each side of the red carpet under the stone canopy. Below them, musicians arranged themselves on each side of the steps. The crowd quietened as they began to play 'Veneta's Song' and the children joined in with their pure, young voices. One girl's soprano soared above the others.

First Iraina then her two priestesses were helped from the chariot by Vortin's assistant priests, Selvid and Sharma. Iraina smiled as she noticed Veneta close her eyes, as if to shut out Sharma's thick, groping hands. The crowd roared its approval at this little drama.

The priests led the way up the steps, along the carpet and through the double doors of the Temple, followed by Iraina and her priestesses. The prostitutes disappeared up the spiral staircase.

Inside the Temple, Vortin was waiting impatiently in the holiest place, the sanctuary in front of the altar, for the arrival of Iraina. Selvid and Sharma took up positions on either side of him. The eunuchs were absent.

Jeetuna and Veneta led Iraina forward to the great stone altar, covered now with a layer of soft wool and a pure white linen cloth. They removed her crown and mantle, untied her girdle, and unfastened the chain-linked matching brooches on each shoulder, allowing her robe to fall round her feet.

She did not flinch before the lascivious gaze of Sharma nor the heat in the eyes of Vortin, but was angry when Selvid turned his face away. Even when she was naked he did not look at her in the way she had seen him look at Veneta.

In their turn, Sharma and Selvid moved to Vortin's side and disrobed him. Jeetuna and Veneta appeared unmoved. They were used to Vortin, who took them at his pleasure whenever he desired.

Gathering up the garments, the priests and priestesses carried them to the doorway and held them up to show the waiting crowd. A great roar went up. Iraina knew that some of the men would be wiping the perspiration from their foreheads, while others would be disappearing into the dark ways between the houses for their own purposes.

Returning inside, the four assistants placed the clothes on the floor and returned to the altar where Vortin and Iraina had remained motionless, facing each other. Steps had been placed in position, and first the High Priestess then the High Priest was helped to climb on to the altar slab. Their four assistants then knelt on the floor in front of the altar to watch and wait, ensuring that everything was done correctly according to the ancient ritual. The great stone figure of Ashuba rose above them, an appendage strapped to his loins, his luminous eyes registering approval.

Outside, the crowd was silent. The children sat down in their places, the musicians sat on the steps. And they waited, as they had done in past years, and their forebears before them, and as those who followed would also wait.

Everyone took for granted that their High Priest and Priestess would make sure that all was done correctly and reverently, and trusted that the great god Ashuba and his wife Shubinata would be satisfied with the earthly re-enactment of their union in the spirit world. Thus would be ensured the continuity of the priesthood and the safety and prosperity of the settlement. So it had been commemorated a thousand years since and so it would be commemorated a thousand years hence.

Twenty minutes passed. Some of the virile young men in the square boasted later in the bathhouse that, given the chance, they would not have kept the crowd waiting so long.

On the altar, Iraina was becoming increasingly frustrated. She had used every seduction in her knowledge to rouse Vortin's body, but had not succeeded. She knew that Sharma was watching every movement of her tongue, every caress, every bite, and was contemptuous of Vortin and pitying her. She knew that if Sharma had been on top of her, the crowd outside would have been counting by now. She knew that if she did not produce a more suitable successor than her son, Sharma would most likely succeed to the high priesthood when Vortin died, and then his bulk *would* be on top of her, and he would show no mercy.

To hide her frustration and Vortin's shame, she gave the pre-arranged signal for a coverlet to be drawn over them.

Selvid and Veneta were glad to escape from the intense emotional undercurrents that were replacing the intended glorious coupling of the bodies of High Priest and Priestess, and went outside to face the crowd, closing the doors behind them. A great roar greeted them and then the people began to chant over and over again:

"Ashu-ba!" "Ashu-ba!" "Ashu-ba!"

Encouraging a rhythm, sustaining the rhythm, louder and louder, faster and faster, their fantasies driving them on, their excitement an aphrodisiac. A couple of the women fainted and were left lying where they had fallen. Not a few of the men were preoccupied.

In the house lower down the hill, there was another tune being played to nature's unstoppable rhythm.

"Push, Trifena, push!" encouraged Stalwyn. To her, every birth was a miracle, linking those caught up in it with the dawn of creation.

"There's a good girl, pu-ush! Pu-ush! Pu-ush!"

"I can't!" sobbed Trifena, writhing in the birthing chair. "I can't push any more. It hurts!"

"You must, for your baby's sake!"

"Not much longer, Trifena," Hestig encouraged her, kissing the glistening nape of her neck beneath the rich brown coil of her perspiration-soaked hair. His arms again encircled her strongly under the armpits. "Try, dear heart!"

"I can see his head!" cried Stalwyn, leaning forward excitedly from her stool in front of the chair. "Come on, Trifena – another three pushes and it will all be over!"

"Ashu-ba!" "Ashu-ba! Ashu-ba!"

The first streamers of yellow light were flung like banners from the east over the tops of the trees as the great Temple doors were flung open. Another roar went up from the crowd, greeting the union of night and day. Except that under the coverlet there had been no union, only failure.

At the exact moment that dawn burgeoned across Byden wood, a scream from the house down the hill pierced the darkness.

But it was splintered into thousands of pieces by the even louder jagged shriek that it encountered over the shepherd's hovel by the eastern ditch.

CHAPTER X (10)

Two chilling screams. It was as if a great black cloak had suddenly been flung across the sky, smothering the dawn, stilling movement, stifling breath, paralysing thought. Even the cockerels were silent. In no time at all, everyone had gone home. Only the members of Iraina's procession remained, still guarding the entrance to the Temple.

Iraina appeared, having changed into her new purple robe, theatrically framed by the great doorway, but there was no one left to impress. The chariot and oxen were brought round to the bottom of the steps, but she waved them away and ordered the children and musicians to leave.

Veneta ushered her young charges back to their rooms. They thronged around her, clamouring for attention, the little ones clinging to her legs, but she hushed their noise and sent them off with hugs and kisses, telling them she would see them in the Temple the following morning, when the new intake of children arrived and the twelve-year-olds would be dedicated for adult service.

Then the two priestesses stood attentively in front of the two pairs of great pillars, waiting to carry out Iraina's wishes. The events of the night and her failure with Vortin had tipped the High Priestess into a well of darkness, added to which she was seething with jealousy. If she had been jealous of Jeetuna, with her self-confidence, swinging hips and overt sex appeal, she would have understood, but to be jealous of Veneta – that inhibited, plain, soft creature who had more learning than was good for her – was too much!

Iraina brought her thoughts back to the matter in hand. She guessed the reasons for the screams and despatched her priestesses in two different directions – Veneta to the shepherd's hovel, and

Jeetuna down the hill to the new house. She asked them to gather news and report back to Vortin, and also to herself after she had rested.

Then she went back inside and climbed the spiral staircase to the floor above, to eat and drink and relax with the women who lived there, and retire to her suite of rooms, her official quarters.

But tonight she longed to discard her priestly robes, to become plain Irene, and lie in her secret refuge where the bed was wider and she did not have to sleep alone.

Hearing a slight sound in the courtyard below, she moved across to the window and peered through the thick glass. The black horses and carriage had returned. Vortin was waiting for them. Two robed figures climbed down from the vehicle and the taller one stood in conversation with the High Priest, his mouth close to Vortin's ear. Iraina saw the other, a fuller figure, slip quietly out of the yard without their noticing.

Later in the morning, visitors began calling at the house down the hill with their congratulations and wax blessing tablets to lay on the house shrine, and home-made gifts for the baby: a jar of honey, a diminutive pair of leather shoes, a bone rattle jingling with tin bells, a glass bead bracelet and a rag doll.

Hestig was sitting on the mattress, his arm around Trifena's shoulders as she sat propped up on pillows, her head resting against his chest, the baby in her arms. She thanked Pulcher warmly when he proudly presented a bone hairpin he had been carving all morning.

"Are you disappointed your godchild is a girl, Pulcher?" she asked.

A grin spread across his misshapen face from ear to ear, which answered her question. Trifena wondered how she could ever have thought him ugly.

"Would you like to hold her?" she offered. He nodded and Hestig gently picked up the white swaddled bundle and placed the baby in Pulcher's arms.

The dwarf looked in wonderment at his goddaughter's dark skin and fine black hair. She gazed back at him and his grey eyes filled with tears.

Trifena knew then that she would never fear for her daughter while Pulcher was near. She had not yet forgotten the terrifying incident that started her painful labour.

"Name again," Pulcher demanded.

"Bron," replied Trifena, and repeated, "Bron. Hestig, if you bring me a wax tablet, I'll write it for him."

Hestig replaced the baby in her crib, then found a folding wooden frame containing two tablets of honey-coloured beeswax.

"See," said Trifena, "B - R - O - N," and she wrote it for their friend. "Now you try it, Pulcher."

He sat on the floor in a corner and concentrated, busily scratching shapes, the metal stylus held clumsily in his left hand.

The blacksmith's wife paid them a visit while he was engaged on this task and confided that she had slipped away from the forge house while her husband slept off his night's debauchery.

"Why 'Bron'? It's nothing like Trifena or Hestig," she commented.

Hestig looked at his wife. "We like the name," was all Trifena said.

After Bron's afternoon feed, which was not accomplished very successfully, so that the baby was still crying in her crib, Trifena wondered again where Selena was.

"I can't understand it," she said to Hestig in some distress. "Why is she avoiding us, just when I need her? She'll know how to get the baby to feed. The poor little mite must be hungry. I don't like to ask Pulcher to call on her again."

"Trifena," Hestig began, and took her hand. "I have something terrible to tell you. It's difficult to believe, but you can talk to Selena about it later."

"You think she will come, then?"

"I don't doubt it, when she's ready. She has good reason for staying away."

Then he told her of that night's dreadful happenings, which Stalwyn and their visitors had whispered to him. Trifena guessed that he was concealing some details, to save her distress.

"In nine years of Midsummer Eve coupling, Iraina has only produced Nobilianus," he reminded her. "As we have heard, he is crazed, which is why he is kept hidden in a room above the Temple. Of course, there may be a reason she is barren."

"I can't believe it," whispered Trifena, "but they say in the bathhouse that she is Vortin's daughter."

"I've heard that too, from the men," said Hestig. "Anyway, one way or another, when Vortin dies, Nobilianus, Sharma or Selvid will take his place. Most likely it would be Sharma, because he'll get there by foul means if he can't do it by fair.

"If he takes Iraina as his High Priestess, she has nothing to fear – but if he doesn't, or if he casts her aside when she gets too old to satisfy him, he could bring someone else in her place – and you know what that means."

Trifena shuddered. "She will die like the High Priestess she replaced, and all her entourage with her – set alight in the wickerwork god. We couldn't let that happen to Veneta!"

Hestig continued. "However, if those two produce another child, preferably a daughter, Nobilianus and his sister could, before their parents die, take over their priestly roles. That would ensure the continuity of the line and the safety of Vortin and Iraina at the same time."

He drew a deep breath. "So Vortin came up with this idea – that Ashuba might give them a daughter if one was sacrificed in exchange."

"But human sacrifice is against Roman law, and I thought it was abolished by Vortin's grandfather," Trifena whispered.

"It was," replied Hestig grimly, "but Vortin saw fit to reintroduce it this Midsummer Eve."

Trifena held out her arms for Bron, and Hestig placed the baby in them. She held her daughter close, rocking her gently. Bron stopped crying.

"But who – ?"

"The shepherd's new-born daughter."

"Hoad and Louca's baby?"

Hestig nodded. "Stalwyn told me that she was asked to attend the sacrifice, but had the courage to say that her skills were dedicated to bringing life into the world, not sending it out, and Vortin accepted that. Then he asked Selena, as a matron of the village."

Now Trifena understood her friend's long absence. "She could have refused," she said.

Hestig shook his head. "She thought that, by accepting, she could offer most support to Louca and could make sure that the baby did not suffer at the hands of –"

"Who? Where?" asked Trifena.

"Brocchus, he cut her throat in the wood. There had to be blood, you see, as there is at birth. As no man is allowed inside Shubinata's temple, Selena was told that she must lay the body on the altar. Can you imagine how she felt? And that's why she has stayed away – she couldn't face you with the baby's blood on her hands. But she'll be here, I'm sure, as soon as possible. She was up all last night, of course, so needs some rest first. You'll be able to ask her yourself, though perhaps neither of you will want to talk about it."

"And supposing a baby is not born to Iraina?" Trifena wondered, in tears.

"Then I imagine Vortin will do the same again next year, and the next, and the next, until they do conceive a child."

Hestig could not bring himself to point out, and the obvious truth had not yet seared through Trifena's haze of happiness, that a girl baby *had* been born that night, at the precise moment the terrible sacrifice had taken place.

And Vortin knew! Pulcher had reported that Jeetuna accosted him outside the house shortly after Bron's birth, her only purpose being to take any information back to the High Priest and Priestess.

Veneta was first back at the Temple, with news of the anguish in Hoad and Louca's home. The report from Jeetuna about the birth visibly elated the High Priest and he went straight away to the altar to thank Ashuba for the god's miraculous intervention.

As soon as she could, Veneta slipped like a brown shadow back to the shepherd's house. Selena, having discarded her black cloak, was already there, together with a crowd of friends and neighbours.

Compassion had emboldened two of the women to ask the priests at the Temple if they might retrieve the baby's body from the altar in the wood. The macabre deed having been answered already, in a way not even Vortin could have contrived, he gave his permission.

Hoad wrapped his little daughter in black cloth woven by Dagvald, carried her outside to the door post and tenderly laid her in the hole already dug. The baby's mother could not stand upright, and she had to be supported by caring arms while Veneta spoke the few words she hoped would bring some comfort, before consigning the little body and soul to the afterlife.

In her prayers, Veneta did not mention Shubinata, whose priestess she was, who appeared powerless before the great god Ashuba and his High Priest. She prayed instead to a god whom she did not know, who had no name, but who she was beginning to believe was there, waiting in the shadows – a god who loved, and who would welcome this mite and take care of her until her parents could reach her again.

The baby's mother raised her eyes to Veneta's.

"Do you believe that, Louca?" Veneta asked her.

"If you say so, Veneta, I believe it," was the trusting answer.

As they watched Hoad filling the pit, Louca was overwhelmed with such grief that she had to be helped back into the little round house. Kendrus, the physician, and one or two others followed, but all those who were not needed dragged heavy feet homewards.

Only Hoad and Veneta were left outside. He pushed a stick into the ground to mark the grave then straightened his back and looked towards the Temple. Veneta guessed that his thoughts were as black as the little bundle he had just buried.

CHAPTER XI (11)

Selena and Dagvald visited the new family later in the day. The two women clung to each other, without speaking of the event that had taken place.

"I need your advice." Trifena sounded desperate. "You've had so much experience."

"I'll help, if I can. What's the problem?"

"I don't know where to start. I don't seem to have any milk, and anyway she won't suck, so she's hungry and keeps crying – she'll die if I can't feed her. How often should I try? Then I know that Hestig will want me to be a proper wife to him at some time, but I can't bear the thought at the moment, and anyway, I don't want another baby too soon. There's so much I don't know!"

"The first thing to do is relax," smiled Selena, "and tackle the problems one at a time."

Using experience and common sense, she answered all Trifena's questions, and finally managed to persuade Bron to hold on to Trifena's nipple. They all cheered when the baby started to suck.

Neither Trifena nor Hestig managed to get much sleep that night, the few dark hours being filled with the wails of both mother and daughter, attempts at feeding, experimenting with changing Bron's napkins, and checking, when she wasn't crying, that she was still breathing.

So both were feeling less than their best next morning when Trifena heard the notes of the trumpets and the insistent beating of the drum.

"Listen, Hestig," she called to him. "A band! I wonder what it's about."

Hestig looked terrified. "I think they may be coming here," he said, his voice hoarse.

"Why here?" Trifena was mystified. "Hestig – what's wrong with you?"

"I'm going for Pulcher," he told her. "He'll fetch Selena and Dagvald," and he disappeared through the door into the courtyard. Minutes later he returned. The music was not any louder.

"They seem to be processing round the village. I'll help you to dress, Trifena, so that we can receive them."

"Who?" asked Trifena, still puzzled.

"Vortin and his minions. I'm sure they're coming to see our baby."

"That's an honour, Hestig. Why are you looking so grim?"

"Just get dressed!" he ordered, so harshly that she obeyed without further question.

Vortin's retinue was making its way slowly round the settlement. Sharma and Selvid led the way, carrying between them a processional statue of Ashuba. Behind them, dressed in red, the High Priest stood in a golden chariot pulled by the six eunuchs.

Jeetuna and Veneta followed, with difficulty, carrying a statue of Shubinata, resplendent with her flowing hair, huge breasts and stomach.

Iraina's smaller chariot, also gold, was pulled by the Temple women and the older children. The High Priestess, too, was robed in red.

As they proceeded, more and more people joined the end of the procession, the children running and dancing in time to the rhythms.

The cavalcade passed the carpenter's workshop and between the stonemason's and metal worker's houses, then followed the path to the corn dryer by the bank and ditch on the eastern edge of the village.

It turned right outside the house of Hoad and Louca. Vortin was quite unaware of whose house it was. He didn't notice the freshly dug grave nor see Hoad come to the door to curse and spit in the direction of his receding priestly back.

The procession continued along the line of the bank, between the farm labourers' tumbledown houses, and past the sheep pens and cow byre and the stables at the back of the inn.

It went past the forge and continued between the craftsmen's homes to the public latrines and the house of the sewer cleaner, before turning west towards the beekeeper's, then passed Pulcher's door.

Those pulling the chariots enlisted help from the crowd now. Vortin chose to ignore the barely audible grumbling and cursing as they struggled and strained up the hill, finally arriving, breathless, outside the Roman-style house. There they stopped.

Sharma nodded towards Brocchus, who strode to the door and banged loudly.

In the courtyard, Trifena waited excitedly, Bron in her arms.

"What an honour!" she exclaimed, and could not understand the fear on the faces of her husband and friends as they looked at each other but said nothing.

Hestig swung round to face Dagvald, who was standing behind them all.

"As a member of the council, I have some influence in secular affairs," Dagvald said in reply to Hestig's unasked question, "but am no match for Vortin. He insists that everything he does and says carries the approval and authority of Ashuba."

Hestig nodded to Pulcher to open the door.

The priests and priestesses had placed the statues of the god and goddess on each side of the doorposts, like sentries on guard, keeping the crowd at a distance. Vortin climbed down from his chariot and walked between the statues into the courtyard. He glanced about him, then at the little group standing before him. Trifena was at ease, but only because she still did not understand the purpose of the visit.

Iraina, as lovely as always, came through the doorway, followed by the priests and priestesses. Veneta was looking troubled and did not return Trifena's welcoming smile.

"Trifena, I bid you good morning." Vortin had addressed her directly. She bowed her head to him. "And you, Hestig." Hestig nodded. The High Priest reached out a thin arm towards the baby.

"So this is Bron."

Trifena was surprised and pleased that he had remembered all their names.

"I have much of import to say to you both."

Hestig led the way into the triclinium. Vortin and Iraina indicated to the priests and priestesses that they should also follow, but Pulcher stayed with Brocchus at the doorway to the elegant room and Selena and Dagvald were left standing in the courtyard.

The maidservant, Bettina, was sent to bring wine and snacks for everyone assembled. Vortin and Iraina sat on a couch and indicated that Trifena should sit on a chair. Everyone else remained standing.

Trifena nursed Bron on her lap, still confused and wondering why her family had been singled out for this unusual distinction.

Vortin signalled to Selvid, who brought forward a small, carved wooden box on a silver tray and laid it at Trifena's feet. Then Iraina signalled to Jeetuna, who brought another carved box on a silver tray and placed it by the side of the first. Trifena was at a loss for words and sat staring at the gifts.

"Open them!" ordered Vortin impatiently. Hestig took Bron from Trifena's arms so that she could. Nervously, she lifted the boxes on to her lap and raised one lid and then the other, releasing their sandalwood perfume. When she saw their contents, she gasped and stared in disbelief. In Vortin's box lay the most exquisite, incised gold finger ring, and in Iraina's, matching gold drop earrings.

"Thank you, but – but why?" Trifena stammered.

Vortin stood up and so did Iraina. His reply sent the young mother's senses reeling.

"We have come to claim our daughter," Vortin announced.

"Your daughter?" Trifena cried. She jumped up, scattering the boxes and their contents at her feet. Sharma scooped them up in his large, acquisitive hands and hid them in his robe. Grabbing Bron from Hestig, Trifena held her tightly. "She's our baby!"

Hestig moved across and put an arm around her shoulders, pulling her protectively to him. Veneta stood motionless, all colour gone from her face.

At the doorway, Pulcher took a step forward, but was restrained by the outstretched arm of Brocchus, who towered over him.

"Ashuba has commanded it," Vortin continued with absolute confidence. "At the exact moment he received the spirit of the sacrificed child – the shepherd's daughter, I believe – he sent this baby to us – not from Iraina's womb, I allow, but from yours."

"You're not making sense! Take back your gifts! She's not for sale!" screamed Trifena hysterically. "Tell him, Hestig, tell him!"

"It's as my wife says," Hestig said quietly. "The baby is ours. The fact that she was born at dawn on Midsummer Day is just coincidence."

Vortin ignored him. "Young woman, there is no argument. At eight days you will bring her for purification and naming, not to the temple in the wood but to the High Temple. You will take care of her until she is three years old and on her third birthday you will bring her again, to join the Temple children."

"No! No!" screamed Trifena, managing to stay upright only because Hestig's arms were around her and the baby.

"She will be educated in the ways of our ritual and worship," Vortin continued implacably, "and when she is twelve years old, she will be given a new name and become a priestess of Shubinata, in training for High Priestess and consort of Nobilianus. I have decreed it shall be so! Ashuba has decreed it shall be so! There is no appeal!"

With that, Vortin swept out of the room, his red cloak swirling behind him. Iraina and their retinue followed. Veneta was last.

"I didn't know! I didn't know!" she whispered in great distress as she too left the room. "I'll be back as soon as I can!"

With noise and ceremony, the procession continued up the slope on its way back to the Temple.

Selena and Dagvald hurried into the triclinium to offer what comfort they could, but Trifena was inconsolable.

"I won't give her up, I can't! She's my flesh, my bone, my blood! It would be like tearing out my insides! I'll kill him before I part with her!"

"We'll leave the settlement," Hestig said, "leave during the night."

"It'll be no use," Trifena sobbed. She remembered her encounter with Ashuba in the Temple the day after they arrived in Byden, and again on the night her labour began. "We can't fight Ashuba! He had this planned before we arrived in Byden. It is punishment for my wrongdoing!"

She crouched before the shrine, Bron clasped close to her. "Have pity!" she pleaded. The eyes in the stone faces of the gods appeared unmoved. "Punish me, if you must, but not my baby! Not my Bron!"

"Hush, hush, my darling. There was no wrongdoing." Hestig tried to comfort her, crouching beside her and rocking them both in his arms. "Come and lie down. You must rest or you won't have enough milk to feed her."

Pulcher was hovering in the courtyard, obviously not fully understanding the threat to his goddaughter. Selena sent him to Stalwyn, to ask for a sleeping potion that Trifena could take without harming the feeding baby.

Dagvald left to consult Severus, though he said he feared that the old man would be powerless to help.

Late that evening, Veneta slipped away from her suite of rooms above the schoolroom and out into the warm air. Her urgent knocking at the front door was heard by Pulcher, who opened it. He led her into the bedroom where Selena was doing her best to comfort the stricken family. Trifena, with eyes swollen, held out her arms to Veneta.

"Can you offer us any hope?" asked Hestig desperately.

"Perhaps, a little," she replied.

And so it was that, by the time Bron's third birthday was imminent, she had spent so much play time with the children in the Temple that it was a second home to her, and Veneta had become a second mother.

Sometimes, Veneta brought her youngest charges from the Temple to the Roman-style house, where they could enjoy a normal, happy, home environment.

"Bron will be well cared for," promised Veneta, "I'll see to that. She will be fed, clothed and educated. Start saving now and, when she is twelve years old, you can pay the sacrifice money and buy her back."

Trifena did not believe for one minute that Vortin would let them have Bron back and she guessed that, if Veneta was being honest with herself, neither did she believe it.

Section II

VENETA

CHAPTER XII (12)

AD 388

Bron's third birthday – Midsummer Day – was warm and sunny. As usual, the settlement was beginning the day's holiday by sleeping late, recovering from the night's pleasures.

The crowd that had collected outside the Temple at dawn had dwindled in number from previous years. Iraina was beginning to lose her wild, youthful beauty. She had remained barren and many had secretly begun to ridicule the suspected lack of activity on the altar slab beneath the coverlet.

However, there had been no more baby sacrifices. Apparently, Vortin had decided that there was no further need.

Trifena and their slave, Bettina, were early in the kitchen, making ready a birthday meal for Bron. The girl lit the fire in the oven and prepared honey cakes ready for baking when the ashes reached the right temperature, then mixed eggs, herbs, milk and oil for omelettes. Trifena meantime stuffed dates with pine kernels and rolled them in salt before frying in honey. She also whipped fresh cream from their cow to pour over a dish of early raspberries and strawberries picked the previous day.

When Bron came running into the kitchen to find her mother, her excitement and laughter filled the room with sunshine, or so it seemed to Trifena. She swept her daughter up in her arms and hugged her close, wishing her a happy birthday.

"How many thleeps before I go to live with Veneta?" Bron wanted to know.

Trifena sighed at the lisped question. "No more sleeps, Bron – it's today you go."

She settled the little girl's legs around her waist above her stomach, which was swelling again, and carried her across the covered courtyard towards the triclinium. They stopped on the way so that Bron could kiss the stone lion 'good morning' and slurp a mouthful of the refreshing cold water cascading from its open mouth into the shell-shaped basin.

Then the child looked enquiringly at her mother and Trifena smiled and nodded. Bending over, still anchored around her mother's waist, she stretched her bare arm into the lion's mouth and down by the side of the water pipe. Reaching to the bottom where the stone was flat and the pipe emerged from the plinth, and not caring that she was wet to the shoulder, her fingers found a small package wrapped round with leaves and tied with grasses. On withdrawing her hand and opening the parcel, Bron laughed to find a piece of honeycomb filled with honey.

"Just what I wanted!" she declared.

Trifena laughed too and kissed Bron again.

Hestig was already in the triclinium. Their son, Hestigys, not yet two years old, was running round him, and baby Trifosa was happily wriggling about on his lap. None of them was yet dressed.

Since Bron's birth, Trifena had made sure that the red curtain was pulled securely across the house shrine when it was not in use, although Ashuba's eyes had not sought hers in the intervening three years.

"Why should they?" Trifena asked Hestig. "He got what he wanted – he's got our Bron."

Neither of them fully understood what had happened the night she went into labour, but the outcome was in no doubt.

Still in their night attire, the family played the children's favourite games and sang their favourite nursery songs, before gathering at the table to enjoy the birthday breakfast. In Roman style, Hestig and Trifena reclined on the couches, resting on their left arms, while the children made themselves comfortable on the cushions around them.

Pulcher arrived as the omelettes were being served, and Bettina was sent back to the kitchen to make some more.

"When is it prethent time?" lisped Bron with obvious impatience.

"Now," said Trifena. "Look, I've made you a toilet bag and everything in it is for you to take with you to the Temple."

Bron's little hands reached into the linen bag and found a circular polished metal mirror secured in a wooden frame, combs carved from antler, a pottery night lamp made by her father, a pair of blue, soft-leather slippers, and a variety of other gifts to make her life at the Temple more comfortable. Selena had made and sent a long white dress with sleeves to the wrist, and Pulcher gave her a bracelet he had painstakingly created from painted bone beads.

"Just what I wanted!" Bron exclaimed as she discovered each present and thanked the giver.

The moment Trifena had dreaded for three years had arrived. Veneta came for Bron before the sun was high overhead. Dressed in her new white dress, with summer flowers playing hide-and-seek in her dark curls, and carrying a bouquet Trifena had lovingly created, Bron trustingly took Pulcher's hand and together they followed the priestess to the Temple.

Trifena, her sight blurred with unshed tears, walked behind with Hestig, each carrying one of their two younger children. Selena and her grandson Soranus, hand in hand, brought up the rear.

As they reached the Temple steps, they were joined by other families, and together passed through the great entrance. For all the children, this annual ritual of dedication was a day of honour and rejoicing.

Many of the children were orphans or had parents too poor to feed them, so they had been sold to the Temple. All had the option of leaving at twelve years old if someone could afford to buy them back. This happened to very few, so boys became eunuchs or trained for the priesthood, while girls learnt the arts of prostitution or trained as priestesses to serve Iraina.

The boys chosen as eunuchs would become the responsibility of Brocchus, and their excruciatingly painful ceremony would take place at a later date.

Each year Veneta made sure that all the girls who from now on would be living on the second floor were virgins, and that initiation did not take place before her charges were twelve years old, in accordance with Temple law as written in the great Book of the Altar. Their initiation, almost like an examination, was the prerogative of Vortin, followed later by Sharma, and Selvid if he wished, which he never did, before the girls were made available to pleasure any man who could pay the high fees charged.

Any children not wanted were sold off. Byden Temple was renowned over a large area for the excellence of its discipline and instruction, and many individuals and groups were prepared to pay inflated prices for its discarded twelve-year-old children. These had left the Temple the previous day.

Now the three-year-olds were to be ceremoniously presented to Ashuba at the outset of their training.

Once inside, Bron was cheerily greeted by the children already living at the Temple and was happy to sit with her friends, cross-legged on the floor. Every now and then she turned and waved to her family. Pulcher grinned and waved back.

Once she ran back to Trifena.

"Mummy, I don't like the god today," she whispered. "He's looking at me and his eyes are red."

Startled, Trifena knew she must not show her own fear and reached for Hestig's hand.

"Don't look at him, Bron. Look at Veneta."

"She has a cloth over her head."

Trifena smiled. "It's not a cloth, dear, it's a veil. Look at the High Priestess, then – that tall lady in the golden gown."

"She's pretty," whispered Bron, "but who's that old man? He's looking at me, too."

"He's the High Priest. Now, go and sit down again, there's a good girl."

Bron did as she was told but continued to steal glances at the High Priest. She thought he looked a lot like Ashuba, who stood behind him, though he was not so tall and was much thinner than the stone god.

As the ceremony continued, music from lyre and tibia accompanied young voices, then all present listened enchanted as a pure soprano soared above their heads and into the ceiling's shadowed recesses.

The final notes of the chants died away and the priests and priestesses left the holy sanctuary.

No one had noticed the white face pressed close to the thick glass of a window high up in the wall. Nobilianus, now seven years old, had heard about the bride his parents had picked for him, and was curious to see her for himself. Instantly recognisable from the description he had wheedled out of Veneta, his first sight of Bron did not displease him, and he returned to his room happier for the secret inspection.

Trifena knew that her daughter was anxious to show the family the bedroom that would be hers for the next nine years, although Bron could not comprehend that timescale. She allowed the child to take her by the hand and lead them up the spiral staircase, opposite the one used by the prostitutes, to a small room. Its walls were plastered and painted a muted green, and light came from a window in the tiled roof.

Three mattresses were laid against the walls and each occupant had a bedside cupboard, a chest of drawers, hanging space and a shelf.

Only when the last little pottery ornament, lovingly crafted by Hestig, had been filled with flowers and arranged on the shelf, and her special toys had been placed on her pillow, did Veneta ask Trifena and the family to leave. With heavy hearts, they rejoined Pulcher and Selena with her grandson, Soranus, who had been waiting patiently below.

Trifena reached no further than the top of the Temple steps outside when she burst into tears.

"We'll soon be home," Hestig said sympathetically, putting his arm round her.

"But it's not home without Bron," sobbed Trifena.

Slowly and sadly, the little group made its way down the hill. When they reached their house, Pulcher left them, saying that his voices were giving him a headache so he was going for a walk to listen to them in peace.

Once inside, Hestig took the children to the kitchen to ask Bettina to serve lunch, while Selena sat with Trifena in the triclinium, holding her hand.

"Bron has been a bright star in my sky," Trifena said through her tears, "and suddenly she's shot from view. All I have left is the darkness."

"That's not true, Trifena," Selena remonstrated. "You have your husband – and you know how much he loves you. You have two beautiful children and another coming, and they all need you. Besides, Bron's not very far away."

Up on the hill, the children were excitedly playing follow-my-leader as Veneta led them on a tour of the Temple and introduced her newly-arrived charges to those who worked and lived in the precinct.

By the time she took Bron back to her room, two young girls were already there, waiting for her.

Bron regarded them seriously. The taller of the two had yellow hair that fell in wisps past her shoulders and kind, dark eyes that slanted upwards at the corners and looked at Bron inquisitively. She could not see very much of the younger girl, who was partially concealed behind her friend's shoulder.

Veneta made sure they were happily settled before leaving to organise supper, promising to return before they went to sleep.

"What did Veneta say your name was?" asked the older girl. Bron told her.

"That's easy to remember," said the younger of the two, emerging from behind her friend. "I'm Naila and Sorin's name is Sorin. She sings."

The older girl laughed, then explained to Bron, "Naila's only five, she's little. I'm big, I'm six. How old are you?"

Bron remembered it was her birthday. "Three."

"That's very little," commented Sorin. "Veneta says we've got to look after you. Are you an orphan?"

Bron didn't know. "I am," said Sorin. "My mummy and daddy took sick and died two years ago."

"I've got a daddy and mummy," Naila added proudly and Bron saw her eyes shine dark blue. "Daddy's a farmer."

"I'm hungry," Bron then realised, and began to cry. She was also very tired.

Sorin and Naila sat on her mattress and each put an arm round her shoulders.

"Supper will be here soon," Sorin comforted her. "I know – let's play with your spinning top."

When one of the oldest girls arrived with their pottage, all three were taking turns in bouncing Bron's big, red leather ball round the room.

After supper, her two new friends helped her undress and then they took time to comb each other's hair, wondering at the different colours of black, yellow and light brown. Sorin returned Bron's used chamber pot to her cupboard, and tucked her into bed.

"Will you wet the bed?" asked Naila.

"I do sometimes," replied Bron.

"Don't worry about it," Sorin advised. "Veneta's left a linen napkin for you, and she will have put a layer of lamb's wool over your mattress."

Veneta was delayed on her nightly round, having had to settle most of the youngest children by playing with them or telling them stories, and did not reach Bron's room until deep dusk. When she did, she smiled to see Bron, her face still wet with tears, cuddled up to Sorin and both fast asleep in the older girl's bed.

CHAPTER XIII (13)

"The water's cold," complained Bron.

"You'll get used to that," Sorin told her.

Veneta, helped by Sorin and Naila, were washing and dressing Bron on her first morning in the Temple.

The girls brought her a straight calf-length tunic with short sleeves, the colour of the sky above the village on that bright summer morning. The girdle at the waist, a deeper blue, was hidden by an ample overhang of material.

"It's too big," complained Bron.

"That's because you're going to grow much bigger," smiled Veneta, "and when you do, it will fit perfectly."

At that moment, one of the older girls brought in their breakfast of bread and pomegranates and a jug of Stan water. Bron looked doubtfully at the fruit.

"It's a pomegranate – try it," urged Veneta. "They've come a long way – from North Africa."

"It's all right to eat the pips," Naila assured her, helpfully.

After breakfast, the children gathered outside in the portico and Veneta organised them into a column, three abreast. Bron held hands with her two new friends. Veneta led them down the Temple steps and to the right alongside the stone wall on which the covered walkway stood.

"Where are we going?" she heard Bron whisper to Sorin.

"To school – you'll enjoy it," her friend whispered back.

As they turned the corner of the wall, Soranus was standing with his grandmother in the doorway of her house. Bron waved happily and they waved back, before Selena hurried off down the hill, presumably to report to Trifena.

Veneta led the children to the school at the top of the settlement, behind the Temple, backed by Byden Wood. It was indistinguishable from most of the round houses in the village, though bigger, and had a base of large stones built up in several courses, covered by a steeply sloping roof of interwoven branches and turf.

Once inside, they all stood still, blinking and unable to see anything for a moment. From the depths of the darkness, a soft and richly-textured voice, of deeper timbre than any local speech, and with a strange accent, wrapped itself around them.

"Well, and what have we here?" asked the voice. "If I am not mistaken, the Temple children have arrived – and I do believe that they are the cleverest and most beautiful children I have ever seen – wouldn't you say so, Veneta?"

Veneta laughed. "Yes, I would say so," she agreed.

The darkness began to lighten, but still they could not see the person standing at the end of the room.

"Children, say 'good morning' to Africanus."

The children obeyed in their sing-song fashion, "Good mor-ning, Afri-can-us!" The voice responded, "Good morning, children, and welcome."

Then from the darkness moved forward a giant of a man, as black as ebony wood. Bron, obviously startled, caught hold of Veneta's hand.

"Bron, this is Africanus. He will teach you many things, so you must listen well."

"I will also tell you some exciting stories," promised the big man.

"About Africa," explained Sorin.

"Where the 'granates came from?" asked Bron.

Veneta replied, "That's right. It's a country a long way from here, Bron."

"Where the sun always shines," added Naila.

"It's where I was born," and the African threw back his head and laughed so infectiously that the children began laughing with him.

"I'll leave them in your care, Africanus."

"We'll have our lessons outside today, Veneta. You little ones come with me and I'll find you a writing tablet and a stylus each. The older ones collect yours from the cupboard and wait outside."

"I will call for you at lunch time," Veneta told the youngest, "and we'll find something exciting to do this afternoon. Be good, now," and she left.

At the end of the morning, when she returned, she found them happily playing the Roman game *terni lapilli*. Africanus was helping Bron and the other young children take turns to place their coloured stones on the nine-square wooden board, trying to line up three in a row in any direction. The older boys were playing each other and making a lot of noise every time a game was won.

"How has she coped?" Veneta quietly asked Africanus.

"I believe she enjoyed the morning – they all have," he reported. "I gave them a writing lesson, then we went into the wood to find different barks and leaves to draw. We had a break only when the farmer's wife came to give them all a drink of milk – it was still warm from the cow – and again when the baker called in with his cheese cakes."

"Splendid!" exclaimed Veneta with pleasure. "Now, I'll take them off your hands till tomorrow."

"See you later, Bron," chorused Sorin and Naila as she left with Veneta and four other young children, two boys and two girls.

"How would you like to eat your lunch by the stream?" Veneta suggested and had no need to ask twice. "Bron, shall we call in at Selena's on the way and invite Soranus to join us?"

"Yeth, please," said Bron, "and let's call on Mummy, too."

"Not today," replied the priestess. "I will make sure you see your family regularly, but I want you to settle into your new home first."

After leaving Selena's house, with six children at her heels, Veneta passed the Temple and headed towards the eastern boundary of the village, not wishing to pass Bron's home.

As they reached Hoad's house, Louca came out to greet them. The priestess's eyes were drawn to the plot of ground outside the entrance, where lay Louca's first born. There was little sign of the grave now. Veneta knew that it had taken a long while for Louca to come to terms with the sacrifice of their daughter. For two years she would not let Hoad come anywhere near her, but he had waited patiently, and now Louca held a baby in her arms.

Veneta had thought that the young couple would loathe the sight of Bron, who most people accepted had taken the place of their murdered baby, but unexpectedly the couple displayed genuine affection for the little girl and were deeply upset when they learned the future Vortin had planned for her.

"Trifena and Hestig were pawns in his game as surely as we were," they admitted to Veneta.

Now, Louca crouched low so that the little girl could look at her son.

"Mummy's going to have a baby soon," Bron confided. Louca smiled and ruffled the dark curls.

The little party reached the animal pens and Veneta let the children stop to talk to the cows, sheep and goats, before following the beaten path down to the ford.

With delight, they removed their sandals and paddled about in the stream. The water was so clear it was almost invisible. When they became too boisterous and the boys splashed too vigorously, Veneta called them on to the bank to eat their lunch. She had brought hard-boiled eggs, bread, raw carrots, cucumber and junket. They quenched their thirst with water from the stream.

"Veneta, may we go to Stanmere?" asked Soranus.

"Of course, as long as you all behave yourselves when you get there," she replied. "Bring your sandals with you."

The priestess led them, wading uphill for half a mile, until they reached the spring where the star-flashing water bubbled up from under the ground. It formed a pool before streaming down to the settlement below.

Veneta silenced the children's chatter as they approached, and in the sudden quietness, thought she heard a rustling in the undergrowth. The mere was encircled by a high bank and thin clusters of trees. She gazed all round but could see nothing untoward, and presumed it must be some woodland creature seeking cover.

"Shubinata's nymphs look after this sacred grove," she told her charges. "See, people have thrown coins and things they value into the pool."

"My mother threw a shale bracelet in there a few days ago," volunteered Soranus. "The man who sold it to her had oiled it well and she thought it was jet."

The children looked down among the sacrificial pots, the much-valued shiny pebbles, an ox skull and baby shoes, but it had gone.

This time they all heard the unexplained noises in the bushes, too loud to be caused by a wild creature.

"Who's there? Come out and show yourself!" ordered Veneta, moving across to protect Bron.

"Nymphs!" called a squeaky voice.

The children were ready to take flight, but were reassured by Veneta's reply.

"Nonsense! Come out, Pulcher, and stop playing silly games!"

Pulcher emerged from the trees, looking as guilty as Trifena's new puppy, Skeel, when he was caught with the family's lunch in his jaws. Bron squealed with delight and ran over and took his hand.

"Lad, you've no need to hide," Veneta scolded him. "You're welcome to come with us at any time, you should know that."

Pulcher smiled down at Bron. "Sorry, Veneta. Not sure. Everything changed."

"Nothing has changed," Veneta assured him, "except that Bron is living away from home."

She watched as they all played hide-and-seek with the dwarf among the trees, and then it was time to return.

Veneta and Pulcher took turns to carry a sleepy Bron back to the Temple.

"How did you get up to the mere without me seeing you?" Veneta asked him.

"Crossed lynchets. Through sacred pits of the dead," he explained. "Quiet – hear my voices."

"What are your voices saying, Pulcher?"

He told her in his halting speech. Veneta said she understood. "I will help you all I can," she promised.

CHAPTER XIV (14)

On their return, Veneta found the Temple staff gossiping about a Roman soldier who was staying overnight at the inn on his way back north. He had told the innkeeper's wife that he intended visiting the Roman temple on the following morning.

"First thing," Iraina instructed Veneta, "take some of the children with you and make sure all is in order in there. No one has been near the place for months." She smiled and added, "He probably won't be around very early – he said he'd be spending the evening in the bathhouse."

The simple Roman temple, circular in design, pillared and open to the elements, stood solidly on the eastern side of Ashuba's Great Temple, near Byden Wood. It had been built there as a nod towards the population's fealty to their Roman masters but was only used when any of the military or a Roman family passed through on their way to more important towns.

Veneta was aware that Vortin was never quite sure of Rome's religious allegiances and had played safe by erecting two altars, in front of the only solid wall.

One was dedicated to the deified emperor, displaying a bust crowned with a laurel wreath, which could have portrayed any one of them.

The other was for the middle-eastern god, Jesus, who was represented by a Portland stone slab on which had been painted a stylised emblem of a fish, the Christian symbol.

The High Priest was highly suspicious of the Christian religion. It challenged the existence of Ashuba and the hitherto unquestioned authority of the Temple, and he said he would have none of it. Consequently, apart from the very few who had travelled, the people of Byden lived in ignorance of Christian beliefs and practices, and obviously Vortin intended to keep it that way.

Veneta woke Sorin, Naila and Bron early next morning.

"Girls, we've a very important job to do," she told them. "Breakfast is on its way up. Hurry and get dressed and meet me at the entrance as soon as you can."

When they had gathered, she explained, "There's a Roman soldier staying at the inn and he will be visiting his temple during the morning, so Iraina has asked us to give it a good clean before he gets there. Sorin, I want you to find suitable flowers and grasses to fill the temple containers. You young ones, take what you can carry of these cleaning materials, and follow me."

They set off with twig brooms, bristle brushes, a mop, sheep's wool dusters, and oil for the lamps. The young lad, Vitius, brought a wooden bucket full of water for washing the stone floor.

Veneta tried to make the work into play for the children, although she could see they were not quite convinced. She also used the occasion to give them a lesson on housework and the religious beliefs of the Romans.

They were chatting happily when the slipping and sliding of iron nails on stone caused them to turn, and there stood a young Roman equestrian tribune. Now it was Veneta's turn to be embarrassed as she stammered her apologies in her best Latin, and offered to leave, but the young man would have none of it.

"I can wait," he said. He removed his bronze helmet and laid it on the stone floor.

Just then Sorin arrived with an armful of greenery and he asked Veneta if he might help fill the containers on the floor around the walls. She kept a motherly eye on them all, but relaxed when she saw that no harm was afoot and the job was taking half the time with the young man's assistance. He was talking to Sorin in her own tongue and making her laugh.

"Bron," Sorin said, "I told the tribune that your father made the flower containers. He asked if his name was Hestig."

"Do you know my daddy?" asked Bron in surprise.

"No, but I have a message for him," replied the Roman and asked Veneta if he might talk to Bron outside. Veneta nodded and they all sat on the steps in the sunshine.

"So your name is Bron," said the tribune. "That's a pretty name, and you're a beautiful little girl. How old are you?"

"Three," said Bron.

Veneta watched him thoughtfully as he studied Bron's black curls and intelligent dark eyes, and her flawless baby skin well browned by the summer sun, and wondered what he was thinking.

"I know your father is a potter and his name is Hestig. Is your mother's name Trifena?"

Bron nodded, obviously amazed that this stranger should know anything at all about her family. He addressed Veneta, again in Latin.

"I'm on my way back to Eboracum but have come via Byden at the express request of Adrianus Maximus, our retired provincial governor. Bron's parents were his long-time slaves and I will take news of them. Would you tell me the way to their house?"

Veneta gave directions and offered to have one of the Temple boys take him there, but he declined the favour.

"I will make my offerings here then find my own way. Thank you for your courtesy."

Veneta and the children left him to his religious observances and returned to the Temple to report to Iraina.

An hour later, the High Priestess decided that she should inspect Veneta's work and the cleanliness of the Roman shrine. She found all in good order, and a gold coin on the altar to the emperor.

The coin never reached the Temple's coffers.

CHAPTER XV (15)

Bron was delighted when Pulcher began working at the Temple.

"My voices told me to come," he confided to Stalwyn. "Veneta help me. She ask Selvid, Selvid ask Vortin. He say yes. I am useful, only want a mid-day meal."

He became a runabout for the staff and anyone else who gave him orders, enduring the occasional beatings and thrown missiles.

"Bron cries when I hurt," he told Stalwyn on more than one occasion, "but I happy near her."

The High Priest and Priestess showed an intense interest in 'their' daughter, and everyone involved in her upbringing was required to report to them at regular intervals.

"Vortin wants to know about even the slightest stomach cramp, sniffle, cough or rash she has," Iraina had said, and Veneta was often at the physician's house, asking him to visit Bron.

Stalwyn made sure she herself reported the outcome of these visits to Bron's mother, Trifena, to allay her fears. Trifena was reassured to know that her daughter was receiving such excellent medical attention without it costing Hestig any fees.

Stalwyn had been charged with overall responsibility for Bron's general health. It was not an onerous job as life continued pleasantly for the child, mostly in the schoolroom, where Bron enjoyed her lessons and, like an Illyrian sponge, soaked up everything that Africanus taught her. She whispered to Stalwyn that she loved the huge African almost as much as she loved her daddy and Pulcher.

Bron's afternoons were spent with Veneta or in the Temple with Selvid, who taught the rituals and ceremony according to Atrebatis tradition, as laid down in the great parchment rolls in the clay cylinder on the altar.

All her free time was spent playing with Sorin and Naila, and there was hardly a squabble between them.

Stalwyn was often at the Roman house, as Trifena was not at all well during her fourth pregnancy. On one occasion, calling unexpectedly, she found the doors unlocked and Trifena lying on her bed, sobbing loudly. Hestig was at work in the market place, and Trifena had sent Bettina, their slave, to play with the children at the stepping-stones.

"Whatever's the matter?" asked Stalwyn. "Are you ill?"

Encircled by the midwife's arms, Trifena gasped, "No, it's just that I miss Bron so much, and I'm sure she thinks of Veneta as her mother."

Stalwyn stroked the masses of pale chestnut hair and reassured Trifena that her fears were unfounded.

In the kitchen she found an old dish, brought it back to the bedroom, and kindled a lump of jet, purchased in Calleva, which the tradesman said had been picked up on a beach south of Hadrian's great wall.

"In case you have suffocation of the womb," Stalwyn explained, and confided to Selena later that the vapours did nothing to relieve Trifena's dark mood.

"It's all in her mind," replied Selena. "She's been so restless lately."

Stalwyn nodded. "It's only natural that she should be missing Bron."

Selena hesitated. "It began about the time that Bron moved into the Temple," she said slowly, "but I think it has more to do with the visit of that young Roman soldier. I was there when he called, bringing news of Eboracum and the people they used to know, and all the excitement of the town. Life here must seem very dull in comparison."

"How is Hestig coping with her?"

Selena shook her head again. "Things are not right there, either. I know you will treat this in confidence, Stalwyn –"

"Of course."

"I called to take the children off her hands a couple of days ago. Bettina let me in and they didn't know I was there. She and Hestig were in the triclinium, having an almighty argument. You know, I've never heard them quarrel before – he usually looks at her as if he can't quite believe his good fortune – but he was shouting at her mercilessly, and the children were crying, and then there was such a crash! I'm sure she threw something at him. I told Bettina not to let them know I'd called, and went home. It really upset me to hear them going at each other like that."

Trifena was not happy that Hestig was spending more and more time at work. He had added a small extension to the back of the house with wheel, kiln and storage space, working in there by oil lamp during the evenings and at his booth during daylight hours.

He told Trifena that he had many orders to fulfil, which she believed because she saw the increasing popularity of his table and kitchen ware. Jugs, jars, bowls and dishes were stacked high in the storeroom. His cream-coloured flagons embellished under the rims with heads of goddesses were especially popular with local housewives, and further afield. Many of the merchants who passed through Byden left orders for collection on their next visit.

His earnings provided an increasing surplus. This was even after laying money aside for Temple and village taxes and providing a portion of his crop for the Roman corn tax, to feed the military. He began saving towards what he and Trifena called 'Bron's account', the money they were accumulating to buy Bron back from Vortin and Iraina when she was twelve years old.

One evening, when the children and Bettina were asleep, and the hour was late, Trifena decided that she was spending too many evenings on her own and, oil lamp in hand, crossed the courtyard to the kitchen, went out by the back door and so into the workshop. The room was in darkness, and there was no sign of Hestig.

She lay awake in their bed for a long time, waiting for him to come home. When he finally slipped under the cover beside her, she asked him where he had been.

"Are you still awake?" he asked in surprise.

Trifena asked him again where he had been.

"I needed some air," he told her. "My head was spinning as fast as the wheel. I needed some air."

"Oh, and where did you go that you were out so long?" she asked. She felt her chest tightening and a cramp in her stomach, which had nothing to do with her pregnancy. It was strange, but at six months this baby was not moving as much as the others had.

"Along by the Stan, up to the mere. Go to sleep now." He turned his back, as cold towards her as she was being towards him, and was soon breathing deeply.

Next day was a religious holiday, one of the many minor festivals throughout the year. Hestig led the family up the slope to the Temple, to take their offering and observe the rituals and see Bron. Selena and Dagvald followed them in. All the inhabitants of the settlement were expected to attend at some time during the day.

Trifena saw that Bron was busily engaged with her friend Naila, under the supervision of Veneta, in topping up a cauldron of vinegar and egg white. Bron had boasted to everyone that this was their special job for a year. With all the candles and tapestry hangings, it was inevitable that small fires occasionally occurred in the Temple, and the mixture was kept ready to smother them. The wooden pump on wheels, used for larger fires anywhere in the settlement, was kept behind the Temple precincts.

Trifena was reassured to see that Pulcher was not far away. He was hurrying here and there, fetching and carrying, taking messages, and generally making himself useful.

She also looked around for Sorin but could not see her. However, once the simple observances began, she heard her. It was Sorin's first solo performance. A little hesitant while she found confidence, her unaccompanied soprano voice gradually gained strength and vibrancy. Trifena wondered how so small a pair of lungs could contain so much volume. Sorin only had to open her mouth and out came these breathtaking, perfectly pitched notes, seemingly without effort.

Voices were hushed until the last echo had been caught and held by the ancient building before being released into silence, then there was a ripple of appreciation. Sorin would be singing at intervals throughout the day, as the rituals were continuous until sundown. As soon as they could, the family and Selena approached Bron, and Trifena handed over an egg sponge she had cooked especially for the girls and Pulcher. Then they went in search of Sorin.

When they found her, Trifena gave her a hug.

"That was so beautiful," she whispered.

"No one has hugged me like that since Mummy died," Sorin delightedly whispered back.

When they returned to the altar area, Trifena noticed that Dagvald was deep in conversation with Severus. As the family left the Temple, Severus walked with Hestig down the steps and spoke quietly to him.

"Severus wants to see me in the council chamber," Hestig told Trifena. "I'll go and see what he wants, though I think I can guess."

When Hestig arrived in the chamber above the covered market, he was greeted by the members of the village council, who were seated at the long table. Severus, the oldest by far, sat at the far end. Dagvald was there, and Africanus, also the doctor, and four of the most responsible and respected tradesmen and craftsmen in the village.

"Thank you for attending, Hestig," Severus said. "I expect you can guess why we have invited you here. It has been our unanimous decision to ask you to join the council."

For some time they chatted about the extent and content of their work and answered Hestig's many questions. Their authority was always subject to the dictates of the Temple.

"They said that I shouldn't give them an answer straight away," Hestig told Trifena later, "but I should think about it carefully. They know how busy I am, with both the family and the business growing so fast. I must make sure that I will have time to attend to the affairs of the council without everything else having to suffer.

"They also hinted that, if I accept, they will ask me to become treasurer in time, once I settle in and learn the rules and procedures."

"And what answer will you give?" asked Trifena dully.

"I believe I will accept," Hestig replied.

"It will give you yet another excuse for staying away from home," she complained, "and I'll be spending even more hours on my own."

Hestig reflected that a few months ago she would have been excited about the honour offered to him.

The family spent the remainder of the day in a leisurely fashion, visiting friends and playing with the children. After dinner, Hestig decided that he would call on Dagvald, and spent most of the evening talking to him about the obligations and responsibilities of village councillors.

Selena, aware that Trifena was alone, sent him home before he would have left of his own accord. It was summer dusk when he crossed the courtyard. He thought how tired Trifena looked, felt a rush of guilt, and kissed the top of her head.

"You go to bed," he said, "I'm going for a walk."

CHAPTER XVI (16)

Trifena woke late next morning. Hestig had already left the house for the market. She felt like staying in bed but decided that it would lift her spirits to go for a stroll round the settlement and perhaps to the schoolroom in the hope of seeing Bron.

Her children were washed and dressed and had breakfasted. They were in the courtyard, playing knucklebones with some smooth flat stones.

"The master gave them to Hestigys," Bettina told her. "He picked them up in the Stan last night."

Trifena decided she might also visit the temple in the wood and speak to Shubinata about the baby. She was sure something was not right inside her. An offering would be required – perhaps a visit to the jeweller's would give her some ideas. She would then stop at Hestig's booth and ask if he had made up his mind about becoming a councillor.

The jeweller looked up and smiled when he saw Trifena. "Something to welcome the baby?" he asked.

Trifena shook her head. "I need an offering for Shubinata."

He was showing her bracelets of jet, shale and ivory, finger rings, necklaces and brooches of glass beads, all suitable for an offering, when footsteps approached.

"Good morning, Trifena."

Trifena turned and looked into the flashing green eyes of Septima from the inn, she who ogled Hestig whenever she met him, not caring whether Trifena and the children were present or not. Hestig had taken to studying his feet whenever they met, which didn't happen very often because the girl spent most of her time at the inn or in the bathhouse.

"I'll be with you in a moment," said the jeweller.

"No matter, I can wait," she said. "I don't want to hurry over my purchase as it's rather special."

Trifena was having difficulty in making up her mind. The girl's presence unsettled her. One after another, pendant, brooch and necklace were chosen then discarded.

The blacksmith's forge stood on the opposite side of the path. Trifena disliked the big bully of a man and, when she heard his deep voice behind her, fumbled a lucky charm she was inspecting, but he was addressing Septima.

"So, where were you last night?" he demanded. "I asked for you but they said you were out."

"A girl's got to have a night off, sometimes." She was obviously trying to lure him out of his black mood, but though her mouth laughed, there was no laughter in her green eyes as they looked at him.

Like a cat, thought Trifena – but a frightened cat.

The blacksmith placed a large hand on each side of Septima's tiny waist and held her so tightly she was having trouble breathing.

"Just don't make a habit of it." It sounded like a threat.

Septima laughed again, still without warmth. Trifena guessed that she dare not upset a client.

"I'll be there tonight," she promised.

"Good." He released his iron grip, slapped her on the buttocks, and strode back to his forge.

The jeweller looked uncomfortable and Trifena blushed. She quickly chose a colourful glass bead necklace. While he was wrapping it for her in sheep's wool, Septima let her arrow fly.

"I hear you are to be congratulated," she said, her voice as slippery as rare Chinese silk that the merchants sometimes brought into the market.

"Congratulated?" asked Trifena stupidly.

"On your good fortune," continued Septima, then when Trifena did not respond, "On Hestig becoming a village councillor. I think he's made the right decision, don't you? Surely he discussed it with you before accepting."

"Accepting?" repeated Trifena.

"Yes, he was going to see Severus first thing this morning."

Trifena looked at the girl. The prostitute's face was expressionless but her eyes, her green cat's eyes, told Trifena all she did not want to know – meetings by the stepping-stones in the moonlight, the fierce passion just where they fell, the laughter and strolling up to the mere with their arms around each other, kissing as they went, and then the cool grass by the water and pleasure taken more leisurely. Was his gratitude now paying for the trinket she was about to buy?

How was it possible to read so much in someone's eyes? Oh, this girl surely *was* the seventh daughter of a seventh daughter!

Trifena looked away, paid for her purchase, and blindly made her escape. Without knowing how she got there, she found herself outside the temple in the wood. It was always open and well used by the women of the settlement. Trifena hoped no one else would be at the altar, and there was no one.

Barefooted, she approached along the red carpet and placed her gift before the goddess, then fell to her knees. She knew that whatever had happened was not Hestig's fault. She had driven him to it. There was a time when he had never looked at another girl, although he was a strong and handsome young man making his way in life, and there were not a few young women in the settlement, a couple of them married, who enjoyed his company.

For an hour she poured out her heart to Shubinata, acknowledging her fault and asking to be shown the way forward to put things right between herself and Hestig again. "I will do anything," she promised.

For good measure, she picked up one of the lead curse tablets lying on a side table. With the stylus also left there, she scratched on it a picture of a cat with flashing eyes and wrote underneath it the Latin number VII and the first letter of Septima's name, rolled it up and laid it with some coins on the altar.

About to leave, she remembered the reason she had decided to come to the temple in the first place.

"I nearly forgot," she said, turning again towards Shubinata. "It's our baby – something seems not quite right. Of course, I may be imagining things. You know, though, so I leave everything to you."

She asked for blessing on family and friends, prayed for Bron's eventual return – of course, the Temple would be well compensated – then left to make her way back to the settlement.

She wondered just how Shubinata was going to put things right between Hestig and herself.

CHAPTER XVII (17)

Trifena walked at a leisurely pace. The path, dry and firm beneath her sandals, eased her progress through the luxuriant foliage, and the songs of unseen birds among the leaf-laden branches brought her a calmness of spirit she had not felt for some time.

This calm was abruptly shattered when, as she was passing through the gap in the boundary bank, she started to bleed.

She felt the thick warm liquid creeping down the inside of her legs, stopped dead in her tracks and began to panic. No one was around but it was not far along the path to Hoad and Louca's house. Tightening all the muscles inside her as best she could and keeping the insides of her thighs in contact with each other, while shuffling one foot in front of the other, she made her way to their door. Gasping in fright and doubled up, she banged on it urgently, which brought Louca to her aid.

One look at Trifena's face and the blood dripping on to her sandals, and Louca took her inside and helped her down on to the mattress.

"Lie quite still," she commanded. "I'm going to find Stalwyn. My baby's asleep in his crib – he shouldn't wake."

When Stalwyn arrived, the contractions had already begun. Louca returned with Hestig a few minutes later. Trifena clung to him.

"Hestig," she sobbed, "Hestig, I don't know what's happening to me."

"Louca, revive the fire and heat a pan of water!" ordered Stalwyn, in charge of the situation. "Hestig, find a cloth and bathe her face in cold water! And Trifena, lie still. We may yet be able to stop your baby from being born. It's too early, much too early."

But there was nothing any of them could do. First came the blood and spongy, tubular mass that should have been born after the baby, then the cord, and finally the baby, starved of blood and air and nourishment.

"It's a boy!" exclaimed Hestig, kissing and bathing Trifena's face alternately.

"Louca, bring me a sheepskin or sheep's wool – anything soft and warm," instructed Stalwyn. She clamped and cut the cord and wrapped the tiny, tiny body in the wool newly shorn, and gently placed the soft bundle in the arms his mother reached out towards him.

For two seconds he opened his eyes, and Trifena looked into their pale blue innocence, then he closed them again and was gone.

Trifena began to wail inconsolably and would not give up her baby.

"No! No!" she cried over and over again. "No, he's mine! No one shall take him away! He'll feed from me in a while and then he will be well."

"But Trifena, dear heart, you can't – you mustn't –" Hestig pleaded helplessly.

"Stalwyn, leave me with her for a while," Louca whispered. Stalwyn nodded and, taking Hestig by the arm, led him outside.

He told Trifena later that Stalwyn had done her best to comfort him. She said that it was no one's fault, these things just happened, and Trifena would be fine in a few days' time. She had then gone on to admonish him to be a sensible man and stay away from the inn because it wasn't for the likes of him and no good would come of it! Extremely embarrassed, he had shuffled his feet and looked down at them to hide his face, though he knew his neck must be as red as his cheeks, and she had laughed and said, "Take her home, young man – and give her another baby!"

Meanwhile, inside the house, poor in material wealth but rich in love, Louca was talking quietly to Trifena, who was still nursing the tiny corpse.

"He's only asleep. He will feed in a moment," Trifena insisted. "If we wait, he will feed, and grow strong like our other children," and she tried to bare her breast.

Louca stayed the fingers that were fumbling with the brooch fastening the front of her bodice, and bathed her face with the cloth

Hestig had laid down. She spoke so quietly and lovingly that, hearing the local accent, Trifena was confused into thinking her mother was in the room with her, and finally handed the baby over without anxiety.

Louca looked down at the little screwed up face, bloodied and without any fat to plump up the cheeks. "For the whole of your earthly life you were loved and wanted, little one, which is more than can be said for a lot of folk."

Hestig returned later and found Trifena sleeping peacefully. He wrapped her up in her woollen cloak and carried her home, only half awake, in his arms.

The bleeding gradually dried up and, as Stalwyn had promised, within two weeks Trifena had completely recovered physically, although she had not been strong enough emotionally to attend the burial of the baby. They took him into Byden Wood and laid him under soft earth, covering the grave with last year's brown leaves.

Then there was recovery to be made in other matters, for both of them. Hestig only left his wife's side to go to work, and they spent every evening in each other's company, often just sitting in the dark, holding hands.

Hestig was first to raise the subject.

"Trifena," he began, in such a low voice that she guessed what was coming, "there are things between us that have to be said."

"Yes, Hestig," she replied, relieved that he had had the courage to initiate this conversation and had not left it to her, because she would not have known where to begin.

"Things have been done of which I am very ashamed now."

"It wasn't your fault," she interrupted him, "it was mine. I was treating you so abominably that it was no wonder you went elsewhere for comfort."

"You knew?" he asked in surprise. "How did you know?"

So Trifena told him about her meeting with Septima at the jeweller's and how the girl had let her know that she had been with him the previous evening.

"The vixen!" He was so angry.

Then she told him how she had gone to the temple in the wood and the content of her prayers, and writing the curse tablet.

"I thought you'd stopped caring for me altogether," he said, "and

103

that's why I went to Septima. She'd always let me know I could go to her at any time, day or night. She said as much every time I met her when we were living at the inn. It was only that one evening."

Trifena was surprised. She didn't know whether to believe him until she looked into his serious blue eyes and knew he was telling the truth.

"But you were always going out. It seemed you couldn't bear to be with me any more," she cried.

"Only because I thought *you* didn't want to be with *me*," he replied. "On that one evening only I took Septima up to the mere but, by the time we reached it, I had cooled off – and that's all there was to it, nothing more. We walked back in silence. That's probably why she was so vindictive towards you."

As an afterthought he asked, "Is talking to her what started the baby coming?"

"Probably," agreed Trifena, and added, "but it would have happened anyway."

"Trifena, my sweet, I adore you. I always have. I always will. Do you think we can begin again?"

Later, as they lay together in the darkness, she was amazed at her foolishness in gambling with such high stakes and so nearly losing him.

She also wondered at the speed with which Shubinata had answered her prayers.

Thinking again about the curse tablet, she was sorry she had left it on the altar, and next day was at the temple early in the faint hope of retrieving it, but necklace, coins and tablet had gone.

On her knees, she thanked the goddess for answering her prayers about Hestig, then added, "But I'm sorry I left the curse tablet. I'd like to take it back. I realise now that Septima is not a threat, and never was, and in fact I feel rather sorry for her. So please forget the curse."

Trifena could not tell whether or not the goddess had heard her or would take any notice of her plea. She would have to wait and see.

And not long afterwards, she realised she was pregnant again.

CHAPTER XVIII (18)

As soon as she was sure, she chose a moment when they were alone, put her arms around Hestig's neck and whispered her news into his ear. He made an announcement at the council meeting later that day.

"You look as if you'd lost a siliqua and found a solidus," Dagvald commented, and everyone laughed.

A few days later, Hestig was working at his booth when he smelt a perfume he recognised and, raising his head, found himself looking straight into a pair of green eyes. He knew this meeting had to take place some time and was glad it was in broad daylight with plenty of people about.

"You've been avoiding me," Septima said.

"Not particularly," replied Hestig, "it's just that we haven't been in the same place at the same time."

"Come back to me, Hestig," she pleaded. "I know your wife's expecting another baby, but what of that? Most men have more than one woman. Come back to me," she continued to plead.

The green eyes bored into his, like a carpenter's gimlet, reaching into the back of his head, searching his thoughts. For a wild moment his pulse quickened, but the desire quietened and dissolved and he shook his head.

"But I love you," Septima hissed at him.

"And I love Trifena," he replied. "Septima, it's over – not that it ever really started."

"I'll wait for you tonight by the stepping-stones," she said, and left. Hestig sighed.

That evening, Trifena went to bed early. Hestig stayed at home, though he knew that Septima would be waiting for him by the stepping-stones, and when, later, there was a knock at the door, he sent Bettina to open it.

"What do you want?" he heard her ask.

"To see your master. Please tell him that Septima is here."

"I will do no such thing!" Bettina answered her. "Go away. We don't want your sort here."

"You're only a slave. Who are you to speak to me like that?" bristled Septima, raising her voice.

"Hush," the girl commanded, "do you want my mistress to hear you?"

It was obvious that Septima was not going to leave until she had spoken to him, so Hestig came out of concealment.

"I'll deal with this," he said to Bettina and went out, closing the door behind him. He took hold of Septima firmly by the arm and led her away from the house.

In the light from a flaring torch on a wall, her green eyes reflected back flecks of yellow. Oh, those eyes! Hestig knew that a man could get lost in them – lose himself and all sense of reason and responsibility – but at what cost?

His voice was harsh. "What do you want?"

"I've been waiting for you an hour since –" Septima began.

"And you'll wait for me a lifetime," he told her. "Go back where you belong!"

"I'll get a beating for being out again, but it'll be worth it, Hestig, if you come down to the stream with me now."

"Not now, not ever! The beating will be your own fault – anyway, they'll make sure it isn't severe enough to put you out of action and lose them money!"

Tears began running down her cheeks, smudging her heavy make-up. Hestig looked at her with scorn.

"You're not fit to tread the same ground as Trifena!" he said and took hold of her roughly by the shoulders, turned her around, and gave her a strong push away from him.

The prostitute fled, heading for the market place and the inn.

She was not seen in public for several days after that and it was rumoured that she had been kicked by one of the horses.

Two weeks later, the settlement was preparing for the mid-winter feast of Unvala.

Part of the preparation was licensing the inn and Temple prostitutes. A day was set aside when they came to the council chamber with their certificates of health from Stalwyn and their money for a licence for the next six months.

Not all council members needed to attend, but Hestig was present as he was gradually taking over the duties of treasurer.

He had not seen Septima since the night she had called at his house, but she was required to attend that morning and he had to take the licence fee from her. He took no more notice of her than he did of the other girls, but as she sat down opposite him and put the coins into his palm, her fingers closed round his so that he had to pull his hand away. Then she sat on the edge of her chair and under the table opened her legs and caught his leg between them and squeezed hard.

"Next!" Hestig called to the line of waiting girls and she had to go, but he noticed the nudging and the eyes flitting in his direction, and heard the giggles, and knew he had to do something about Septima, but didn't know what.

And that night she came to the house again. Trifena was at Selena's, being measured for a tunic for the festival, and Bettina was in the house with the children. Hestig was busy in his pottery at the back of the kitchen. For several evenings he had been hard at work, fulfilling orders from housewives, inn and Temple, all preparing for the festival.

He was loading the kiln with dishes and pots when there was a tap at the door, and before he could cross the room, Septima was inside, the door closed behind her.

"Hestig!" she cried and threw herself at him, arms round his neck, covering his face with kisses.

"Septima, stop it!" he ordered her, as best he could when he was able to free his mouth and draw breath, but she paid no heed.

He planted his hands on each side of her waist under her cloak, intending to push her away, but found she had very little clothing on. He was caught unawares by the firmness of her young body and before he knew what was happening, his arms had slipped all the way round her waist and he was responding, pulling her tightly to him, smothering her face with wild kisses, lips closing her eyelids, pressing on her open mouth, slipping down to her chin.

Throwing back her head in triumph as his mouth slid down her neck, she opened her eyes wide – those green eyes flecked again with yellow – and something in his head snapped.

"*Bitch*!" he screamed at her.

He strode over to the door and flung it wide open, then picking her up in his arms, and holding her so tightly that she could barely draw breath, let alone move, with great angry strides he covered the ground between his workroom and the little round houses, across the market place, and to the front entrance of the inn.

"Don't leave me here, Hestig," she pleaded with him. "If they know I've been out again –"

"You deserve everything you get!" His passion of a moment ago now fuelled his seething rage and he could barely restrain himself from punching her, but he was sufficiently aware to recognise the part he had played in the whole affair. He walked round to the back door of the bathhouse and deposited her roughly on her feet.

"Don't you ever – don't you ever – come near us again!" His voice spat from between his teeth and he was almost choking with rage. "If you do, I swear I'll kill you!" He turned and strode away.

"Who was that?" The voice came from the shadows and the boy who stabled the horses moved into the light.

"Never you mind!" Septima replied.

"'E sounded like 'e meant it."

"I think he did," she said, "and I'll do to you what he threatened to do to me if you breathe a word!" She slipped back into the bathhouse as unobtrusively as she had slipped out.

CHAPTER XIX (19)

The Festival of Unvala at the winter solstice gave the people two days' holiday. During this time, everyone was required to fast for twenty-four hours before sitting down with family and friends to the lavish Unvala evening meal. They were hardly aware of their hunger cramps, however, because there was so much work to be done.

At this time of year, Ashuba was at his most distant. The hours of darkness were creeping forward, gradually overwhelming the reluctant daylight and threatening to extinguish it altogether.

The air became cold and morning and evening mists as thick and grey as horse blankets smothered the settlement and hid the valley below. Sometimes the wind took notice and swirled the blankets away, but then it blew from the east and bit into people's bones. The leaves had succumbed to its bitter breath and now lay dead beneath the trees, which creaked and groaned in mourning. The grasses were dead and the flowers had vanished long since.

"There are lands to the north," warned generation after generation of old folk every Unvala, "where the sun doesn't shine for six months of the year, the crops don't grow, the people go hungry and their babies die."

"But it's never happened in Byden," the young people always protested.

"Not yet, but if Ashuba deserts one place for long periods, why not another?" their grandparents argued. "That's why, every year without fail, we must remind him of his days of strength and vigour, and persuade and bribe him to return."

So the men were busy in the Temple amassing light – candles and torches and oil lamps, mirrors, glass beads and polished coins. They decorated the god with amulets, necklaces, and bracelets hung with pendants that looked like spoked wheels and represented sunrays.

Greenery and berries that were surviving the winter, mostly holly, ivy and mistletoe, were carried in to decorate the altar. In the wood, skeleton trees were garlanded with cloth leaves in greens, yellows and reds, sewn on to intertwining leather thongs.

The extra shopping and house cleaning finished, the women stayed at home to prepare the evening feast. Children were sent out to hen houses to collect eggs, and bring in wood pigeons from the family's columbarium. Joints from cows, pigs, sheep and deer were prepared for roasting. Hares were skinned, spicy sauces prepared for pheasants and partridges that had been hanging too long, pastry rolled out for ham, stuffing mixed for recently-butchered sucking pigs, and offal with cereal pounded for the sausages. Fattened snails were given their last clean, fish were gutted, and winter salads, vegetables and nuts prepared.

Fires would soon be lit everywhere – in market place, streets, and in compounds outside houses. A hearth was being built under the stone canopy of the Temple portico, and branches and logs that had been dragged up the front steps were piled high on each side of the great pillars of the doorway, ready to feed the flames.

In the early evening, representatives of all the families would bring their offerings to Ashuba's fire. Then, fat dripping from wild game and joints turning on spits would cause the blazing wood to sizzle and sputter. Inside, the altar would disappear under a pile of home-produced fare: crusty spelt wheat bread, cheeses, bottled fruit, fresh seasonal vegetables, herbs, spices, pickled oysters, wine, and glass storage jars containing liquamen, the fermented fish sauce popular with the Romans.

Bron watched all the preparations, eyes wide in amazement. Selvid gathered the children together in a group, out of the way of the work, and explained the traditional rituals and their meaning.

"Vortin supervises the whole operation, making sure that everything is done according to tradition and the writings on the parchment scrolls," Selvid told them. "It is the only evening in the year when all the Temple staff share a meal. Iraina and the priestesses are organising the feast in Vortin's house. Come and see."

He took them across to the house, which stood behind the Temple, just inside Byden wood. Bron watched the girls from the second floor scurrying about, laying clean white cloths and napkins on tables, polishing crockery and goblets, knives and spoons.

"Where's the food?" asked Bron.

"It will all be brought across from the altar," explained Selvid. "We eat the offerings."

They returned to the Temple and he sent them away to help wherever they could.

Pulcher beckoned to Bron. "We find your father," he offered.

They found him at the altar.

"What are you doing, Daddy?" Bron asked, from where she and Pulcher stood on the other side of the altar rail. She was intrigued. It was not often that anyone not important was allowed in the sacred area.

"I'm looking for cracks in the pottery ornaments and candle holders, so I can replace them. This is our family's Unvala offering."

"You mustn't touch Ashuba."

"I'll be careful," he promised.

It was tradition that Africanus and the Temple children ate together, the schoolroom having been cleared for this purpose. Women from the village prepared and served the early evening meal, then the children were sent to bed before the adults sat down to eat.

"Africanus, where do you go at Unvala?" asked Bron thoughtfully, before leaving the schoolroom.

She was sad when he answered, "Nowhere, Bron. I spend Unvala evenings on my own."

All the activity and work in the settlement each year was rewarded because, from each Unvala evening, imperceptibly at first, the hours of daylight began to lengthen.

"You see," said the old folk smugly, "we were right. You young people always think you know everything about everything, but the ancient wisdom reaches back to the beginning of creation."

Vortin liked to reward those who had been particularly helpful to him during the year, and to secure future co-operation, distributed gifts from the Temple coffers. Not entirely trusting some who served him, he usually asked Iraina to send one of her priestesses with the bags of coins. On this occasion, Veneta was busy in the schoolroom, so Jeetuna was asked to make the calls.

She planned her route round the settlement to include the innkeeper, who kept Vortin supplied with fine wine, Severus as leader of the village council, Stalwyn for keeping a health check on Bron, and Trifena for carrying and bearing 'his' daughter.

This gift had come Trifena's way each Unvala. On the first occasion, when Bron was six months old, she had refused it, but Hestig had encouraged her to take the money. Vortin was unaware that it was being added to the savings for Bron's ransom.

About two hours after sunset, Jeetuna arrived at their door, muffled in her cloak and hood and carrying an oil lamp. Hestig was still at the Temple. Snowflakes were beginning to lay their own pure white tablecloth over the damp earth in celebration of the season. The flakes were causing the fires, now blazing at dozens of sites throughout the settlement, to splutter and protest, but were not extinguishing the flames, and golden sparks were leaping high into the cold air.

The message from Vortin was delivered to Trifena, the small pouch of coins was handed over, and a cold 'thank you' received in return.

"Have you seen Severus?" Jeetuna asked her. "I called at his house but there was no one there."

"Try the wheelwright's," suggested Trifena. "I know he's dining there tonight."

Jeetuna thanked her and set off down the hill towards the craftsmen's houses. She had no need of her lamp as the fires lit the path.

The blacksmith had not been able to get to the Temple with an offering. His drinking had started the evening before in the bathhouse and had continued all day at home between bouts of sleep. Now standing in his doorway, he was trying to clear his head when Jeetuna passed on her way to his next-door neighbour, the wheelwright.

The man had always had a fire in his loins when Jeetuna was near – many of the men had. None of them dared do anything about it, however, because she was a priestess and not for the riff-raff – so it was written in the great Book of the Altar. They knew that Vortin would show no mercy to anyone who violated the young woman, even by touching her in the way of men, and that the full weight of

Ashuba's vengeance would bear down from heaven and extinguish the life out of him.

The blacksmith knew that well enough, and in his sober moments lowered his eyes, turned his head, and either visited the bathhouse or walked up to the mere and immersed himself in the spring's cold water. However, now he was not sober but drunk, though at the moment not too drunk to stay upright.

He drew back in the protection of his doorway until he saw Jeetuna leave the wheelwright's and turn to walk towards the doctor's house. He caught up with her behind the inn.

The surprise of the attack from behind and his great strength brought her down in the snow. Rolling her over, he covered her face with her hood to gag her mouth and muffle her cries and kept one large hand, fingers spread, firmly clamped down on her nose so that she had to fight to breathe. That way, he reasoned in his confusion, she would not be able to tell who he was. He did not realise that she could identify him by the stink of the beer and the smell of charcoal and smoke and iron, and the size of the hand that tore at her clothing.

He took hold of her knee and his huge hand crawled up the inside of her thigh, fingers squeezing and releasing her flesh, like a cat stretching and retracting its claws, drawing blood. Then the probing and poking and the final act of humiliation, trying and trying again, fumbling and unsuccessful, but still roaring his passion above her, until she fainted in the snow.

CHAPTER XX (20)

Cold flakes falling on her face brought Jeetuna back to her senses but she was unable to move. For a long time she lay there in misery, hurting, cold and frightened, but he had gone. She knew she should not stay still for much longer or the cold would kill her, or someone would find her in all her shame!

The fear that overcame her then was more excruciating than her physical pain. She was Vortin's and she had allowed herself to be violated. She was of no use to him now, only fit for life in the inn, or worse! But she had to get up. The doctor's house was near and she would seek Stalwyn's help. So she began to crawl slowly towards the lamp the doctor always kept lit in his window at night.

Hearing a thump as she fell against his door, Kendrus opened it and looked out into the darkness. He saw no one. But when he pushed the door wider, it met the obstruction of her body and he looked down to see a black heap on the ground.

Calling urgently to his wife, he bent and took the body in his arms, carried it inside the house and laid it on the bed. Stalwyn came, wiping flour from her hands. Together they gently pulled back the cloak then looked at each other in disbelief.

"Jeetuna?" Stalwyn asked, smoothing the wet hair off the young woman's face. It was no longer the colour of summer wheat.

"Yes," Jeetuna sobbed, without tears.

"Whatever has happened to you?"

"Don't be stupid, wife!" her husband scolded her. "You can see very well what's happened to her!"

"But who would do such a terrible thing?" Stalwyn was still stupefied.

"Someone with a death wish!" her husband replied. "But enough speculation. Be so good as to clean her up and put warm olive oil on those nasty scratches."

After his wife returned with all she needed and had ministered to the young woman, Kendrus made a brief examination.

"Are you hurting much inside?" he asked.

Relaxing under Stalwyn's gentle ministrations, Jeetuna said she didn't think so, and that her attacker had been one-handed and very clumsy and not successful in what he was trying to do.

"Whoever he was," said the doctor.

"Whoever he was," repeated Jeetuna and left it at that.

"Do you want to go back to the Temple tonight?" Kendrus enquired.

Stalwyn said, "She can't stay here, or someone will notice, and start asking questions."

Jeetuna began to cry inconsolably. "I'm of no use to Vortin or anyone else now. I'll lose my reputation, respect, my position at the Temple – perhaps even my life!"

Stalwyn's face was grim. "We'll see about that! I'm not without some influence in this settlement!" she said. "Look at the state you're in! Did you ask to be attacked? Did you entice him? What were you doing out in this weather, anyway?"

"Delivering Vortin's annual gifts," Jeetuna replied, then added, "I was on my way here with a pouch of money for you, Stalwyn, as a thank-you for taking care of Bron."

"Hmph!" grunted Stalwyn, as if to ask, "Didn't I say I had influence?"

"You're my patient and I say you must rest for a while," the doctor declared, "then we will smuggle you back into the Temple. We will decide how best that must be accomplished."

"My lamp will still be outside the back door of the inn, in the snow, and the money too – unless he's taken it. There were two pouches – Stalwyn's, and one for the innkeeper."

"Stay with her, wife, and I'll see to it." The doctor lit an oil lamp and went out into the swirling flakes.

When he returned, Stalwyn was still sitting, stroking Jeetuna's face and hair.

"It's all done," he reassured them, shaking the snow from his cloak. "There was one pouch with no money in it, but the other one was lying at a distance, so obviously he hadn't found it. I left it with the innkeeper's wife and said it was from Vortin, with thanks for their services throughout the year. I've brought your lamp back, and I smoothed out the snow as best I could with a besom broom I found outside their back door."

"You're a good man," smiled Stalwyn with softness in her eyes as she looked up at her husband, and brushed snow from his greying hair. "Now, how are we going to get her back to the Temple without attracting any attention? I think you must speak to Vortin."

"Does he have to know?" pleaded Jeetuna.

"Will you be well enough to sit at his feast tonight?" Jeetuna shook her head in answer to the doctor's question.

"Then he will have to know. Anyway, if he's not told, and finds out you've been violated –" The doctor left his sentence unfinished.

"Violated – nonsense!" exclaimed Stalwyn. "Kendrus, you must just tell him that she was attacked – for the money she was carrying – but she put up a fight and he only got away with one pouch, which is the truth. Say she needs to rest for a while but we'll smuggle her in by the side door later in the evening. She'll be a bit stiff but as right as a new gold coin by tomorrow."

Jeetuna looked at her with gratitude.

"You can show him the bruises on your face and arms, but say the snow softened your fall. None of that is a lie. After all, there was no penetration, so there's no violation – and more importantly, no fear of a pregnancy."

Kendrus turned to leave. "Don't forget to ask Vortin to keep the side door unlocked," Stalwyn reminded him.

All went according to plan and Kendrus reported that Vortin believed what he was told. The High Priest said that, if anyone enquired, he would say that Jeetuna had a chill, caught while out in the snow delivering his gifts.

Before the revellers had finished their feast and returned to their rooms, Jeetuna was safely in bed, comfortable and asleep.

Meanwhile, the blacksmith had gone home. The stolen coins were as addictive as alcohol and he could hardly wait to get to the bathhouse to spend them – on the other five girls in turn and Septima last. It didn't matter whether or not he could accomplish everything he intended, because of impotency caused by the drink, but he would still have a rip-roaring evening, then go back to his wife. Of course, if his hag of a mother-in-law was in the house, he would have to throw her out first before finishing off the evening in bed with his beautiful Attryde.

He thought hazily that her beauty was the reason he had married her, no doubt about it. She was much younger than he, and she could have married several of the other men in the settlement, but she had chosen him. In those days he had a thriving business and was building a fine reputation for himself – a prospective council member – until the drink got him.

It was strange that the morning after, Attryde was often covered with cuts and blood and bruises and didn't look as beautiful as she did when he arrived home. He never quite remembered how he had caused her injuries – once he had broken her nose and another time her arm – and when he sobered up, he was sorry. But he was so seldom sober these days.

Only his wife was in the house when he arrived home. She had stopped inviting guests to the Unvala meal, even her mother – especially her mother. So he slobbered over his meal, left a mess on the table, complained about the honey cakes and threw the fruit pie at her. Then he belched loudly and left the table, saying he would be back later and she had better wait up for him, or else!

When he had gone, Attryde wondered how the girls at the inn could bear to be near him in the state he was in, but at least they would benefit from the coins she had seen him fumbling to put in his purse, slung on a belt under his tunic. She wondered where he had got hold of the gold but knew better than to ask.

Wearily she cleared up all the mess, then went to bed to sleep while she could. She knew his noise would wake her when he came back from the bathhouse, and by the time he saw her, she would be up and on her feet. Hopefully he would be too drunk and satiated to do more than collapse on the bed and sleep. If not, she would be able to dodge most of his blows. When he sobered up in the morning, he would remember nothing, and a good breakfast might restore him to some semblance of normality.

When at last he returned he had blood on his tunic and was boasting that Septima never refused to do anything he ordered her to do.

Poor Septima, thought Attryde, with little energy for much pity. *I hope he paid her well.*

Leaving his clothes in a heap on the floor, she got him into his nightshirt and into bed, suffering only a black eye and cut lip for her efforts.

CHAPTER XXI (21)

It stopped snowing overnight.

In spite of being late to bed, Iraina was patrolling the corridor outside Jeetuna's room early next morning. As soon as she heard a noise inside, she knocked on the door and walked in without waiting for an answer. Jeetuna was sitting on the edge of her mattress, gradually easing movement from her sore muscles and stiff shoulders.

After the priestess gave her account of the attack, and displayed the bruises on her arms and face, Iraina asked only one question.

"Who was he, Jeetuna?"

The priestess didn't hesitate. "The blacksmith."

"Are you sure?"

"Certain. I could smell him."

Iraina's expression was grim and determined. "Vortin shall be told," she said. "He'll deal with that bully! Don't leave the room until your bruises have disappeared – you're absolved from all duties until then. And," she warned, "not a word of this to anyone – to anyone, do you hear? Not even Veneta and Selvid. As far as everyone is concerned, you have a chill."

She waited until Jeetuna had burrowed under the coverlet again to go back to sleep, then left the room.

In her own room, Iraina sat with elbows resting on her toiletry table, chin in hands, trying to decide what to do. As she moved, she knocked something to the floor. Bending to pick it up, she recognised the curse tablet brought back from Shubinata's altar only two days ago.

Idly turning it over in her hands, her eyes were drawn to the scratched sentence, each word written backwards, as was common practice on these tablets: "Cursed be my son-in-law in blood and sword with Septima his whore", and drawn underneath was a hammer and anvil. Obviously, this had been placed on the altar by Attryde's mother.

Responding to a sudden flash of memory, Iraina pulled open her top drawer and searched among the collection of similar sheets of lead. She unrolled several before finding the one she was looking for. It read simply: "Septima". Iraina had stood unseen in the curtained shadows when the innkeeper's wife had placed it on the altar before Shubinata, and had heard the invective poured out against the girl because of her relationship with the innkeeper.

She searched again and found another tablet she remembered removing from the altar – a drawing of a cat with eyes flashing and "VII S" scratched beneath it. She knew it cursed Septima of the green eyes, seventh daughter of a seventh daughter, who was obviously the cause of a great deal of unrest among the women of the settlement.

An idea was forming in her mind, and she went to find Vortin.

All that day the blacksmith slept. The only time he roused was when Attryde's mother left, taking with her his clothes from the night before.

"I'll wash them for you, dear," he heard her say to her daughter. "It will save you a filthy job." The smell of dried blood and vomit and worse assaulted even his nostrils.

As the door banged, he sat up in bed, his head pounding with blows that resembled those of hammer on anvil.

Smelling the bacon sizzling in the pan on the gridiron over the fire, he rushed to the front door to be sick outside, but didn't quite reach it. Wiping the back of his hand across his mouth and leaving the curdling mess for Attryde to clear up, he crawled back into bed.

It was early that afternoon when a covered wagon drawn by two mules crossed the ford and rolled up the path into the market place, its heavy iron tyres on wooden wheels making deep ruts in the snow. Sitting on the buckboard, holding the reins, was an elderly man, a young girl seated with him. By the side of the mules trudged five members of a company of itinerant performers, preferring to walk than be jolted and jarred inside the wagon.

Tying the mules to a convenient post and slinging leather bags of hay round their necks, the entertainers lost no time in unloading drums and musical instruments and setting out their equipment, which included two poles dug into the ground some distance apart, braced with guy ropes, and a much thinner rope stretched tightly between them.

An audience was already beginning to gather when Trifena and the family arrived, even before announcements made through cone-shaped loud hailers introduced the company, and music and singing proclaimed the start of the performance.

The intense excitement of the crowd was tangible and even the young women and children from the Temple came out to watch. Pulcher had Veneta's permission to bring Bron over to her family, which pleased Trifena, especially when Bron brought Sorin and Naila, her friends, with her.

When young Hestigys ran to pick up a dropped hard-packed snowball, the performers encouraged him to try juggling two of them, while a girl, in colourful clothing and wearing a grotesque pottery mask, spun dishes on sticks. Her companions made eggs appear from behind children's ears then magicked them away in front of the wide eyes of their audience.

Light woollen shawls were passed through wooden cylinders and changed colour, and knuckle bones were tossed into the air but never landed, although the children searched frantically among the feet of their elders. One young man astounded everyone by eating fire. Then the company tumbled and jumped and collapsed in heaps and walked upside down on their hands before flipping over and over until the crowd became dizzy just watching.

A fanfare on brass instruments was the signal for the old man to walk forward. He held up his hand for silence and the crowd hushed.

"For our final act, my granddaughter will walk the tightrope!" he shouted. "To do this, she will first climb a human pyramid!"

There was a loud roll on the drums and the young girl appeared, now dressed in a short, bright red tunic. Three men locked arms at shoulder height and rocked uncertainly as two more climbed on to their shoulders and a sixth man climbed up to form the apex of the triangle.

The girl placed one foot in her grandfather's cupped hands and he practically threw her up on to the first tier, and from there she scaled the human ladder with ease, mounted the wooden platform above their heads and waved to the crowd. The audience gasped, then was silent.

Slowly and with care, one dainty foot after another, arms outstretched, she proceeded to walk along the rope. When almost across, she seemed to lose balance, swayed and dropped to one knee, her other leg dangling. As if with one throat, the crowd sucked in an audible icy breath of alarm, but she regained her balance and ran the last few steps to the platform and safety. Raising an arm in triumph and smiling broadly, she posed and waved again to the crowd, who clapped and clapped and would not let the company pack up their equipment until early twilight had almost vanished into night and lamps had been lit.

Veneta began gathering the children together, so Trifena kissed Bron and her friends goodnight and Hestig took them and Pulcher back to the priestess.

As the people dispersed, dropping coins on to a shawl on the ground as they passed, a clearing happened in the crowd and, looking across, Trifena noticed the girls from the inn. At that moment, Septima looked round. Trifena knew it was Septima although only her eyes were visible, the rest of her face being swathed in a dark blue cloth.

Hestig had confessed the girl's visit to the pottery two evenings previously so Trifena now stayed calm, thinking there were no more secrets, unaware of his momentary loss of self control, as he had omitted to tell her that part of the incident.

She was slightly alarmed when Septima left her companions and walked purposefully towards her, eyes fixed steadily on her face. With baby Trifosa in her arms and Hestigys clinging to her skirt, Trifena turned to seek her husband's support, but he was still talking to Veneta. Turning back, she found Septima confronting her. The swathed face came closer until the green eyes, framed with black eyelashes and sparking like the Unvala fires, filled Trifena's vision with spite. The voice sounded unnatural, and the lips seemed to find difficulty in producing the words.

"Your oh-so-faithful husband says I am not fit to tread the ground you walk on, but he threatens one thing and lusts another! You tell him from me that I won't keep quiet and, if I go down, he'll go down with me! You tell him that!" and she turned and limped away.

The encounter caused Trifena to shiver uncontrollably and her teeth to chatter. She turned again to call Hestig, and saw the black-cloaked figure of Brocchus watching her. She realised he must have seen, and probably heard, Septima's outburst. She called to Hestig, who came straight away, obviously sensing the urgency in her voice, but she would not tell him what had upset her until they reached home.

Later that evening, the boy who slept in the inn stables with the horses was woken from his dreams by a man's voice from the shadows. Sleepily, he lifted his lamp to see who had spoken.

"Lower your lamp," the voice ordered, "and if you want to earn a coin or two, listen and do as you're told."

The boy listened, and did as he was told, then walked away, only pausing once to look over his shoulder.

He saw the snow being shafted suddenly by light from the bathhouse as the door opened. A woman's voice called out into the darkness and then the door closed. As he left, he heard other sounds – a cry, a resistance, a thud muffled by the layer of snow, heavy breathing – then silence. He quickly disappeared into the night.

The blacksmith woke early next morning, a working day after the two-day holiday. Memory was returning, and Jeetuna fighting him in the snow was part of it. He couldn't believe the pictures in his mind and passed a hand across his sweating forehead. He wondered why he was still alive. He must run, and soon, before Vortin came for him.

Roughly he shook his wife awake. "Attryde, I've got to go!"

"Go? Go where?" she asked in sleepy surprise, moving away from the wet patch in which he was lying.

"Anywhere away from here!" he barked. "Pack me up some clothes and food!"

"What have you done now?" she asked with a resigned sigh.

Normally he would have lashed out at her, but he needed her

help and didn't answer. Together they stuffed some things into a sack and he left. Minutes later he was galloping past the forge on a horse stolen from the inn stables.

Its hooves made little noise and only the prints of the horseshoes in the soft snow left evidence of his escape.

CHAPTER XXII (22)

Later that morning, Attryde's mother called to report the gossip that was spreading round the settlement like fire, flaming from mouth to mouth. Septima, one of the prostitutes from the inn, was missing – no one had seen her since the previous evening in the bathhouse. The innkeeper had also discovered that one of his horses had been stolen from the stable. Prints in the snow showed the route taken by the animal and information given by some early risers revealed the flight of the blacksmith, so everyone concluded that the lovers had met somewhere and fled together.

Attryde knew they hadn't and was puzzled, and said as much to her mother. Several times she asked for the return of her husband's clothes, but received only evasive answers and the promise to bring them back when he came home.

Attryde still didn't know why her husband had fled but thought he must come home some time, if only to collect his hoard of coins buried beneath the hearth, which had been forgotten in his rush to leave.

Her mother said that the innkeeper's wife was livid, as the inn was losing money all the time Septima stayed away. Apparently, the girl had run away before and was found once in Calleva and on another occasion in one of the villages north of the Ridgeway, among the Catuvellauni people. She had been dragged back and beaten for the trouble she had caused.

Once again, the innkeeper sent slaves to search the fields and woods locally, and wade in the pool at Stanmere, then to go further into the surrounding area, but a week went by, then two, and still there was no sign of her.

After a month, the mystery ceased to be the main topic of conversation in the village, the speculation died down, and the innkeeper's wife brought in Septima's replacement.

Meantime, the large brazier remained cold and the forge strangely silent.

The first signs of Ashuba's quickening pulse were the Stanmere snowbells that pushed their way up through the earth – not very far, but far enough to make sure that the snow had cleared. And when they discovered that it had, as if in memoria, they drooped their snow-white heads towards the brown nursery from which they had recently escaped.

In spite of intensely feeling the cold, Africanus decided to take his pupils up to the Stanmere. He invited Veneta to accompany them but she was busy elsewhere, so one morning he and Pulcher led the children down to the Stan and climbed along its gently rising banks until they reached the top of the hill. There they all gazed in delight at the snow-like covering of drooping white bells secured to the earth by delicate green stalks.

"I want you older children to study the snowbells and draw them individually," Africanus told them. "I'll help the young ones."

The children sat among the flowers, settling happily to their tasks.

"Don't pick any," Africanus warned them. "Picked snowbells taken indoors bring bad luck."

He had been warned of this by the Roman legionary who had brought the beautiful little plants from across the Channel several years previously. The young soldier had nurtured two pots of bulbs throughout his long march west and had presented them to the village council. He said they were a token of gratitude for nursing him back to health, after he had collapsed at the inn on a previous visit. The councillors had planted the clumps by the water, where they were now flourishing and multiplying year by year.

The children plainly showed that they enjoyed these outings with Africanus. He helped each one with individual work, always ready to listen to their concerns, and was so knowledgeable and imparted learning so naturally that they thrived under his tuition, Pulcher included. And he always made time for games before they returned to the settlement.

As usual, they elected to play hide-and-seek in the trees, taking it turn-and-turn-about to hide The game had been in progress for only a few minutes when Naila made her gruesome discovery and let out a piercing scream, which brought everybody rushing over to her. Pulcher pulled Bron away from the body and she buried her head in his chest, his arms around her.

The cries of the children were heard down in the village and a crowd of anxious men, carrying sticks and staves, came running up the hill.

When they arrived, they found Africanus by the pool, trying to comfort the crying and frightened children who surrounded him.

"Through there," he said, pointing to a cluster of spindly trees at the water's edge.

From the state of the naked body, it was obvious she had been dead for several weeks, whoever she was.

The children were taken back to the schoolroom to be fed and comforted while Africanus and three of the men returned to the village with a wrapped and tied white shape slung from a long branch carried between them. It was laid in the market place, and soon surrounded by an inquisitive crowd.

Africanus and other members of the council held the people back at a respectful distance while doctor Kendrus examined the body. He pronounced it as being the remains of Septima, but only when one of the girls from the inn identified the blue cloth wound tightly around her neck – the cloth with which Septima had swathed her face to hide the fearful cuts and bruises inflicted by the blacksmith during the night of the Unvala fires.

"Didn't you search in the trees round the mere?" the innkeeper's wife shouted at her slaves, and they answered in confusion, some saying they had and others that they had only waded in the pool.

"Not that it matters any more," she commented. "All that does matter is that Shubinata has made sure those green eyes are no longer a threat to any decent woman." Her husband looked away, acutely embarrassed, and remained silent.

Africanus suggested that the only strangers in the village on the second night of Unvala, the last time Septima was seen alive, had been the travelling players. However, suspicion naturally fell on the blacksmith, although Attryde denied that he had left the house that night, he was too drunk and sick. People muttered that a wife *would* say that to protect her husband – even that husband – and her statements were not reliable and could not be produced as evidence in court if ever there was a trial.

Then there was an argument about a temporary resting place for the body. Vortin said he would not allow it to desecrate the Temple, and the innkeeper's wife refused to allow it past her front door. Finally, the doctor agreed it could be laid outside his back door and he and his wife would deal with it.

"No, not Stalwyn!" Vortin stated adamantly. "She must keep away until it's buried. I'll not have her touching that rotting body then touching Bron."

So Stalwyn was invited to stay at the Temple until after the disposal of the corpse. This was not allowed to take place in the sacred burial pits at Stanmere so it was buried one night deep in Byden Wood, the responsibility being given by the village council to the latrine and sewer cleaner.

Then, to everyone's surprise, before any further debate could take place, Hestig was arrested.

CHAPTER XXIII (23)

They came for him at dawn, with no prior warning, just heavy steps along the pathway and a loud banging on the door, a pause, then more banging. Trifena jumped out of bed and threw a wrap around her shoulders then sent Bettina to open the door before it was pounded off its hinges.

The eunuchs rushed in, led by Brocchus, and made straight for the bedroom, pushing past Trifena on the way. She could only look on helplessly as they attempted to drag Hestig from their bed, but Sharma held up his hand to stop them.

"Hestig, we are arresting you for the murder of Septima the prostitute on the second night of Unvala," he announced formally. "Say nothing you will regret when you get to court."

Trifena pleaded with them, clinging to her husband and trying to shield him from them. "He was with me in the house all that evening," she shouted at them.

"Wives always say that," said one of the eunuchs. "You won't be asked to give evidence."

"This is madness," Hestig cried, "I didn't kill her! You're arresting the wrong person!"

"The court will decide that," Sharma stated. "Come quietly or we will take you by force!" and they frogmarched him out of the house, still in his nightshirt, and trying to look back over his shoulder to shout reassurances to his wife.

"I can't believe this is happening!" Trifena cried to Bettina in distress. "Hestig didn't kill that girl. While I get dressed and bundle up some clothes for him, run and ask Dagvald to alert Severus and the other council members. Then come back and stay with the children while I go to the Temple. Be quick!"

On her way to the Temple, she heard Septima's warning voice over and over in her head. "If I go down, he'll go down with me! If I go down, he'll go down with me!" The curse Trifena had left on the altar in the wood had turned full circle.

When she entered the Temple, several of the council members were already there. Hestig was standing before the altar in front of Vortin, hands tied behind him, protesting his innocence. Severus was arguing unsuccessfully that this was a civil matter and not the concern of the Temple. Iraina looked on.

In desperation, Trifena looked round for Veneta, but the priestess was nowhere to be seen. Presumably she was in her bedroom above the schoolroom, unaware of Hestig's arrest.

Vortin read from a scroll.

" 'Don't you ever come near us again! If you do, I swear I'll kill you!' Were they your words to Septima?"

"Yes, but –"

Vortin interrupted him. "And she did come near your family again, didn't she? She threatened your wife and children after the travelling show – on the second night of Unvala."

Trifena remembered Brocchus spying on her encounter with Septima.

"It was a threat in the heat of the moment – I didn't mean it literally," protested Hestig.

"Septima thought you did – and said so," Vortin replied.

"Who to?" demanded Hestig.

"To me," came the reply. Hestig looked surprised at seeing the ostler standing to one side.

"You will receive a fair trial," Vortin assured him. "Meanwhile, you will be locked in one of the rooms upstairs."

"No!" cried Trifena, but was silenced by a look from the High Priest.

"Severus, I am conscious of his position in the community," he continued. "One of our rooms will be more comfortable than the village cell."

Severus nodded. "May I go with him? We have to prepare his defence." Vortin waved his assent.

As Hestig was led away, Severus took the clothes from Trifena's arms and suggested she went home.

"We will do all we can," he promised her. "One of us will call on you later to let you know what is likely to happen."

Dumbly she obeyed.

"Iraina! Sharma! Brocchus! To my office – *now*!" ordered Vortin.

When they had gathered round the table in the room behind the altar, Vortin turned on them in anger.

"Would one of you mind explaining how this came about?" he demanded.

"It was that stupid stable boy gossiping all over the village about Hestig's threats, and reporting them to the council," Sharma explained, using his wide sleeve to wipe away the perspiration from forehead and face. "We couldn't risk our plans being sabotaged, so we had to take some action."

"So, what do we do now?" Iraina asked. "We know Hestig didn't murder the slut. We should have guessed the blacksmith would make a run for it after his attack on Jeetuna."

"But not as soon as he did," said Sharma.

"When I enquired, he was still in a drunken stupor," added Brocchus, "and I thought there was plenty of time to arrest him."

"Prove the blacksmith guilty and Hestig goes free," Sharma reasoned.

Vortin asked, "Is Attryde's mother still willing to co-operate?"

"We've only to give the word and she'll produce the bloodstained clothing," answered Sharma. "It's a pity we haven't already caught up with the man and have had to wait this long –"

"– and were forced into producing the body," added Brocchus, "but it was really getting over-ripe, and if we'd waited much longer, there wouldn't have been anything recognisable to find – except the length of cloth, of course. Using that was much easier than using my hands."

"I am still angry that Bron saw it," said Vortin.

"If we had let Veneta into the conspiracy she would have made sure the children weren't up at the mere yesterday," added Iraina. "She must be told now – and Selvid."

Sharma, who should have known better, said, "Bron will be very upset when she finds out that her father –"

"*I* am her father," Vortin interrupted icily.

"Even so, she should not be told about the arrest of Hestig," Sharma warned.

Iraina was adamant. "Then you'd better get the dwarf away from the Temple before he tells her."

"See to it, Brocchus," Vortin ordered, then added, "I mean temporarily, this time. Pulcher can come back when it's all over."

Brocchus nodded and left the room.

"The question now," said Iraina, "is how do we get the blacksmith back to face our trumped-up murder charge?"

"Well, my dear," said Vortin, turning to her, "the murder of Septima, and getting the blacksmith executed for it, was your idea. You think of something."

Iraina considered the problem. "He won't have got further than the first inn," she said, "which probably means he's still in Calleva. The eunuchs can make a few discreet enquiries there."

"Then what?" asked Vortin.

"Once we find him, we could get him word that Hestig has been arrested for the attack on Jeetuna and the murder of Septima. That will lower his guard. His mother-in-law says that when the money in the stolen purse runs out, he will sneak home – he has money hidden in the house – untaxed money –"

Vortin tutted with annoyance. "See to it, Iraina. Do whatever you have to do. Sharma, go with her."

Sharma bowed and they left the room.

Fear had hounded the blacksmith further south than Calleva, to Venta Belgarum, where he was finally found, working for a Roman employer by day and frequenting the inns, bathhouses and brothels by night.

"So you're from Byden!" exclaimed his newfound friend, who offered to buy him beer after the money in his pouch ran out. "Now that's a coincidence! I passed through Byden market a week ago. A lot of gossip and great excitement there!"

"Why so?" asked the blacksmith warily, inspecting the man from under bushy black eyebrows.

"One of the priestesses was roughed up recently – can you imagine? What sort of fool would do that? It was dark and she couldn't see her attacker. Then one of the inn girls was murdered, and they've just arrested a man for both offences. He'll likely be executed."

"Do you remember his name?" the blacksmith was quick to ask, breathing heavily.

"Not sure –" was the reply. "It began with an aitch, I think."

"Hoad?" guessed the blacksmith.

"No – longer than that." The man was playing with his prey, who might have been suspicious if he had been less drunk.

The blacksmith scratched his head and made two more guesses, then asked, "Hestig? Couldn't be Hestig?"

"That was it!" cried the man, "I remember now! Do you know him?"

"Vaguely," said the blacksmith, "but why him?"

"Something about some threats he made, and no alibi – only his wife and their slave, but they don't count in law."

Thus it was that late one evening, when there was no moon, a soft tapping brought Attryde to her door, to open it just a little. It was pushed back so violently that she was nearly flattened against the wall and in strode her husband. Attryde shrank from him, he looked so wild and dishevelled.

"Pleased to see me, Wife?" he asked with a low laugh. "Don't wet yourself – I'm not staying long, not taking any chances – just long enough, though. Get me a beer and some food, and be quick about it, then douse the fire so I can get at what I came for."

Afraid of what he might do if she disobeyed, Attryde filled a jug of beer from the barrel and brought it to him with a beaker, then threw a few more root vegetables into the cauldron suspended above the central hearth.

"How long before it's ready?" he demanded, belching. "Good Byden beer, this."

"Soon," she replied nervously. "You won't have to wait long."

He eyed the mattress. "There are some things a man can't wait for," he said. "The pot will take care of itself. Get over there on the bed."

As she didn't move he caught hold of her hair and dragged her to the mattress, throwing her down on to it.

"Don't, please don't –" she begged him, but he took no notice as he disrobed and tore at her clothes.

She screamed and received a blow across her mouth.

"Scream again and you're dead!" He spat the words into her ear. "It makes no difference to me! I'll be far away from here, where not even your witch-of-a-mother will find me!"

It was then that the door banged back against the wall and he was set upon by a swirl of black. He was heaved off his wife, bound by cloaks and rope, and struggling and blaspheming, was half-carried, half-dragged from the house, sending the cauldron flying and scattering its contents over the floor.

For a while, Attryde lay where he had left her, breathing deep sighs of relief and thanking Shubinata for her rescue. Then she slowly got to her feet and began to clear up yet another mess occasioned by her husband.

Next morning, Attryde's mother arrived and was obviously shocked to see the state her daughter was in.

"I've been to the Temple," she said, "with your husband's clothes. They're still spattered with Septima's blood."

"But, mother," Attryde remonstrated, "Septima was still alive the evening *after* he knocked her about. She watched the performance in the market place with the other girls – they all said so – although she was hiding her face behind that cloth. My husband had been in bed drunk all that day and the following night. He left very early next morning. He couldn't have murdered Septima."

"Attryde," her mother said, "there are forces at work here that we must not question. Shubinata has honoured my curse tablet – that's all you need to know. Stay away from him, let matters take their course and don't interfere."

Later in the morning, Sharma and two of his eunuchs arrived at the house to confiscate her husband's undisclosed savings. Having beaten out the fire, they kicked the ash and half-burnt faggots clear, then dug up the cache of coins in a leather drawstring bag that had been buried beneath the hearth. Most of the money they took for unpaid taxes and to cover the cost of her husband's trial, but they left a considerable sum with Attryde and she understood that it was the price of her silence. It was more money than she had ever seen in her life.

The trial was fixed for a week later and was to take place in the council chamber above the covered market.

Meantime, the blacksmith was locked in the cell next to it, where Attryde visited him, though he was unaware of her presence. His craving for alcohol not being satisfied, he raged for three days and nights, keeping the settlement awake. Then he tried to climb up the walls and banged his head on the floor, and finally crawled into a corner and refused to speak to anyone.

CHAPTER XXIV (24)

Bron was distressed by the unexplained absence of Pulcher. Sorin and Naila brought her news one evening before going to bed, having overheard the matter being discussed by the girls on the second floor.

"Bron, your father is locked up on the top floor. No one is allowed to visit him, except Severus," said Sorin.

"That is why Pulcher was sent away," added Naila, "so he wouldn't tell you."

"But why is he locked up? I want to see him," said Bron.

"You mustn't," Naila told her.

"But I want to," insisted Bron and began to cry.

"Hush," warned Sorin. "Let's ask Veneta when she comes."

Veneta looked surprised that the children knew.

"Iraina has given strict instructions that you are not to be told, Bron," she said, "so I can't take you to see him."

As soon as Veneta had left them to sleep, Bron got out of bed in the dark and told the two girls that she was going to find her father.

"You mustn't," said Naila again, but Bron would not be dissuaded.

"I can't let you go on your own –" Sorin said, "I'll come with you."

Naila wanted to go too, but Sorin said she should stay safely in the bedroom and make snoring noises if anyone came along the corridor.

So the two girls left their room, shawls thrown over their shoulders, hand in hand, oil lamps lit. From their wing, they crept along the dark corridor that skirted the circumference of the walls, high up in the roof, past the huge entrance, to the wing on the opposite side of the Temple.

"Which room?" whispered Bron, shivering not only from the cold.

"I don't know."

They went a little further. They could hear giggling and strange noises from the rooms the prostitutes were occupying. Then they saw a candle coming towards them. Sorin pulled Bron against the wall and they tried not to breathe and to disappear into the shadows. Gradually the candle drew nearer until the light picked up the white of their night shifts. The candle was held higher and revealed a thin white face peering at them through the darkness.

The face belonged to a boy, older than Bron, about the same age as Sorin but much taller. He had a mass of blonde hair in natural tight curls all over his head.

"Who are you? And what are you doing here?" he asked Sorin suspiciously.

"Who are you and what are *you* doing here?" Sorin countered.

"We live here," said Bron. The light from the candle swung down to her level.

"And so do I," he said defiantly.

"You're Nobilianus," said Sorin, with sudden understanding.

"And she's Bron," he replied. "I've seen her before, through the window. We're going to be married one day."

"What's married?" Bron queried.

"Do you usually creep about these corridors at night?" he asked.

"No, do you?" Sorin came back at him.

"You're not to talk to me like that," he complained. "I'll tell my father."

"Who's your father?" asked Bron, in ignorance.

"Vortin, the High Priest," responded the boy with pride. "I will be High Priest one day. See, I wear the ring of office." As he waved his right hand about, an emerald crystal flashed green in the candlelight.

Bron remembered their errand and said, "We've come to find my daddy. He's locked up somewhere."

"I know where he is," taunted Nobilianus. "What will you give me if I tell?"

"What do you want?" asked Sorin.

"You could come and see me sometimes," he suggested. "It's

lonely up here with only the old priests visiting and that black African."

"We're not allowed," said Sorin, adding, "we'd get into the most fearful trouble."

"Then I shall tell on you both," he threatened, with obvious pleasure at the prospect.

Sorin was not daunted. "And we will tell on you," she said.

He pulled a face in the candlelight. "I still won't show you where her father is!" Then he laughed, blew out his candle, and relented. "Oh, all right then. Follow me."

He led them by his voice in the dark to a door on the opposite side of the corridor, and knocked softly twice.

"Who's there?" Bron recognised her father's voice.

"Daddy, it's me, it's Bron, Daddy!"

"Bron! You shouldn't be here! Are you on your own?"

"I'm with her," Sorin reassured him, "and Nobilianus is here, too."

Hestig was silent for a moment. "Sorin, take her back. You'll all be in trouble if you're found here."

"But I want to come in to see you." Bron was near to tears.

"I can't let you in, sweetheart – the door's locked and I haven't got a key. Go back now. I'll be out of here soon. Go back to bed."

"We must go," Sorin urged her.

"Goodnight, Daddy," said Bron.

"Goodnight, sweetheart. Sleep tight."

"Sleep tight, Daddy."

The children crept away.

"Daddy sounded funny," commented Bron.

"I think he was crying," Sorin told her.

"My Daddy doesn't cry," insisted Bron.

"What about me?" whined Nobilianus.

"We'll ask Veneta if we can come to see you sometimes," Sorin promised, then took Bron back to bed.

Next morning, Veneta told the two girls to wait in their room after breakfast and not to go to the schoolroom.

"I am disappointed in you," she scolded Sorin. "You were put in here to look after Bron, not lead her into trouble. You are not to leave the room after bedtime – you know the rules, yet you deliberately disobeyed them! As for you, Bron, you are old enough to know right from wrong!"

"I wanted to talk to Daddy," Bron explained.

Sorin was chastened but asked, with head bent, how Veneta had found out. Both girls knew that Naila would never have divulged their secret.

"Nobilianus told me," said Veneta, "and I hope for your sakes he hasn't also told Vortin."

Seeing Sorin's surprise, she added, "I suppose he promised he wouldn't tell?"

Sorin nodded. "Yes, if we visit him sometimes."

Veneta's reply was sharp. "Keep Bron away from that boy – do you hear?"

"But I thought Bron was going to marry him."

"Don't think! Just do as you're told and don't ask questions. Now off you both go to school."

Veneta shooed them from the room.

CHAPTER XXV (25)

Everyone who could spare the time came to watch the trial of the blacksmith, Trifena among them, and there was standing room only in the council chamber. The long table had been pulled to one end of the room and faced the crowd.

Severus presided and on either side of him sat the councillors. The absence of Hestig was noticeable to all. No official from the Temple was present but there were several in the crowd who would be reporting back to Vortin.

When the blacksmith was led in, tied to his warders, the crowd fell silent.

He had been cleaned up but was very thin as he had not eaten for seven days. Now, there was little to remind the expectant onlookers of the large, drunken, bullying man they knew. Skin hung slack from his pallid cheeks. The only colour on his face was in his eyes, which stared unseeingly ahead, red rimmed and black and sunken under heavy eyebrows. His shoulders drooped beneath the burden of his fear and misery, and his feet shuffled. Only once did he acknowledge the presence of the crowd, when he looked round the room, seemingly searching for a friendly face, but found none.

"Bring him a chair," ordered Severus. Africanus, acting as clerk, read out the charge.

"Did you kill Septima?" asked Severus.

"No," replied the prisoner.

One by one, witnesses were brought forward to testify to his drunken, brutish behaviour. All the girls from the inn had some evidence to give, as well as the innkeeper and wife, and his mother-in-law. There was little need for the testimonies, as all the settlement knew of his excesses.

"Now," said Severus, "we come to the second night of Unvala, and the visit of the travelling entertainers. I want to establish the events of that evening."

One of the inn girls was called back to the table to confirm that all the girls had attended the performance, and had then gone back inside the inn to have a meal and start work.

When the stable boy was called, murmurs of surprise rippled round the crowd.

"State your name," instructed Africanus.

"You know my name," retorted the boy.

"State it anyway," ordered Severus, "for the record." The boy complied.

"Now tell us what happened on the second night of Unvala," prompted Severus.

"I was in the stables, see, with the 'orses," he began. "This man come in, but I couldn't see 'im proper in the dark, 'e was dressed all in black. I didn't know 'oo it was."

He hesitated. He knew the figure had been too tall to be the blacksmith. He now had his own thoughts about who the man in black was, but he had been paid well by Sharma the priest, so held his tongue.

"Well, what then?" asked Severus.

" 'E gave me a coin and said I should do as 'e told me, then disappear, and that's what I did."

"So tell the court what you were instructed to do," said Africanus.

"I went into the inn by the back door and found Septima, and told 'er she was wanted outside. She followed me out – she warn't afraid of anything, that one – then I disappeared. I never saw 'er again."

"Have you thought, since, who the man was?" asked Severus.

"Yes – 'im," and he pointed to the blacksmith.

"It's a lie!" shouted the accused man.

"What makes you think so now, when you weren't sure at the time?" persisted Severus.

The truthful answer was that the silver coins in his purse had convinced him, but he couldn't say that. He searched about for an answer.

"I think I 'eard 'er speak 'is name – before I left," he said, confused.

"So *she* recognised him when you hadn't, though he was dressed in black and it was dark?" enquired Severus.

The boy brightened. "Well, sir, she knew 'im better'n I did."

Everyone laughed and Africanus had to order the people to be quiet.

Dagvald, sitting at the long table as a member of the village council, asked for permission to speak to the boy.

"There is another man locked up for this murder," he said, "also on your evidence. They cannot both be responsible. What is your answer to that?"

The ostler became even more confused. He reasoned in his head that he heard Hestig make threats, but *he* had to be found innocent, while he had not seen the blacksmith anywhere near the inn on the night of the murder, but *he* had to be proved guilty. He concentrated on the coins in his purse and knew he needed to sharpen his wits on their edges.

"It was true what I said –'Estig did make those threats, and I thought it must be 'im that did it, but then I got to thinking again and I remembered –"

His mind cleared as if by divine intervention and he told his lie with such confidence that the court believed him. It was such a brilliant lie that he wished he could have told someone about it, but dare not.

"If I 'ad been more awake, I would 'ave taken more notice of the 'orse –'e let me know. That blacksmith did a good job but 'e was never very kind to the 'orses, see. They was frightened of 'im. There was one in partiklar 'oo 'ated 'im – got a fearsome jab in the 'aunches once with a 'ot shoe – and 'e reared up anytime the man came near 'im. 'E nearly went wild that night – I could 'ardly 'old 'im down."

The boy saw the blacksmith look up in amazement. "He's lying!" he shouted.

"You'll get your turn in a minute," Africanus reprimanded him.

The ostler was told to sit down and Attryde's mother was called. She displayed the bloodied clothes, which she identified as her son-in-law's.

Finally the blacksmith was called. He protested his innocence but without hope. Attryde could have given him an alibi if she had been allowed to speak, but she was not in court, and had more reason to loathe him than anyone else. He recognised the hatred that had piled up evidence against him, and knew the reason – not the murder of Septima, of which he was innocent, but the attack on Jeetuna, which had not been mentioned. This was Vortin's revenge and there was no escape.

After short deliberation, Severus advised the court of the conclusion reached by the councillors – that the blacksmith was guilty of the murder of Septima and he had hidden her body at Stanmere before escaping on a stolen horse next morning. Grimly, Severus pronounced the death sentence.

Under Roman law the court was not allowed to execute him, so it was announced that they would send to Calleva for permission to have the sentence carried out there.

Severus gave one final command. "The clerk will go now to advise Vortin of the court's decision and request the release of Hestig immediately. He shall receive a document confirming his innocence."

This directive was greeted with a cry of relief from Trifena.

Africanus was despatched to Calleva the following morning, to present the court's findings and request the execution. He returned three days later with a document granting permission, signed and sealed by a member of the ordo, the Roman civil council of Calleva.

During those three days, Attryde visited her husband in his cell and they made their peace and said their farewells. Humiliated and repentant now that he was sober, he welcomed the release the Roman sword would gift him.

The ostler was absent when they brought the prisoner, bound, to the stable and threw him across the saddle and tied him to the horse he had stolen on the morning he fled. His warders were nervous and discussed the trouble they were anticipating from frightened horses, as the stable lad had testified at the trial, and expressed their surprise when the animals took no notice of the blacksmith. He shrugged with resignation.

It was well before dawn when the little procession trod the path down to the ford, passing the house opposite the forge on their way.

The blacksmith knew that Attryde would be inside, listening to the horses trotting by, and he wept as he had not wept since a child for the wife he had lost forever.

CHAPTER XXVI (26)

AD 391

Two years had passed since the murder of Septima and the execution of the blacksmith, and life in the settlement had settled down again into the mundane.

One morning early in the year, Veneta stood at the Temple altar, on duty at a minor religious festival, of which there were many, watching the worshippers streaming in through the entrance doors.

She saw Attryde enter with a handsome young man at her heels. He had taken over the forge and was working hard there and making a success of the business. Attryde smiled at the priestess, who nodded in acknowledgement.

Veneta thought how much better fed and better dressed Attryde looked these days, and at last she seemed to have found contentment. Some of the women were nudging each other and looking somewhat enviously towards the couple, but Veneta had not heard any of them say they begrudged the young woman this newfound happiness, and no questions were asked directly.

Bron was chatting animatedly to Sorin and Naila. Veneta felt sure that the child was as happy as possible living at the Temple, almost entirely due to her friendship with the two girls, but also in part because of the affection she herself and Bron felt for each other.

Presently, Hestig and Trifena and the family came in. Naila saw them first, then all three girls waved enthusiastically.

The family now included Aelia, not yet two years old. Bron adored her baby sister. The toddler was blonde and blue eyed and Hestig said she reminded him of his younger sister, whom he had not seen since he was captured.

Veneta had asked him some time ago to tell her that story.

"I was a boy, only twelve years old," he related. "My sister and I were playing on the beach near our home in Jutland when this band of Roman seafarers suddenly appeared. Apparently, their ship had been blown north by the gale that had been raging all the previous week. They asked us where they were. At the time, I couldn't understand what they were saying and we just stared at them. Then they picked me up and flung me into a little rowing boat and took me back to their ship. We left my sister screaming on the beach. That was the last I saw of her, or my family."

After the service, Iraina announced to Veneta, "Now that Bron is five years old, Vortin has decided it's time she and Nobilianus got to know each other. Please see to it, Veneta." So a meeting was arranged.

Veneta and Bron arrived at the altar at the same time as Selvid approached with Nobilianus. Selvid looked grim and Veneta knew why.

Both of them hated being a party to bringing these two children together for the purpose that Vortin had in mind. Veneta shuddered whenever she thought of the intended union, which she felt sure would damage the girl's personality irreparably and blight her whole future. But priest and priestess had to do as they were told. Veneta hoped that Bron's courage would serve her well, and anyway, circumstances could change in the seven years that lay ahead. Once again, she pushed the matter to the back of her mind.

"Son, this is Bron, your wife-to-be," said Vortin.

"I know," said Nobilianus, "I've seen her before."

"You have? Where?" asked Vortin, raising his eyebrows.

Nobilianus turned his back to his father and only Veneta and Bron saw his sly wink.

"Up there," he said, "through the window."

"Now you are nine, Nobilianus, it's time you two began to spend some time together," said Vortin.

The children didn't move. His father impatiently clicked his tongue against the roof of his mouth.

"Take her for a walk, son," he said, "just round the interior wall. It's too cold outside. Talk to each other. Veneta and Selvid, go with them."

The four walked in silence for a while, two by two.

"Bron, tell Nobilianus what you learned in school this morning," prompted Veneta.

"Africanus has written a play about Boudicca," Bron explained with enthusiasm. "Her army of Britons burnt down three big towns –" She hesitated and looked at Veneta, who helped her out.

"Camulodunum, Londinium and Verulamium," she said.

"She killed all the Ninth Legion," Bron added.

Nobilianus knew the story. "But Governor Suetonius with the Fourteenth and Twentieth Legions defeated Boudicca's army and she poisoned herself. What's clever about that?" he asked.

"My friend Sorin is going to be Boudicca," Bron persevered.

"I remember her," Nobilianus said, frowning, and added in a whisper that Veneta and Selvid couldn't hear, "I told on you two, creeping round the corridors at night – I hope you got into trouble."

"Well, we didn't!" retorted Bron.

"Pity," said the boy, and then in a louder voice, "I'm not interested in a silly play."

"It's not silly!" Bron defended what all the children in the schoolroom had agreed was their teacher's masterpiece. "Veneta has written some music for it and Sorin sings a song by herself."

"When are we going to see this play and hear the music?" asked Selvid.

"Not quite yet – when it has been well rehearsed," Veneta told him.

"So what do you like doing?" Bron asked the boy.

"Pulling wings off flies," he answered, and laughed.

"Ugh!" said Bron and rubbed her ear, as if to rub away what she had just heard.

"Well?" asked Iraina when they returned to the altar. "How did you get on together?"

"She's too young – she bores me," Nobilianus said, dismissing Bron by turning his back on her.

"I don't like him," said Bron. "I would rather play with my friend, Soranus."

Vortin was clearly displeased. "The sooner you get to like each other, the better," he snapped.

"They're only children," Iraina soothed him. "They'll grow to love each other, as you and I do, Vortin, and one day they will secure the priestly line."

After he had walked away, Iraina turned to her priestess. "They must meet more often," she ordered sharply. "Organise it, Veneta," and she too left.

During several such meetings, the relationship between the two children grew steadily worse. Veneta noticed Bron sticking out her tongue whenever she caught sight of Nobilianus spying on her from the upstairs window. If Sorin and Naila were near, she nudged them and raised her eyes upwards, and they also looked up and stuck out their tongues. Nobilianus retaliated in like fashion.

Veneta, at once relieved and concerned, consulted Jeetuna.

"Arrange for them to meet outside the Temple," Jeetuna advised, "and with other children."

A few days later, Veneta walked down the Temple steps followed by Nobilianus, Bron and her two friends, and a few other boys and girls. They were joined by Africanus. Noticing Soranus in his grandmother's compound, Veneta invited him to join them.

It was February, the lambing feast of Imbolc, and everywhere carcases turned on spits and fat dripped into fires so that the faggots sizzled and spat. The aroma of roasting sheep basted with vinegar and mint was so strong that it almost fooled the palate into thinking the meat was already succulent in the mouth. Everyone was looking forward to the evening meal.

Crossing over the stepping-stones, the children removed their sandals, and with noise and laughter began splashing each other with cold water until, as usual, their play became too rough and Africanus had to intervene. Then they followed him and Veneta up to the mere. Only Nobilianus had not joined in the game, and was looking very uncomfortable in the children's company.

The snowbells were still glowing white in their drifts, but were making way for pale yellow primroses. Around them the bright green moss was soft, but the crackle of running feet on broken branches and twigs sounded like breaking ice.

Most of the trees were still spindly bare but some had remained green throughout the winter. Many were wound round with ivy and other creepers, which also clung precariously to the bank encircling the pool, as if to keep from sliding down into the water.

Africanus spent time with his pupils, pointing out the shape of a leaf here or the colour shading on a branch there, as they picked up moss, twigs, stones and flowers to take back to the classroom.

While they were occupied in this way, Veneta looked about for a figure she guessed would not be very far from Bron, and smiled to see Pulcher lurking behind a bush.

She would not let the children play in the water until Africanus had tested its depth. Near the highest part of the bank on the far side of the pool, with water up to his waist, he broke off a branch from above his head and stuck it firmly into the mud.

Wading back, his tunic dripping wet, he warned the children: "Don't go near that branch, it's deepest there. Everywhere else is shallow enough."

"Now I have a special job for you, children," Veneta told them. "Iraina has asked us to collect all the coins and jewellery people have thrown in, and take them back to the Temple. See what you can find."

With shouts and laughter, there was a general jostling to be first into the water, some entering cautiously, while the more adventurous jumped in from the top of the bank.

Bron had immediate success. "Look what I've found!" she called and held up a copper bracelet.

Bare toes were soon treading on coins of all denominations, and the sun's fingers, searching through skeletal branches, were helpfully pointing out the glint of glass beads on the muddy bed.

"Aren't you coming in, Nobilianus?" teased Soranus, in water up to his chest.

"I don't like cold water," said Nobilianus, sulkily.

"It's not *very* cold," encouraged Naila, with only her ankles covered.

Africanus came to sit beside Veneta.

"I'm worried about the boy," he confided to her. "He should mix more with the other children. Being on his own so much makes him – well, strange. And as for him and Bron –" He shook his head. "She's such a normal, happy little girl."

Veneta's reply was never voiced because of a commotion on the far side of the pool. Nobilianus had wandered round the top of the bank, and the soft earth at the edge had given way under his clumsiness.

She jumped up and watched apprehensively as he slithered down the slope on his back, yelling as he went. When his feet had almost reached the water's edge, he rolled over and scrabbled for a handhold, but grass and ivy came away in his fingers. He managed to turn on to his back again and tried to dig his heels into the mud, but to no avail, and he slipped into the water, disappearing altogether where the warning branch was standing guard.

As Veneta cried out, Africanus leapt to his feet and ran into the shallows and began to wade out, but Soranus was already there, diving, coming up for a deep breath, then diving again to locate the boy. He found him as Africanus reached them, and together they dragged the struggling Nobilianus to the edge of the water, where he collapsed in a heap.

The children gathered round and gazed down at the High Priest's son, plainly horrified at what had happened to him. As soon as he recovered breath, he began crying and shouting and blaming everyone except himself.

"It was no one's fault, it was an accident," Veneta said sharply, as she knelt by his side.

Pulcher came across sheepishly when she called him from concealment, and set off for the Temple to collect a change of clothing for Nobilianus.

The boy started hollering again. By now the children had wandered away from him, their contempt obvious, and were putting on their sandals. Veneta had turned her attention to Soranus and Africanus, who were both soaking wet.

"I've lost it! I've lost it!" Nobilianus began wailing over and over again.

"Lost what?" asked Veneta.

"His ring," answered Bron.

"Well, no one is going back into the water to look for it now, so you might as well be quiet," Veneta told him. "We'll drag the pool later."

"Veneta's going to get into such trouble," the priestess overheard Sorin say to Bron, and thought she was probably right.

"I'll dive for the ring tomorrow," Soranus said, then hesitated. "If I find it, Bron, will you let me kiss you?"

Veneta smiled to herself. Bron looked surprised but nodded shyly.

It was a subdued party that made its way back to the settlement. Africanus had to give Nobilianus a piggyback as the boy refused to walk, and as the man's clothes were still wet and clinging, Nobilianus was soaked again by the time they arrived at the Temple.

Vortin was plainly embarrassed by his son's behaviour but verbally disciplined Veneta for her lack of supervision. She felt this was grossly unfair.

"Africanus, you are saved from loss of privileges only because of the part you played in the rescue of my son," Vortin told him.

Later, in private, Iraina spoke sharply to her priestess about her irresponsibility and threatened to hand Bron over into Jeetuna's care – *or lack of it*, thought Veneta.

Soranus came to the Temple next afternoon, again dripping water over the mosaic, but with the emerald crystal ring irreverently displayed halfway down his fore finger. Passing Bron as he entered, he grinned cheekily at her.

"I searched for almost an hour," he told Vortin. "I found it in a clump of moss near where Nobilianus was trying to find a handhold."

Vortin sent for his son, who was brought down to receive the ring and thank its finder. He did as he was told but obviously felt humiliated, and his expression was not one of gratitude.

CHAPTER XXVII (27)

Bron did not meet Nobilianus for several weeks after the incident at the pool, though she often caught him watching her through the window on the second floor.

One evening, Sorin came up to the bedroom with the news that she had met Nobilianus coming out of Vortin's office.

"He wants to see us," she said. "Tonight."

"I don't want to see him," Bron pouted.

"Nor do I," said Naila, in support.

Sorin explained that he had something very important to say.

"I don't want to hear it," insisted Bron.

"It's a secret," whispered Sorin. "Oh, do let's go, Bron. I want to know what it is."

Bron also wanted to know what the secret was, but she mistrusted Nobilianus completely and felt sure that anything he suggested would ultimately lead them into trouble. Sorin continued to wheedle, and finally Bron agreed.

"Tonight," said Sorin.

Naila was concerned that Veneta would get into more trouble if they were found where they were not supposed to be. As yet, they knew nothing of Iraina's threat to place Bron in Jeetuna's care.

"Then we must be careful not to get caught," said Sorin.

They waited until their supper trays had been collected and Veneta had called in to wish them goodnight, and all was quiet along their corridor. Then, throwing shawls round their shoulders, they crept in the dark along by the walls and across to the corridor that ran parallel to theirs, past the women's quarters, towards the room where Nobilianus spent most of his time. He was waiting for them in the doorway, his hand shielding the light from a candle.

"Come in," he invited and shut the door behind them.

"Well, what do you want?" demanded Bron.

"I've been somewhere special on my own at night – you won't guess where!" he announced.

Where? thought Bron, but kept quiet.

"Where?" asked Sorin.

"To a really sacred place – the pits!" he told them, triumphantly.

"Among the dead?" asked Naila in disbelief.

"Yes," replied Nobilianus.

The interest of all three girls was apparent, even in the semi-darkness.

"I'll take you there one night, if you like – that is, if you're not afraid. I'm not afraid," he boasted. His fearful reluctance to go into the pool was a recent memory for all of them.

"Children are not allowed up there without grown-ups," said Bron.

"You'll tell, like you did before," Naila accused him.

"No, I won't," he said.

"I don't believe you," said Bron.

"Do let's all go, Bron," Sorin tried to persuade her.

Bron shook her head.

"You don't do everything she says, do you?" Nobilianus sneered at Sorin.

"We'll come if Soranus comes, too," stipulated Bron.

"We don't want him along," Nobilianus objected, though not very convincingly.

"I do," said Bron, "or I won't go."

The boy agreed. Bron thought afterwards that she had played directly into his hands.

"I don't want to be left behind this time," Naila told them nervously.

"Of course not," Bron assured her.

"When shall we go?" asked Sorin.

"The first night of the full moon," Nobilianus decided. He was already beginning to sound less confident.

Having agreed the time and place of their meeting, the three girls crept back to their room.

Once there, Bron said, "I don't believe he's ever been up to the pits on his own, in the dark. He's making it up to look brave."

Next morning she found Pulcher in the Temple and told him of the plan, asking him to get in touch with Soranus. Pulcher remonstrated as best he could, but finally agreed to do as she asked. His only condition was that he went with them. He said he would keep his distance so that Nobilianus wouldn't know he was there. Secretly, Bron was glad that he would be near, caring for her, as he always did.

It was a day of sunshine, still cold in the shade, but with a sky deep blue and not a cloud in sight. Africanus told the children that the sky was almost as blue as it was above his homeland. As he talked, Bron saw in his eyes such a sad and faraway look.

Veneta returned from market as the sky paled to an all-over blue wash. Bron asked her why the full moon looked so different, and Veneta said the brightness of the sky hid the glow that usually smudged the edges of the circle. For a while, it hung like a gold medal over to the south, full and perfectly round, its face clear and friendly. As daylight faded, the halo returned, and the moon lit up the evening like a lamp.

The children's plan was that the five of them would meet at the gap in the western bank. Pulcher had been persuaded to unlock the side door of the Temple. One at a time, Nobilianus then the three girls, crept down the iron staircases, out through the side door, and turning right made their way past the back of Selena's house and so to the gap in the bank. Soranus was waiting for them. Bron was conscious of the speed at which her heart was beating.

Without a word, Nobilianus led them down into the shallow curve of the boundary ditch and up on to the lynchets, the low banks that divided the farming strips. They stumbled across the rough earth and into Byden Wood.

It was dark in the wood but the moon gave sufficient light through the trees for them to tread their path. None of them had brought a lamp for fear of being noticed. Behind their guide, Sorin held Naila's hand, then came Bron, followed by Soranus at the rear. Only Bron was aware of Pulcher following at a distance.

In silence, they climbed the gentle slope running parallel to the Stan, which was a field away. When pheasants suddenly rose from the trees with a sound like flapping tablecloths, presumably to look for roosts where there was less disturbance, Bron's heart jumped and she guessed that none of them felt as brave as they had when they planned the adventure. She certainly didn't.

Then they left the wood and stepped out into the open. The pits covered an area the size of the settlement. The three girls and Soranus had been there before and would be there again at the feast of Rosalia in May, when families picnicked among the flower-covered graves. However, the visits were always in daylight, never at night.

Fortunately, it was almost as bright as daylight now as the full moon glistened the frost on the chalk foundation, which was dug all over with shallow graves. Mounds of rich earth cosseted their dead, generations of ancestors, their decapitated heads placed between their knees, with treasured possessions and grave goods around them, to ease life in the next world.

There was peace and stillness out in the open with only the dead for company. In the distance, an owl hooted. Bron saw Naila shiver as she clung to Sorin's hand. Nobilianus was looking nervously about him and Bron stayed close to Soranus.

"Well, what now?" Soranus asked, after nobody had spoken for several minutes.

"We shouldn't be here," whispered Naila.

"The dead are not going to hurt us," reasoned Bron, "because they're all our friends."

To keep warm, she suggested that they began chasing each other among the pits, the one caught becoming the catcher in turn. Then Sorin wanted to play hide-and-seek, and had to explain the game to Nobilianus.

Soranus volunteered to hide first and concealed himself in a shallow in the chalk, pulling his cloak over him. As soon as he heard the others coming near, he sprang up with a ghostly wail, arms flailing the air. This sent them all running away in different directions with laughter and squeals, except for Nobilianus, who complained that Soranus wasn't playing the game according to the rules just explained to him.

When it was her turn, Sorin hid behind a tree on the edge of the wood and was soon found. Naila nervously refused to hide, then Nobilianus said he wanted a go. Soranus said it was Bron's turn, but Nobilianus insisted, and Bron gave way.

With their backs to him, they could hear the cracking of twigs and knew he was in the wood. Presently there was silence.

"Coming, ready or not!" called Sorin and the four children made straight for the trees.

Five minutes later they had still not found Nobilianus.

"I didn't think he was clever enough to stay hidden this long," said Soranus.

"Perhaps he's gone back to the pits," Bron suggested. "Race you there!" and she ran towards the edge of the trees, the others behind her.

In the open again among the pits, there was still no sign of Nobilianus.

"Perhaps the dead have got him," Naila suggested, a tremble in her voice.

"I do hope so!" exclaimed Soranus.

"They're welcome to him!" said Sorin. "Come on, let's go before they send him back!"

As Bron turned to follow, she awkwardly caught her foot in a depression in the ground and fell heavily, twisting it under her. Her cries brought the children running to her. They raised her to her feet and Sorin gently moved her foot out of the hole, which caused Bron intense pain. They tried to bear her weight between them as they made their way through the trees, but the strength needed was more than they could muster and they came to a halt.

"One of us will have to go for help," said Soranus.

"But we'll all get into such earth-shattering trouble!" worried Naila.

Then Pulcher was there. No one expressed surprise. They were all used to Pulcher being around exactly when Bron needed him.

"I carry," he said simply, and the children moved out of his way. The dwarf was not tall, but his legs and arms were strong, and he picked Bron up as if she were a bag of chicken feathers.

CHAPTER XXVIII (28)

They were descending through the wood when they saw torchlights crossing the lynchets towards them.

"How have they found out we're missing?" asked Naila, surprised.

"Nobilianus," replied Pulcher. "He run – I saw."

"Go round them," Bron urged the other three children. "You don't need to get caught."

"They'll have missed us, anyway," said Sorin. "I'll stay."

Naila hesitated then said, in what was obviously meant to sound a brave voice, "So will I."

"Let no one suggest that I leave," Soranus warned, before anyone spoke.

The group met the priests and eunuchs at the edge of the wood. There was no sign of Nobilianus.

As Sorin had predicted, there was earth-shattering trouble at the Temple next morning. Nobilianus was present at the investigation before Vortin and Iraina, who were seated in front of the altar on their two ornate, gilded, stout wooden thrones. He told how he had seen Pulcher unlock the side door so that the three girls could escape from the Temple, and how Soranus had met them at the ditch. He said he had followed them into the wood, realised they were headed for the sacred area, and returned to raise the alarm. Vortin believed him. Iraina seemed not so sure.

"Nobilianus, my son," she said sweetly, "you are not wearing your ring again. What have you done with it this time?"

The boy's usually white face flushed pink and he pushed the fingers of his right hand, from which the ring was missing, through his blonde curls. "I think I must have lost it in the wood, Mother," he said.

Pulcher was beaten heavily with staves under the supervision of Brocchus, and dismissed without being given the chance to say goodbye to Bron. She learned later that, if it had not been for the nursing care lavished on him by Stalwyn and Trifena, he would have died alone in his house.

A punishing fine was levied on the family of Soranus, who were also prohibited from worshipping in the Temple for three months.

"A great sorrow to us," his grandmother, Selena, said.

Naila was sent home in disgrace to her family, who were similarly forbidden to worship. She confided to her friends that her greatest punishment was that her parents would have to feed her now, when they couldn't afford it, and she had resolved to eat only enough to keep herself alive.

Sorin was treated more leniently but she said it was only because her voice would one day earn money for the Temple. She was banished permanently from Bron's room to one much smaller, and confined for a long time on bread and water, so that her yellow hair lost all its sheen. The play written by Africanus was eventually performed without Sorin taking any part in it, which caused her many tears.

Veneta was punished, but she would not tell Bron how. Whatever the punishment, it caused Selvid to look very angry for many days.

And Bron was put into Jeetuna's charge.

Under the supervision of Kendrus, her sprained ankle healed within a week, but not so her grief for her friends. When she cried herself to sleep, there was no Veneta to smooth her curls and kiss her cheek, or Sorin's motherly love to take her into bed for comfort.

Bron thought about the whole affair and realised that Nobilianus had got his revenge on everybody.

On Vortin's instructions, Africanus now came to her room to give her lessons, and she told him the truth of what had taken place that night.

When preparations were being made for the feast of Rosalia, Africanus said he had spoken to Selvid privately, and there was just the chance of some welcome news.

Two days later, as Bron and the other children were receiving instruction from Selvid, two of the eunuchs came hurrying into the Temple and excitedly asked the priest for an immediate audience with Vortin. The children were still sitting cross-legged round the mosaic when the High Priest appeared and was soon joined by Iraina with Nobilianus. Vortin dismissed the children, with the exception of Bron. Then he turned on his son.

"What have you got to say about this?" he demanded and held up the green crystal ring.

"Oh, Father, I'm so glad you've found it," exclaimed Nobilianus, with evident confusion. "Where was it?"

"It was found at the pits," declared Vortin, looking hard at his son, who turned pale and began to fidget. "Perhaps we should hear the truth of what really happened that night."

"It was as I said," spluttered Nobilianus.

"Then how did your ring get up to the pits?" thundered Vortin. "Did it walk by itself?"

"It could have walked with the help of two human legs," blustered the boy.

"Bring him in!" ordered Vortin to the eunuchs, and they ushered in Soranus, who had not been allowed to set foot in the Temple since the night of the escapade. As he passed, he gave Bron a cheeky smile.

"Now," said Vortin, "let's hear your version. There is no sense in lying because you've already been punished."

Soranus looked at the ring held in Vortin's long fingers, at the cowering Nobilianus, and stated exactly the part the High Priest's son had played in the episode, including their having to explain the game of hide-and-seek to him, and his saying Soranus wasn't playing fair, and then taking Bron's turn.

Vortin must have believed him because he almost exploded with anger. Nobilianus visibly shook with fear, tears ran down his pale cheeks, his teeth chattered, and he sank to the floor. He bowed his forehead to the ground, stammering and crying.

Soranus was ushered out quickly, his face wearing a much wider grin than when he arrived.

Africanus told Bron several days later that Soranus had visited Naila at her home among the shepherds' houses by the east ditch, to tell her what had happened.

"He was upset to see how thin she had become in only a few weeks, and she looked so tired and worried."

"Poor Naila," said Bron. "I wish I could help her, but I can't."

"Soranus was able to brighten her up a little. She was so pleased to see him and hear his story, and they laughed together at their memories, and he said she almost became the Naila you all knew."

Bron smiled.

"She sent her love to you and Sorin and Veneta. Soranus told her that things aren't the same at the Temple and it's more difficult to get messages through."

"But this one got through, thanks to you," said Bron, smiling affectionately at her teacher.

No one in the Temple was allowed to see Nobilianus for a long time after that, not his mother nor Veneta nor Africanus.

He stayed in his room and food and wine were left outside the door and collected from there, though the women along the corridor told Africanus that it was barely touched. Rumours were rife that his father had beaten his son black and blue, not so much for the escapade as for the lie.

Whatever the truth, everyone in the Temple could hear the wailing and yowling that came from his room, sounds that seemed to Bron more animal-like than human, and she covered her ears rather than listen. Only when the noise stopped each night, and she thought he must be asleep, was she able to fall asleep herself.

Section III

JEETUNA

CHAPTER XXIX (29)

AD 391

There was no love in their relationship. In fact, Bron decided that Jeetuna did not like her very much. The priestess certainly spent as little time with her as possible, visiting only to make sure she was well and provided with her daily needs. Bron thought she was as lonely as Nobilianus must be.

Her only joy was the daily visit of Africanus. He seemed to know what she needed and he led her in imagination out of her situation and into realms of fantasy. With his spell woven round her, she walked among the stars, whose names she learned, or sailed across great seas to lands of searing heat or icy wastes, climbed to fires burning on tops of high mountains, or descended into rock caverns of precious stones mined by strange-looking people.

After he left her, she spent hours exploring in her imagination the lands he had shown her.

Often she fancied she could hear Pulcher calling. She never quite saw him, but knew he was there, looking after her in every adventure so that she never came to any harm.

So it was on the night of the fire. She had slept restlessly for several hours and was awoken by his voice, which was as clear and loud as if he were standing in the room by the side of her mattress.

"Come, Bron," his voice said, "put on wrap – follow me."

Obediently, she pulled a blanket off the bed, wrapped it round herself, slid her feet into slippers, and stepped through the now open door into the corridor. No one was in sight.

She could immediately smell smoke and was suddenly wide awake. Without panic, she descended the iron staircase to the floor below.

Acrid black clouds thickened ahead of her, swirling up into the roof, and through them danced a strange flickering light, bright yellow and orange, accompanied by a low roaring sound. With shocked surprise, Bron saw that the tapestry hangings and altar frontal were ablaze, with exploring fingers of flame reaching ever higher and higher. The eunuch who should have been on night duty was nowhere to be seen.

Through drifting smoke and framed by the fire, Ashuba stared straight at her, his piercing eyes glowing red, willing her to take action. Her first thought was to run to the cauldron of vinegar and egg white, but with dismay she saw it lying on its side, its contents streaming across the floor well away from the fire.

Fortunately, at that moment, two men clattered down the iron staircase from the women's rooms. She called to them for help. One ran to raise the alarm. The other man began pulling down the sanctuary hangings with his bare hands, trying to stamp out the flames as the tapestries heaped up on the floor. He shouted to Bron to run upstairs and bring down the children and warn the women.

As she turned to obey, she thought she saw a shadow detach itself from the darkness along the opposite wall and dissolve into the half-light on the far staircase. It was such a fleeting movement that Bron wondered if she had imagined it, until she was halfway up her own staircase and looked across to the high window opposite. There was no doubt about the shadow that passed across its thick green glass. Bron, who had by now discarded her blanket, shivered and wondered.

She ran along her corridor, banging on all the doors and calling to the children to get downstairs as quickly as possible, then asked Sorin to go with her along the other corridor to warn Jeetuna and the women and their visitors. There was no need to knock at Iraina's suite of rooms because the High Priestess was away at Shubinata's temple, ritually preparing herself for the Midsummer Festival.

When she reached the room of Nobilianus and briefly knocked on his door, his sleepy voice asked what the commotion was about.

"Fire!" answered Bron and gave no further explanation. She had decided that he knew, anyway.

After the blaze had been quenched and the still-smoking hangings had been dragged outside on to the portico, Vortin ordered everyone to stay downstairs. All were accounted for, except the missing eunuch. After a brief search, he was found lying in the area behind the altar, just beginning to regain consciousness. He said he had heard someone shuffling about and had gone to investigate but remembered nothing more. A heavy length of wood lay nearby where his assailant had dropped it.

Vortin sent for the doctor, then ordered everyone back to bed but to reassemble after the service of early-morning prayer.

Next day all of them looked bleary-eyed with the exception of Veneta, who had slept soundly in her room above the schoolroom, unaware of the fire. Vortin was wearing the same robes as on the previous day and looked as though he had been up all night.

They all regarded the devastation that greeted them, especially the state of the altar, with horror. The wooden hanging rails and upright supports that were still in place were burnt or scorched and the others were just heaps of ashes on the floor. The few remaining tapestries hung in tatters, blackened with smoke and flecks of soot. Everything still smelt of smoke and Vortin got annoyed with the continual coughing and sneezing that everyone was trying to suppress.

Melted candle wax had run over Ashuba's feet and had hardened into a pool, dripping stalactites from the edge of his plinth. The god needed cleaning and repainting.

The mosaic and tiles were sticky with the fluid from the cauldron, which had a large dent in its side where it had hit the floor.

"I have conducted a thorough investigation but have not come to any conclusions," announced Vortin. "The torch used to set the fire was found by the altar, still blazing. Obviously, the arsonist had to be tall enough to remove it from its bracket on the wall."

Sharma suggested that, as the side door had been found unlocked, the culprit could have been someone with a grudge who had come in from the settlement, but no one was named as a possible suspect.

Bron was thanked for the part she had played in rescuing everyone. The two men involved were given free passes to the second floor for the rest of the year, and Vortin ordered that a very large bronze warning gong should be installed by the entrance doors.

Selvid was put in sole charge of the clean-up operation, as Sharma was away on Temple business. Everyone, including the children, was set to work. Only the priests and eunuchs were allowed to touch Ashuba, and as Brocchus was away with Sharma, it was left to the remaining five eunuchs to repair the damage to the stone god.

Bron was glad to see Dagvald, who came to consult with Vortin and measure up for new tapestries. He was able to smuggle in a packet of cakes, made with home-made wine, which Selena, helped by Soranus, had baked especially for Bron.

"Tell Selena they're just what I wanted," she whispered.

All the work had to be accomplished at speed to make ready for the approaching Midsummer Festival. When all was complete, Vortin sent Veneta to Iraina's cell in the wood, to summon her back for the rededication of the altar. Bron was there when she arrived with Veneta.

"You look very well, my dear," Vortin told her, "but then you always do after your annual retreat. It always surprises me how you can stay in that bare cell for so long."

"It does me good just to be alone with the goddess," Iraina said, "but, of course, if you had let me know about the fire, I would have come back sooner."

Sharma and Brocchus also returned and the rededication was performed with customary ritual and reverence.

Ashuba's eyes glowed an even deeper red for Bron and she again read the message in them. She went immediately and found Jeetuna, and conveyed to her what she had seen, or thought she had seen, on the night of the fire. Jeetuna said that the flicker of the flames must have played tricks with Bron's imagination, and that she should not repeat her fancies to anyone else.

Bron understood that message, too. She had done her duty to Ashuba and now left the matter in Jeetuna's hands, not mentioning her suspicions to anyone else, not even Africanus. As much as she disliked Nobilianus, she would not be the cause of his having another beating from his father. She could not think that he would live through it, as thin and pale as he was.

Late that evening, Nobilianus received a visit from Jeetuna in his room. He was flattered by her obvious devotion to him and enchanted by her beauty when she turned the full force of her sexuality on him with her dark blue eyes and wide smile. Not understanding the strange emotions unsettling his mind and body, he knew only that he needed to reach out and touch her hair.

When she whispered that she didn't know why he had set fire to the altar, though she was sure he had a very good reason, his sharp intake of breath and tensing facial muscles revealed that she had hit the mark.

"But, my dear Nobilianus, I am your most loyal servant, *as I am your father's.*" He understood she was warning him that she could tell of her suspicions if she chose. She continued, "But no one shall hear it from my lips for as long as I live. This meeting and our conversation will be our secret."

"You are right, I had good reason," he bluffed, "and I will not forget your loyalty to me when I am High Priest."

"I am honoured to be your friend," she replied and took his right hand in hers and kissed his ring.

When she left, he strutted about his room for a full hour, imagining himself as High Priest. Bron featured nowhere in his mind pictures, but Jeetuna had secured for herself an honoured and protected place as priestess.

Bron always saw her family at a distance during services, but still wasn't allowed any close contact. The Midsummer Festival was celebrated as in the past but for Bron was a day like any other, in spite of Midsummer Day being her sixth birthday. Certainly Jeetuna did not acknowledge it in any way. There were no presents from her family and Pulcher as in previous years, and no special cake or sweetmeats. Bron knew that a birthday parcel from her mother would have been delivered to the Temple, but Jeetuna had not passed it on to her.

Now banned from the Temple, Pulcher could occasionally be seen wandering around the covered walkway outside, obviously hoping to catch a glimpse of her, but only occasionally able to send an unobtrusive smile or wave.

Neither were Sorin and she given any opportunity to speak to each other. Sorin's voice was growing stronger and sweeter and Bron took comfort from a message whispered to her by a member of the young choir: "Sorin says she is singing for you, Bron."

Eventually, however, Vortin relented and Bron was allowed back into the schoolroom and was given freedom to come and go, though Jeetuna kept her under strict observation. Bron knew that Africanus and Veneta were trying to make up for Jeetuna's dislike of her by showing all the love and kindness they could, but that they were anxious not to step outside the bounds of their duties because of the repercussions that would follow.

One morning, Bron was delighted to see Pulcher back at work. She ran over and kissed him on the cheek and said how pleased she was to see him there. He flushed with pleasure.

The same morning, she learned from Jeetuna that she was to have a room companion, who would be moving in after school. Her excitement turned to disappointment, however, when the orphan Edreda appeared at her door, carrying a bundle of belongings.

Everything about Edreda was plain and round – in fact, she gave the appearance of an uninteresting brown circle. Bron knew that she worshipped Jeetuna and would report back to her idol everything that Bron said and did.

So Bron became more isolated than ever and found release only in the schoolroom and the stories told by Africanus. One day it occurred to her that she, in turn, enjoyed telling stories to the other children. At first they were retellings of those she had heard from her teacher, but as she gained confidence, they became her own stories, drawn from her wild imaginings.

Edreda particularly enjoyed the stories, which brought excitement into her life. Bedtime became a source of pleasure for both girls as Bron created a world where they could become whatever or whomever they pleased, maybe princesses fighting the Romans, shy deer living in the woods, or hunters tracking one of the strange striped or spotted jungle creatures Africanus painted for them with words.

In this way, Bron began an uneasy friendship with her roommate that relaxed over the succeeding months. Edreda still reported to Jeetuna, but less frequently and eventually only what she and Bron decided the priestess should be told.

Because Edreda was able to wander freely, a privilege earned by her spying work, she began carrying messages from Bron to her family and friends and back again – a secret known only to those involved.

Edreda told Bron that Trifena always welcomed her during these brief visits. When Edreda arrived, special treats were brought to the table, and afterwards she played games with the children, especially little Aelia who, she said, was as blonde and beautiful as she herself was insipid and plain.

So Edreda became very important to a small group of people. She seemed not to notice any discomfort from adverse weather as she carried messages to and fro, and many times returned to Bron dripping rainwater and dishevelled.

"Oh, Edreda, I'm sorry you're so wet," sympathised Bron late one afternoon during an April of prolonged and very heavy rains. "I'll find you some dry clothes."

"I slipped over in the mud, but I'll be all right," insisted Edreda stoically between sneezes, beginning to undress.

Bron looked at the girl anxiously, fearing that she had caught a chill.

"Where have you been?" she asked.

"To the market, and to see Naila. I didn't stop long because she was so busy nursing her mother and father. They both have a fever."

CHAPTER XXX (30)

AD 393

Plague! As soon as Kendrus confirmed it, the word flew round the houses only just ahead of the pestilence, terrorising every family.

The doctor was first summoned to the hovels of the poorest, where the outbreak began, among the farmers and shepherds and animal keepers by the eastern bank. The pig breeder was the first to die insane. Kendrus guessed he had brought the death back from the market in Calleva, where it was now rumoured to be rife.

He was followed into the afterlife by several of his neighbours, then Naila's mother and a day later her father, then the butcher's wife and children and the butcher himself, all within five days of onset.

When fomentations prescribed by Kendrus didn't prevent sores and buboes from spreading into people's armpits and groins, the High Priest acted swiftly, unceremoniously ejecting from the Temple those who had come to pray for healing, then barricading the massive doors. Kendrus was dismayed to see his patients lying on the stone steps, abandoned to succumb to the sickness without their god's comfort.

Vortin himself left hurriedly one morning, and later the same day Iraina disappeared into the wood.

On Vortin's instructions, Sharma and Brocchus took Nobilianus to safety. They also took with them Vitius, the boy now grown into a young man. Sharma and Brocchus were expected back but didn't return.

Vortin also made special arrangements for Bron. Jeetuna took her to Shubinata's temple in the wood, to live in Iraina's retreat cell. The priestess returned to the Temple because she had nowhere else to go, but shut herself in her room and refused to come out.

Veneta and Selvid told Kendrus they would not leave the children, and as well as caring for them and the rest of the staff, they kept the religious life of the Temple operating as best they could. However, as one after another of their charges became sick, all observances were abandoned in order to nurse those who needed their care.

Kendrus was given his own key to the side door and he and Stalwyn came and went as required, but were overstretched by the needs of the sick and dying inside the Temple and in the settlement, although they recruited as much help as they could. But families were terrified and locked themselves in their houses, only emerging to lay their dead outside for the sewer cleaner to collect and bury in the wood, until he too died, followed several hours later by his wife, after which bodies were left rotting along the pathways.

When Bron was taken to the cell in the wood, she expected to find Iraina already there, but the High Priestess was nowhere to be seen.

Every day, a rota of volunteers organised by Veneta took Bron's requirements to a collection point some way from the little temple. Apart from food, everything delivered had to be protected from rain and left there for one week, before Bron was allowed to collect and use it, in case the pestilence had been brought alive with it.

Stalwyn also arrived daily to make sure she was well, always keeping at a distance for fear of passing on the sickness.

Although on her own, Bron found a freedom that she had not known since her punishment. At first she was afraid of sleeping alone in the dark cell and brought the mattress into the temple, where she always kept candles or torches burning. However, after a while she became used to the rustlings and small noises in the dark, and as she began to recognise the creatures whose home she now shared, she gained confidence. Finding that the wood was, in fact, a friendly place, she took the mattress back to the cell.

She asked Stalwyn if Africanus could sometimes give her lessons, from a distance.

"Africanus, I'm so pleased to see you!" called Bron when he arrived one afternoon a few days later. "Are you well?"

"I'm hungry, but well enough," he replied, "thanks be to Ashuba."

"And all the children?" she asked.

"It's best not to ask, Bron. There's nothing you can do. I'm pleased to see you looking so fit."

"But I'm lonely here," she told him pitifully.

"Then I'll try to keep you busy so you won't have time to think about it," he smiled. "Look around you, Bron. What do you see?"

She looked about, puzzled. "Trees, of course, and grass, flowers, the temple, and the cell, and the sky through the branches."

"Nothing else?" he asked.

"There is nothing else," she said.

"How many greens can you see? I can see at least seven. And browns? Four or five."

Bron understood the lesson. "There are three or four blues in the sky, and not all the clouds are white."

"You've got the idea," her teacher smiled. "Now look at patterns, shapes, texture. Use your senses, Bron. How many sounds and what are they? When the dawn chorus wakes you up, can you distinguish the different bird songs? Be aware of stillness, and movement. Touch objects – barks of trees, stones, thorns, petals – run water through your fingers. Breathe in deeply – flowers, damp earth, the pungent smell of a fox. Be careful what you taste, though."

"I know what's poisonous," Bron assured him, "which berries, and all the flat-headed and parasol toadstools."

"Then tell me about it when I come next – in about a week's time – or better still, write it all down, or paint it. It will be a record of your time spent here."

Spring passed and summer came and went, and Bron continued to report to Africanus when he visited. She sometimes asked him or Stalwyn what was happening in the settlement, and always about her family.

"It's bad, Bron – don't ask," they both replied. So she ceased questioning, but made them promise to tell her if her family fell sick.

Then one day Louca appeared instead of the nurse.

"Is Stalwyn dead?" asked Bron, fearing the answer.

"Not yet," replied Louca, tears running down her cheeks.

"Are you all right, Louca?" Bron asked, "and Hoad and the children?"

"So far," Louca told her. "Pray to Shubinata for us, Bron. We need help. We've had a good harvest this year but there's not many of us left who are healthy enough to bring it in, and some of our people are starving."

"And Mummy and Daddy, and my brother and sisters?" Bron persisted.

Louca hesitated. "Your family has had the fever, but they seem to be over the worst. Your mother sends her love. She is so glad that you are safe here. You must never think of coming home until the plague has left us."

Bron wondered how Louca knew that the thought had crossed her mind.

So she continued to spend time in the temple, polishing and dusting and arranging fresh flowers and grasses. It gave her something to do and she thought that it pleased the goddess who, she hoped, was listening to her prayers.

CHAPTER XXXI (31)

Bron was at this work one morning when there was a sound behind her and there in the entrance stood Iraina. She wore a simple, short-sleeved stola that Bron hadn't seen before, which did not disguise the weight she had put on, and Bron couldn't help but compare her radiant good health with the gaunt looks and sunken eyes of those who daily came from the settlement.

"Bron!" Iraina exclaimed in surprise. Bron was not sure that the High Priestess was pleased to see her. "What are you doing here?"

Bron told her about the arrangements Vortin had made for her.

"If you want to sleep in your bed, I can sleep in the temple," she offered.

"I'm not staying," replied the High Priestess. "I only came to find out what's happening in the settlement and whether it's time to return."

"It's not safe yet," said Bron and told her the news as far as she was aware of it. "Someone will let you know when to go back, if you tell me where you're staying."

"That won't be necessary," smiled the High Priestess, "I'll find out for myself."

"Do you want me to leave while you pray?" asked Bron.

"I won't be staying long enough to pray," replied Iraina.

She turned to go then came back and asked casually, "Any news of Vortin and Nobilianus?"

"No," replied Bron.

"Just thought I'd ask," Iraina said and disappeared through the trees.

Bron was intrigued. She wondered where Iraina was living. Did she have another cell somewhere in the wood? Why had she never come to the temple to pray? She was shamefully neglecting her high priestly duties. Bron gathered up her courage and made the decision to follow Iraina. It would give her something different to do, though she knew she must proceed cautiously.

She waited a few minutes until she judged it was safe, then took the same path. By now she knew the footpaths well and was used to following deer, tracking quietly, keeping herself hidden. Once or twice the High Priestess glanced back, but Bron was invisible.

After about two miles the trees thinned and revealed a strip of grassland. Bron clambered up into the lower branches of a beech tree to get a better view.

Beyond the strip rose a very high grassy bank running as far as the eye could see in both directions – the mysterious and mighty Ridgeway, believed to have been built by gods long ago. Bron hadn't seen it before, but recognised it from the descriptions given by her mother and Africanus.

She stared in amazement at the people and ox-drawn carts thronging the highway, at horses with riders in the saddle, and flocks of sheep ushered along by their shepherds.

A century of legionaries passed, led by their centurion and his second-in-command. Marching four abreast in twenty lines (Bron counted them), their helmets and breastplates reflecting back the sun's rays, they scattered anyone and anything in their path.

She was so enchanted with the spectacle that she forgot momentarily why she was there and quite lost sight of Iraina. When she did find her again, the High Priestess was climbing the slope to the top.

What Bron then saw came as a complete surprise. Iraina was shielding her eyes against the sun and waving to a man Bron had never seen before, who was leaping and slithering down the slope towards her. Bron thought he looked a lot younger than Iraina. He lifted the High Priestess off her feet and swung round with her in his arms, then kissed her stomach before setting her down. He then kissed her full on the lips. She laughed and said something to him before, hand-in-hand, they walked to the top of the ridge and disappeared out of sight.

Bron was amazed. She knew that on the other side of the Ridgeway lived the Catuvellauni people. She had been told that at night, in the woods, they still coloured their bodies blue with woad and danced naked under the full moon and ate their babies.

She stayed where she was in the branches for several minutes, trying to make sense of what she had just witnessed. Thoughtfully, she climbed down and returned to the temple the way she had come.

Who could she tell? Should she tell at all? Iraina belonged to Vortin. Bron knew it was written in the Book. She thought of his fury and fearful retribution and knew she could tell no one. She also knew now why Iraina had put on weight. Had she not seen her own mother look that way only four years ago, before Aelia was born? It was a heavy secret to bear alone.

Bron recalled Iraina's not infrequent absences from the Temple, when she went into retreat, and forbade anyone to disturb her vigil. She always returned with a spring in her step and lights in her violet eyes. People were awed by the close communion the High Priestess obviously had with her goddess. Now Bron was not so sure...

The months passed and it was November. One morning, when Bron emerged from the cell, she found Pulcher waiting at the collection point. She waved a greeting to him.

"You're early!" she called. "Not bad news?"

"No," Pulcher called back, "but my voices give no peace. Something wrong, don't know what."

"I'm glad to see you, anyway," said Bron.

They shouted to each other about nothing in particular for some time then Bron happened to glance up and gave a small cry. Pulcher's eyes followed hers. The sky was the colour of faded blue dye with few clouds, so that the sun was clearly visible, but strangely no longer a complete circle. In one corner, a small crescent-shaped piece was missing.

They could not look for long because the brightness hurt their eyes.

"Under trees, Bron - look through branches."

They ran into the wood, Pulcher keeping a safe distance between them, so that he would not pass on any contamination he might unknowingly have brought with him. As they stared from underneath the branches, which cut down some of the glare, the hole in the sun gradually grew larger.

"I'm frightened," Bron said.

"Inside temple," he instructed her, and she obeyed.

"Don't leave me," she pleaded with him.

"I stay outside here," he promised.

Bron prayed to the goddess. "What is eating the sun, Shubinata? It will get cold and dark! We can't live without Ashuba!"

She went back to the door and helplessly she and Pulcher watched as the monster, or whatever it was, gobbled up more and more of the golden circle.

Then Hestig arrived. Bron ran towards him.

"Don't come any closer, Bron," he warned her. "Are you all right? Your mother sent me so that you wouldn't be on your own."

"I stay," promised Pulcher. "Not leave Bron."

"Thank you, then I'll go back," said Hestig. "You're a kind friend to us, Pulcher. Selvid has opened up the Temple and everyone who is clear of the sickness is gathering there to pray to Ashuba. The others know they're probably going to die anyway. Even Selvid and Veneta don't know what's happening."

Looking very anxious, he hurried away. By now, the sun had almost completely disappeared. It grew dark and the temperature dropped abruptly. The birds stopped singing and there was an unnatural silence. It was as if the world was holding its breath.

Then the sun disappeared altogether except for a perimeter circle of light and a flaring on one side.

Peering through the Temple doorway, Bettina, with her arms round young Trifosa, forgot her fear and was enchanted.

"Oh, to have a diamond ring just like that!" she said to Trifena.

Her mistress was thoughtful. *If we live through this,* she decided, *and the plague doesn't kill us all, I'll make sure Bettina receives such a ring. We've never given her a present and it's time we did, for all her loyalty to us.*

The sun was absent for several minutes while the people wailed and prayed aloud, fearing the worst. Then someone shouted, "Look! It's coming back!"

Everyone crowded into the doorway and tumbled out on to the steps. As the monster spewed out the bright circle, the world lightened, the temperature rose and the birds began to sing again.

The people praised their great god Ashuba, and thanked him for their deliverance, but made sure they stayed in the Temple for the hours it needed for the whole sun to be regurgitated. Trifena then sent Hestig back into the wood to make sure that Bron was safe.

Pulcher stayed talking to her until nightfall, when she went into the cell to sleep. Then he wrapped himself in his cloak and spent a cold night under a tree, hardly noticing the discomfort in his desire to protect his goddaughter. He didn't leave until next morning, when he had made sure that the sun had risen normally and light had returned to Bron's world.

CHAPTER XXXII (32)

Winter came. Temperatures were mild and there was little snow, but morning frosts were heavy and enchanted the wood as they outlined trees, leaves and blades of grass with white crystal. Bron walked every day, wondering at the intricacy of thousands of spiders' webs trembling and glistening in the pale sunshine wherever there were stalks or blades of grass to support them.

She had gained a healthy hardiness by living so much out of doors and was always warm enough in the thick clothes that Louca brought her, which Dagvald and Selena had woven. Benefiting from the distant tuition of Africanus, she had learned to build and light a charcoal fire and both cell and temple were kept warm and inviting.

She stored a large selection of wax tablets and slivers of wood covered in writing, rolls of drawings and paintings on parchment, embroidery worked for Selena, and several misshapen pottery jugs and bowls made from local clay her father had sent, which had hardened in the sun.

One day a familiar figure approached along the path through the trees.

"Stalwyn!" cried Bron.

"Don't come any nearer, Bron dear," warned the nurse. "I'm better, but we mustn't take any chances."

"I'm so pleased to see you!" Bron laughed delightedly. "I thought you were going to die."

"So did I," smiled Stalwyn, "but thanks to Ashuba, the fever and boils and raving passed. My husband is better, too, so we will be taking plenty of thank-offerings as soon as the Temple is open for worship again."

"How long?" asked Bron.

"Have a little more patience, dear – we will bring you back as soon as we can. There have been no new cases for a week, but people are still dying, though it's taking longer from the onset of the fever."

"I want to go home," said Bron.

"Your mother will come with Veneta to bring you home as soon as Vortin gives the word."

"Is he back?"

"Not yet – none of them are."

"Is Veneta well?" Bron wanted to know.

"She is now. She and Selvid have worked themselves to a standstill looking after the people in the Temple, and we nearly lost them both, but thankfully they have recovered. Jeetuna escaped the worst because she hasn't come out of her room since she left you here. Strange, though, but no one seems to know where Iraina is hiding."

"I know –" The words had escaped before Bron could stop them.

"You do?" asked Stalwyn, showing her surprise. "Where?"

Bron could have bitten off her tongue for its indiscretion. She hesitated. Stalwyn looked mystified.

"Is she well?"

Bron hesitated again. "I-I think so," she said.

"Bron, don't tell me if you feel you shouldn't," Stalwyn said. "It doesn't really matter as long as we can get in touch with her."

"When I last saw her, she said she would find out for herself when it was safe to go back to the Temple."

"How long ago was that?"

Bron remembered following Iraina through the wood when the leaves were just beginning to turn yellow.

"Last autumn." She paused, then blurted out in a rush of words, "Stalwyn, can you keep a secret? It's a big secret and you mustn't tell anyone, not ever."

"If it's so secret, Bron, should you be telling me? Have you promised Iraina not to tell?"

"Iraina doesn't know that I know. I can't keep it to myself any longer, but you must promise not to tell."

"Very well, I promise not to tell anyone, ever," smiled Stalwyn.

Then Bron told what she had seen on the Ridgeway, and because Stalwyn was a midwife, asked if her conclusion could be true.

Stalwyn looked very grim. "You could be right, Bron. Of course, it may not be so –"

"What would Vortin do?" asked Bron.

"He would have no choice," Stalwyn answered. "He would have to make an example of her. There would be no mercy for her and her priestesses and anyone else he had a mind to punish."

"I've heard about the wickerwork god they put people in, then set on fire," said Bron in such a tiny voice that Stalwyn probably didn't catch every word.

"You're right, Bron, no one else must know – not Veneta nor your mother, not anyone. I only hope that Iraina comes back as soon as Vortin wants her."

They came for Bron a month later. She saw them coming as she sat outside the temple, filling her pots with wild daffodils, and nearly knocked her mother over as she rushed into her arms. Then there was just as big a hug for Veneta, and they were all three laughing and kissing and crying.

Trifena stood her daughter at arm's length to have an objective look at her.

"Bron, you've grown so in these eleven months, and you look so healthy," she exclaimed with great pleasure.

From where she stood, Bron looked from her mother to Veneta and back again. Their faces were those of old women, tired and lined and grey.

"You're both so thin," she remarked sadly.

"It's been a very unhappy time," said Veneta. "You'll see changes, Bron, and you must be prepared for it. A lot of the people you knew are not around any more, and you will be very sad. But the plague has spent itself now and those of us who are left will have to start all over again."

"Come, darling," said Trifena, "let's take you home."

"Real home?" asked Bron with excitement.

"For today," said Trifena. "Tonight you'll sleep in your own little room, but tomorrow we'll have to take you back to the Temple."

"Because Vortin returns tomorrow," Veneta explained, "and I know he will want to see you straight away. But there are only just over three years left until you are twelve and then your father can buy you back, and think what a sophisticated and educated young lady you will be by then!"

Bron wanted to collect together all her belongings.

"Leave them," advised Veneta. "I'll arrange for someone to pick everything up tomorrow."

"The wood has never looked so beautiful!" Trifena exclaimed as they walked towards the settlement, Bron running ahead.

"Happiness colours it all," said Veneta.

Before leaving the wood and crossing the shallow defence ditch, Veneta turned right. Trifena and Bron followed her. She continued along the edge of the trees until they were behind the Temple, then turned north again, deeper into the undergrowth. Bron was puzzled.

"Bron, dear, we want to show you something," whispered Trifena. "You've got to know and we thought this was the best way."

They reached an area cleared of trees where no grass was growing and bare earth formed a large mound. Bron looked at her mother, questioning.

"It's the plague pit," explained Trifena.

Veneta led them a little further to another such area, but here was light green moss and dark grass newly growing and multi-coloured spring flowers in pots. As Bron looked, she saw that each pot stood on top of an individual mound. Wooden uprights were pushed into the soft, newly-turned earth and names were written on pieces of wood nailed across them.

Bron looked from her mother to Veneta. The priestess said simply, "They're all the children."

"Bron, be prepared for the worst," warned her mother. "I can't shield you from this."

Bron walked along the lines, recognising the names of friends from the Temple and settlement, children she had grown up alongside and played with in the schoolroom and in the Stan and up at the mere.

She paused in an area where four graves were grouped together. Afraid to look, she hid her face against her mother's breast.

"Read the names, Bron," encouraged Trifena, her arms tightly clasped around her daughter. Bron turned her head, still clutching her mother, and read aloud with increasing hysteria, "Edreda... Naila... Sorin..." and burst into tears.

Trifena was crying, too. Because her vision was blurred, Bron was unable to read the last name.

"Whose is it, Mummy?" she whispered.

"It's Aelia, your baby sister," said Trifena.

"I didn't say goodbye to any of them, I didn't say goodbye," sobbed Bron.

"They understood," Veneta said soothingly, "and they gave me their messages for you. Naila died before I could get to her, but Sorin wanted you to know that she loves you, and wherever she is, she is still singing, and Edreda said thank you for being her friend."

It was a slow and distressing walk back to the settlement, but the sights that greeted Bron there stopped her tears, though they had been in full flow. She wouldn't look at Naila's house, but turned her head to the corn dryer and animal pens. There was no corn in the dryer and the pens were empty.

"The animals were all eaten long ago," explained her mother.

Louca came to her door as they passed, her young children around her. Hoad stood behind and waved a greeting. Stalwyn too came out of her house to welcome Bron home.

The pathways were almost deserted. The few people who were out and about looked like walking skeletons and Bron did not recognise most of them.

Everything looked derelict. There were gaping holes in walls and thatch and roof turfs. Doors were hanging off hinges and inside the houses Bron could see cold hearths and pools of dark water where rain had gathered.

Some of the skeleton-like figures were emerging from empty houses, dragging pieces of furniture.

"They're stealing," explained Trifena, "but what does it matter? The owners won't need their goods any more. Some are finding money hidden away – but that doesn't matter, either. We need all the help we can get."

The inn was quiet and dark, the stables empty, the young ostler gone, and there were only one or two booths open in the market place. One of them was Hestig's.

"Daddy!" shouted Bron, and ran over to him, to enjoy her father's loving welcome.

And there was Pulcher, grinning from ear to ear. He lifted Bron up in his arms and danced with her round and round until they both became dizzy and he was forced to put her down.

"Let's all go home," suggested Trifena wearily.

"I'll go back to Selvid," said Veneta. "We have a lot to do before tomorrow, when Vortin arrives, but I will try to persuade him to rest for an hour or so. Jeetuna has finally emerged from her room, and it's time she pulled her weight." She turned to Bron. "I'll see you tomorrow, Bron."

As she walked away, Trifena sighed.

"There's nothing you can do for them," Hestig told his wife, "so don't try. Selvid and Veneta must sort things out for themselves."

Bron ran ahead of her mother and knocked at their door. Bettina opened it, with Skeel bouncing round her feet, giving Bron a noisy welcome home. Bettina kissed Bron on the cheek then called Hestigys and Trifosa, who came running to greet their sister.

"Hestigys, you look so grown up!" exclaimed Bron admiringly, "and Trifosa, how pretty you are!" The little girl tossed her long dark chestnut hair with pleasure. Bron looked about for the youngest member of the family before she remembered where she lay.

The day and evening passed, catching up on all the news. Pulcher arrived, then Bettina answered the door again and invited in Selena with Campania, her daughter-in-law, and young Soranus. Both women had been widowed.

Bron had no doubt that Soranus was a good-looking boy, in spite of being so much thinner. As soon as he could, he manoeuvred her into a corner of the courtyard.

"I'm so pleased to see you home, Bron," he told her. "I wonder, do you remember the time I dived in the mere and found the ring that Nobilianus lost?" She nodded. "It was three years ago, but do you remember what you promised me then?"

She remembered very well and blushed. "May I take that kiss now?" he asked her.

Bron was so pleased to be home that she would have let the whole world kiss her that evening. Nodding, she closed her eyes and received the gentlest kiss on the cheek. She opened her eyes.

"Aren't you going to say that it's just what you wanted?" he teased, and would have kissed her again, but she laughed and ducked under his arm and ran off to join the family.

"I nearly forgot," exclaimed Trifena. "The lion has some very special presents for everyone, as it's such a happy occasion."

Hestig turned off the water and one by one they all reached down into the lion's stone mouth, fingers groping, and brought out a wrapped gift. There was a great deal of laughter as Hestigys minced around with a fan chosen for Selena, and Soranus unwrapped a bone meant for Skeel, and Pulcher a little ring with a pretty glass gemstone that looked like sardonyx. Bettina cried tears of joy when she put the ring on her finger. The others received gifts equally unsuitable that were eventually sorted out. Trifena had not bought a gift for herself. "I already have mine – Bron's home," she said.

"Now, Bron," said her father, later in the evening, as Hestigys and Trifosa were being put to bed, "how about telling us one of your stories?"

"I don't tell stories any more," replied Bron.

CHAPTER XXXIII (33)

AD 394

Next morning, Hestig left early for the council chamber. Trifena explained to Bron that the plague had killed old Severus, and with Dagvald also dead, Africanus busy helping out at the Temple and Kendrus still employed doctoring the sick, it had fallen to her father to take over the leadership.

She took Bron back to the Temple during the morning. Later, Jeetuna found her lying on her mattress, staring into space. All around were Edreda's belongings, scattered where her friend had left them the day she was taken ill.

"Oh, Bron, there you are," said Jeetuna. "I'm glad to see you back. Vortin is asking for you."

Vortin was in his office behind the altar.

"Come in, Bron," he called when she knocked at his door. "Thank you, Jeetuna, you may leave." Jeetuna withdrew.

Vortin looked Bron over with obvious approval. "I'm happy to see you looking so well," he said at last.

"You look well, too," she replied, politely.

"We are the lucky ones," he admitted. "Now, tell me what you've been doing this past year."

So Bron told him all she had learned and accomplished while living in the wood.

"That's good, Bron. Now there is much work to be done in the Temple and you and the children who have survived must help the priestesses all you can. The school will be opened again as soon as possible. You will be pleased to hear that I don't intend to restrict your movements in any way. You are free to come and go as you please, provided that there are no more escapades. Do you understand?"

"Yes," said Bron.

"Nobilianus will not be confined to his room, either, and will be starting school. I want you two to become friends. Will you try?"

"Yes," said Bron again, her fingers crossed behind her back.

"Very well, you may go now. And Bron –"

"Yes, sir?"

"I wish you to start calling me 'Father'."

"Yes, sir," Bron replied.

"And Bron," he added as another afterthought struck him, "you probably know that you're growing into a very beautiful young lady."

Suddenly, she was wary. "Thank you, Father," she said and escaped from the room.

Outside she almost bumped into Iraina.

"Hello, Bron." Bron stared at her. "You seem surprised to see me."

"I am," said Bron. "How did you know when to come back?"

"When you left the cell, I knew it was time for me to return."

"Were you spying on me?" asked Bron.

"No, dear, just keeping an eye on you," replied the High Priestess.

She turned to open the door to Vortin's office and Bron took a quick look at her waistline, which appeared normal.

"Have you kept well?" asked Bron.

"Never better," replied Iraina, and closed the door behind her, leaving Bron wondering.

Sharma, Brocchus and Vitius were next to return, accompanying Nobilianus. He was taller than ever and had a more robust complexion. Bron passed him in the corridor upstairs.

"Hello, you're back, I see," he said to her without warmth. "Father says we've got to be friends. Not much hope of that, is there?"

"None at all," replied Bron.

"Though we don't have to like each other just because we're going to be married," Nobilianus said spitefully. "Once a year on the altar – that's all you're likely to get!"

Bron was aghast. She had never considered for one moment that their marriage was a probability, and as for the rest –

"That's what you think!" she retorted. "My family will have bought me back long before anything like that happens!"

"Just let them try!" he shouted at her retreating back. "My father won't allow it. *We* are your family! Here you are and here you'll stay!"

Bron fled to her room and flung herself down on the mattress and cried for an hour, then went in search of Veneta.

Next morning, Vortin instructed everyone in the Temple to gather for Morning Prayer. It was the first service held there for almost a year.

After the service of thanksgiving for survival, which included miscellaneous sacrificial offerings that nowadays replaced the animal sacrifices of the past, the High Priest addressed those assembled. Their number was greatly depleted, though not as much as in the settlement where, Vortin told them, only about one third of the population had survived the greedy plague.

"There is much work to be done, people," announced Vortin. "The Temple has to be thoroughly cleaned from top to bottom. Any necessary repairs and redecoration will have to be carried out. In addition, all the living quarters, offices and stores will have to be cleaned. The belongings of those who have died will be disposed of, and there will be some rearrangement of rooms.

"Of course, I realise that there are not enough of you to undertake all this work by yourselves, so we will be bringing in labour from the settlement. I want the Temple open in time for the Midsummer Festival. My priests and priestesses are in charge and will direct you as necessary. Work will start straight away."

One of the first of the settlement's work force to arrive was Pulcher. He found Bron where she was helping to strip the sanctuary. The rule allowing only the priests and priestesses into the holy area had been relaxed until all the work was completed.

"Hello, Bron," he greeted her excitedly, as he lifted a heavy tapestry from her arms. "Vortin going to ask me come back, work here."

"Going to?" queried Bron. "How do you know?"

"My voices," he whispered.

Bron was scraping wax from the tiled floor and Pulcher was collecting up the candles when Vitius arrived to tell him that Vortin wanted to see him. Pulcher winked at Bron and hobbled away.

"Hello, Vitius," said Bron, smiling at him. "Have you kept well?"

"Well enough," he answered. "I can't stop, Bron, I'm busy," and he walked off.

"He's changed," remarked Veneta as she and Bron folded the altar cloths. "He used to be such a pleasant young boy. I don't know what Sharma's done to him but it's difficult to get a civil word out of him these days."

Hestig arrived next day to inspect the pottery containers. Bron's belongings had been brought over from the cell in the wood and her father asked her to show him all the work she had completed there. As they passed the entrance door on their way to Bron's room, Africanus arrived to keep an appointment with Vortin, and they took him upstairs with them.

Hestig was delighted at the progress Bron had made, and Africanus took the work to show Vortin. "We'll display it in the schoolroom," the African said.

"He's a good man, whatever his colour," Hestig remarked.

"What colour?" asked Bron. Hestig smiled.

"I must go back to the booth now and relieve your mother or she'll be fretting about getting back to her working party."

"Mother's in a working party?" Bron was surprised.

"Everyone in the settlement is in a working party," Hestig explained. "Besides, it gives her something to think about – other than missing little Aelia."

"So what is everyone doing?"

"Cleaning up, and there's so much clearing out work to do in the empty houses. We can ill afford to lose the labour of the people who've come up to the Temple, but Vortin says it's our duty to Ashuba, so we can't refuse."

"What will happen to all the empty houses, Father?" wondered Bron.

"The Temple has confiscated them and the village council has to try to find new people to move in and live here."

"That's exciting!" exclaimed Bron.

"I don't know about exciting – it's a headache for the council, especially as we're short on numbers."

Vortin was pleased to see the people's health improving and their strength returning, so that the work in Temple and settlement continued with growing energy and enthusiasm.

He was concerned to increase the population, not least because the people's offerings and payment of Temple tax had dwindled to almost nothing. A few, such as Hestig, were able to meet their commitments, but only because a steady stream of merchants was returning to the market and business for all was increasing spectacularly.

Having consulted Kendrus, one morning Vortin sent criers running throughout the settlement, announcing that he had, for the time being, outlawed all abortion and infanticide, even by the girls at the inn. He and Iraina had agreed to take all unwanted children into the Temple at the age of three years.

The innkeeper's wife had survived the plague, though her husband had not been so fortunate, and was back in business. She reported to Vortin that she had decided to increase the number of girls she managed, especially now that one or more of them was likely to be pregnant at any given time. As Kendrus advised her not to import any girls from outside the settlement, the High Priest suggested Selena's widowed daughter-in-law as one possible replacement.

Campania declined, but Attryde accepted when approached, in spite of her mother's entreaties. The young blacksmith who had worked the forge after her husband's execution had died in the pestilence. Horseshoes were not required as the horses had been killed and eaten and no one was ordering new household utensils while they could pilfer from the empty houses. Attryde's money had run out, so she was glad of a job, even that job.

Iraina said she was concerned that the women and girls had lost their good looks to the ravages of the plague and on May Day morning led all those of child-bearing age in a long procession to Shubinata's temple. Veneta and Jeetuna had been sent ahead to collect the May dew into every available vessel, and there was much chatter and laughter when the women returned with glistening faces.

The woods were uncannily quiet as there were no young men with cow horns waiting in the trees... but perhaps next year.

Whether it was the May dew working its magic or not, Vortin was pleased to receive reports of lean figures putting on shapely weight, colour once again glowing on plump cheeks, eyes lightening and fullness returning to young lips.

By the time of the Midsummer Festival, everyone was tired from all the hard physical work they had been doing, but everything was finished on time and the whole settlement was looking forward to the holiday.

As Vortin expected, Iraina disappeared into the wood to prepare herself for the great festival, forbidding anyone to intrude, on pain of Shubinata's displeasure.

The Midsummer licentiousness took place as before, encouraged by the High Priest.

"Vortin," asked Iraina under the coverlet on the altar, "do we have to go through this sham every year? It's obvious you have no desire for me any more."

"Yes, we do," he replied firmly. "Once we start ignoring the practices laid down since time began, the whole edifice will start crumbling and you and I with it. The rituals are very important. It's not your fault, my dear. We're both getting older. I'm fifty-four. You can't expect the passion of twenty years ago. You're a clever actress when you need to be. You can fake it again – after all, it's only once a year."

Next day, almost the entire settlement came to the Temple with their sacrificial thank-offerings for having survived the plague, and everyone was in jubilant mood.

This year, Nobilianus was allowed to stand among the children gathered before the altar. Vortin was not pleased to see that his son and Bron stood as far away from each other as it was possible to get.

He was also irritated that Nobilianus looked uninterested and bored with the proceedings as he idly watched the families filling the space in front of the altar. Suddenly, however, the boy began to take a lively interest and seemed to be searching for someone in the crowd.

As the worshippers disciplined themselves into regular lines, Vortin caught a flash of flaming chestnut hair and saw the subject of his son's attention – a young girl with exquisitely pale skin and large eyes. Nobilianus appeared unable to stop ogling her. Vortin wondered who she was then realised she was with Bron's family and must be Bron's younger sister, Trifosa. He resolved to warn his son not to entertain any notions in that direction.

For the first time ever, there were no three-year-olds to admit.

During the service, the remnants of the choir tried their best with the choral works, but Sorin's soaring soprano was missed, and Bron's cheeks were not the only ones wet with tears.

Vortin had again assigned her to Jeetuna's charge. Having apparently sat out the plague in her room, sidestepping the work and worry that Veneta had suffered, Jeetuna had survived unblemished.

Selvid was not letting Vortin forget the part Veneta had played in keeping the Temple functioning and its people nursed back to life, or comforted when dying. There was no need because the gaunt face and thin body of Veneta made very obvious the overall effect the deprivations had had on her physically. The High Priest was amused by Selvid's devotion to Veneta but the couple had served him well and faithfully and he knew he would be greatly inconvenienced without them.

Until now, Sharma had been his favourite, but at the moment he was displeased with him and Brocchus. Their instructions had been to return to the Temple once they had delivered Nobilianus and Vitius, acting as servant, to safety in a friendly settlement north of Byden. However, they had stayed away for the duration of the epidemic. Vortin had decided to say nothing on their return, but he stored away their disobedience in his memory.

He questioned Iraina about her flight and was not surprised when she said she had 'gone home' to escape the sickness.

Vortin's heart softened as he remembered Iraina's mother. She had been one of the Temple prostitutes in the time when his father was High Priest and had captured the heart of the young High Priest-in-training.

Normally, when one of the Temple girls became pregnant, the baby was aborted, but she had pleaded to him for the life of their child, and he had been unable to refuse her. Before anyone else knew of her pregnancy, he smuggled her across the Ridgeway to a Catuvellauni village. He was devastated when she survived only three days after the birth. Iraina, known as Irene to the Catuvellauni, had been brought up there by a foster mother, who was still alive.

It had taken him years of secret grief to recover from the death of the girl he had loved to the exclusion of all others, but recover he did, eventually. Iraina reminded him of her mother, and when his father died, he brought her to Byden as his High Priestess. He guessed that some of the older people suspected the relationship, because of Iraina's likeness to her mother, but no one knew for sure.

The only slight cloud on Vortin's horizon was the affluence of Hestig. He saw that the potter's work was much sought after and orders had been flooding in now that the market was open again. Hestig was also earning money, as Severus had, in a consultancy role as leader of the council. Even so, the large amount of the family offering, given in memory of their little daughter, Aelia, surprised Vortin. Hestig had also asked if he could pay for his son to attend the Temple school and later pay for Trifosa to follow.

Nobilianus had recounted to his father Bron's outburst about being bought back. Vortin was apprehensive. He had plans for her and his son.

He was also surprised at the great pleasure he found in just watching her. One way or another, he purposed to keep her in the priestly family.

One way or another...

CHAPTER XXXIV (34)

A few days after the Festival, Iraina sent for Stalwyn.

"Thank you for coming," she said. "How many of our women are pregnant at the moment?"

Stalwyn listed them, twelve to her knowledge.

"Vortin and I wish to honour them," Iraina told the midwife. "I am arranging a special service before Shubinata and want you to be present."

Stalwyn agreed, and the mothers-to-be were summoned to the temple in the wood two days later for an early morning service of thanksgiving and dedication, with prayers for safe deliveries.

After they left the temple, each carrying an infusion of powdered saffron to ease labour, Iraina asked Stalwyn to stay behind. A few minutes later, the High Priestess was leading the way through the wood towards the great Ridgeway.

They didn't arrive home until early evening, just as Kendrus was becoming anxious. Stalwyn confided her news to him over a bowl of hot stew.

"We crossed the Ridgeway – what a busy highway that is! – and she still hadn't told me why she needed me or what she wanted me to do. There was a horse and cart waiting for us, with a young Catuvellauni man driving it. Then she produced a cloth and asked if I minded being blindfolded. I was too curious to object! We drove for about another two miles, and from the sounds around us, it was obvious we had entered a village. I was helped out of the cart and, when Iraina took the blindfold off, we were in a round house like the ones here."

Kendrus was as incredulous now as Stalwyn had been when Bron confided her suspicions.

"She said it was a friend's baby, but it was so obvious it was hers. A mother can't disguise the fact when she holds her own baby. She's a dear little mite, and looks just like Iraina, but she isn't thriving. The wet nurse seemed competent enough, but she is also suckling her own child."

"So what did you suggest?"

"It's obvious that Iraina can't stay and feed her daughter. She has either got to find another wet nurse, although the change of milk may upset the little one, or – I know it's hard – that woman has got to feed Iraina's baby first and her son second, if she has enough milk. We all know that the boy may not survive, but Iraina has promised to pay her more, and the woman is widowed and needs money for her young family."

Kendrus was concerned for his wife's safety. "My dear, do you realise that this could put your life in danger? If you had a mind, you could blackmail Iraina for evermore."

"No one there is going to admit that the baby is hers. She trusts me, and I think you'll find I shall be well paid, but you're right, of course. Unfortunately, I'm not the only one who knows," and Stalwyn told her husband about Bron's discovery. They discussed whether they should tell Bron this latest news, but decided against it, for her own safety.

Whenever Bron was not needed for duties and could get away, she wandered off into the wood behind the Temple and sat quietly near the four graves of her sister and friends. She brought to them news of her good days and bad days, her quarrels with Nobilianus, her loneliness, her happy memories. Sometimes she would wander further into the wood, exploring paths, aware of the sights and sounds around her, as Africanus had taught her.

She was not afraid of getting lost as she knew that Pulcher always followed. He would not intrude on her solitude, and she never saw him, but she knew he was there.

On one such afternoon late in October, she had wandered further than usual. The path underfoot was soft after rain, and her footsteps made no sound. Suddenly she was aware of familiar voices ahead, through the trees to one side of the path. Curious, she crept towards the sounds, unseen and unheard.

Among the trees were three figures in various stages of undress. Bron knew she should leave but instead stayed hidden, transfixed.

Sharma stood, his priestly robes dishevelled, legs spread-eagled, pushing against the naked figure of Vitius who was bent double in front of him, hands clutching the trunk of a tree for support. Brocchus lay on his black cloak spread out on the ground, laughing and urging them on.

Bron was not ignorant of what took place in the rooms on the second floor, and what the girls talked about, but she had always thought that these adult games needed men and women. She didn't know that a woman wasn't necessary.

She continued to watch, horrified, but at the same time fascinated by the pulsing movement and the panting and ribaldry and strange noises. What surprised her most, though, was the sight of Brocchus. She thought she understood what being a eunuch meant, but obviously she was mistaken, because Brocchus looked complete in every way.

Bron suddenly felt sick and wanted to run, but knew she must make no noise. Quietly she turned and moved step by step slowly back the way she had come, expecting any minute to hear a shout, her presence revealed, her name called, but the three figures through the trees were too preoccupied and making too much noise to notice her intrusion.

She reached the path and fled in shame and panic, not heeding the direction, on and on, until she was thoroughly lost, with the sky growing dark above her. When she could run no further, she sank to her knees.

Pulcher, frantic with anxiety, at last found her sitting among damp leaves and tree roots, scoring the insides of her arms again and again with a sharp flint picked up on the path, and drawing blood.

"No, Bron, no!" he implored, taking the flint from her and throwing it far into the trees. He sat and enfolded her in his arms, laying his cheek against her hair and gently rocked her backwards and forwards as she shook and sobbed without tears. She attempted to tell him what she had seen, not knowing how to describe what she had seen, but he quietened her rush of words.

"I know, I saw too," he said.

When she had stopped sobbing, he worried for them both.

195

"Got to get back, got to get back," and he warned her, "Bron, never tell what you saw – danger, much danger." Bron nodded.

It had been dark for an hour by the time they reached the Temple. Bron was still far from calm. Pulcher left her and walked towards the side door, intending to look for Veneta, but Jeetuna appeared.

"Oh, Pulcher, there you are!" She came over to him. "Have you seen Bron? I've searched everywhere."

"Asleep in bed?" he suggested.

"That's where she should be, stupid," Jeetuna retorted, "but I've looked there and she isn't." They went into the Temple together.

Several minutes later, Veneta emerged and found Bron shivering in the shadows.

"Bron, dear, Pulcher told me you were out here. You look exhausted! I've sent him home and promised I'd smuggle you inside. He wouldn't tell me what has happened to you, but insisted you need safe arms."

Bron began to cry. Veneta could see that this had not been just another escapade.

"Hush, hush. Come, now."

The priestess took hold of Bron's hand and drew her inside the Temple. With a finger to her lips, she led her up the spiral staircase nearest to them and crossed to the children's corridor.

Once inside Bron's room, she helped her undress.

"Oh, Bron, what's happened to your arms?" she asked, aghast. Bron started crying again. "Hush, child, do you want Jeetuna up here? Bathe them in cold water while I get some bandages. You can't go to bed in that state."

Once Bron's arms were bandaged and she was washed and had put on her nightshift and slippers, Veneta explained her plan.

"I'm going to put you in one of the empty rooms for the night. I'll tell Jeetuna I found you there. If she asks you about it in the morning, you can say you must have sleepwalked."

"Thank you, Veneta."

As the priestess made Bron comfortable in the strange bed, she asked, "Do you want to tell me what happened to you tonight?"

Bron shook her head. "I can't."

"Then I won't ask any more questions. You're home safe, that's the most important thing. Keep your arms hidden until they've healed. I'll come and see you in the morning."

She kissed her gently on the cheek and left her to sleep.

Bron lay awake in the dark for several hours, listening to the owls hooting and hearing again the rhythmic grunting that accompanied Sharma's frenzy and sweat. And Vitius. The young man's face haunted her – white and expressionless and somehow dead. Bron knew he wished he were dead.

When Jeetuna came to find her in the morning, Bron had a fever and her ramblings made no sense. Stalwyn was summoned to examine her and advised that she should stay where she was for several days until her temperature returned to normal.

She made no comment to anyone about the injuries to Bron's arms underneath the bandages.

CHAPTER XXXV (35)

AD 395

The Midsummer Festival, the second since the passing of the plague, and Bron's tenth birthday were approaching. One morning Vortin summoned Jeetuna and Sharma to his office. He was pacing backwards and forwards, flushed and excited, eyes gleaming, though he tried to keep his voice controlled.

"Sharma, I am making some changes to the Festival this year. It is time that Nobilianus was present at the dawn ritual. He is fourteen years old and should know what is done. After all, he will be taking part as High Priest when I am no longer here. I want him fully instructed and present. Selvid and Veneta also need to be informed. Please see to it."

"Of course, Vortin," replied the priest.

"That is all, you may both go."

Sharma left the room. Jeetuna, looking puzzled as to why she had been summoned, was about to follow when Vortin stopped her.

"Jeetuna, my dear –" His breathing was quick and shallow. "I also want Bron present. Please prepare her." Jeetuna stared at him. "Shut the door as you go out."

Jeetuna could not wait to tell Veneta about this new development. Veneta was aghast at the news.

"It's not right – Bron's too young," she exclaimed.

Iraina's cool voice interrupted them. "Too young for what?" She had been passing and overheard the last remark.

"To watch the Midsummer ritual," answered Veneta.

Iraina's surprise was obvious.

"On whose instruction?" she asked icily.

"Vortin's," Jeetuna answered.

"Indeed?" Iraina spoke between gritted teeth. "I'll see about that!" She stalked off in the direction of Vortin's office.

"She didn't know," whispered Veneta.

Jeetuna laughed. "It won't make the slightest difference," she said with conviction. "He's made up his mind. Nobilianus was just cloud cover."

Veneta looked alarmed.

"Your precious Bron – why not? She'll be available to him anyway in a couple of years' time."

"A lot can happen in two years," insisted Veneta, "and meantime she's still a child."

"Then this will help to mature her." Jeetuna laughed again. "I'll tell her when she comes out of school."

When she had gone, Veneta cornered Selvid behind a pillar and told him.

"Veneta, there is no power on this earth that can stop Vortin doing what he wants once he has made up his mind, you know that."

"I can't let it happen, and I won't! Bron is only a child. She will have to grow up soon enough without indulging his fantasies at ten years old!"

Selvid looked at her tenderly, and she knew he wished he had a solution for her. He placed his fingers over her lips.

"Hush, Veneta, hush. Criticism will put you in certain danger."

"There's no one else to hear, and I trust you completely."

"There are many in the Temple – most, in fact – who would happily carry such comments back to Vortin if it would gain them his favour."

Veneta lowered her voice. "I've got to make some effort to stop it happening."

"But what? You know Vortin says that everything he decrees is according to Ashuba's will."

"Nonsense! Everything Vortin decrees is according to Vortin's will!"

"There you go again!"

She wanted him to take her face in his hands and kiss away the lines of her anxiety. Instead he smiled and gently tapped her on the nose.

"Selvid, there has been something going on that I don't understand," continued Veneta and told him about Bron's late night out and the injuries to her arms. "Stalwyn examined her next morning – she must have noticed them, but she said nothing. Perhaps she knows what caused them."

"I'll support you in anything you decide to do, Veneta – but be careful."

"Do you think that everything Vortin says and does is by divine decree?"

"Vortin is High Priest, servant of our great god Ashuba, but he is also very much a man, and a lonely one at that."

"You haven't answered my question."

"Yes, I have. Do take care, my dear, take care."

Veneta wondered if he had also just described his own position.

She made up her mind to confront Ashuba in person. As soon as she was alone in the sanctuary, she swung the censer around the altar and knelt before the statue of the great god. As the incense swirled about her, bearing her words upwards, she asked outright, "Ashuba, great god of light, of fire, of power, I kneel here as your most loyal servant and priestess to ask if this is your divine will or only Vortin's fantasy."

She raised her face to the god's in supplication. One hundred candle flames leapt higher and were reflected in his eyes. They glowed bright red through the clouds of incense but there was no pity in them, no understanding, no compassion.

As soon as she could, Veneta made an excuse to visit Stalwyn. The midwife greeted her kindly. Veneta unburdened her problem.

Stalwyn hesitated. "We are all subject to the will of Ashuba as interpreted to us by his High Priest."

"But don't you think that sometimes Vortin the man gets in the way of Vortin the priest?"

Stalwyn was silent.

"My friend," Veneta continued, "do you know how Bron got those strange injuries to her arms?"

"No, I thought you might. She was too feverish for me to make sense of anything she said."

"There's one person who does know." Veneta told Stalwyn about the night Pulcher and Bron arrived back late at the Temple.

"Shall I invite Pulcher here one evening, soon?" asked Stalwyn. "I think we should know all the facts before we decide what's best to do for Bron." Veneta agreed.

The meeting took place two evenings later. Pulcher was very reluctant to tell what he and Bron had seen in the wood until Veneta explained to him, "The more people who know, the better. It means that Bron is not the only one who holds the secrets."

The two women listened, appalled, as Pulcher described the scene, haltingly but in detail. He left nothing out. The women were silent.

Stalwyn spoke first. "I should let you into another secret, although I promised Bron I wouldn't tell a soul, and only do so now to protect her."

Stalwyn then recounted Bron's suspicions and her own trip to the Catuvellauni village to see Iraina's daughter. Now it was the turn of Pulcher and the priestess to listen in amazement.

Next day, Veneta visited Shubinata in the temple in the wood, taking with her an offering of Stalwyn's cakes.

"Majesty, I have consulted Ashuba and he has no pity, but you are a woman and will understand. Bron is innocent in mind and body. She will be twelve in two years' time and then will be a woman, but for now –" She paused, then threw out her challenge.

"Of course, you may have no influence with Ashuba. Perhaps you have to do as you are told by your man, like the rest of us."

Shubinata gave no indication that she had heard, and Veneta withdrew.

Her next call was to see Africanus at his round house near the school.

"Africanus, I need your help," she said and explained her fears about Bron's innocence being jeopardised by Vortin, then asked, "How familiar are you with the Book of the Altar?"

"Not very," he confessed.

"Then this is your chance. I will give you the parchment to study and I want to know if there is anything in the writings – anything at all – that I can use to prevent Bron from having to attend the Midsummer ritual."

His reply a few days later was disappointing.

"Nothing, Veneta – but neither does it say anything to support Vortin."

He unrolled the parchment until he found the section he was seeking. Veneta held the end of the roll containing the earlier writings while he pulled the parchment towards himself and flattened it out on a table.

"See here, among the Abominations of Ashuba. After the tenth, which forbids the practice of homosexuality, the eleventh states –" He read aloud in the old language, occasionally helped by Veneta when he stumbled over an unfamiliar word. "'No girl child of the Temple shall be entered until she is twelve years old. At the start of her thirteenth year, on the anniversary date and precise time of her birth, she becomes a bride of the Temple. First in order stand the virgin priestesses, lower in order the virgin prostitutes. The High Priest first and his assistant priests as subordinates shall have lordship over the women, who shall be obedient to their commands. However, each woman shall be nurtured by the Temple with respect and dignity.'"

Veneta smiled wryly at this. "Nothing more?" she asked.

"Only warnings – 'If any priest shall transgress and take one of my children before her time, he shall be disgraced before the people –' and so on."

Veneta sighed.

She sought out Selvid again in his apartments at the back of the Temple and repeated all she had learned from Pulcher and Stalwyn. For a moment he said nothing then commented that he was not surprised.

"I've thought for a long time that something was going on between those three, but I couldn't decide what. Veneta, times are changing. Do you realise we have enough information here to bring down the whole Temple structure and with it all the laws and practices that have underpinned life in Byden for generations?"

Veneta was suddenly afraid. "But what would replace it?"

"What, indeed!"

He took her hands in his and looked into her eyes. She could not know that her face haunted his every waking moment and filled his dreams.

"Whatever happens, we're all right, aren't we, Veneta? We'll survive?"

She left her hands in his for a few moments before gently withdrawing them.

"I must go," she said. An onlooker would have perceived that it was not a decision either of them desired, but he opened the door for her and she left.

On a whim and on the pretext of a visit of inspection, she made her way to the little round temple in the north-eastern corner of the settlement and stood before the elaborately carved, marble altar of the present Roman emperor, Honorius.

"I need all the help I can get," she told him. The space between them lay sterile.

She was about to leave but decided that there was another appeal she could make, and walked across to a simple stone altar. It was surmounted by a slab on which was painted a fish and a monogram formed by the first two letters, chi and rho, of the name Khristos in Greek.

"I'm sorry, I've forgotten your name. I've not spoken to you before. I don't know who you are and you don't know me, except that I bring the flowers in sometimes. It's Bron, you see – she's only ten, and very innocent, and I'm afraid for her. Vortin doesn't take his eyes off her when she's around. He calls himself her father but it's not as a father that he looks at her. I'm sorry to have bothered you."

As she left the temple and came down the steps, Pulcher was hurrying towards her, looking tense and anxious.

"They said you here," he panted, short of breath. "Iraina says please to return."

"What's going on?" asked Veneta as she hurried along beside him, leaving a space between them to allow for his uneven gait.

"Big row – Vortin and Iraina."

"What about?" It was not often the pair argued, especially in public. Usually what one wanted was in the interests of the other, and if it was not, Iraina shrugged and gave in.

"Bron, my Bron," he answered.

Veneta put a hand on his shoulder and turned him to face her.

"Tell me, Pulcher. What about Bron?"

"Vortin – Midsummer Festival. He say 'Yes'. Iraina say 'No'."

"Good for her!" exclaimed Veneta, as they climbed the steps to the Temple entrance.

Inside, voices were raised. Iraina was screaming at Vortin. He was trying to reason with her as they faced each other in front of the altar. With them stood Jeetuna and both priests. Several of the eunuchs remained at a distance, as did some of the Temple women, who were whispering behind their hands and nudging each other, clearly enjoying the spectacle. Nobilianus stood with Brocchus but neither had any say in this matter.

"Oh, there you are, Veneta," called Iraina. "Let's hear what you have to say. Tell Vortin what *you* think about Bron attending the Midsummer Festival."

For a moment Veneta was at a loss. She looked from one face to the other. She knew that Iraina's opposition stemmed not from any concern she felt for Bron, but because of her jealousy. However, if Iraina was this jealous, there must be good cause, and Veneta's throat tightened with fear. She tried quickly to assess the situation.

Jeetuna, whose responsibility Bron now was, had no love for the child and would only be interested in keeping Vortin happy and placated. Sharma would have reacted in the same way. Three votes.

Veneta's eyes met those of Selvid, who sent her a silent message to be careful. However, she knew he would already have supported Iraina.

Three against two, and Veneta held the balancing vote. Whatever the politics of the situation, she had no choice. Taking a deep breath, she was firm in her reply.

"I think Bron is too young to be present at the Midsummer ritual."

"Three against three!" exclaimed Iraina, triumphantly.

Veneta understood why the High Priestess was so opposed. She was afraid that Vortin's physical reaction to Bron's presence would shame her, who had been unable to rouse him for years.

"You seem to forget, my dear, that you are only my advisers. I do not need to act in accordance with any advice. I can please myself."

Iraina was adamant. "If Bron's there, I won't be!" Stalemate.

Selvid intervened. "Vortin, I believe this will not be a popular command. The people will consider she's too young. Hestig will not approve, and as leader of the council, he has great influence in the settlement."

Vortin remained silent while he considered the possible opposition.

"Very well," he decided, "I will go along with your advice. Bron and Nobilianus need not be present this year – but next year will be different." With that threat, he dismissed them.

Veneta and Pulcher joined hands and danced a jig, unseen behind a pillar. Then she left him and went to thank Shubinata and the unknown god for answering her petitions.

The only shadow was Vortin's threat "... but next year will be different."

CHAPTER XXXVI (36)

AD 396

Throughout the years, on the night of the Unvala fires, Vortin had continued to send his gifts to those he wished to favour.

"He's buying us off," Trifena complained every year to Hestig, but always accepted the bribe, adding the coins to the savings for Bron's release from the Temple.

This year, in the late afternoon of Unvala, there came the expected knock at the door. As usual, Hestig was assisting with preparations at the Temple. Trifena was in the kitchen with Bettina, preparing the festive evening meal, and sent her to open the door.

When Bettina returned, she announced with some surprise, "It's Vitius, madam."

Trifena wiped her hands. "Show him into the triclinium."

When she entered he was standing admiring the mosaic.

"This is a surprise, Vitius. Please sit down."

"Vortin has sent me to deliver his gifts," explained the young man. Trifena accepted the pouch and asked him to convey her thanks to the High Priest.

"May I offer you a drink of wine?"

He refused, and added, "Our twenty-four-hour fast is not quite over."

Trifena smiled. "I won't tell if you don't," she said and rang the bell for Bettina.

"It's one of our favourites," Trifena confided, when the girl had returned to the kitchen. "Every spring, Hestig bleeds the rising sap from the willow trees along the Stan. It produces the sweetest of wines."

Bettina brought back a tray with glass beakers and pastries and a glass jug of white wine that sparkled with a hint of gold. While Trifena was pouring a drink for her guest, Vitius helped himself to the pastries Bettina offered. Trifena saw him smile at her slave. She knew that both young people had been born in Gaul and on several occasions, when they had met accidentally, she had heard them conversing together in their own language.

She thought what a handsome lad he was, especially when he smiled, but he usually looked so pale and tense.

In the months after that visit, Vitius was often at the house, sent by Vortin whenever he had a message for Hestig or an order for pottery, and it seemed that more and more frequently Bettina returned from market with a flush on her cheeks, saying that she had happened to meet him there.

"I hope you're not falling in love with him," Trifena teased her. "He's going to be a priest one day, and out of your reach."

She watched the sparkle in the girl's eyes vanish and was sorry then that she had mentioned it. *There are going to be tears,* she thought, and sighed for the heartbreak she understood and knew would follow.

Much to Bron's excitement, one morning, Hestigys appeared at school as a new pupil. Africanus sat him next to Nobilianus, probably hoping that he would be a calming influence on the High Priest's son, but Nobilianus was just as restless and unable to concentrate.

Bron felt proud of the speed with which her younger brother learned his lessons, but it showed how slow Nobilianus was, although he was older by five years. It was not long before any contact between the two boys was as sour as the relationship between Nobilianus and herself.

Hestigys confided to Bron that he especially resented the sly way the boy always managed to be standing near their younger sister, Trifosa, whenever she came to the Temple with the family.

On one such occasion, Bron was surprised to see Nobilianus and Trifosa in quiet conversation, and reported the fact to Hestigys. He went over to the couple, took Trifosa by the arm and marched her back to their parents.

"Don't talk to him!" he hissed in her ear as they passed their sister.

"I shall talk to whoever I like!" Trifosa retorted.

Bron watched as she shook herself free and tossed her head, and the flames from the torches on the walls burnished her hair with copper lights. Nobilianus had noticed it, too.

Hestigys sighed and Bron smiled to herself. He always complained that it was his misfortune to be sandwiched in age between two such strong-willed sisters. She looked round to see if anyone else had noticed this little drama and found Jeetuna watching from a distance.

Jeetuna was frustrated. She had been told often enough that she was beautiful and desirable, but lately had been forced into near celibacy. Vortin had no interest in Iraina and rarely in herself these nights. Iraina seemed not to care, but Jeetuna was unfulfilled. The reason for his neglect was obvious. He had hunger only for Bron. Selvid was energised only in Veneta's presence, and even Sharma lately seemed preoccupied.

When desire was in her at night, she would knock on Sharma's door, however late, and invite herself into his bed. This amused him and he would laugh and move over to make room for her. She always made worthwhile his several hours of lost sleep.

It was on such a night, their passion subsiding, that the priest kissed her hard on the lips again and commented that Vortin was a fool to be missing out on the joys of her body. Jeetuna humphed.

"His eyes are full of no one except Bron," she said.

"That child will be his downfall!" exclaimed Sharma with such vehemence that Jeetuna didn't know how to answer. As High Priest, Vortin should have been beyond criticism or reproach.

"And what then?" she asked, teasing and kissing him and rousing him again. "What then, my love, my lord?"

"Then," he replied unwisely as he bound her to himself once more, "then I will be High Priest."

He was exultant as he rode surging wave after wave, then reaching the highest crest, teetered with held breath before his passion exploded and he fell submerged in the undertow. As the current receded and he lay exhausted, he promised, "Then, with you at my side, my luscious Jeetuna, you – only you –"

"What of Iraina?" Jeetuna asked, but he laid a finger over her lips. "Our secret," he warned, and she nodded. She also wanted to ask, "And what of Nobilianus?" but said nothing.

The thought returned to her again and again as she pondered Sharma's indiscretion, uttered in the waning of his passion. *What of Nobilianus?* He stood in line, and would succeed his father, unless something happened to him in the meantime.

One day she approached the boy on his way home from school. She told him how well he looked and how handsome, and said she was surprised at Bron's lack of respect for him.

"But in truth, you like Trifosa, don't you?" tempted the priestess.

"I didn't realise it was that obvious," he said.

"It is to me, because I have your welfare in my heart," Jeetuna purred, "but, fortunately, I don't think your father has noticed. She's lovely, of course, and has much more character than Bron."

"That girl!" he exclaimed with exasperation. "What my father sees in her, I don't know."

"But your father intends her to be your High Priestess, one day."

"After he's finished with her, I hope she'll be a submissive wife," Nobilianus said. "She's my path to her sister."

"I know the family keeps Trifosa away from you, I've seen them," sympathised Jeetuna, "so you hardly have a chance to speak to her. I could change all that."

His cheeks flushed and his eyes shone. "You could? How?"

Jeetuna didn't know how, but determined to find a way.

"Leave it to me," she said.

She raised his hand to her lips, kissed his ring of office and again pledged her loyalty to him, as she had done when she visited him in his room after the fire in the sanctuary.

"I will not forget this," he promised her.

Jeetuna knew she had handled the situation well.

It was the first of May again, the beginning of summer. As was the custom, a group of young girls, smaller in number since the plague, all dressed in white, met together at the edge of the wood before setting out for the temple to beautify their faces in May dew.

Although only ten years old, Bron had obtained permission from Jeetuna to join them this year and had brought with her a hooped garland of greenery and flowers, hung with brightly coloured ribbons, which Veneta had helped her prepare.

They were just about to set out when a small, excited figure ran towards them, flaming hair emphasising a pale complexion above her white dress. She carried a small bunch of freshly picked bright yellow sunstars – *lion's teeth* the slaves from Gaul called them, *dents de lion* – which were already wilting in her hot hands.

"Trifosa, what are you doing here?" demanded Bron with exasperation. "You're not old enough. Go home."

"I won't!" exclaimed her sister. "I'm coming with you!"

"Does Mother know you're here?"

"Of course not," Trifosa answered, and added illogically, "If she did, I wouldn't be here."

Bron saw that argument was useless and, as she was not prepared to take her sister home and miss the fun, she reluctantly agreed that Trifosa could go with them.

"But stay near me and behave yourself!" she ordered. Trifosa meekly nodded.

Having bathed their faces in the dew trapped in the folds of the leather mantle laid outside Shubinata's temple, the girls grouped and began to run back along the path, knowing that the boys with cow horns would be hiding in the trees, waiting for them. For once, Pulcher was not in attendance on Bron. He had sent her word that he had been ill during the night.

It was not long before the long low notes of the horns told them it was time to run faster, or be caught, if that was their wish. The noise increased and the young lads appeared from their hiding places, jumping over thick undergrowth or swerving round trees, blowing the horns and shouting and laughing, chasing a group of girls or singling out one special quarry.

Bron dropped her hooped garland and ran as fast as she could, ahead of the others, intending to escape, but suddenly became aware that Trifosa was no longer at her side. She stopped abruptly and turned, allowing most of the girls and their pursuers to rush by. One of the lads stopped.

"Bron, in all modesty, you're supposed to run," he chided her. Bron knew him well from the days when they used to play together before she entered the Temple. "If Soranus knew you were in the wood this morning, he wouldn't still be lying in bed," he teased her.

"Have you seen Trifosa?" she asked anxiously. "My mother will kill me if I let anything happen to her!"

"No. Do you want to go back and look? I'll come with you," he offered.

The pair set off, retracing their steps, until Bron was amazed to see, in the distance, her young sister running round the trees, giggling. In pursuit was a much older lad.

"Trifosa!" Bron called, sounding like her mother. "Come here at once!"

The pair stopped in their tracks and the boy stayed out of view behind a tree. Trifosa came over.

"Bron, you spoil all my fun!" she pouted.

"You're too young to be playing chase with a boy," scolded Bron. "Who is he, anyway?"

"Never you mind," Trifosa retorted. "Let's go, if we must."

Bron was suspicious.

"Leave it to me," said her friend, and making a wide circle, approached the figure now hidden in the undergrowth. With a rush he bounded towards the lad, who was obviously very reluctant to be discovered. There were shouts and a tussle, then a thud, and the sound of cracking twigs and a flurry of dry leaves as a figure ran off. Then silence.

Bron grabbed Trifosa by the hand and dragged her over to where their friend lay on the ground.

"Are you all right?" she asked anxiously, bending over him.

"Just winded," he said. "I'll be on my feet in a moment. The idiot kneed me."

"Who was it?" asked Bron, knowing the answer from the defiant look on Trifosa's face.

"Nobilianus," he replied, still clutching his stomach.

They helped the lad back to the settlement.

"Bron, don't tell, please," wheedled Trifosa, widening her pale brown eyes.

"I may or I may not, I'll decide later. Now go straight home – and keep away from him!"

"I'll take her home," the boy offered, having recovered. "Shall I give your love to Soranus when I see him?"

Bron laughed. "Yes, if you think it will make him happy," she said.

"Think? I know it will," he replied, smiling broadly.

Bron was puzzled. *What I wonder is, how did Nobilianus know that Trifosa would be in the wood this morning?* She turned to her sister. "How did *you* know that *I* would be here?"

"Jeetuna told me," Trifosa said.

CHAPTER XXXVII (37)

Bettina, Trifena's slave, lay awake in her little iron bed, listening to the sounds in the courtyard. Once or twice she thought she detected a soft footfall and held her breath, straining her ears to listen more intently, but all she heard then was her own heart thumping painfully in her breast. There was no soft knock on her door, no hesitant creaking as it was pushed open and closed again, no rush into young arms, and drowning in whatever followed.

In the early hours she heard Skeel growling in his kennel in the courtyard and went out to him.

"There's nothing to growl about, you silly old thing," she reassured him. "Do you want to come into bed with me? You might as well, there's plenty of room, but don't let our mistress know!"

The dog needed no second bidding and followed her back to her little room at one end of the kitchen. He leapt on to her bed, then burrowed down under the coverlet, reappearing again to lay his head on the pillow, his eyes regarding her with great solemnity.

As the hours passed, she began to sob quietly into his soft brown fur, and crying, she eventually fell asleep.

Skeel woke her next morning, licking her face and whining to be let out. Bettina's thoughts were only of Vitius. A thousand things could have happened to prevent his coming. She was sure he would have a good explanation next time they met, and they would try to be together again during another night. She thought she would die of a broken heart if he had no explanation. Perhaps Trifena was right and he would always be out of her reach.

Her routine had to continue normally so that no one would guess her heartache. None of the family was about, and after washing and dressing, she left her room and began to prepare breakfast for them, remembering to shut the window she had left open all night so that her hoped-for lover could gain access.

Later that morning, Hestig arrived home with Brocchus, who had brought him from his stall in the market. Trifena ambivalently welcomed their guest and offered him some refreshment, which he refused.

"Sharma has sent him to collect the Temple tax," Hestig told her.

"I didn't think it was due yet," she said, surprised.

"It isn't," Brocchus explained, "but Temple expenses have increased lately. If Hestig, as our representative, has received it from the people, it might as well be in our possession as in his."

Since their meeting in the market when she first arrived in the settlement, Trifena had always felt uncomfortable in the presence of the eunuch. He looked her over so insolently. She was annoyed when Hestig left them to converse together in the courtyard, but her duty as hostess did not allow her to walk away.

In moments, Hestig returned with a face as grey as a plague victim's.

"It's gone!" he said hoarsely.

"What's gone?" asked Trifena and Brocchus together.

"The bag, the settlement's funds," he said. "It was there yesterday – I know because I added money to it – but it's not there now!"

"It must be!" Trifena exclaimed. "You've made a mistake! Go and look again!"

"Come and see for yourselves!" he said to them, and they followed him into the triclinium and across to the shrine. The red curtain was pulled back.

"I keep it here, in the wooden plinth beneath Ashuba," he informed Brocchus. "See, it has a door at the back. The cavity's empty! Look for yourselves. There's nothing there!"

They searched but there was no place that the large bag of money could have dropped without being seen.

"How much was in the bag?" asked Brocchus, suspiciously.

Trifena gasped when she heard the amount.

"Someone must have got in, somehow!" she cried. "Bettina! Come here, girl! Follow us and we'll all search!"

Bettina came from the kitchen, her face white. They moved from room to room, but there was no sign of a break-in, no damage, no evidence anywhere of an intruder. All was as it should be.

"No one is to leave this house!" Brocchus ordered. "I shall return with Sharma. I'll collect your son from the schoolroom on the way."

When he had left, Trifena threw her arms about her husband.

"I don't understand what could have happened," she said. "It doesn't make sense!"

"Someone must have got in," suggested Hestig, "but when? Bettina, have you any explanation?"

Bettina stammered "No - no, sir." She looked as if she was going to be sick.

Trifena tried to soothe her slave's nervousness. "It's all right, my dear, no one suspects you," she comforted her. "Let's all go into the triclinium and await the arrival of Sharma."

"It doesn't look good for me," muttered Hestig.

His fears were justified. Sharma arrived with Brocchus and three of the other eunuchs. Hestigys was with them.

"This is a bad business," said Sharma. "Be so good as to stay in the triclinium, all of you, while my men search."

The search was thorough but fruitless.

"I regret that I am going to have to arrest you, Hestig, until we have a satisfactory explanation of what has happened here. Eunuchs, take him!"

Trifena protested as her husband's arms were bound behind his back and he was led away. She threw a shawl round her shoulders and followed to the cell in the courthouse.

"Trifena, there's nothing you can do for me here," Hestig told her. "Send Bettina with some lunch, and you and Hestigys go round the settlement and talk to everyone – everyone – and see if they can shed any light on this affair. Ask if there have been any strangers passing through or staying at the inn. Ask if anyone is spending a lot of money – anything. Tell everyone I didn't steal it. There must be some other explanation."

Trifena sent Bettina with every practical comfort for Hestig and the girl assiduously hurried to and fro between house and cell, providing food and washing water and clean clothes as he needed them.

Meanwhile, Trifena and Hestigys visited every house in the village, enquiring, discussing, surmising, listening. Most believed Hestig was innocent but no one could offer any explanation.

Hestigys was taken out of school to run his father's pottery as best he could, and Trifosa had increased responsibilities as she helped her mother manage the livestock.

"The trial date has been set for the end of June," one of the councillors told Trifena, "after the Midsummer Festival."

Suddenly, something seemed to make sense to Trifena. Having been thwarted last year, Vortin had already indicated that he wanted Nobilianus and Bron present at this year's ritual.

Trifena went to see Veneta and voiced her suspicions: "I think Vortin arranged the theft to keep Hestig out of the way until after the Temple ritual."

"If so, there is nothing any of us can do about it," said Veneta. "Your husband will be released when the money turns up – as it will, no doubt."

Trifena also confided her fears to Bettina. "But I don't want to burden you with our problems, my dear. I know you have your own heartache. It hasn't escaped my notice that Vitius hasn't called here since before the theft."

CHAPTER XXXVIII (38)

The May feast day of Rosalia was welcomed as a day off work. A mid-morning procession led by Vortin and Iraina had left the Temple and was making its way through the settlement down to the Stan, before following the stream up to the mere and across to the sacred burial pits.

Trifena, with Bettina and Trifosa, walked with the women and girls, singing as they went, and were accompanied in their song by a persistent cuckoo. They carried posies and woven garlands of flowers and greenery, while Hestigys among the menfolk struggled with wickerwork baskets full of food and beer.

Trifena led her group to the graves of grandparents and other members of her lineage, and spread the floral tributes. The other women were laying flowers on their family mounds, and soon the whole area resembled a wild garden.

Then everyone crossed to the mere to enliven faces and hands in the cold water. Clouds of mayflies were there already, frantically dancing away the only day of their lives. Trifosa threw into the pool a handful of coins her mother had given her as an offering, then filled an earthenware jug with the pure, life-giving water to solemnly sprinkle on the mounds. All the women were following this ritual.

That done, families were united again as they sat to eat and drink, those above ground sharing with those below by laying out a selection of everything they had brought with them.

"Children, breathe in deeply," Trifena instructed her son and daughter.

They already knew that, by doing so, they were absorbing the unseen vapours of knowledge and wisdom released by those who had travelled before them into the next life.

It was a great grief to everyone that the plague victims lay in the pit in the wood and were not also lying beneath their feet. As usual, the Temple staff who had no family graves were forming groups at the unattended mounds. There were many such, after the pestilence.

Bron went across to her mother. For Trifena and the family this was not the usual enjoyable occasion, but they went through the motions to show that nothing had changed for them and Hestig was innocent of the charge brought against him.

Africanus had joined the procession but was now standing alone, apart from the proceedings, and Trifena sent Trifosa over to invite him to join them for the picnic. He came across and thanked her, ate little, and took his leave of them as soon as he was able.

"Please forgive me, Trifena, but I like to be alone with my thoughts at Rosalia time," he explained. "I too wish to remember my family and childhood. The west coast of Africa is such a long way away."

"I understand," she sympathised and watched as he left them and wandered off into the wood.

The priests and priestesses mingled with the families, accepting any delicacies offered and speaking words of comfort where required.

Trifena was surprised when Jeetuna made a point of coming over to assure her that no one believed Hestig had stolen the settlement's funds. She congratulated Hestigys on keeping his father's business solvent and whispered a few words to Trifosa. Trifena was grateful for her concern, and said so.

The people returned to the settlement whenever they were ready. Trifena and Bron, Bettina with them, sang the old songs with the other womenfolk as they made their way home, so that the course of the stream and lynchets and woods burgeoned with melody and harmony. It did not worry Trifena that the youngest member of the family was not with them, as she assumed Trifosa was with her friends.

Trifosa had not been so deep into the wood on her own before and was beginning to feel anxious when a voice called her.

"Trifosha! Over here!" Nobilianus emerged through the trees. He looked flushed and a little unsteady on his feet, and Trifosa guessed he had been drinking a large quantity of beer.

"Jeetuna said you had something to say to me," Trifosa told him. "What is it? I'm not supposed to be talking to you."

"Then why did you come?" he asked unsteadily.

She didn't answer.

"Anyway, talking can't hurt," he said, and hiccupped.

They walked a little way and she let him hold her hand.

"Well, what is it?" she asked again.

He stopped and turned to her. "I jush wanted you to know that I think you're very pretty," he said, breathing hard.

"Is that all?" she asked. "I thought it was something important."

"It ish important," he said.

"You're supposed to be marrying my sister," Trifosa reminded him.

"Oh, her!" he said, dismissively. "I'd much rather it wash you."

"I'm not going to marry anyone!" declared Trifosa with conviction.

"Wash a waste!" he said, drawing nearer to her, so close that she backed up against a tree.

Suddenly she was alarmed. "I've got to go now," she said, flustered. "The family will be missing me."

"You don't have to go yet, Trifosha, not just yet. Give me a kish – a little kish can't hurt."

"I don't want to kiss you," she told him. "Let me go, Nobilianus, let me go!"

"Just a kish –" He looked down at her with eyes half closed. His body had hers pinned against the bark of the tree so that its roughness hurt her back. She began to struggle and push him away but his weight was too much for her.

Then she could not move at all because with his left hand he was holding her firmly by the shoulder while pressing his lips on hers, using his right hand to fumble with his clothing. Then it was underneath her tunic and travelling up the inside of her legs. He was still trying to kiss her.

All she could do was bite him hard on the top lip. He cried out in pain and the offending hand flew to his mouth and came away dripping with blood.

"You little witch!" he yelled, but laughed with pleasure, and lunged at her again, this time pulling her tunic up around her waist and thrusting his exposed and erect penis between her legs.

Suddenly there was a roar and a huge pair of black hands pulled Nobilianus off his victim. An arm as hard as iron held him firmly round the waist and off the ground while he kicked and struggled and mouthed language that shocked the little girl and their teacher alike.

"Go home, Trifosa," Africanus ordered her. "Go home! I'll speak to you tomorrow. As for you, young man –"

Trifosa heard no more because by then she was well out of earshot. She ran all the way home and was too frightened to tell anyone what had happened.

After Africanus had said all he had to say, he walked Nobilianus back to the Temple. The boy remained silent, which gave Africanus opportunity to consider the situation.

He was worried. Usually he would have known how to discipline his pupils and what to say to the families concerned, but this incident was entirely unprecedented in his experience.

Attempted rape was bad enough, but for the High Priest's son to act so, with a girl who was not associated with the Temple, who was only eight years old, and the sister of his intended consort, broke all the rules.

Finally, he decided not to tell Vortin what had occurred, only because he knew the ferocity of the punishment the High Priest would mete out, even to his own son, and that Iraina would not intervene on the boy's behalf.

Vortin laughed at his son's dishevelled state, flushed face, bloodied lip and red eyes. "The local beer is strong stuff," he said, "but you'll get used to it. How's your head?"

"It aches."

"Then you'd better spend the rest of the day in bed, son."

Africanus confided in Veneta, who was horrified at the behaviour of Nobilianus.

They decided that Trifena must be told, but not yet, as she had as much as she could bear with the imprisonment of Hestig and the disgrace in which the family already stood in the eyes of some in the settlement.

However, Veneta went with Africanus to talk to Trifosa at home while her mother was visiting her father. There was no need to say much. Trifosa had had the biggest fright of her young life, although she had not fully understood what Nobilianus had tried to do, until Veneta explained it to her. The priestess promised not to tell her mother at the moment, as long as Trifosa stayed well away from the boy. The child needed no second warning.

Nobilianus was in school next morning, his lip swollen, and meeker than usual, but once Africanus told him that Vortin would not be informed of the incident, his attitude changed and he was unrepentant. In fact, he became quite bumptious.

In the absence of Hestigys, who was still working at the pottery stall in the market, there was no one who would stand up to him.

CHAPTER XXXIX (39)

Iraina was looking pale and Vortin was concerned about her. He wanted her strong and healthy for the Midsummer Festival. He sent Veneta to fetch Stalwyn, who came immediately, arriving at the Temple early in the morning.

She climbed the spiral staircase without letting anyone know she was there. Approaching Iraina's rooms, the midwife heard a noise all too familiar. Iraina was being sick.

Embarrassed at intruding at such a moment, Stalwyn returned the way she had come. After several minutes, she again climbed the staircase, singing this time, and found Iraina waiting for her. The room smelt of sandalwood, but Stalwyn's experienced nose could still detect the sour odour of vomit.

The High Priestess brushed aside Vortin's concern and said she had not been sleeping too well lately. Stalwyn gave her sleeping draughts and left. She knew that Vortin could not be responsible for this sickness, as there was little physical contact between the couple these days.

Iraina was in a dilemma. She was pregnant again by the Catuvellauni boy. It was early days yet, which gave her opportunity to make a decision, but she thought that this time, whatever she decided, there would be no going back.

It was a simple matter, *Vortin or her illicit lover?* – her life of ease and wealth and status with her father, or a new life of near-poverty, housework and babies, but among her own people and with the boy she loved, or thought she loved.

Iraina was not entirely sure what was love and what was infatuation, or lust even. She knew she was hurting and unhappy when away from Cullum and their daughter, but had not been able to bring herself to turn her back on her life of privilege. Of course, she had managed to cream off a respectable amount of savings over the years – money that rightly belonged to the Temple – but that wouldn't last them a lifetime, especially with her expensive tastes.

Cullum said that life had no meaning without her, but Vortin had also said the same at the beginning. She recognised that Cullum was not all-in-all to her. But there was the new baby – could she get rid of it? It all hinged on that one question. If she kept it, she would have to leave Byden. If she got rid of it, she could stay, and life could carry on as now.

It was Sharma who reported to Vortin that there was a Christian in the settlement.

"How come?"

"Apparently, Hoad found him lying injured in the wood and carried him to the inn. Stalwyn bathed his wounds and Kendrus put his arm in a splint and sling. Of course, everyone is waiting for a miracle."

Increasingly, Christians were passing through the village. Vortin knew that some of the simple people were attracted to the stories of the miracles attributed to Jesus, the god-man, whom the Romans had crucified. It was even claimed that he had come to life again.

The High Priest decided there would be opportunity to hear the man's strange tales, as he was going to be at the inn for some time – unless, of course, this Jesus healed him overnight, which he thought was highly unlikely. So he sent Sharma to invite the pilgrim to the Temple.

Word came back that the man would be happy to explain his religion, but he wouldn't enter a pagan Temple, and would prefer to talk to all the people, not just those of the religious life.

Vortin was amazed that his authority should be challenged in this way, but had to bear in mind that Christianity was now the preferred religion of their Roman masters, so perhaps it would be wise to comply. Anyway, he was curious to find out what sort of man the pilgrim was.

So, early on the arranged evening, he and Iraina and their retinue arrived in the market place on foot but with great ceremony and a lavish show of vestments and jewellery. Their golden priestly thrones were carried by several struggling eunuchs and placed in a prominent position in the square. Once the High Priest and Priestess were seated, the people crowded round in a great circle, jostling for places so that they could get a good look at the pilgrim when he arrived.

Vortin was expecting an equally lavishly-dressed representative of the new Middle East religion, and was surprised when he was approached by an elderly man in a long grey woollen garment girdled at the waist, sandals on his feet, a cloak around his shoulders and a Jewish prayer shawl over his head, which hid the bruising and lacerations. In his right hand he carried a long staff and his left arm was bandaged to the elbow to keep the two pieces of wood in place, and supported in a sling.

"Greetings, Vortin, and to your lady, Iraina. May the peace of God be with you." Vortin nodded acknowledgement. The old man continued, "My name is Asher. I am a traveller and also a Christian."

The people waited quietly, probably hoping for some wonders, some tricks, but Vortin pondered that, with only one working hand, tricks were most likely out of the question. All the Christian could offer was talk.

Asher indicated that the people should sit down on the ground, and sat down himself next to the thrones, laying his staff by his side. Vortin looked at Iraina and guessed that, like him, she was feeling slightly ridiculous as they towered above the assembled company in their finery.

Asher began: "There was once a man who was travelling by donkey through a dense wood, on his way to worship at the Christian church in Calleva, when he was set upon by thieves, who beat him up, stole everything he had, and left him barely conscious on the path."

The crowd was listening intently.

"Many people were passing to and fro, including some who should have shown compassion, priests and business people, but none stopped to help him.

"After a few hours lying on the pathway, he found strength enough to remount his donkey, who was the only creature to show him any consideration and had not wandered off, and he rode on through the wood. However, weakness overcame him and he finally fell, where he was found by a stranger and brought to an inn. Doctors tended his wounds, the innkeeper provided bed and board, and her ladies looked after him and showed him the greatest kindness."

The crowd was quiet. Even the children who had been running about settled to hear the end of the story. The teller of tales was silent.

"Is that all?" asked Vortin.

"It is one strand of a two-stranded rope," replied the old man. "Love your neighbour. That is what this village has done for me. The Kingdom of God is already among you."

"And the other strand?" asked Iraina.

"That is harder," came the reply. "The second strand is to love God, the one true God."

"But I thought you Christians worshipped three gods," called Sharma.

"Three parts of one whole," explained the traveller. "You believe in a creator god, don't you?"

"Certainly," replied Vortin. "His name is Ashuba. I am his High Priest and behind me is his Temple."

"And you believe that he once walked the earth?"

"Indeed," answered Sharma.

"The same god?" asked the old man.

"The same," replied Sharma.

Vortin had signalled to the Temple women, who were busy pouring wine for the priests and priestesses. Asher was offered a golden goblet and accepted with thanks. Selvid helped him to his feet.

"There is a third aspect to God. Look at it like this," he said. "Christians believe that Jesus was God walking on earth. Jesus said he was the vine. But the vine stays in one place – in this case, on a hillside in Italia. But the *wine*, now – put your nose to the goblet and savour the aroma, dazzle your eyes with its jewel red colour, catch its sparkle in the flare of the torches, and finally taste it –"

He took a sip of the wine then passed the goblet to the nearest person on his left, and it was passed from hand to hand, each taking a tiny sip before letting it go. Vortin blanched to see his fine goblet besmirched by so many dirty hands, but Iraina laid quietening fingers on his arm and he said nothing.

The traveller was still speaking. "The wine contains the essence of the grape – its perfume, colour, flavour, the sunshine and rain and soft Italian air, and the fertile earth that nurtured it – and it is exported all round the world. Just so, the Spirit is the essence of God, sent all round the world – the third part of the Trinity – but still one God."

"That is easy to understand, traveller," said Iraina. "Thank you for the story."

"It's more than just a story," replied the old man.

Vortin fidgeted until the empty goblet was safely back in his hands.

"We will talk again," he said, and ordered his retinue to return to the Temple. This time he and Iraina did not move. The eunuchs struggled to lift the thrones, without success, so commandeered several of the strongest men standing by to do the job for them.

"Father, you don't believe all that nonsense, do you?" Nobilianus asked, once they were inside the Temple again.

"Of course not," replied the High Priest, "but you've got to know what the enemy is saying."

CHAPTER XL (40)

Veneta was intrigued. Early next morning, she sent Pulcher to wait outside the inn and report to her immediately the stranger visited the Christian altar, as she was sure he would do. As soon as she received word from the dwarf, she slipped out of the side door and across to the little Roman temple.

She surprised the old man on his knees on the cold stone floor in front of the altar with the fish symbol, and coughed to announce her presence. He began to rise, slowly and painfully, and she hastened to help him.

"Every picture tells a story," he laughed. "I'm afraid my knees are not as young as they were."

"I'm so sorry that there's not a praying stool here," Veneta apologised, "but this temple is seldom used. I will bring one across later in the day – no one in our Temple will miss just one."

"I expect your Temple is lavishly furnished," commented Asher, looking at the simple altar before them. Veneta felt ashamed. "It's all right," he hastened to reassure her.

"Is it?" she asked. "Ashuba wouldn't think it was all right if this was his altar."

The old man winced. "How is your arm?" she asked him.

"It still hurts."

"I'm surprised he hasn't worked a miracle, your God, and healed it during the night."

Asher smiled. "It will heal in time. A miracle is no less a miracle because it happens slowly."

"I need a miracle," mused Veneta, and paused.

"Do you want to tell me?" he asked. "You don't have to, of course, but I may be able to help."

So Veneta told him about the Midsummer Festival and her anxiety for Bron in the face of Vortin's lust, which he barely bothered to conceal any more, and the silencing of Hestig by his arrest and disgrace.

"Last year I pleaded with Shubinata and the Roman emperor-god and your God. At least one of them heard me because we were able to talk Vortin out of it, but he is determined to have Bron present this year so he can stand before her naked. I was going to make the rounds again."

"Why not relax and just ask *Him*?" Asher suggested, nodding towards the altar. "You could pray now – or let me pray for you."

"Please," nodded Veneta. "He knows you better than he knows me."

"Don't be so sure of that," Asher smiled.

So she let him pray for Bron, joined in with his "Amen", then thanked him.

"Just trust Him," said the old man, "and remember what I said about miracles."

When Veneta left, she felt more at peace than she had for a long time. As promised, she brought a praying stool over from the Temple, then went to find Selvid.

"I need to talk to you," she whispered.

"I'll come to the schoolroom tonight," he promised.

At his quiet knock, she opened the schoolroom door, locking it again behind them and slipping the key on her girdle, then led Selvid up the steps to her suite of rooms above the false floor.

She had spent time preparing light refreshments, and as she poured wine and they ate together, she told him of her conversation with the Christian and the old man's prayer for Bron.

Their talk drifted from what they had gleaned of the new religion to their growing dissatisfaction with many aspects of life in the Temple. Of paramount concern to Veneta was the fast approaching Midsummer Festival.

"Bron is like my own daughter, Selvid, like the daughter I can never have. She replaces the baby I had aborted." Then, more quietly, "The child would have been fifteen now."

Subconsciously, she folded her arms tightly across her stomach and bent over them as if once again suffering the pain of her loss.

Selvid sat helpless. "I have never asked you, Veneta, whose baby it was."

"How should I know? Vortin's? Sharma's? Yours?" He flinched. "I only know that Kendrus said I would never have another. I still cry for her at night sometimes, though not so much now."

Selvid sat at the other end of the couch, motionless. She watched him, surprised that he said nothing to comfort her, but he turned his face away. Then he stood up.

"I must go," he said flatly. "I will let myself out," and he hurriedly left the room.

Veneta moved away from the door, her eyes so full of tears that they spilled over and ran down her cheeks.

Then suddenly he was behind her. "You locked the front door," he stated.

When she did not respond, he gently turned her around. Seeing the tears, he pulled her into his arms. Veneta was not sure what would happen next, but he began covering her eyes, her cheeks, her mouth and chin with hungry kisses. She flung her arms round his neck and began kissing him too, with just as much fervour.

"I love you, I love you, I love you," he was saying over and over again, as they remained locked together in each other's arms, spinning round and round and round.

"And I love you, Selvid, with my life," she said, laughing and crying again and not knowing which way was up and which down.

He stopped spinning then and looked at her, his grey eyes serious. "I used to take you to bed," he said, "but that was in the old days before I loved you so much. It's different now. Do you understand what I'm saying?"

"I think so," she said, "but you have Ashuba's permission – it's all right."

"No, it isn't," he answered. "I'm not going to take you just because I can, because I'm allowed. One day, Veneta, we'll be free, and then I will."

"How, free?" she asked him.

"We must get away before Sharma or Nobilianus becomes High Priest. Neither of them will want us around. If Vortin's out, we'll be out, too."

"I couldn't bear the pains of the wickerwork god," Veneta whispered. "Jeetuna is terrified, too. You know how she sucks up to all of them, not knowing which one to favour."

"I'll get you out of Byden if your life is in any danger, I promise. Now I really must go."

"But –" began Veneta.

"Don't ask me to stay, please don't ask me to stay, or I will. I can resist my own desires – just. But I can't fight both of us."

Veneta let him release her. "Go then," she said reluctantly, giving him the key. "I'll see you in the morning."

After he left, she went to bed and lay curled up, hoping that sleep would cure the heavy ache in the pit of her stomach.

The pilgrim left the settlement two days later, his arm still bandaged and held in the sling.

It was Midsummer Eve. Veneta was deeply disappointed. She had put her trust in Asher's God but there had been no miracle, fast or slow. She decided that the old man's faith was misplaced, his belief a folk tale, and his God, if he existed, lacked compassion or power, or both. She wished now that she had run to Shubinata instead.

Vortin had commanded that Bron should not go with the other young girls to the temple in the wood, to bring back Iraina from her long ritual purification, but should wait in the Temple. When the procession arrived, she would help the priestesses disrobe their High Priestess. Nobilianus would help undress Vortin as he stood in front of the altar, facing Bron, and she would watch. The two children would kneel with the priests and priestesses as Vortin mounted the altar and mounted Iraina.

However, this year there was to be a change to previous arrangements. This year, Vortin had decreed (it was Ashuba's wish, of course) there would be no coverlet. Veneta knew that this year Vortin would be sufficiently aroused to do what he had been unable to do for several years past and would enter Iraina. Except that he would have his eyes fixed on Bron, and not on his High Priestess.

She knew this because he had been in a fever of expectation all week and everyone in the Temple was aware that his masculinity was reacting to Bron every time he saw her.

Veneta had tried to prepare Bron as best as she could. "Don't close your eyes, whatever you do, or you will anger him," she advised. "But you don't have to look at anything except his eyes. Stare him out. You might even make him feel ashamed, though I doubt it."

Bron told Veneta that Nobilianus winked at her whenever he caught her eye. Once, he had got close enough to whisper, "You and me, Bron – that will be you and me on the altar one day. You can't wait, can you?" She had stared at him in alarm then run away to seek comfort from the priestess, leaving him roaring with laughter.

The women had worked all afternoon to make sure that everything was in order in the temple in the wood. Now it was an hour before dawn. Outside, the simple structure was encircled by three rings of lit candles and there were seven thick round candles burning on pedestals inside. The red carpet was strewn with white rose petals, as was the wooden altar, and the statue of Shubinata wore a crown of red and white roses.

The two priestesses, the women and girls, had arrived in plenty of time. All wore white with red trimmings of flowers, ribbons and jewellery – white for innocence and purity, red for blood.

The women musicians were in place. Behind them, the young flower girls lined up, carrying their bunches of red and white roses, and behind them, two white oxen waited patiently for the whiplash that would tell them it was time to start trundling the chariot along the path towards the village. The barefoot prostitutes lined up along each side of the chariot, and surrounding them all, the older girls held their flaring torches high.

Veneta and Jeetuna, gently holding the long daisy chain between them, waited for their summons, Iraina's traditional double clap, to tell them she was ready to be escorted to the High Priest.

Back at the settlement, Vortin stood at the top of the Temple steps. He surveyed the crowd of people in the square below as they waited in silence, preparing to cheer as the first notes of the trumpets in the wood announced that the procession had begun to move forward.

Returning to the sanctuary, he paced backwards and forwards impatiently, hardly taking his eyes off Bron, who was kneeling meekly to the left. Her dark curls fell round her face and hid her eyes, which were studying the tiles on the floor.

Nobilianus was irritating him, fidgeting about on his prayer stool to the right, changing his weight from one knee to the other and crossing and uncrossing his ankles behind him.

At each side in the sanctuary stood Sharma and Selvid, while the eunuchs were hidden in shadows round the walls.

So they waited... and waited...

Suddenly there was a disturbance at the entrance doors, which were flung open as Jeetuna ran in, closely followed by Veneta.

"She's not there!" Jeetuna panted. "Iraina's missing!"

"What do you mean 'missing'? She can't be missing!" shouted Vortin. "Go and look for her!"

"We have," wailed Jeetuna, "and she's nowhere to be seen!"

Vortin was nonplussed.

"Even if we find her, there's no time to get her back here before sunrise," said Sharma practically. "Without Iraina, there can be no ceremony."

The truth of his words slowly dawned upon Vortin. Unbalanced by his overwhelming disappointment and frustration for the second year running, he transferred his fury to his priests.

"Find her!" he screamed at them. "Send all the men to scour the woods. Find her and *drag* her back, if necessary! We'll show her who's master here!"

Sharma and the eunuchs fled from the Temple. Leaving more slowly, Selvid passed Veneta on the way and they exchanged a few whispered words.

"Selvid, go!" Vortin yelled at him. "Now!" and he left.

Outside, Sharma could be heard announcing to the people that Iraina had been spirited away, and he needed the youngest and fittest men to form parties to search the woods.

Standing in the near-empty Temple, the priestesses awaited their instructions. Vortin glared in the direction of Bron.

"Get her out of here!" he shouted.

Veneta took the young girl by the hand.

"Come, Bron, I'll take you to see your father," she smiled, and led the way outside.

Nobilianus also escaped from his father's dark presence, so that only Jeetuna remained. She sidled nearer to the High Priest.

"Vortin, I understand your anger with Iraina."

"I wonder," he replied, bitterly.

"There may be a perfectly good explanation, of course, but you need comfort tonight. Let me love you. See, the light is coming –

dawn is breaking – you don't need to be without a lover on Midsummer morning."

He looked at her, considered the offer for a moment, then thought of Bron.

"Get out!" he ordered, and she left.

CHAPTER XLI (41)

Iraina could not be found. Vortin sent eunuchs to the Catuvellauni village but everyone there remained tight-lipped. After a few days, he called off the search. He didn't know why she was missing, but realisation dawned that her absence played into his hands. In fact, he could not have managed it better if he had organised her disappearance himself.

Bron would be twelve in a year's time, and with Iraina out of the way, he could make her his High Priestess and take her to his bed, and never leave it if he had his way. He would be discarding one daughter for another, but as there were no blood ties, there was little chance that Bron would bear imperfect babies.

Nobilianus, usually obtuse, nowadays looked at his father as if clearly understanding what was afoot. Vortin knew that his son was not at all concerned about Bron and had probably decided that, when he was High Priest, he would get rid of her, anyway.

Vortin's eyes followed her everywhere. He touched her whenever he could. He thought he would go mad before the year was up, but there was always Jeetuna, and he would make do with her in the meantime. She was clearly anxious to take Iraina's place, and might have done so if it had not been for Vortin's unmanageable obsession. She would be more than pliable as long as she thought she had a future as High Priestess, so he would dally with her until he announced his plans for Bron on next Midsummer's Day.

In the meantime, there must be no impropriety and no conduct that was contrary to the teaching in the Book of the Altar, as that would undermine his currently impregnable position as High Priest.

Stalwyn was concerned for Iraina. She guessed where she was – not spirited away by Shubinata, as the people believed, but gone to her young lover in the Catuvellauni village. She spoke to Kendrus about it, and with his agreement, set out one morning to cross the Ridgeway.

Having made enquiries of travellers she met on the way, it was not too difficult to pinpoint the village where Iraina had taken her previously, although blindfolded at the time. She was recognised and greeted as soon as she entered the settlement, and was directed to the hut of the wet nurse.

"Gone north," said the woman, "out of danger."

"Was she well?" asked Stalwyn.

"Sick a lot, but well enough," came the reply.

"And her daughter?"

"You guessed, did you? Oh well, I suppose it was obvious. She's thriving now – two and a half years old."

"And your son? What about him?" Stalwyn enquired.

The woman shrugged. "He died. What did you expect?"

Stalwyn began to say how sorry she was but the woman interrupted her. "It's one less mouth," she said, "and the gold coins will feed the rest of us for life."

Two days later, Brocchus found the missing leather bag of money. He told Hestig it was lying at the bottom of the mere, in the deepest part, caught up in the weeds. None of the coins was missing.

"How strange – just where they found Septima's body," Trifena commented sourly when she welcomed him home after the trial was cancelled.

"Next time, I will bury the bag where no one can find it," he decided. "I'll not tell anyone, not even you," and he kissed his wife on the nose, "then nobody will be able to let on where it's hidden."

Next morning, he returned to his market stall and his son was able to go back to school, "Much to the chagrin of Nobilianus," Hestigys reported.

"Of course no one can prove I stole it, because I didn't," Hestig told his customers when they enquired. "Why would I want the settlement's money? I have enough of my own without stooping that low!"

Vitius was resting on his bed in his room when there was a knock at the door and Sharma walked in.

"Sharma!" exclaimed the young man, jumping up in surprise. "You don't usually –"

"It's nothing more than an errand for Vortin," Sharma was quick to explain. "He wants to find out where Hestig hides his money – his own money. It's another job for you. You'll have to get on the right side of that girl again."

"But I haven't seen her for weeks," Vitius argued.

"Come, now," wheedled Sharma, "you're not lacking in boyish charm – as I know only too well. Just turn it full on her and she'll not be able to deny you anything you want."

"So why does Vortin need to know?"

"You might guess it has something to do with Bron – he's panicking that her parents intend to buy her back from the Temple. Now be a good boy and find out, and you'll be well rewarded – I'll see to it."

Bettina was an experienced shopper and Vitius watched as she and the stallholder in the market enjoyed their good-natured haggling.

"They're so fat already, they won't need many nuts to finish 'em off," the man advised. "Cheap at the price – and I'll throw in a fattener as well."

"All right, I'll take six – six of the plumpest, mind," Bettina stipulated. The stallholder pulled out six dormice by their tails and dropped them into a metal container, covering them with the lid. "Feed 'em well and they'll be ready for eating in about three days' time," he told her. "Just stuff 'em with minced pork, season with poppy seeds and honey, and bake – delicious!"

Bettina paid for her purchase and turned away, and nearly fell over the young man.

"Vitius!" she gasped. "I've been trying to get in touch with you for weeks."

"I know," he said. "Bettina, can we go somewhere to talk?"

"Not now," she said, "I'm due back home to prepare lunch. We could meet somewhere this evening, though."

If she had made any resolve to treat him coldly, it had melted in the warmth of his prepared smile.

"I'll wait for you outside the house, after dark – can you get away that late?"

"I'll be there," she promised.

She wasn't able to slip out until the family retired to bed, but Vitius was waiting for her. He drew her to him and, putting his arm round her waist, led her away from the light and down the slope towards the Stan.

It was a beautiful night with a sky covered in stars and a bright full moon floating high among the illuminated clouds.

"Vitius, it's been awful! The money was stolen, and my master was arrested and put in that dreadful cell, and it was me who left the window open all night. I left it open for you, but you didn't come. How could you, Vitius? You promised you would come! I lay awake all night waiting for you."

"You haven't told anyone about the window, have you?" he asked quickly.

"No, of course not. I didn't want to get you into trouble – or myself, for that matter."

"I wanted to come," he said, turning towards her and taking her hands in his and clasping them tightly to his chest, "I really did, but –"

He had practised this lie over and over, reasoning that he was only doing what Sharma had told him to do. He had always obeyed Sharma since he was a little boy and now it was second nature.

Admittedly, there were some things that Sharma made him do that he hated, and it was worse when Brocchus was with them. However, if the priest threw him out of the Temple, as he threatened to do if Vitius told anyone what the three of them got up to together, he had nowhere else to go. Sharma would make sure that no one gave him food or shelter. *Then what would become of me?* he thought.

So he continued with his lies, with shame because he knew that Bettina loved and trusted him. He had believed that he was not capable of loving a girl, so could hardly comprehend the emotions he was feeling now. Still, he had a job to do.

"I was ready to come, but Brocchus was sick and I was told to sit with him all night and tend him." That lie gave them both an alibi. Of course, it was Brocchus who had climbed in through the window and stolen the bag of money, hidden exactly where Bettina had let slip that it would be.

"I knew you weren't the thief!" Bettina exclaimed. "But who –?"

"Someone must have been passing and noticed the open window," Vitius said.

She accepted the explanation, without questioning why the thief had thrown the bag, with the money still in it, into the mere. All she seemed concerned about was whether Vitius would come another night.

"Yes, soon," he promised.

"But no more open windows," she said.

"You can let me in the front door next time," he replied, then surprising himself added, "Bettina, I think I'm falling in love with you."

"I know I'm in love with you, Vitius."

He kissed her tenderly and it felt clean. In fact, he felt so good about it that he kissed her again. She was soft and plump, and he laughed and said she reminded him of one of the dormice. She laughed too and let him kiss her again and again and the kisses lasted longer and longer. Bettina would have let him go further, but Vitius was unwilling. He had had enough sex of a sort to last him a lifetime, and wanted to keep intact the memory of perfection, of Bettina with the light of the moon falling full on her face. Besides, he had a job to do – a job he was beginning to detest.

"Not here," he said. "We can wait."

"You may be able to," she complained.

"Come on, dormouse, I'll walk you home," he teased her.

On the way, he remarked innocently, "I'm glad the money was found. Let's hope it's never stolen again."

Judging by her reply, Bettina trusted him without question. "Hestig has hidden it in a safer place this time – buried it, I think – and not even Trifena knows where it is."

"But he must have a lot more hidden – his own money, I mean. Everyone says how rich he is now. He can't go digging holes all over the place. We have the same problem hiding the Temple taxes."

"If he has a lot more, I don't know where it is," Bettina told him, "although I did once find a bag with money in it hidden in a barrel of grain. It disappeared later. I think bags must be hidden all over the house and he moves them about."

They reached the entrance door and he put his arms round her waist and looked down into her face again.

"Dormouse!" He laughed and enjoyed kissing her once more. "I'll be back."

He returned to the Temple, light of heart. He was glad that he possessed the information Sharma had demanded and there was no need to deceive her further. But he must be careful and not let Sharma suspect that he had suddenly and wonderfully fallen in love. He wondered whether Bettina would be brave enough to run away with him.

They often discussed it during his subsequent visits. They realised that it was the only way they were ever going to be truly free to love each other. Bettina thought that Trifena would not let Hestig pursue her, but Vitius said that Sharma would never rest until he had caught up with them and brought him back for punishment – probably a death sentence.

By her twelfth birthday, Midsummer's day, Bron would have completed a long apprenticeship of nine years at the Temple. She knew that her parents would be coming to pay Vortin the money saved for her release, and she would be leaving on the evening before the great Festival. Of course, Vortin would be furious, but all she could think of was that she would be going home and leaving the Temple for good.

Her only regret was parting from Veneta, though they would often see each other out and about in the settlement. There were also memories she was reluctant to leave behind, but she would still be able to visit the four graves in the wood. After her last experience, she never ventured further unless Pulcher was with her.

She was sitting among the graves one afternoon in May, chatting to him, when Soranus approached.

He had grown into a tall, handsome lad with dark brown tousled hair, a nose that was a little too large in Bron's opinion, eyes that nearly closed when he laughed, and full, rounded lips. At fourteen years, there was still some growing and filling out to take place, but his shoulders were already broad.

Bron looked up at him and smiled. Only recently, he had told her that he couldn't remember a time when he had not been in love with her.

He looked at Pulcher pointedly, but unusually Pulcher stayed where he was and would not leave them alone together. Bron knew her friend was aware of the feelings Soranus had for her, and his growing towards manhood, and would not allow her to be compromised or put in any danger. Sometimes Bron wondered whether Pulcher was jealous of the man that Soranus was growing up to be.

Soranus sat down with them, knees up to his chest, his firm brown arms clasped round them.

"So, what have you been learning today?" he asked Bron.

"Africanus has been telling us about Rome," she replied with enthusiasm. "He says it is a beautiful city with temples and statues and fountains and arches, and has a huge amphitheatre, like the one in Calleva, but much bigger. I'd like to go to Rome one day."

"Dream on," laughed Soranus. "You haven't even been to Calleva yet. The only way you'll get to Rome is if you marry a Roman soldier."

"That's not very likely, because I've only ever met one," laughed Bron, "but it doesn't do any harm to dream, sometimes."

"Would you like to go for a walk in the wood?" suggested Soranus hopefully. "I promise I won't let her come to any harm, Pulcher."

"No! No walk, no wood, no, no!"

Soranus looked surprised at the vehemence of his reply.

"Not today," said Bron more gently. "Perhaps another time." She got up to leave.

"I'll hold you to that," Soranus said. "I won't forget.

CHAPTER XLII (42)

After the harvest rejoicing at Samhain, as soon as Trifosa was nine years old, Bettina began escorting her to school.

When Vitius asked why the escort was necessary, the slave girl confided that there had been some unsavoury incident involving Nobilianus, who was never very far away.

"Nothing would surprise me about that young man," Vitius replied.

"Hestigys and Bron have been told not to let him anywhere near Trifosa," said Bettina, "and Africanus seats him as far away from her as it is possible to be."

As usual, the passage of time was marked by the main traditional religious feasts: Unvala in mid-winter, Imbolc at lambing time, May Day again, then everyone began preparing for Rosalia and the picnic with their dead at the sacred pits.

Throughout this time, Vitius would not accede to Bettina's plea to visit her at night. She spoke of their being together so often and so longingly and wondered aloud why he remained so reserved. He knew, if their relationship was to prosper unencumbered, he must tell her the truth about himself, but it took him weeks to pluck up courage. Several times he began a sentence, only to abandon it half-said.

"You don't know anything about me," he told her on one occasion.

"Vitius, you can tell me anything. You won't lose me – I love you too much," she assured him. "Just trust me."

One evening when the family had retired for the night, they were in the kitchen together and he was watching her wash up the dishes after the evening meal.

"Bettina," he began, "I've something to tell you. Come and sit beside me."

Hearing the anxiety in his voice, she dried her hands and did as he asked her.

"While I am telling you this, I want you to remember that I love you. When you've heard what I'm going to say, if you decide you want me to go, I will."

"Never!" she said, and turned her eyes to his face, ready to listen.

As he spoke, the colour drained from her cheeks. He told her that the abuse began almost as soon as he entered the Temple, at the age of five. Vortin had become High Priest the previous year and had subsequently appointed Sharma as his assistant, so the priest had not been in office long. He had taken an immediate fancy to the little boy.

Soon Brocchus joined the Temple staff and very soon became aware of what was going on between priest and child. Vitius always did as he was told, in those days without understanding, but knowing he had to keep it all a secret. Sharma realised that the eunuch, who one night took great pleasure in displaying himself as a fraud, would tell all if he were not allowed to take part in the sexual activity.

The abuse had continued into adulthood and now it was a way of life and he knew no other. That was not to say that he enjoyed it, quite the opposite, especially since he had met Bettina.

She stood up and looked at him as if he were a stranger.

"Go!" she said. "Please, just go!"

"But Bettina –" He took a step towards her.

"Don't touch me!" she cried, backing away from him and passing her hand backwards and forwards across her eyes as if to wipe away the images he had described so vividly. "Don't ever touch me again!"

She ran from the kitchen into her room and slammed the door. Vitius heard her bed creak then the awful sound of her sobs. He waited a moment, then left.

He did not see her for three weeks after that, but one morning while he was sitting on the floor in a quiet corner of the Temple, studying the altar scrolls, he saw her crossing towards him, determination written all over her face.

"Is that why you won't come to bed with me?" she asked him without any preamble.

"That's most of it," he said.

"Have you – you know – during these three weeks?"

"No," he said. "I've refused – for the first time ever."

"It will be different with me," she said.

"I can't, Bettina, not in Byden – never in Byden."

"Then there's nothing for it," she decided. "We've got to get away."

"Sshh!" he warned.

He now determined to play his own game. Vortin had chosen to put his current plan into operation during the feast of Rosalia, when everyone, almost without exception, would be at the pits for the picnic. Vitius was to ask Bettina to make some excuse to delay setting out with the other women, so she could let him into the house. Once inside, he would find an opportunity to secretly open the door and let Brocchus in. The eunuch would then hide in the house until the young couple had left to join the festivities at the pits.

Brocchus had received his orders directly from Vortin. Vitius guessed that the High Priest was scheming to impoverish Hestig, so he wouldn't be able to buy Bron back. He assumed that Brocchus would make a thorough search of the house and steal all the money he could find. To be deprived of their savings would be hard luck for the family and hard luck for Bron, but Vitius couldn't worry about that. For once he had to think of Bettina and himself.

When they left the house, he and Bettina would not go up to the pits. Instead, they would make their escape, and hopefully would not be missed for several hours.

CHAPTER XLIII (43)

AD 397

Accompanied by the songs of the women, Sharma followed Vortin as he walked alone at the head of the procession, leading his people from the Temple into Byden Wood, on their way to the burial pits.

Sharma had already checked that Hestig and his family had joined the column and that Bettina had not.

Jeetuna tried to edge her way forward so that she was almost abreast of Vortin, but Selvid kept her in her place. Sharma was amused at this little drama. He admired her single-minded determination to be wherever she could gain most advantage. Decreasing his pace, he drew level with her.

"Nice try!" he told her. "We make a good pair, you and I. Always an eye out for number one."

She turned the beauty of her wide smile on him.

"You're not jealous are you?" she teased in a whisper. "He's lonely without Iraina and if I can offer him a little comfort, where's the harm? You know where my true delight lies, Sharma – in your bed."

"In any bed, my dear, that's going to gain you some advantage. Not that I'm blaming you. We must all gather our harvest where we can."

When Vitius knocked at the door, Bettina opened it and he slipped quietly inside.

"Are you ready?" he asked.

"I couldn't collect my things together until they'd gone, but it won't take me long."

"I'll come and help you," he said and followed her into her room. She had so few possessions that they were soon tied in a bundle.

"I'll make sure no one's around," said Vitius. "Stay here."

Obediently she sat on her mattress to wait. He went to the front door and found Brocchus outside and let him in. He indicated that the eunuch should hide in the triclinium. Brocchus nodded and entered the room and quietly closed the door.

Returning, Vitius found Bettina in the kitchen, kneeling on the floor with her arms around Skeel. She was massaging his floppy ears and the dog was grunting his pleasure.

"I think I've changed my mind!" exclaimed Bettina. "I can't leave them for I don't know what. Everything's so safe here."

"I'm going," Vitius told her, "with or without you. I have to get away. If you're coming, it's now or never."

With a sigh, she returned to her room for her bundle.

Vitius kissed her. "We're a couple now," he said. "In future, whatever happens to you, happens to me."

Together they crossed the courtyard and went out through the front door.

Skeel watched them go, but Vitius guessed that the dog would return to his kennel and lay down, head on outstretched paws, patiently waiting for the family to return. He might growl a little when Brocchus came out of the triclinium to set about the task Vortin had given him to do, but as the eunuch had been in the house before as a guest, hopefully the dog would decide there was nothing amiss and go back to sleep.

Hand-in-hand, Vitius and Bettina hurried down to the stepping-stones, crossed over, and started up the hill on the opposite side of the stream. They had gone some way when Bettina stopped.

"I've got to go back," she gasped between breaths.

"Whatever for? You haven't changed your mind again, have you?"

"No, of course not. But I've forgotten my ring – the one Mistress gave me. I can't leave without it! It's the only piece of jewellery I possess."

"I'll buy you a ring as soon as I can," Vitius promised her.

"I don't need your ring if I have you," said Bettina, "but this is all I will own to remind me of the family."

"We haven't time," Vitius said, but Bettina was insistent.

"Oh, very well, but you know we must be far from here before they all return from the picnic."

Together they hurried back the way they had just come. As they crossed the Stan stream, Bettina noticed smoke rising from somewhere up the hill.

"Where's that smoke coming from, Vitius?" she asked. "Is it Pulcher's house?"

"No, it's higher up than that," he replied.

A yellow light suddenly flared in the smoke, then another, and another.

"Vitius, our house is on fire!" screamed Bettina. "Hurry! Hurry!"

Trifena lay with her head on Hestig's chest, well content. The gathering was as noisy as usual. Children were playing among the decorated mounds while the young people gossiped and flirted, parents relaxed, and the older folk reminisced about the 'good old days' when their families were complete.

One of the women nearby noticed smoke down in the settlement and mentioned it to her husband. He stood to get a better view.

"What's the smoke?" he asked his neighbour. "Is someone burning rubbish down there?"

One by one, people's attention was drawn to the fire. They began scrambling to their feet, Trifena and Hestig among them. Suddenly, flames became clearly visible and a woman shouted, "Someone's house is on fire!"

Without hesitation, there was a general stampede down the hill, led by the men and young people. Trifena, with the women and children and elderly folk, followed as quickly as she could. She sent Bron over to Vortin, who was leading his group down at a more leisurely pace.

It soon became apparent which house was on fire. The cry passed from mouth to mouth. "It's the Roman house! It's Hestig's house!"

Meantime, Vitius and Bettina had reached the front door. Bettina hadn't brought a key with her and all she could do was pound on the door with her fists.

"Out of the way!" ordered Vitius and moving back, launched his shoulder at it with as much force as he could. It took three assaults before the door gave way.

Inside, the fire had taken firm hold. The courtyard roof was not allowing the smoke to escape and thick black billows met them as they stumbled across the threshold. It became trapped in their hair and filled their eyes and lungs. Nothing familiar was visible and flames were leaping upwards and sideways from several places at the same time.

"You can't go any further, Bettina!" shouted Vitius, gasping and choking. She was only a grey shadow now in the enveloping smoke.

"I've got to!" she shouted back between violent coughs. "I've got to find Skeel!" and she disappeared into the thick blanket.

Vitius hesitated only a moment. "I'm coming with you," he shouted. "Wait for me! Bettina, wait for me! Where are you?"

Then he followed her into the unknown.

When the crowd reached the settlement, Trifena was appalled at the sight that met them. Some of the men ran to release Hestig's animals and shoo them away to safety while the younger and fitter ran to the Temple for the fire appliance, and the womenfolk who lived nearest raided their houses for pots and pans. She watched as everyone else formed a human chain from the house down the slope to the Stan.

As soon as they could, those nearest the stream filled whatever utensils were to hand with water, and neighbours began passing them from one to the other until those nearest the house were able to throw water through the open doorway and up towards the roof.

Pulcher organised the children into another chain and they passed the now empty containers back down to the stream for refilling.

As hard as they worked, with backs twisted and arms aching, the small containers of water made little, if any, difference to the ferocity of the fire, which was by now consuming the entire house.

It was some time before the wheeled fire appliance arrived, hauled by several men. They placed it as near the house as they could, but by now the heat was intense. Two of them stationed themselves each side, and grasping the ends of the handle, began to pump, squirting water through the open door. As the men tired, others took their places. The last person in the human chain now changed tactics and threw his bucket of water into the wooden container in which the pump was fixed, thereby constantly replacing the water used.

Their efforts were of little avail but they continued pumping until Hestig came across to thank them and told them to rest, as they had done all they could.

Helplessly, everyone stood at some distance, watching as the yellow and orange flames elatedly took full possession of the house, raged as victor for a while, then slowly began to calm down.

Hestig stood with the men, discussing how the fire had started and how it had caught hold so quickly and completely.

Trifena had been watching in stunned silence, but was now crying in the arms of Selena. Stalwyn joined them. Veneta, Pulcher and Soranus stood with Bron and her brother and sister, doing their best to comfort them. Young Trifosa was beside herself at the thought of the horrific death of Skeel.

Suddenly Trifena raised her head and grabbed hold of Selena's arms.

"Bettina!" she cried. "Where's Bettina? I left her in the house."

"She must have got out," Selena said hopefully, looking round.

"Then where is she? Where is she?" cried Trifena.

"I'll look for her," offered Stalwyn and hurried away.

When she returned, shaking her head, Trifena collapsed against Selena's ample chest and the older woman's arms tightened round her.

Hestig came over to his family. "I can't understand it, I can't understand it," he said over and over. Trifena began to cry again and clung to him and told him of her fears for Bettina.

"If she was in there, there's no hope," he said. "Our only consolation is that the smoke got to her and Skeel before the flames did."

"We've lost everything –" Trifena sobbed, "our friend, our home, the business, our savings – even our dog! Everything!"

"But we're safe," Hestig said, kissing the top of her head, and speaking with more confidence than he could be feeling. "There may be things Hestigys and I can salvage in the morning. I'll build up the business again, and we'll have another house – and we're safe, that's the most important thing."

"You must come home with me," said Selena. "There's only me in my house now, and there's room for you all."

"That's so kind of you, but the four of us will crowd you out," said Trifena, "and if – when – Bron comes home, there will be even less space."

Hoad and Louca were standing near. They held a whispered

conversation, then offered Selena a home with them until Hestig could rebuild and move the family out of her house.

"We haven't much room," confessed Louca, "but you're very welcome to what we have."

"If I go, it will give you more privacy," Selena said to Trifena, and accepted the offer gratefully.

Veneta put her arm around Bron and took her back to the Temple, and the family dejectedly walked away from their house, leaving the fire to burn itself out.

Even in her shock and grief, Trifena asked Hestig, "What now of our plans to buy Bron back from Vortin before the end of next month?"

"Yes, the fire has been very opportune for someone," he replied.

CHAPTER XLIV (44)

The family spent a restless night in the house that had once been Trifena's home, 'topped and tailed' in Selena's bed. It rained lightly in the early hours but next morning, when Hestig and his son returned to inspect the damage, and passed through the hole that had been their front door, they found that the fire was still smouldering in timbers and piles of rubble. As they surveyed the devastation, Soranus and Pulcher joined them.

Hestig began picking up broken bricks and tiles and aimlessly dropping them again.

"Come, Father," said Hestigys, taking him by the arm, "I think we need some plan here, or nothing will get done."

Hestig straightened his shoulders. "Yes, you're right. Soranus, will you and Pulcher start in the triclinium – see what condition the shrine is in. If the statues are not too badly damaged, we'll ask Vortin if we can store them in the Temple until we build again. Hestigys, come with me."

Father and son began their tour of inspection. Hestig expressed his delight to see that at least the lion fountain, though cracked and blackened, was otherwise undamaged.

Above was a gaping hole where tiles from the courtyard roof had fallen in – or had been removed? Spreading out from there, wooden rafters were either missing completely or, if in position, were as black as if someone had painted them that colour, still smouldering, and unstable. As they looked, one crashed into the courtyard.

In the kitchen, the lead utensils had melted but otherwise the metal pots and pans were salvageable. The pottery workshop was least damaged but most of the stock was charred, cracked or broken.

Bedding was burnt and scorched and draperies had disappeared or were shredded and flapping in the heat still rising from the smoking remains. Hestigys touched the charred outline of a wooden table and it disintegrated and fell at his feet so that he had to jump back to avoid the hot, flying cinders. The acrid smell of smoke permeated the air they breathed and everything was covered with flakes of ash and soot, which were still falling.

Finally, Hestig noticed that the wooden trapdoor giving access to the hypocaust had been burnt away and the fire had also raged underneath the triclinium, though what had fed it was a mystery. That was one of the places in which he had hidden their savings. He searched when the area had cooled down, but no cache of money had escaped the flames and the family was seemingly penniless.

"Father," said Hestigys, "it surprises me that the fire seems to have started in several places at the same time."

"That surprises me too, son," Hestig replied.

It was then that they made their gruesome discovery. As they kicked aside smouldering debris in the courtyard, mostly fallen rafters, which lay criss-cross on top of each other, they found all that was left of the dog kennel and, near it, the charred remains of Skeel in the arms of an equally-burned body. To their surprise, another body lay not far away. Neither human being was recognisable, but they could guess both identities.

Pulcher was sent to request Kendrus to come to deal with the dead, while Soranus went up to the Temple to ask the favour of Vortin.

He returned with Vortin's permission to store the statues of Ashuba and Shubinata, closely followed by Brocchus, who made the excuse that he was there to accompany the statues as they were carried to the Temple. Hestig guessed that he had been instructed by Vortin to find out what was happening at the burnt-out house.

The eunuch expressed surprise at how many people had gathered to help with the clean-up operation. However, out of superstition or respect, none of them would step across the threshold until Kendrus had organised the removal of the bodies, Skeel's included.

Then Brocchus watched as everyone set to work with a will, before leaving with the statues, carefully placed in a cart pulled by the eunuchs.

After the workshop had been cleaned out, Hestig decided to use it as a storeroom for everything that could be salvaged, which included bricks and tiles for rebuilding.

Finally, rubble and rubbish were carted away and tipped into a pit dug for the purpose. Neighbours and friends came and went as they were able throughout the week, and by the end of that time the site had been cleared.

Only then did Hestig bring Trifena back to the house. As they stood in what had been the courtyard, she told him about the lesson Vitius had been giving the children on the occasion of her first visit to the Temple. He had asked them who was most powerful, the sun god Ashuba, lord of fire, or his wife Shubinata, goddess of water.

Now the fire god had raged and killed and the Stan water had not been sufficiently strong to quench it.

He gently kissed the tears from her eyes. "I promise you that we will build again," he told her.

Trifena looked up at him. "I know," she said.

"Now we have one last task." He smiled.

Hand-in-hand they walked across to the fountain and he thrust his arm down inside the gaping mouth of the lion. Trifena watched as he withdrew a small package, wrapped in cloth, and transferred it to the leather pouch fixed to his belt.

"Vortin hasn't won yet," he said, and together they left to walk back to Selena's house.

CHAPTER XLV (45)

June was drawing to a close. Vortin had spent a restless night, his expectations at fever pitch, impatient at the prospect of taking Bron. At dawn on the following day, Bron would be twelve years old and ritually a woman. She had become a woman physically several months ago and had offered blood from a newly slaughtered lamb during a rites-of-puberty service at Shubinata's altar.

Vortin seldom thought of Iraina these days, except to bless Ashuba for her absence.

Having turned from one side to the other and back again in an endeavour to sleep, he got up and gulped down a beaker of cold water, but still felt hot and flushed. Returning to bed, the sweat poured off him. *One more night alone and then the comfort of Bron in his arms, yielding her innocence and virginity to him. In his old age, she would give him back his youth and vitality.* The only slight relief he could give himself now was self-indulged.

On the morning of Midsummer's Eve, he fidgeted on his throne in front of the altar. His priests and priestesses were with him, as were representatives from the village, to witness any transactions taking place. They were waiting for any parents who came with bags of money to buy back their children.

Of those who had entered the Temple at the same time as Bron, two boys had died of the plague, one girl had been sold, and another was to start life upstairs. So no parents had arrived this year and none was expected.

Vortin stood, about to leave, when two figures appeared in the open doorway, silhouetted against the sunlight. Surprised, he sat down again and beckoned them forward.

His surprise increased when the couple materialised from the shadows and he saw that they were Hestig and Trifena. Vortin's complacency was suddenly overlaid with apprehension.

"Hestig, is that you?" he called. "What are you doing here?"

"We have a right to be here, Vortin, as parents of one of the Temple children," was Hestig's calm reply.

"Bron?" asked Vortin, stupidly, not believing what was happening.

"Of course, Bron," replied her father. "We have come to buy her back."

There was a stunned silence before Vortin challenged him, in a somewhat squeaky voice, "But you can't, you haven't any money."

Sharma interrupted, "We hear you are living on charity these days. How is life in Selena's house?" Hestig ignored him.

Vortin continued, "Everyone knows that all your savings were destroyed in the fire."

"Not quite all, Vortin," Hestig replied, "though that was obviously the arsonist's intention."

"Father?" All eyes turned towards the entrance again, where Bron stood, a tiny figure between the great pillars. Vortin saw Trifena make a move as if to go to her daughter but Hestig caught hold of her hand and she stayed where she was.

Slowly Bron approached, past the clusters of villagers, past her parents on her right and the priestesses to her left, stopping in front of him. She looked up at the High Priest, Ashuba towering behind and above him.

"Bron, my dear," he addressed her, his heart and loins churning. She didn't answer.

Vortin's deep-set eyes blackened.

"So what?" he asked, speaking to her parents but unable to take his eyes off Bron. "So what if you still have a little money to offer the Temple? It won't be enough – Bron is beyond price."

"We know that," replied Hestig, "and because she is beyond price, the gift we are offering Ashuba for her return is also beyond price."

Those who had come in from the settlement clustered forward, obviously anxious not to miss a word.

Out of the corner of his eye, Vortin saw a movement as Trifena stretched her hand out towards her husband, palm upwards, and unclasped her fingers. Lying there was a cloth package. Hestig took it from her and handed it to Selvid, who stood nearest to him. Selvid brought it across to Vortin.

The High Priest stared at the small parcel in Selvid's hands as if transfixed. "What is it?"

Trifena held her tongue no longer. Stepping forward she invited, with words falling over each other, "Unwrap it, Vortin, and see for yourself."

He was unable to move so Selvid carefully unwrapped the cloth.

"They are gathered from the sea," explained Trifena. "Amber stones, their hearts reflecting the sun, for our great god, Ashuba –"

"And pearls," interrupted Veneta, "– drops of the sea's night fluorescence – for the goddess, Shubinata."

There was a gasp from Bron and those watching as Selvid held the necklace up to the light. A sudden draught flared the candles around Ashuba's feet. The gems flashed and behind Vortin the god's red eyes gleamed.

"Where did that come from?" asked Bron in amazement.

Sharma seemed afraid that Vortin was going to refuse the necklace and said quickly, "It is priceless, indeed. Ashuba is pleased. Vortin, you must accept it. Vortin!"

The High Priest shook himself out of his stupor and said slowly, "I accept it, on behalf of the Temple." In the circumstances, he could do nothing else.

He took the necklace from Selvid and handed it to Sharma, and quick as a flash, Jeetuna stepped forward and took it out of Sharma's hand and again held it up for inspection.

"Then I am free?" asked Bron quietly.

Vortin nodded. "You are free," he confirmed, then suddenly seemed to wake up. "But not before this evening, and in the meantime, you will continue to serve here. Jeetuna, keep her occupied all day!"

Trifena asked if they could collect together Bron's belongings. Vortin's reply was sharp.

"She can do that herself. She's not a child any longer!"

Hestig reminded him firmly, "Officially, she is a child until dawn tomorrow morning, the time of her birth – you would do well to remember that."

Vortin felt as if he was going to have an apoplectic fit. Sharma was studying his face, which was growing redder by the second.

Veneta asked Hestig to leave. "There is nothing more to be done here. Come back this evening at the appointed time to take her home. I will make sure she is ready."

Hestig nodded, and with a smile to Bron, took Trifena by the hand and led her out of the Temple.

Vortin turned his fury on Bron. "Take her away, Jeetuna! I want her out of my sight! And keep her busy!" And with that he pushed his way through the villagers and stormed off.

The gathering dispersed, whispering together.

As soon as everyone had gone, Jeetuna clasped the necklace round her neck and stroked the gems. She was annoyed when Sharma unclasped it and took it off her.

"That, my dear Jeetuna, is for the neck of Ashuba and not yours! And not even you can charm it off *him*," he said and laid it on the altar.

"Sharma, who do you think will be High Priestess now?" she asked him.

"More to the point, my love – how soon, do you think, before *I* am High Priest?" he asked her.

She was mystified. "What do you mean? Vortin's still in office – he isn't going anywhere."

"We'll see," Sharma replied. "I have my own agenda to follow and I do believe it starts now. I am going to find Vortin – I think he needs my support," and after pinching her so hard on the buttocks that it hurt, he also left.

She suddenly remembered Bron, who was still standing there, and Vortin's orders. "Come along, girl, I've got to find some jobs for you to do."

Bron meekly followed her out.

The young women on the second floor had seen the developing incident through the window in the corridor and one of them had knocked at the door of Nobilianus' room to tell him to come and look. He was delighted that Bron was about to leave the Temple and amazed that the threat of a future spent with her had been removed so suddenly and easily.

As soon as the lower floor was empty, he ran down the spiral staircase and stood leaning up against a pillar in the portico. From there he could look down on Selena's house and was occasionally rewarded with a glimpse of Trifosa. She and Hestigys had been taken away from school because of the reversal in the family fortunes and he was desperate for a chance to talk to her.

Sometimes, Trifosa seemed to sense that she was being stared at and would look up. Then she would turn her back and go quickly inside the house. The knowledge that she was aware of his presence always delighted him.

Bron did not see Vortin for the rest of the day. Jeetuna kept her at work, then lost interest, and it was Veneta who said it was time for her to go upstairs and clear out her room.

The Temple was unusually quiet for Midsummer's Eve. For the second year in succession, without Iraina, the Midsummer ritual could not take place, so there were no preparations to be made.

Bron had noticed Sharma and Brocchus leaving together and guessed where they were going. Jeetuna was taking advantage of her free time and said she would accompany the women at the inn to the bathhouse. Selvid was engaged on Temple business and Veneta was with Africanus and the children in the schoolroom, occupying them until bedtime. She had promised to return at the time Hestig and Trifena were due to arrive to take Bron home.

Bron could hardly remember what it was like to live with her family. Looking back, much of her time spent growing up in the Temple had been happy, and the rituals and routine had become very familiar and comfortable.

She spread a blanket over her mattress and began to collect her possessions together. Among her clothes lay gifts she had been given over the years, such as a small hinged doll made of bone from Veneta and a wooden trinket box with tiny lock and key from her parents. She put to one side a silver bracelet Vortin had given her, deciding to leave it behind. She also bundled up her old spinning top and red leather ball, now flattened because of a hole in it, made years ago when Nobilianus laughingly punctured it with a metal hairpin because he knew it would upset her.

There were also mementos of her friends – a blue ribbon that had been Naila's; a little metal triangle which, when struck with a metal baton, now lost, gave Sorin the note from which to start her vocal exercises; and a braid for Bron's hair, which Edreda had made and shyly given when they first became friends.

A slight sound in the doorway caused her to turn, but before she could see who was standing there, a blanket was thrown over her head and she was fighting against arms that were closing tight round her, lifting her off her feet and carrying her down the spiral staircase.

CHAPTER XLVI (46)

Hestig and Trifena arrived back at the Temple in good time. Veneta met them at the entrance.

"She's bundling up all her belongings," the priestess told them, "though it's taking her rather a long time. I'll go up and see if she needs any help."

At the bottom of the spiral staircase she paused and turned. "I know Bron is very happy to be going home, but there are *some* things here she will miss."

"And some people – you especially," smiled Trifena.

"I like to think so," Veneta replied. "It will take her a little time to settle back into family life, especially as she won't be going to her real home."

"We understand," nodded Hestig.

"I'll miss her so much," said Veneta, and added, "You know I love her dearly."

"Yes," replied Trifena kindly, "but you'll still be able to see each other. We are so grateful to you for being her second mother all these years. We won't forget."

Veneta returned a few moments later. "She's not in her room," she said. "Her bundle's neatly tied up on her bed, but she's not there. Perhaps she's gone to see the children or the girls, though she's already said goodbye to them once this afternoon. I'll have a look in their rooms."

"I can't understand it," said the priestess when she again returned without Bron. "She knew you were coming for her."

Pulcher walked in at that moment, having completed an errand for Vortin. Veneta despatched him to look in the schoolroom, but he came back, shaking his head. Trifena's face showed that she was beginning to panic. She and Hestig left to scour the settlement while

Pulcher was sent up to the plague graves and Veneta went to search the temple in the wood and Iraina's cell. All drew a blank.

By now Selvid had returned and was told of Bron's disappearance. His eyes met Veneta's.

"I will go and find Vortin," he said and walked in the direction of the High Priest's office. Vortin came back with him.

"We must look everywhere," said Vortin, unusually helpful. "Veneta, you must allow a search of your rooms. You, too, Selvid. I have keys in my office to Sharma's suite and the rooms of the eunuchs."

The party split up to search the places Vortin had mentioned. Bron was still nowhere to be found.

"She must have run away," concluded Vortin. "It was obvious she didn't want to leave the Temple."

That was not obvious to anyone else.

"There is only one place we haven't searched," said Hestig slowly. "You said we must look everywhere, Vortin."

"So I did," he agreed. "What place have you in mind, Hestig?"

"Your private apartments."

The High Priest hesitated momentarily, then agreed and handed over his keys.

"You are welcome to look," he said. "In fact, we will all go over there."

The little group left the Temple by his private back door behind the altar and traversed the path to his house. Trifena was apprehensively clutching Veneta's hand. They searched, but there was no sign of Bron.

"It's as I said," repeated Vortin as he locked the front door, "she didn't want to leave and has run off. I'm sure she'll be back. Go home, Hestig. We'll let you know when she returns."

"There really is nothing more we can do," Hestig said to his wife. "She knows where we are, and Veneta will send us word if she comes back to the Temple. We might as well go home." Trifena nodded.

"I go, too," muttered Pulcher, following them.

Hestig looked closely at their friend. "Are you feeling all right, Pulcher?"

"It's my voices," explained the dwarf, quietly so that Trifena couldn't hear. "All say 'Bron in danger!' over and over again."

"Nothing more?" asked Hestig anxiously.

"They shout at me but I not understand them!" Pulcher replied, clearly in great distress. "I go home to listen."

Later in the evening, ignoring his own advice to wait at home, Hestig called for Veneta and Selvid and, together with Trifena and other friends, they began to search the pathways and back places in the gathering darkness, asking all those they met if anyone had seen Bron. No one had.

When Soranus came out to join the search, Veneta wondered why Hestigys had not joined them.

"He's at home with Trifosa," Trifena explained. "We've seen Nobilianus loitering about outside again."

Returning to the Temple, they found it unusually deserted, except for the eunuch on duty. He said that Sharma and Brocchus were not back from their errand, whatever it was, the children and other eunuchs had retired for the night, and Vortin presumably was at home.

Veneta suggested that she and Hestig should visit the bathhouse, as it was the only place they hadn't looked for Bron. Jeetuna was there. Hestig blushed furiously when he saw that she was naked in the water. She laughed and made no attempt to cover up. She also said she hadn't seen Bron since the afternoon.

"Let's go," said Veneta, conscious of his embarrassment.

"Aren't you coming in, Hestig?" teased one of the inn girls as he followed Veneta out.

"Dishy!" they heard another girl comment.

"Yes, he is rather," agreed Jeetuna.

It was also quiet in Vortin's house. He had returned after the search and tidied up, then prepared a meal from some of the Temple offerings, though he ate very little and threw most of it away. Then he lay on a couch and slept awhile to pass the time and refresh his strength.

When he woke, the oil lamps were burning low and one or two had sputtered out. He stood at his door and looked into the deepening gloom. No one was about, though there were lights and noise in the settlement where some of the people were obviously intent on following traditional Midsummer practices.

Midnight had passed. If Iraina were here, they would have been preparing the altar now with a layer of soft wool covered by a pure white linen cloth. But it was still not time.

He was surprised at how calm he was feeling, although he became more agitated as the hours passed. At last he decided that he had reached the end of his barely tenable self-control and it was time now for indulgence and fulfilment.

Was not he Vortin, High Priest of Ashuba, that great god's representative on earth and, as such, infallible in all he said and did? What he now planned was against Temple law, because Bron had been bought back by her parents, but he was determined that she should still be his High Priestess, and tomorrow he would change the law, if necessary – on Ashuba's instructions, of course. He only had to make sure that, when the ritual climaxed, it was daybreak and she had attained twelve years of age and womanhood.

He filled a pottery lamp with olive oil and blew out those that were still burning in the room. Taking the lamp with him, he drew back a corner of the richly woven carpet and bent to raise the trapdoor beneath it. Holding the lamp high so that he had light to see, he descended the wooden steps, closing the trap behind him. This small room was where he stored money and treasures stolen from the Temple by his father and latterly by himself.

In one corner, a wooden chest and boxes had been pushed aside to make room for a mattress. It was covered in a layer of soft wool, over which he had spread a pure white linen cloth. On the altar cloth lay Bron, hands tied behind her back, feet tied together, and a gag pulled tight round her mouth. At the sight of Vortin, her dark eyes opened wide with terror, but as he approached and she accepted her helplessness, they narrowed into a look of intense repugnance. By now, all logical reasoning had deserted him, and nothing could have changed his intention.

He put the lamp on the wooden chest and knelt beside her.

"There's no need to be afraid, little Bron, my darling," he said soothingly, stroking her dark curls. She moved her head away from his touch. "As Iraina was my daughter and my love, so will you be. She has betrayed me, but you will be with me forever, in this world and the next. You may not love me now, but you will, in time. Just give it time.

"I know I meant you for Nobilianus but he is only a boy and wouldn't know what to do with you. I know, and soon you will know, too. We just have to wait a little, until daybreak when you are twelve years old, so that the law is observed in that respect at least. They wanted to take you from me, your mother and father, and thought that a necklace of amber and pearls would trick me into giving you up – and it almost did – till I conceived this plan.

"Talking of conceiving, that is exactly what you and I will do, and we will have babies – all the babies Iraina could not give me. That will be fun, won't it, conceiving babies night after night? Just you and me, Bron, night after night."

She tried to scream but could only make unintelligible noises at the back of her throat, then she retched against the gag.

"Hush, hush!" Vortin said. "I'm going to untie your gag – but it's no use screaming because no one will hear you, and anyway I will cover your mouth with kisses. Then I will untie your hands, because you will want to use them, and your feet – that will be necessary – but I want you to lie quite still, at first anyway. I will show you what you have to do, how to welcome me inside you; I will show you, my darling little Bron. Then we shall pleasure each other, for always and always."

Lying on his bed at home, Pulcher covered both ears with his hands, shaking his head from side to side, his eyes screwed up tightly, trying to disentangle the cacophony of warnings his voices were repeating so insistently. Standing up, he staggered to the door and threw it open. A gentle breath of fresh warm air bathed his face. He took his hands away from his ears and ran up the slope, past the blackened ruin of the Roman house and on towards Selena's, to waken Hestig. He found him dozing in a chair, still fully dressed.

Vortin's excitement was mounting in spite of his intention to pace himself. As soon as he lay down and turned towards her, Bron began to fight him, arms and legs flailing, repulsing him with all the strength her horror gave her, but this only served to heighten his enjoyment and growing passion. What he had intended to be a controlled, sophisticated exploration of her young body, progressing through layer upon layer of pleasure, became a fighting entanglement of limbs and a roll around the mattress that would have been applauded by the lustiest of shepherds out in the fields.

While Bron was trying to defend herself so forcibly, Vortin was pulling off as much of her clothing as he could, and also his own. He finally succeeded, revealing his hot desire for her, and could contain himself no longer.

Meantime, Pulcher and Hestig had reached the Temple. No one else was there to help them, as Vortin had given the eunuch on duty a night off. Hestig led the way, running round to the back of the altar and out through Vortin's private door. Halfway along the path towards the High Priest's house, they heard such a scream of pain. It stopped them in their tracks.

"Bron!" shouted Pulcher, racing awkwardly towards the front door. As they reached it, the sun rose above Byden wood, washing the sky pink and streaking it with streamers of gold.

At that moment, Bron became twelve years old and a woman. In spite of all his planning, in his uncontrollable passion, Vortin had climaxed moments too soon.

Section IV

SORANUS

CHAPTER XLVII (47)

AD 397

Vortin's locked front door crashed open under the onslaught of two determined shoulders and Hestig and Pulcher fell into his living room. Hestig was making for the bedroom when Pulcher noticed the carpet pulled away from the trapdoor. Wrenching it open, he almost fell down the steps in his haste, with Hestig following.

In the lamplight, Bron lay crying on the mattress, bare below the waist and her tunic torn off her shoulders. Alarmed by the sound of the banging and crashing above, the High Priest was hurriedly disentangling himself from her and was shakily beginning to stand, his tunic falling in place to his feet, fear widening his eyes.

Having stumbled off-balance to the bottom of the steps, Hestig gripped the handrail to steady himself and stared in disbelief at what followed.

Pulcher had already reached Vortin in one bound, seemingly unperturbed by the difference in height between them. His left fist connected with the High Priest's crutch, and as Vortin doubled up, gasping open-mouthed in pain and clutching his groin with both hands, Pulcher pulled back his right arm.

Fascinated, Hestig watched the fury building in Pulcher until it overwhelmed his small body and exploded from his fist, already heavy because of its deformity, which was sent smashing into the side of Vortin's jaw. There was a loud crack. For a few seconds, no one moved.

Then Vortin's expression of pain and surprise faded as his black eyes rolled upwards in their sockets, and he sank to the floor. Pulcher licked his tingling right fist and rubbed it against his hip. Bron stopped crying and sat up and began to pull her clothes down to cover herself, then began crying again.

Hestig ran across to his daughter and would have wrapped her in the now-stained white cloth covering the mattress, but she shrank away from it, so he gathered her up in his arms as she was and made for the ladder.

Vortin was regaining consciousness and beginning to groan so Pulcher kicked him in the ribs and he was quiet again.

Hestig was grateful for the dwarf's support from below as he managed with difficulty to carry Bron to the top of the steps and through the still-open trap. They hurried to the front door, which was swinging on its hinges, and so to Selena's house.

The streets were empty, everyone having gone to bed after the night's activities.

Trifena had been awakened when Hestig and Pulcher left the house in such a hurry, and she was waiting for them. Her husband explained briefly and her face turned white.

"I know what has happened is devastating, but we'll need all our strength to help her deal with it," he whispered to her. "There will be time for our own grief later."

Trifena led Bron, stunned and silent now, into the back bedroom, once Selena's workroom, and woke her younger daughter. While Trifosa talked quietly to her sister, Trifena brought warm water, so she could gently wash away all physical signs of Vortin's intrusion, as well as oil to soothe her bruises.

Pulcher, who had offered to run across to Stalwyn to ask her to come straight away, hurried out.

Her ministrations completed, Trifena reappeared and, while they waited for Stalwyn to arrive, she put her arms round Hestig's waist and leant her head on his chest.

"The harm he's done to Bron's mind will probably never heal," she said wearily. "At this moment, my hate for Vortin is all-consuming."

Hestig wished he had been a better father, wished he had insisted on searching Vortin's house more thoroughly, wished above all he could take all this pain away from his family.

Stalwyn arrived grim-faced, having heard Pulcher's account, and followed Trifena into the bedroom.

Hestig, his son and Pulcher then held a council of war, seated round the cold hearth.

"What can I say to you, dear friend?" Hestig asked Pulcher. "You were magnificent! I shall never forget the look on Vortin's face when you hit him – not once, but twice!"

The men would have laughed aloud if it had not been for the plight of Bron in the next room.

"No need to thank, Hestig. I give my life for Bron, and you all," Pulcher said. "Never been so happy."

"We've got to decide what to do now," said Hestig. "It may become a matter of life and death if we're not careful. Vortin won't forget this night."

"Vortin not say what happened – against Temple law," Pulcher reminded them.

"Yes, what he did to Bron was against Temple law on two counts, but that won't stop him trying to get his own back on us."

"Surely, Father, you're going to let everyone know what happened?" exclaimed Hestigys.

"It's tempting, but the implications need thinking about," Hestig replied. "How will Bron feel if everyone knows? No, we must act tactically, not emotionally, but I'll have that evil old man if it's the last thing I do!"

Next day was traditionally children's day at the Temple, when the three-year-olds were presented to Ashuba. There was an unprecedented number this year because of all the babies who had been born and allowed to live after the plague. Sharma announced to the assembled families that Vortin was unable to officiate because he was confined to his bed – unfortunately, he had fallen down the Temple steps on the previous evening and had broken his jaw.

As Sharma presided over the ritual, he wondered what had really happened to Vortin. On the previous day, after accepting the necklace in payment for Bron, the High Priest had stormed off to his office, where Sharma found him minutes later, pacing up and down in frustration and anger.

Sharma had sympathised with Vortin's "natural feelings for this beautiful young girl about to become a woman," and had complimented the High Priest on his great self-control, which he said he would have found impossible to exercise himself. He said that these young virgins knew only too well the power they wielded over older men, and used their subtle allure and non-verbal enticements to entrap even the most highly principled, as Vortin was.

"So what is a paltry piece of jewellery against the loss you're suffering, Vortin?" he asked. "What compensation is that? Taking Bron would be a diadem, not merely a necklace. Bron has been gasping for it ever since becoming a woman physically, and deserves all she gets."

That was a blatant lie, but in his feverish state of mind, Vortin was nodding in agreement, obviously appreciative of his priest's understanding and support. He thanked Sharma for his clear thinking.

Sharma left him almost a nervous wreck, in a weakened state of indecision. Surely, Vortin could not hold out much longer, and would take some precipitous action in contravention of Temple law, which would compromise his position, if not actually destroy him as High Priest.

When Bron disappeared, he thought that his plan was beginning to work, but now everyone had been told that she had unexpectedly turned up at Selena's, having run away then thought better of it. So Sharma continued to wonder what had really happened to Vortin last night.

If the High Priest could be got out of the way, the only person left standing between himself and the high office he coveted was Nobilianus.

The children were now standing before him in a long line and were approaching, one at a time, for the laying-on of his hands on their young heads. As he mechanically intoned the words of dedication, without thought or expression, he looked around for Nobilianus.

It was not long before he saw him wandering about, his eyes darting this way and that, probably searching for Trifosa. However, for the first time in nine years, Hestig's family appeared not to be present.

Sharma guessed that Nobilianus would be elated to be free of Bron, and also free of his father for the time it took his jaw to mend. He would probably take advantage and spend even more time amusing himself with the Temple girls. At first they had seemed to enjoy introducing him to the pleasures of the second floor, but as Nobilianus grew older, Sharma became aware of other words creeping into their conversation when they were discussing the boy – at first only "insatiable", but later "weird" and finally "pervert".

Hearing the whispers, Vortin had questioned Nobilianus in Sharma's presence, and did no more than shrug his shoulders, but from then on had withheld his priestesses from his son.

Trifena watched her daughter's physical injuries heal gradually, but not so her mental state. Bron was sharing a bed with Trifosa, but night after night Trifena had to sit up with her, trying to coax her to sleep, and on many occasions her sister had to calm her when she awoke screaming from a nightmare. This continued for several weeks, during which time Bron would not venture out of doors.

Hestigys, who slept in a curtained-off section of the same room, said he found it less stressful sleeping at Pulcher's house, and finally went to live there. Pulcher told Trifena that he was glad of the company.

Soranus called often, wanting to spend time with Bron now that she was home, and walked away with head bent when he was not allowed to do so. Trifena asked his mother and grandmother to reassure him that the fault was not his, but begged them to say nothing more, so Soranus continued calling, looking mystified and upset.

Selena reported to Trifena and Hestig that Vortin had appeared in the Temple again after about a week, his jaw fixed in place with bandages. He was unable to speak and directed his staff with sign language.

Shortly after this, whispers circulated that a craftsman from Calleva had arrived at the inn and had told the innkeeper to submit all his board and lodging bills to the Temple. The same afternoon, the man had accompanied Vortin to an open plot of land beside the Temple, and had begun his work.

Trifena and Hestig joined the gathering crowd to watch. Eunuchs were dragging long strips of willow to the site and the craftsman was bending and weaving them. It gradually became obvious what was being constructed and, as soon as the people realised, in silence and fear they returned to their homes.

"Is this Vortin's revenge?" Trifena asked her husband.

"I'm afraid so," he replied.

For three days the craftsman applied himself to his work. He began with the legs, set apart, then worked on the torso and outstretched arms. Throughout the body were platforms, one above the other, none leaving sufficient headroom for a man to stand upright. A ladder ran up each side of the figure, and gates at various levels gave access to the platforms. Crowning all was the head, created with a closer weave, with wide grinning mouth and holes for nostrils and eyes. If a fire was set, as it ate its way up towards the head, smoke then flames would escape through these holes, lighting up the face in a horrific grin.

The grotesque figure towered above the settlement. It was a fearsome sight and people averted their eyes whenever they passed. They discussed among themselves why the god had been constructed or who was being targeted.

Trifena and Hestig heard the whispers. They understood Vortin's message only too clearly. The wickerwork god was a threat to silence them. Vortin had already imprisoned Hestig twice and burnt down his house and ruined his business. There was no doubt that he had power to do whatever he wanted, and for the moment caution was the best option.

However, Hestig told Trifena that one day he would make Vortin pay for what he had done to Bron and the family.

CHAPTER XLVIII (48)

Several weeks later, Trifena persuaded her daughter to venture out and visit the bathhouse. Bron had been obsessed with washing herself, and her mother hoped that a prolonged session in hot water and steam would make her feel cleansed in body and, more importantly, in mind.

She invited Selena to accompany them and chose a day when the people were at the Temple for a minor religious festival. In the shadow of the wickerwork god, the settlement was punctilious in following every religious observance.

The family and their closest friends did not feel the necessity for attending every Temple service. They recognised that, as long as they kept their mouths shut about what had happened to Bron, this was all that was required of them. In any case, she would not go anywhere near the Temple and sobbed bitterly whenever the word was mentioned.

Trifena and both her daughters were enjoying the unusually quiet and relaxed morning. They luxuriated in the soothing water, allowing the heat to reach deep, so opening pores and releasing all impurities, which the attendants could then scrape away with strigils.

On the turquoise-painted walls above them, exotic fish, mermaids and other strange sea creatures swam round scallop shells or stretched long wavy legs towards the bathers.

The heat was making Selena feel somewhat dizzy. She was also complaining of a headache and distorted vision, so climbed out of the water and sat on the side of the bath.

No one had said a word for several minutes when Bron mentioned to her mother that the hot water was making her breasts hurt. Trifena and Selena exchanged alarmed glances.

"Oh, no!" prayed Trifena, under her breath. She gathered Bron into her arms and kissed her cheek.

As they were getting dressed after their cold plunge, Trifena unobtrusively studied her daughter's small, developing breasts and then her waistline. She was sure it was thickening.

"I hope I'm imagining things," she worried to Selena, "but she has missed a period."

"You can't be absolutely sure yet," Selena comforted her.

But Trifena was sure as soon as Bron started being sick in the mornings. Bron understood too and there was fear in her eyes.

Trifena decided there was only one escape route and that was the one Umbella offered. She had not seen the old woman since their meeting in the wood twelve years ago, when she and Hestig arrived in Byden, though she had often heard talk of her among the women in the settlement.

She now consulted her husband and they agreed that, for Bron's sake, Trifena would have to approach Umbella and plead for her help. She squirmed with humiliation as she realised that they would not be 'standing so proud' now, as the old woman had foretold. She had never spoken to anyone about the hag's fearful pronouncement – "sword, fire and total destruction". "Nonsense," Hestig had called it, but if she was right about one prophecy, why not about both?

Vortin had revoked his order forbidding abortion and infanticide, made three years earlier after the ravages of the plague. At Trifena's request, Selena asked her daughter-in-law, Campania, to call on Jeetuna at the Temple late one evening to ask a favour.

"Jeetuna jumped to the conclusion that Soranus had got some girl into trouble!" Campania reported to Trifena later. "As if my son would do such a thing at his age! She said she wasn't surprised, as he is a good-looking lad. As a matter of fact, she found it all very funny. She wanted to know the girl's name."

"What did you tell her?" asked Trifena.

"I told her I'd rather not say. I've committed the directions to memory."

Early in the morning several days later, Trifena and Selena, with Bron, left the village unobserved, crossed the stepping-stones, and made for the not-far-distant southern wood.

It was August and already hot, but cool among the trees. Flowers tickled their toes. Whenever the wood opened into a clearing, blackberries were ripening on bushes and dog roses blossomed in delicate shades of pink and white where later there would be rose hips to collect.

Hearing a noise in the undergrowth, they stopped and watched a small deer run from the trees and pound along the path in front of them before turning at right angles to seek safety again in the cover.

They walked until the sun was high overhead. The path split and they continued to the left for five minutes before finding what they were looking for – a very small round hut in the shadow of the trees. It was built entirely of stripped interwoven branches covered with mud and flints.

Outside, an iron cauldron was hanging by chains from a tall triangular framework of crossed branches, above a burning fire. A goat was tied to a tree by a woven grass rope, which it was munching. Rooting about nearby was a pig, and chickens ran in all directions as the party approached. Obviously business was lucrative.

Umbella appeared in the doorway. She looked as Trifena remembered her, enveloped in layers of black so that only her head and none-too-clean hands were visible. Her face was as brown and wrinkled as ploughed earth and her hair was scraped back off her forehead and fastened in a bun at the nape of her neck, from which long, straggly grey strands were escaping.

"So we meet again, Umbella," whispered Trifena, "as you said we would."

The hag chuckled and Trifena felt as icy cold as if she had just plunged into the frigidarium.

"I saw it then and I see it now." She looked at Bron. "Her stars were set in motion on the day you walked into Byden. You laughed at old Umbella then, but I see you are not laughing now. So it continues, and so it will continue until all is fulfilled, as I told you."

Trifena's instinct was to gather Bron into her embrace and run as far from this place as she could reach, but she controlled the impulse and instead put her arm around Bron's shoulders. Her daughter was shaking, and they had to wait while she was sick again, bringing up only bile.

Pushing open a wovenwork door, the woman beckoned Bron through. Trifena went with her. Selena said she would wait outside but would come in if she were needed. The old woman lifted the cauldron from the fire and followed them.

It was dark inside the hovel and for a few moments the visitors could see nothing. Bron clung to her mother. Umbella lit three oil lamps and placed one on a wooden stool and one on each side of a pile of rags. The lights disturbed the cockroaches, which clattered away into dark corners.

She fetched a bucket then indicated that Bron should lie on the rags. Trifena had brought a cloak with her and hurriedly spread it on top of the pile. Bron lay down.

Umbella held out a hand for payment. Trifena produced a package of pots and dishes made by Hestig, which seemed to please the woman, who nodded. Trifena laid them on a small, bare wooden table.

Then Umbella knelt at Bron's feet and indicated to Trifena that she should also kneel and hold the third lamp high for additional light.

"Is it going to hurt much?" Bron asked in a whisper.

"Maybe, maybe not," was the unsympathetic reply.

"You know it's the only way, if you want rid of this baby," Trifena told her daughter, gently caressing her face.

As Bron clasped her mother's hand, Trifena felt the back of her neck crawling, and turning her head, found Umbella regarding them malevolently.

"You know whose baby this is?" Trifena felt foolish asking the question.

"Of course I know whose whelp it is."

"He doesn't know."

"He won't learn it from my lips, if that's what's worrying you. Wouldn't have any business left if I went round pointing a finger at the fathers. Anyway, many of them pay me to keep my mouth shut."

"And this father?"

"This father is different. Too many complications."

The old woman set about her preparations. "Can you do it?" Trifena whispered.

The reply was the same: "Maybe, maybe not."

"But we are paying you well."

"You are paying me to *try*," retorted the old woman.

She was about to examine Bron when Trifena pleaded with her to wash her hands. Umbella shook her head.

"We have more fine kitchenware to give you if you will wash your hands," cajoled Trifena. At her own wise suggestion, Selena had brought another small parcel in case a bribe were needed.

Umbella stood up, grumbling to herself, and poured some water from the cauldron into the bucket and rubbed her hands together.

Trifena looked round in vain for a dry cloth. "Dry them on the cloak," she suggested.

Bron tensed against the internal examination and gripped her mother's hand, but said nothing.

Umbella produced a large metal pump. Trifena flinched and turned her eyes to her daughter's face and began to talk about many things, she hardly knew what – anything to take Bron's mind off what was happening to her.

The pump was inserted roughly but expertly into Bron's vagina and the handle pushed forward, sending a thick solution into the girl's body. Bron screamed. Trifena dropped the lamp and began wiping the perspiration from her daughter's forehead with the end of one of the pieces of rag.

"Light! I need more light!" ordered the old woman crossly.

Selena appeared in the doorway, alarmed by the scream. It obviously took a few moments for her eyes to adjust to the darkness, then she understood the situation, picked up the lamp and held it high.

Bron was whimpering now, complaining of a stinging sensation internally, and clutching her stomach. The pump was just as roughly withdrawn.

"Sit her on the bucket!" came the order. Trifena helped Bron struggle to her knees and perch on the bucket. Fluid and blood were streaming from her.

"Good!" said the hag. "Take her outside. Get her to walk about. Then she can rest on the grass until you're ready to leave. It will all be expelled eventually. If it isn't, come back."

"No, not again!" Bron cried out.

Umbella shrugged. "Please yourself. It won't change anything."

"Sword, fire and total destruction?" Trifena asked in a voice that had no life in it.

"Exactly so," confirmed Umbella, and laughed. "Don't forget the extra payment!"

Selena left the package on the table, bundled up the soiled and dripping cloak, took hold of the bucket handle and followed Bron and her mother outside. Together they helped the child down on to a patch of grass. She was terrified, crying and in great pain. Agonising for her young daughter, how Trifena hated Vortin at that moment!

Although there was a lot of blood with clots, there was no sign of the foetus. Using a ladle to scoop water from the cauldron, which had been hung over the fire again, Trifena and Selena cleaned Bron up as best they could.

They heard the old woman clattering about inside and behind the hut, but she didn't appear again.

"Bron could be dead for all she cares," Trifena whispered to Selena.

Then for a long time her daughter lay quietly.

"Trifena," asked Selena, "what was all that about a prophecy?"

"I should have told you before," Trifena whispered, "but I was afraid what people would say." She then related all that had happened when she and Hestig met Umbella in the wood on the day they arrived in the settlement.

Bron interrupted them. "I'm so thirsty," she said. She was sweating profusely.

Trifena removed the cauldron. The water was too hot so Selena hunted round for lengths of rounded bark and a few broad leaves and managed to pour and cool sufficient water for Bron to drink.

"She can't manage that long walk home like this," Trifena worried. "We need help."

Selena offered to go back to the settlement to alert Hestig, but Trifena said she would be quicker, and set off at a good pace.

The day wore on. The weather was idyllic. Bron lay with Selena beside her, hearing the busyness of the insects in the flowers round their ears and the chattering of the birds in the trees above.

Exhausted, for a while she dozed, but the pain woke her up. By now, the sun was well over towards the west. She said she thought she was ready to start the long walk back.

Selena again emptied the contents of the bucket, rinsed it out and left it tipped upside down on the grass, then they set out, but they had not gone very far before the bleeding started again. Bron's legs crumpled under her and she lay down on her side with her knees up to her chin to relieve the severe pain in her stomach. There was still no sign of the foetus.

It was dusk before they heard noises through the trees and Hestig appeared, accompanied by his son and Pulcher, carrying a litter between them. They looked appalled at the sight of Bron, white-faced, shivering and covered in blood.

"You'll be all right now, Bron," her father soothed her. "Stalwyn will be waiting to help you when we get home."

Hestig and Selena helped her on to the litter, spread over her the covers that Trifena had sent, and together the rescue party began the difficult journey back to the settlement.

CHAPTER XLIX (49)

One of Bron's duties at the Temple had been to lay out Vortin's vestments for his daily services. He had insisted that no one except Bron should do this for him. Now she had left, he had to rely on Jeetuna, but she was never able to please him.

He was aware that she had never studied which stole or cope he liked to wear on which days and, as he had so many, she sometimes made a mistake. Neither did she always know which colour girdle to choose, or how tight or loose to tie the knots, or which rings were suitable for which vestments. Bron never got it wrong, because if she did, Vortin would convince himself that her choice was best, after all.

While his jaw was healing and it was painful to talk, he tolerated the mismanagement, but as soon as he was able to speak more freely, he began to berate Jeetuna for her failings, comparing her unfavourably with Bron's perceived perfection.

During one of these tirades, Jeetuna snapped back at him. She clamped her mouth shut immediately and did not finish the sentence. Normally, challenging Vortin was unforgivable and harshly punished, but the comment she made so wrong-footed him that he was not conscious of her misjudgement.

"What did you say?" he asked, stunned. "My precious Bron, what?"

Jeetuna gulped. "It's nothing, I should not have said it. I beg Vortin's pardon."

He swore at her. "Repeat what you said!"

"I said," began Jeetuna slowly, "that Bron is not as perfect as you think and that the moment your back was turned, she gave up her virginity to one of the boys in the settlement." As he did not reply, she warmed to her subject. "He *is* a boy, too, only fourteen years old." She paused. Vortin sensed that there was more to come.

"What else?" he asked.

"She tried to have an abortion – but it didn't work."

"How far gone is she?" asked Vortin, hoping that the tremor in his voice would not betray his secret to Jeetuna.

"From what Umbella said, it must have happened almost on the night she left the Temple, or very soon afterwards."

Vortin dismissed the priestess and, as soon as he was alone, punched the air with his fist.

"I'll have her back yet!" he yelled to no one in particular.

That evening, the house below the Temple steps received a cloaked and hooded visitor.

"I've been expecting this meeting," Trifena whispered to her husband, "it was unavoidable. You'll have to let him in."

Bron flew into the workroom and shut the door with a bang. Trifena stood stolidly in front of it, shielding it with her body as the High Priest entered.

Vortin was invited to sit down and came straight to the point. "I hear that Bron's pregnant," he said.

Her parents were silent so he continued, "Is it my baby?"

There seemed to be no point in lying, and Trifena reasoned that the truth might prove of some advantage to Bron.

"Who else's?" she asked. "My daughter is not a slut!"

"Yes!" he hissed, obviously with great satisfaction.

Trifena could see that Hestig's hands were quivering and knew they longed to be round Vortin's neck.

"I further understand," continued the High Priest evenly, "that she tried to abort our baby."

Trifena said nothing but again thought that Bron and her baby (she balked at referring to her first grandchild as 'their' baby) could gain protection from Vortin, as he seemed pleased, if not positively delighted, at the prospect of being a father again.

"Right," he said, taking control of the situation, "there is to be no further nonsense about abortions. Bron will have this baby and you will make sure she does so. For my part, I will make sure she has the best of everything during her pregnancy and labour, and afterwards as necessary."

"We want none of your help!" blurted out Hestig. "We are quite capable of looking after Bron ourselves!"

Vortin turned to face him. With apprehension, Trifena saw their eyes lock in combat.

"You will do as I say," said Vortin, "exactly as I say. If you do, no further harm will come to your family or your business, but if you do not, there is a wickerwork god up on the hill who is very hungry…" He left the sentence unfinished.

"And when the baby is born?" asked Trifena.

"You know what to expect," replied Vortin. "At three years old, he or she will be brought to the Temple, as Bron was, and this time there will be no buying back because the baby is my own flesh and blood. Bron will sit at my side as mother of my child and my High Priestess, which is where she should be. So, after all, I have only to wait another three years and all my patience will have been rewarded."

Trifena hoped that her daughter, on the other side of the door, could not hear what was being said, but clearly she had heard every word. The door was wrenched open and Bron pushed past her mother and stood before Vortin, eyes blazing, chest heaving.

She shrieked at him, "No, I will not!"

"Yes, you will, Bron," he said evenly, "or your family will suffer."

He looked her up and down.

"Goodness, Bron, pregnancy suits you. You're looking more beautiful than ever."

He turned to leave, then turned back as if with an afterthought. "By the way," he said, "no one is to know that this baby is mine –" he smiled at Bron with relish and corrected himself, " – ours." He looked at Trifena. "Who knows?"

She listed the names. "I have made a mental note of that list," he said, "and no one else is to be told. To save any questions, you will marry her off as soon as possible."

"Marry?" repeated Bron in disbelief.

"Who to?" questioned Trifena.

"Anyone," said Vortin. "How about this fourteen-year-old boy Jeetuna presumes is the father?"

"Soranus?" asked Trifena.

"Yes, he'll do," replied the High Priest and walked out, leaving behind him a stunned silence.

In spite of Bron's tearful objections, Trifena and Hestig could see no other way but to obey Vortin.

"You'll be safe with Soranus – he'll look after you and the baby, Bron," encouraged Trifena yet again.

"But I don't love him," wailed Bron, wondering how many times she had to repeat it, "and we're not ready to get married. And what happens in three years' time? Do I just say, 'Thank you very much, goodbye, I'm off to the Temple'?"

"A lot can happen in three years," said her mother.

"I hope the baby dies!" Bron blurted out.

"It had better not," said Hestig grimly. "Vortin would never believe it was through natural causes."

Although Bron would not relent, her parents decided to ask Campania and Soranus to visit one evening. Trifena also invited Selena.

After they had arrived and had been served with refreshments, and were waiting expectantly for an explanation, with many apologies and great embarrassment, Hestig explained the reason for the meeting.

"For Bron's safety, she's got to marry," said Hestig, "and if not to you, Soranus, we'll have to find someone else. How about that young friend of yours?" He was referring to the lad who had attacked Nobilianus in the wood at the May Day festival the previous year. "Whoever it is will want for nothing, Vortin will see to that."

The adults nervously left the young couple to talk it over on their own.

Soranus had not been allowed to see Bron in the two months since she left the Temple. Mystified at being asked to accompany his mother that evening, he had nevertheless been looking forward with great pleasure to meeting the girl he idolised, however immaturely. Now he sat dumbfounded. She was no longer pure. She had been violated – and by Vortin! He wasn't sure what he was feeling now, but he did know that he didn't want to get married yet.

As he voiced his doubts, Bron began to cry.

"Please don't cry, Bron. I do love you, you know it well, but Vortin's baby – I don't think I could stomach that!"

There was a pause while they stared at each other, then both broke into uncontrollable giggles at his unconscious play on words.

Bron told him briefly what had happened on the night she left the Temple and about the attempted abortion. These forces of passion and violence were beyond his comprehension and experience and he didn't know how to deal with them. He looked at Bron and realised that *she* was having to deal with them and would continue to do so, whatever his decision.

"I'm not ready for marriage," he repeated. "But I love you, Bron – I always have. If we married, do you think that in time you would grow to love me?"

He asked her so plaintively that she took his hand. "I'm not in love with anyone else," she said brightly.

Soranus was still worried. "But the baby –?"

Bron had obviously been thinking about the answer to that question. "I won't love it. I couldn't! Every time I looked at it, it would remind me of its father. In three years' time Vortin can have it, as far as I'm concerned, but he won't have me! I'll kill myself first!"

"Don't say that, Bron, I couldn't bear that," said Soranus. "We'll think of something." He hesitated. "If we did get married, I wouldn't touch you, not in that way, until the baby was born and your body was clean of Vortin. Do you understand what I'm saying?"

"Yes," she said.

The wedding was arranged for three weeks later, after Samhain, the harvest festival. Bron was adamant that she would not get married in the Temple, and Shubinata's temple in the wood was out of the question, as men were not allowed inside. It was Selena who suggested the courtyard of their ruined home, at the stone lion, and this was acceptable to everyone.

Selvid was asked if he would conduct a short ceremony, but when Vortin heard about it, he insisted on presiding himself. There was nothing the family could do to prevent it. Bron began threatening that she would not attend.

CHAPTER L (50)

Hestig had remained leader of the village council. It was the councillors' ongoing responsibility to attract new families into the mean houses, some of them little more than hovels, left empty by the plague. As well as advertisements in the settlement for the benefit of visiting traders and customers, notices had also been displayed in Calleva.

It was no surprise, therefore, when a Roman arrived at the inn, having come to look round the settlement. He asked to see Hestig and a meeting was arranged in the council chamber above the covered market.

Julius Gaius was a man of about the same age as Hestig, in his late thirties, recently appointed a decurion of the ordo, the governing council in Calleva. This was a civil service position of some standing in the Roman community. He had left his family in Eboracum while he came south to settle into his town house and inspect possible houses and building plots for a home in the country.

As the two men strolled round the settlement, Hestig took an immediate liking to his visitor, and later at the inn they chatted about life in general over glasses of wine followed by mugs of beer. As their tongues loosened, Hestig found himself telling Julius about the life he and Trifena had enjoyed in Eboracum and their move south, Vortin's obsession with Bron, and the fire and destruction of his house and pottery business. The most pressing problem at the moment was Vortin's insistence on conducting the marriage ceremony and Bron's threat to stay away.

Julius said he understood. He also had a daughter, a year younger than Bron, and as a father he knew how he would feel if Flavia were in the same predicament.

They talked earnestly, late into the night. Julius finally stood up to go to his bed, as he intended leaving early next morning, though he said he would probably have a pounding headache. When he reached Eboracum, he would make immediate arrangements for his wife, Lucilla, and daughter to move to Calleva. He had also agreed to run a confidential errand for Hestig.

Soranus visited Bron every day. Sometimes they heard young people of their own age running past the house on their way to and from their games and amusements, and he would turn his head in the direction of their laughter with such a wistful expression on his face.

"Soranus, there is still time to change your mind," Bron said one day. "You don't have to go through with it if you don't want to."

"And see you married off to someone else?" he asked. "I'm not going to let that happen! I just wish that we were a few years older."

He finally persuaded her to walk alone in the wood with him, as he had wanted to do in the days when they were carefree, which now seemed to him such a long time ago. When he forgot about her experience and the baby she was carrying, he teased her and they laughed as in the old days, but at other times he looked at her with wonderment and remained silent.

Pulcher stopped going to the house. In fact, he had not attempted to see Bron since her father told him about the engagement. First Hestig called on him, then Trifena, trying to persuade him to visit, but still he would not. Finally, Soranus called on him, and next day Pulcher went to see Bron.

She sat holding his hand.

"Soranus kind," said Pulcher simply. "He said: *You*, Bron, without *me* – half a person." He looked into her eyes, the darkest eyes he had ever seen, almost black, and sighed. "Bron, *me* without *you* – nothing."

Her eyes filled with tears. "You will always be my very best friend, Pulcher," she told him. "Marrying Soranus won't make any difference."

Pulcher knew that it would, perhaps not to her, but certainly to him. His was an impossible love, except that it was possible because his large heart was consumed by it, but he had long ago accepted that she would never be his and only his. He had guessed that her marriage to Soranus was on the horizon, but was unprepared for it to happen so soon.

Of course, it was all Vortin's doing. Seeing Bron tossing about on that litter, covered in blood, alternately crying and moaning with pain, had driven him to the point of storming up to the Temple for another attack on the High Priest, and this time he knew he would have killed him. It was Hestig who, guessing what was in their friend's mind, restrained him and said that nothing could change what had happened, but perhaps one day in the future...

Trifena and Bron could not decide what she should wear for her wedding, until Selena offered to make her a bridal tunic. Trifosa wanted to help in some way and said she would collect flowers for her sister to carry.

Campania relinquished her own iron wedding ring to Soranus so that he could give it to Bron. As it was too large for her finger, Bron decided to wear it on a cord round her neck. Trifena took a silver wire ring from her right hand and gave it to Bron to give to Soranus. It had belonged to her mother.

Trifena decided there was not enough money for anything more than a modest marriage celebration and Campania offered the use of her house for the reception. When well-wishers wanted to bring gifts, Trifena advised Bron to ask for items she needed for the baby.

It had been agreed that the young couple would live with Campania for the time being.

A week before the wedding, a eunuch from the Temple arrived at the door of the weaver's house, asking for Bron, and gave her a pouch made from tanned salmon skin. He said it contained a wedding gift from Vortin. Bron wanted nothing to do with it and dropped it into her mother's lap. Then she went into the workroom and shut the door behind her. A few minutes later she heard her mother gasp.

"Bron, you had better come out and have a look at this," Trifena called through the door.

When her daughter emerged, Trifena took hold of her hand and placed on its palm the amber and pearl necklace. "Vortin has returned it," she said. "It's yours, now."

"I don't want it, you keep it!" Bron exclaimed.

When Hestig came home from his stall in the market place, Trifena showed him the necklace. He grunted.

"You know what this means," he said to his wife.

"No, what?" asked Trifena.

"He's bought her back."

Trifena placed the necklace in its salmon-skin pouch safely under their mattress, though she thought that no one would dare steal it because of its recent history, which had been gossiped about throughout the settlement.

Next day the eunuch arrived again. This time he brought the silver bracelet Vortin had given Bron and which she had decided to leave behind when she left the Temple. This joined the necklace under the mattress.

The eunuch arrived every day that week with a gift – a glass phial of frankincense, a pair of gold brooches linked by an intricately stranded gold chain, hooped earrings of copper alloy with three different sets of multi-coloured glass pendants, and on the day before the ceremony, a gift for Soranus – a leather pouch of gold coins, sufficient to buy a small house.

When Trifena showed them to Soranus, he was speechless for a few seconds, then stammered that he had never seen so much money in his life. Bron was choking with anger at Vortin's bribes. The pouch joined the other gifts under the mattress.

The eunuch arrived early on the day appointed for the marriage, as the family assembled for breakfast, bringing a sealed letter for Bron. Trifena offered it to her daughter but Bron shook her head.

"I'll not touch anything he has handled!" she stated adamantly.

Hestig asked Trifena to read the letter aloud. It was written on parchment and said: "Darling Bron, I have already given you my wedding day gift, the most precious I possess, so that now our baby grows inside you. Stay well." Ominously it was signed "Forever, V."

The family was silent. Then Bron snatched it from her mother's hand, tore it in pieces and threw it into the cold hearth.

"Will I never be free of that man?" she stormed. "I won't get married if he's coming! I won't! I won't!"

"Hush, dear, it's not good for the baby for you to get so upset," Trifena soothed, unable to help her daughter except to calm her down.

"Can I go and pick the flowers now?" asked Trifosa.

Her mother put her finger to her lips to quieten her youngest child, but nodded behind Bron's back and Trifosa sidled out. She came back immediately to announce that there was a strange man asking for her father, then disappeared again.

Hestig sent a knowing look across to his wife, then went outside. The family could hear the murmur of low voices.

When he returned shortly afterwards, he put his arm round Trifena's waist and kissed her on the cheek.

"It's arranged," he told her and went across to Bron and asked her to sit down.

"Bron, do you remember about three weeks ago I met Julius Gaius, who wants to bring his family from Eboracum and move into the settlement?"

"Yes," she said.

"We had a long talk the night before he left," continued her father. "He has a daughter, Flavia, just a year younger than you, and he was very understanding and sympathetic towards our problems. I begged a big favour of him, which he promised to carry out, and he has been true to his word. The man who just called is a Roman priest who has agreed to marry you today in the Roman temple."

Bron stared at Hestig in disbelief. "Is this true, Mother?" she asked Trifena.

"Of course it's true, if your father says so," Trifena replied.

Bron, who was very emotional these days, burst into tears. Her brother put his arm round her shoulders. Trifena knew that Hestigys had been longing to help his sister but was out of his depth and unable to offer her anything except his support.

Hestig went back to his wife and smiled at her. "Adrianus Maximus arranged it," he said.

"I thought he would," replied Trifena, looking up at her husband. "It's all right, isn't it, Hestig?"

"Yes," he said, "it's fine."

Then he turned to his son. "Hestigys, will you let young Soranus know about the change of venue, and tell Pulcher. Then perhaps you and Pulcher will let everyone else know, so that no one is waiting at the stone lion when they should be at the Roman temple."

"Yes, of course," said Hestigys, seemingly glad to be able to do something useful.

As he left the house, he passed Selena on the way in, carefully carrying the new bridal tunic. She was delighted at the news.

"Right, Bron," she said, "it's time to get you dressed," and she ushered her into the workroom.

Before following, Trifena retrieved from the cold ashes the note from Vortin and carefully placed the pieces under the mattress with the rest of his gifts.

It may be of use, one day, she thought.

Selena and she helped her daughter into the new bridal tunic. The shade of aquamarine contrasted dramatically with Bron's dark curls and dark eyes.

"It's beautiful," Bron enthused.

"And you're beautiful, my dear," replied Selena, wiping away an errant tear.

Bron kissed their friend warmly. "The spray of wild pink roses on the shoulder looks almost real – you are so clever, Selena."

Trifena was regarding her daughter with obvious pride and, to hide her own glistening eyes, turned to Selena with some surprise.

"I thought you told me the roses were cream," she said.

Selena looked nonplussed. "Did I?" she wondered.

CHAPTER LI (51)

Hestig had said that he personally wanted to tell Vortin of the change of wedding plans, and had left to walk up to the Temple.

When he arrived, the High Priest was in his office and Veneta escorted Hestig there, leaving him at the door. He knocked, and entered at Vortin's bidding.

It was with great personal satisfaction, though he dare not show it in his face, that Hestig gave the High Priest the news. Vortin was speechless for a few moments then shouted, "I will not allow it!"

"I'm sorry," Hestig said, lowering his head to hide the gleam that he knew must be shining in his eyes, "but it has been arranged personally by Adrianus Maximus, ex-governor of Eboracum and once our master." He turned and left the room.

He had returned by the time Bron emerged from the workroom in her bridal gown. Overcome with love and pity for her, he told his daughter that she looked like a goddess. Her face and arms were paler than usual because she had spent so many weeks out of the sun, but even so her flawless skin was naturally bronzed. She carried an untidy bunch of wild flowers lovingly picked and tied by her sister - yellow charlock, purple clover and scarlet poppies, all intertwined with feathery white traveller's joy.

He proudly led the way to the temple, with Bron on his arm. Following behind were Trifena, Hestigys and Trifosa, with Selena bringing up the rear. She was apologising to everyone, as they were having to slow down for her because of an unexplained pain low in her back, which she said now reached round to her stomach.

Hestig knew that, since the visit of Asher, the Christian, Veneta had kept the temple dedicated to both the Roman emperor and Jesus the Christ clean and sparkling in its white luminosity. As the wedding party approached, Bron remarked that it seemed to be floating mystically in the September sunshine.

Soranus, in a new cream tunic, and his mother were waiting on the steps for the bridal party. A lump came even to Hestig's throat as he saw Soranus, whose face was alight with the love he felt for Bron. Campania was also wiping away a tear that had escaped down her cheek.

A crowd of friends was waiting at the bottom of the steps, Pulcher among them. Bron left her father's side to go to him and kiss him on the cheek, then she and Soranus led the way into the temple.

The priest smiled broadly as they arrived. He began the service in Latin but then tried a few stumbling words in the local dialect, which encouraged Kendrus to come forward and offer his translation skills. There was laughter when he translated 'cherish' as 'chastise' and that had to be sorted out before the service could continue.

The laughter drowned a disturbance in the crowd at the temple entrance. The wedding party had their backs turned, so did not see people moving aside to make way for a Roman, tall in stature, obviously used to deference, who was edging his way forward to the front. In his middle sixties, with black hair greying, his southern Italian face still extremely handsome, he was earning appreciative glances from the women around him. Their eyes signalled to one another, silently questioning, but all were shaking heads and shrugging shoulders in ignorance of his identity.

The priest was speaking about the difficulties of marriage, that no marriage was perfect, but with love and commitment they could sort out their problems. He obviously knew the circumstances, and Hestig wondered whether he sounded more confident than he felt.

Finally, he asked the young couple to hold hands and make their promises to each other. Bron promised to serve and obey her husband. Soranus grinned at the thought of Bron obeying him. When the priest reminded Soranus that his wife was the weaker member of the marriage, he smiled again, and promised to care for her in every eventuality.

Then they exchanged rings, looking shyly at each other. The priest asked them what they were waiting for, and Soranus kissed Bron full on the lips. Hestig guessed that it was their first kiss. Everyone clapped and cheered.

As the bridal party turned to leave, he heard Trifena's sharp intake of breath and followed the direction of her gaze. It was directed at the Roman. Hestig showed no surprise, nodded his head in recognition and mouthed a silent 'thank you' in Latin.

Adrianus Maximus returned the greeting briefly then Hestig watched as his eyes returned to Trifena. They slid from her to Bron, who was looking so radiant, and his face lit up with surprise and pleasure.

The newly married couple led the wedding party forward, unaware of anyone except each other. They reached the pillars and came out into the sunshine and the crowd of well-wishers parted to make way for them.

It was then that Bron came face to face with Adrianus Maximus, and the black eyes she looked into were her eyes and the mouth smiling so warmly was her mouth, and it was as if she gazed into a mirror. And then she knew. For the first time in her life, she had come face to face with her natural father.

CHAPTER LII (52)

Mouth open, Bron looked from him across to her mother. A flush spread over Trifena's face and neck as she lowered her eyes under Bron's scrutiny, and she wilted a little. Hestig put his arm around her waist, encouraging her to move forward down the steps, and the party continued on its way.

Trifena was able to whisper briefly to Veneta. The priestess waited behind until the crowd had dispersed.

When Trifena looked round during their walk down the hill, she couldn't prevent her heart from pounding as she saw Adrianus Maximus standing like a magnificent statue at the top of the Roman temple's steps.

The bridal party and their guests arrived at Campania's house on the far side of the market place. She and Selena had loaded a small table with homemade snacks and were busy serving local beer. While hurrying backwards and forwards between her guests, laughing and chatting as she did so, Campania was called outside and returned bemused with three slaves from the inn carrying bottles of fine red Italian wine, a gift from Adrianus Maximus.

Veneta arrived after everyone else, saying she couldn't stay long in case Vortin asked where she had been for the last hour, but she just had time to drink a glass of wine and join in wishing the couple happiness for the future.

When she left, Trifena followed her outside and they held a whispered conversation.

"Is he coming?" Trifena asked, a little breathlessly.

Veneta shook her head. "He asked me to tell you that he would be at the inn until sunset, when he would be returning to Calleva. However, he did agree to pay his respects to Vortin straight away."

"Good. Vortin could make trouble today, if he wished. The presence of Adrianus Maximus may deter him."

Trifena returned with disappointment to the party.

She knew that Bron had been trying to speak to her in private, so far without success because Trifena was avoiding her. Finally, however, Bron cornered her.

"Please, Mother – you've got to tell me about my father, my real father!" she pleaded in a whisper.

"Adrianus Maximus gave you life, Bron, but he is not your real father. You know who your real father is. I can't talk to you now, but tomorrow – I promise."

Bron had to make do with that for the time being.

It was a happy celebration. People guessed the reason for the hastily arranged marriage and, by their remarks, all assumed that Soranus was the father of Bron's baby.

Pulcher was making himself as helpful as he could, fetching and carrying and serving the guests and entertaining Louca's lively children. Trifena guessed that he was keeping himself busy to avoid thinking about Bron and Soranus together.

She knew, as Pulcher did, that Soranus had promised to keep his distance until after the baby was born. However, noticing the way the new husband was looking at his new wife and that he seemed unable to keep his hands from touching her arm or cheek at every possible opportunity, Trifena doubted that he would be able to honour his promise for long, if at all.

Among all the general conversation and activity, no one took any notice when Trifena called Pulcher aside and whispered in his ear. He looked troubled and she tried to reassure him.

"Don't be anxious, Pulcher, it will be all right. There's no one else I can trust." He nodded and left.

It was with tears and hugs and kisses that Trifena left her daughter in the care of Soranus and his mother and returned to Selena's house with her family. Even Hestig's voice was gruff as he bid them goodnight.

After Trifosa was in bed, visibly luxuriating in the extra space on the mattress now that her sister had moved out, and Hestigys had returned to Pulcher's house, and the sun was beginning to set, Trifena announced to Hestig that she was going out.

She guessed that he had been preparing himself for this moment since they arrived home, but he looked ashamed as he blurted out, "Trifena, don't leave me!"

"Dearest, I could never do that to you," she said. "I've got to go, but I'll be back. I promise you, I'll be back."

She flew down to the Stan as if she had suddenly grown feathers on her feet and was a young girl of nineteen again. He was waiting for her by the stepping-stones, in response to Pulcher's uncomfortably mumbled message. He held out his arms and she was about to fly into them and get lost in them again, when the memory of the look in Hestig's eyes checked her in mid-flight and she stopped out of his reach. His expression showed his frustration.

"Trifena," he said, "you look wonderful, you haven't changed a bit."

"I have," she said, "of course I have. I've had four children since you last saw me."

He nodded. "Julius Gaius reported to me everything Hestig told him. Does Hestig know you're here?"

"He guesses," Trifena replied. "He didn't want me to come, but I came anyway. He's afraid."

"With good reason." He took a step towards her and she didn't back away. "Trifena, how are you?"

"I'm well," she said, "and happy. How about you, Adrianus Maximus Brontius?"

"The same," he said, "well and happy." He smiled. "You know, no one ever uses my third name except you. Will you walk a short way with me?"

He didn't wait for her answer but turned, as if he knew that she would go with him. They began to climb towards the mere, into the setting sun. The orb was leaving the world in a blaze of red and yellow ochre. He took her hand and she could not gather the willpower to withdraw it.

"Bron is lovely," he said, smiling down at her. "Thank you for naming her after me."

"I had no choice – during her birth my thoughts were only of you. I longed for you, but you weren't there."

He didn't comment except to say, "You and Hestig should feel proud of yourselves for the way you've brought her up."

"Bron's a good girl," said Trifena, "in spite of the independent streak in her – I wonder where she gets that from!"

He laughed. "And I inherited it from my mother. It was a shock to see her looking so much like my mother. Do you remember her?" Trifena nodded and he continued, "I think she guessed about us, long before we knew ourselves."

They walked a while in silence, both engrossed in their memories. Then he stopped and faced her.

"I'd like to get to know Bron better. Will you send her to Calleva for two or three days before I leave? I can arrange for her to stay with one of the Christian women."

Trifena said she would think about it. "I'll have to ask Hestig," she said.

"Of course," he agreed.

"And we must also ask Soranus now that he is her husband," added Trifena, as an afterthought.

"Yes," he said again, and they continued their walk. "Did she know before today that I was her father?" he asked.

"We decided not to tell her, but by now I should think the whole settlement knows. As you two stood together it was like looking at two ears of corn on the same stalk."

"What will that do to your reputation?" he asked anxiously.

"I hope that people know me and the family well enough by now for it not to matter any more," said Trifena. "I don't know how Vortin will react, though, when he finds out, as find out he will – someone is sure to tell him."

"I went to pay my respects earlier today," he said. "He's a slimy character! Do you want me to do anything about him? I could, you know."

"We'll manage," Trifena replied. "We know enough about the hierarchy up at the Temple to bring the whole lot crashing down around their ears."

Her curiosity overcame her. "How's the mistress?" she asked.

"Ageing," he replied, "and not improving in temper."

"And your daughter? She and I were such good friends."

His eyes lit up. "She has five children now."

"Five?" gasped Trifena. "How *does* she cope with them all?"

He laughed. "Nannies, of course – one after another and sometimes two or three at the same time."

They had reached the mere and stood looking down into the clear water. The coins that had been sacrificed glinted in the setting sun.

"Did you hear what happened to the pearl and amber necklace you gave me?" she asked suddenly.

"No," he replied, so Trifena told him about the part it had played in buying Bron back from the Temple and how Vortin had returned it.

"You see," she said, "it saved her at a time when she needed it most."

"I'm glad," he said. "I've always felt so guilty at not supporting her."

"But you have," insisted Trifena. "It was your money that bought us the house and enabled Hestig to set up his pottery, and we're not finished yet. Hestig will get it all back."

"Yes, he always was a good worker," said Adrianus.

"I have the necklace here," said Trifena. "I took it to the ceremony so that you would be there in spirit if not in person. I never imagined for one moment that you would come all this way for our daughter's wedding."

She reached into the salmon-skin pouch hanging from her girdle and handed the necklace to him. He held it up to the light. It caught and held the myriad of hues flung across the western sky and blazed back, burnt sugar through orange flame to molten metal.

"The 'Gold of the North', they call the amber," he mused, "and the pearls, 'Silver from the South'."

Trifena could see reflected in the necklace only his burning passion and her tears on the night she had given herself to him and he had given her Bron.

"I remember when I bought it for you," he said.

"It was just after I found out I was pregnant," she whispered.

"Will you let me put it round your neck again?" he asked her, so appealingly that she couldn't refuse him, and she turned her back to him.

She felt his warm fingers on her throat and his hands caressing her neck as he fumbled with the clasp, fumbling for longer than was necessary, but finally fastening it. He took her by the shoulders and turned her round to have a look.

"It's beautiful," he said, "but it's not more beautiful than the neck that wears it."

"Don't," she said, "please don't."

"I must know," he said, "did you really love me or were you only afraid not to please your master?"

"I really loved you," she confessed, so quietly that he had to come close to hear. He placed his fingers under her chin and raised her face to his.

"And do you still love me?" he asked, holding his breath, as if fearing to hear an answer that somewhere in the dark recesses of his heart would deliver a mortal wound.

"Bron," she said, "I loved you then and I love you now. I have never loved anyone else, never, and it's unlikely to happen to me like that again, it was so perfect."

"Then come away with me, Trifena. Come and spend the rest of your life with me."

"Adrianus Maximus Brontius, you don't mean that," she said. "You have a wife and daughter and five grandchildren you obviously adore. I have my family, and also am soon to be a grandmother. Should we throw away all that for a moment's nonsense?"

"Yes," he said.

"You might think so now, but one morning you would wake up and ask yourself whether it was worth it."

"Never!" he remonstrated.

"If you care so much, why didn't you take me twelve years ago, when I would have followed you to the ends of the empire, instead of giving me away to Hestig?"

He was silent.

"Let's go back," she suggested.

When they were some way from the stepping-stones, he stopped and pulled her towards him before she could resist. He planted her hands on his chest and put his arms round her waist, and kissed her long and hard. Her arms slipped round his neck.

Trifena anticipated it was the last time they would ever see each other, and she thought he felt it, too.

"I meant what I said about Bron," he said, finally releasing her. "Just send me a message when to expect her."

Then he helped her across the stepping-stones and she set off to climb the rise, determined not to look back. But she did, just once, at the point where she knew the stones were about to be hidden from sight by the craftsmen's houses. She hoped he would still be there, where she had left him, but perversely also hoped that he had gone.

He *was* still there, standing quite still, obviously watching her progress. She waved and he bowed to her, then walked away in the direction of the inn.

Hestig was pacing the floor when she arrived home.

"I'm back," she said.

"I'm glad," was all he could find to say in greeting. "You've been gone a long time."

Trifena thought it had not been long enough, but perhaps too long.

"Did he want you to go away with him?" her husband asked.

"Yes, he did," she replied, "but as you see, I haven't gone."

"Why not?" asked Hestig, wanting to hear the answer he needed, but bracing himself for something more honest.

"Because you all need me, and Bron needs me –"

"– and she's his daughter," Hestig interrupted.

"No, Hestig, she's not *his* daughter, she's *our* daughter, and you're her father. It's you who's looked after her and cared about her, worked for her, and done everything in your power to keep her safe and happy. She's your daughter, Hestig, and all your acts of love throughout twelve years have made her what she is today – beautiful, confident, a loving, happy girl, a person in her own right. Yes, she has inherited from him, but all that he gave her you have brought to maturity."

"Gratitude – is that the only reason?" he asked with bitterness.

"There's also our home, or what was our home, and the business," she replied lightly, but seeing the pain in his eyes, was serious again.

"I love you, Hestig," she said. "I always have and I always will and I wouldn't do anything to hurt you, you must know that."

He noticed the necklace was round her throat again. "But not in the way you love him," he persisted.

"I'm here to stay," she smiled. "He and I won't be seeing each other again."

"Do you really mean that?" he asked.

"I do," she said, but it was her head speaking and not her heart.

"And there won't be a repetition of what happened before, when the young Roman tribune brought news from him, and we quarrelled for days afterwards?"

"No repetition," she promised.

For the first time since leaving Eboracum, Trifena thought she could begin, just begin, to banish thoughts of Adrianus Maximus Brontius beyond the horizon of her consciousness, to a place where one day they would no longer be of any significance.

"Trifena, my darling wife, will you come to bed with me?"

"Yes," she said.

CHAPTER LIII (53)

Next day, as promised, Trifena called to see Bron, who was looking relaxed and happy.

"Soon," Bron told her mother, "Soranus will start looking for a house to buy with Vortin's gold coins. I'm sure he had that in mind when he gave them to Soranus, so why shouldn't we use them? We won't be able to afford a house any other way." Trifena agreed.

"I don't want this baby, you know," Bron added. "All it's doing is making me feel sick. Campania made me oxtail soup this morning, which I was able to keep down. Soranus is being very kind. I made him sleep with a pillow between us last night and I forbade him to cross it." Trifena smiled to herself and decided it augured well for the future.

But then Bron looked troubled and explained, "I'm not ready yet, after Vortin. Mother, is it always bad like that?"

"Not if you love each other – you'll realise, in time," replied Trifena. "It might be difficult for you at first, though. You'll have to trust Soranus to help you."

"Did you and my father love each other? After all, you were his slave."

Trifena had prepared herself for this interrogation.

"I loved him very much – it was difficult not to, he was such a kind master. I believed he loved me – you would not have existed, otherwise."

"He didn't force you, then?"

"Never once."

"And Daddy loved you, too?"

"Yes."

"And you chose him."

"Your own father was married. He had a daughter my age. I was her slave. It was impossible to stay in the household once I knew I was carrying you. Adrianus would not turn me out, so he gave me to Hestig, freed us both so that we could marry, and helped us get back to Byden."

Then hesitantly Trifena told her daughter about the meeting on the previous evening between herself and Adrianus Maximus.

"We won't be seeing each other again," she said, "but he wants to get to know you, Bron, and to spend time with you in Calleva for a few days before he leaves. Your father has agreed and all we need to do now is ask Soranus for permission, then approach the carriers to see if one of them can take you. It will be a four or five-hour journey. Do you think you are up to it?"

Bron nodded excitedly. Soranus came in at that moment and she asked his permission. Trifena said this would probably be Bron's only opportunity to get to know Adrianus Maximus, so Soranus agreed, surprised and pleased at being consulted.

He had news of his own. He had been asked to meet Attryde at the forge that morning and she had put to him a proposition that surprised him and which he had come home to think about and discuss with his mother and wife.

Attryde had worked as a prostitute at the inn for more than two years but was not enjoying what she was being asked to do and was looking for an escape, any escape.

It occurred to her that Soranus, fourteen years old and now married and needing work, could be asked to take over the smithy, which was still closed. Everyone requiring the services of a blacksmith or farrier was grumbling about the inconvenience of travelling several miles further down the valley to the next forge. Having watched her husband then her young lover working the forge, she thought she could instruct Soranus, and for the rest he would learn as he went along. Then he should be able to earn enough to recompense her as his benefactor, as long as she lived frugally, and at the same time, support Bron and the baby.

With the encouragement of his womenfolk, Soranus returned to Attryde to accept her offer.

Two days later, Hestig and Soranus helped Bron into a carrier's wagon and she set off for her first visit to Calleva Atrebatum, the administrative centre of the *civitas*, or territory, of their Atrebate tribe.

The uncovered wagon swayed as the mule crossed the Stan ford and leisurely climbed the hill on the opposite side of the settlement. Bron waved to her husband and parents until the conveyance breasted the brow of the hill and all that was familiar to her was lost to sight.

First of all the track took them south-westwards to ford the River Lambburnan at Spinis, a roadside station, where the carrier loaded up some sheepskins. Then their road continued in a south-easterly direction to cross the Chenet River at Enedburna, and here the carrier halted his wagon outside a beautiful white, red-roofed villa.

With help from the owner's slaves, he unloaded a consignment of blue fineware pottery especially made by Hestig for this wealthy customer, incorporating the Roman official's own crest. The carrier was paid and the man and his wife waved to Bron as once again the wagon set off to join the road from Durnovaria, gradually turning eastwards, leaving the Chenet valley behind them.

Bron was so excited about her first journey and absorbed everything around her, just as Africanus had taught her. The road was busy and her arm ached waving to all their fellow travellers, local and Roman, on foot, on horseback or in farmers' and traders' carriages and carts.

The mule plodded onwards. Small farmstead settlements were scattered throughout the gently-rolling, green hills. Around the settlements lay large, golden, stubbled areas, as they lay around Byden, where spelt wheat had recently been harvested. The yield was taken as the corn tax, the Annona, that was required to feed the Roman army in Britannia and abroad. The farms' orchard fruits had also been harvested and the leaves on the trees were showing rusting signs of autumn.

A kestrel hovered above them against an overcast sky and the carter drew her attention to a skein of mute swans flying in the distance, on their way to the coast.

When their path led through woods, the mule taking his time, the carter sang in his deep country voice, enticing the blackbirds to join him, their rich, melodious, whistling song filling Bron with delight.

Aware of her condition, he kept apologising for the swaying and lurching of the wagon and an hour into their journey had to stop, as she was being sick over the side.

She slept on a pile of hides and sheepskins after that until woken by his kindly voice telling her that Calleva was now in view, only two miles distant. Sitting up eagerly, she stared at the magnificent town, surrounded on three sides by woodland.

The mighty flint and stone wall rose fifteen feet high, casting a shadow like a great cloud as they approached.

To give Bron a better view, the carrier turned right and skirted the perimeter until he reached the massive west gateway into the town, crenellated like the wall, with double entrance for vehicles and a postern for walkers. The carrier manoeuvred the wagon through bustling crowds and ox carts, past the ancient earth rampart behind the wall, and so into Calleva.

Bron's eyes opened wide in astonishment at the number of people in the streets and at all that she saw. On either side of the thoroughfare were narrow-fronted shops selling goods of every description, and one-storey houses. All were of timber frame, mud-and-wattle construction, supported on dwarf stone walls, with thatched or slated roofs.

Their route was intersected on both sides by street after street running at right angles, all thronged with people about their business, and children and dogs in the gutter, playing dangerously near passing iron wheels.

Towering above the houses and shops to their right, much higher than the town wall, Bron could see an impressive building with a long roof.

"The basilica," explained the driver.

They turned into one of the side streets, quieter than the wide thoroughfare, the houses larger. Through open gates and doors, Bron caught glimpses of peaceful courtyard gardens. She was enchanted.

The carrier reined in his mule outside the entrance to a stone building. On one door jamb was chiselled a bed and on the other a bunch of grapes, indicating bed and board.

Her father was waiting for her inside the inn. When the wagon arrived, he hurried out to greet her. Bron was very shy of him at first, but the genuine warmth of his welcome soon put her at ease. He paid the driver then gently lifted her down, took her bundle, and led her inside.

They walked into a low-ceilinged room with a fire in the centre hearth, surrounded by wooden tables and chairs. Her father had reserved a table in one dark corner, lit by a candle in a glass bottle and two torches on the adjoining walls.

He ordered vintage wine for himself, and water at her request. He encouraged her to chat about herself and her life in Byden, but she was too exhausted to converse, except to thank him for giving her this opportunity to 'see the world', as she put it. He smiled at this.

"Bron, this is not 'the world' – there is far more out there than you can begin to imagine. I wish I could show you Rome, magnificent Rome. Perhaps one day, when you are older, someone else will. I'm too old to make such promises."

He ordered a meal of local trout, roast venison with cooked pennycress and other wild vegetables, followed by a compote of soft fruits, which he said he was disappointed that she hardly touched. Then he walked her to the nearby home of Chrystella, a Christian who had agreed to look after Bron while she was visiting Calleva. Middle-aged, widowed, her children having left home, Chrystella welcomed Bron with open arms.

"She'll be all right, sir, I'll look after her," she promised Adrianus, then said to Bron invitingly, "There's a lovely soft mattress waiting for you. I'm sure you're ready for a sound night's sleep."

"Goodnight, sweetheart, I'll call for you in the morning," promised Adrianus Maximus, and left.

"You're so like him," smiled Chrystella as she tucked Bron into a real bed. "Anyone can see you're father and daughter."

Bron smiled back, wished her hostess goodnight, and was soon fast asleep.

CHAPTER LIV (54)

Chrystella did not wake her till the sun was high. She had already laid out Bron's clothes on the bed and, as soon as the girl's eyes were open, brought in warm water, olive oil and towels with which to wash, and invited her into the front room of the house as soon as she was ready.

"Your father has called once," she said, "and he's coming back again later."

Bron enjoyed a breakfast of hard-boiled egg, herb-flavoured curd cheese and bread and honey, ending the meal with sparkling well water. Refreshed, she eagerly awaited her father's return, looking forward to exploring the town.

As they set out, she thought how comfortable she felt with him, and he seemed at ease with her.

"Well, what do you want to see?" he asked her.

"Everything!" she replied enthusiastically.

"Then we'll start with the Forum – but you must tell me if you feel tired."

The Forum stood in the centre of the town, on a site of about two acres. They walked through the elaborate main entrance with its foot-high lettering dedicating it to the thirteen-year-old Emperor Honorius, son of Theodosius. They bowed before his new bronze statue, and so into the thronging market. Shops and offices ran along three sides, fronted by a shady, colonnaded walkway.

On the fourth side, the three-storeyed basilica stretched before them with its seventy-foot-high roof.

"The whole *civitas* is administrated from in there," her father explained, "as well as the region's justice system. Now, would you like to go shopping?"

After they had taken all Bron's purchases, mostly clothes for herself and the baby, back to Chrystella's and had lunched at the inn on delicious River Chenet salmon, it was time to look round one of the Roman temples and the Baths. Afterwards, Bron was tired and had had enough sightseeing for one day.

They returned to the inn for an evening meal, sitting at the same table as previously. As he was finishing his wine, Adrianus Maximus said to her, "Bron, a friend is coming to meet me here, to conduct some business. Would you mind waiting a while, and then I will take you back to Chrystella's. I'll ask for a basket chair and you can sit by the fire."

The evenings were drawing in and becoming chilly, and she was content to rest by the hearth in a chair they found for her, imagining pictures among the charcoal and flames, mesmerised and allowing the warmth to ease her aching legs and lull her into a dreamy world.

She suddenly became aware of her father's laughter and that he was calling for more wine, and sat up and took notice. Seated with him was a young Roman legionary about six years older than herself. Bron thought how handsome he looked in his uniform, with his muscular arms and strong legs, and she noticed the golden lights in his dark blonde hair, which was cut short without eliminating its natural curl.

The two men were deep in conversation, speaking Latin, which she did not understand. Her father handed the young legionary a vellum scroll, which he put under his helmet placed next to him on a bench.

When the wine was brought and poured, they toasted each other, then the young soldier turned his eyes towards her and raised his glass and put it to his lips, still looking at her.

"Oh, Bron," said her father. "You're awake. Come over and meet legionary Aurelius Catus. His father and I have been good friends for many years."

Bron shyly crossed to their table and sat down.

"Can we order you anything?" the legionary asked her. Bron shook her head.

"Aurelius and his cohort have been stationed here while on their way to fight for the emperor in Gaul. His father asked me to supply him with a good reference to help him make his way up through the ranks."

"A letter from your father, ex-governor of Eboracum, will carry great weight on my behalf," explained Aurelius Catus, speaking to Bron in the local dialect.

Quoting a blessing she had learned in the Temple, Bron said politely, "May the sun god protect you with his warmth and the water goddess grant you fast currents and fair winds".

"Thank you, I'll remember you for that blessing," he said, smiling.

"You asked me if there was anything you could do for me in return," Adrianus interrupted. "There is one thing."

"If I can," said Aurelius.

"My daughter is very dear to me. I'm far away in Eboracum, and the number of my days is shortening. When you return to Calleva after your tour of duty, I would esteem it a great favour if you would be at her service should she need you at any time. She could get a message to you here in a day if necessary. It would relieve my mind if I felt that there was someone in authority she could turn to."

"Of course," replied Aurelius Catus, "I would be happy to do that for you."

When Bron said goodbye to her father that evening, as they stood at the door of Chrystella's house, he suggested she had a rest next morning and he would take her to the amphitheatre in the afternoon.

"There are public executions there in the morning, which I wouldn't like you to see," he said, "but in the afternoon there will be bull and bear baiting – you may enjoy that. I've asked Chrystella to feed you and the little one, and I'll call for you after lunch."

Legionary Aurelius Catus arrived back at his quarters to learn that immediate embarkation had been ordered. In his haste to pack up and prepare for the march to the coast, he dismissed to the back of his mind the young girl he had just met and the promise he had made to her father.

CHAPTER LV (55)

As Chrystella and Bron breakfasted together next morning, Bron said she was curious. "Chrystella, Christ star, has that always been your name?"

"No," explained her hostess, "I changed it when I became a Christian. I'm an Atrebate, like yourself."

"What made you change religions?" wondered Bron.

"I became a follower of Jesus."

"We've got a Jesus altar in Byden," Bron told her. "He shares a temple with the Emperor. I was married at the imperial altar."

"We can go one better than that," said Chrystella. "We've got a special Christian church in Calleva. Would you like to see it?"

"Yes, please," replied Bron, "I've never seen a Christian church before – come to that, I've never seen much of anything before. I'm beginning to think that Byden is a dump. It's much more exciting here!"

Chrystella sighed, and Bron wondered why. She could not know that her new friend was sighing for the youthful years that Bron was losing before she had found them, through no fault of her own.

"You'll have excitement enough when your baby comes," Chrystella said.

The church where the Christians worshipped on Sundays was small, built less than twenty years previously, erected opposite the entrance to the Forum.

Round the church was a walled garden and Chrystella showed Bron the font where she had been baptised. It stood on a tiled base in front of the entrance and was protected by an overhead stone canopy supported by four pillars.

Inside the church, light came in through tall round-headed windows high up in the walls. Chrystella led her reverently along the red tessellated central nave to an altar standing on a fine black and white chequered mosaic.

A rough wooden cross stood on the altar. Bron was shocked that these Christians should worship an instrument of Roman torture. Perhaps it was a warning to them to behave, like putting a model of the wickerwork god on the altar of Byden Temple.

"Is that you, Chrystella?" asked a voice.

"Asher, how are you?" Chrystella greeted him. "Come and meet my guest, Bron. She's from Byden."

"I was in Byden last year," he said.

"I remember," said Bron. "Has your arm healed?"

"As good as new," he laughed, holding it out straight in front of him. "Kendrus is a very clever physician. Is Vortin still High Priest?"

Bron frowned and said that, unfortunately, he was.

"Bron, Bron," the old man murmured, more to himself than to her. "That name rings a bell. There was a priestess –"

"Veneta –" suggested Bron.

"That was the name. She was very concerned about you and asked me to pray for you. Well, you look all right."

"Except that I'm expecting a baby – Vortin's!" Bron blurted out.

Asher's eyes narrowed. "I'm so sorry," he said, "obviously I didn't pray hard enough."

They continued to look round the simple church until it was time for Chrystella to take Bron home for a meal. She invited Asher to join them, which he said he would be pleased to do.

When the pilgrim learned that Bron was returning to Byden on the following day, he asked if she would mind if he shared her conveyance.

"I might as well go to Byden as anywhere else," he said, "and the ride will save my old legs – and I'd like to talk to you."

Bron said she would welcome his company, if her father agreed. Adrianus Maximus gave his permission, then he and Bron set out for the amphitheatre.

They made their way on foot, in company with an ever-increasing crowd, towards the Londinium Road gate, but turned left before they reached it and passed through the great wall by means of a postern gate. Ahead in the countryside, the ten feet high, brown ironstone and flint walls of the colosseum rose like a giant torque.

The lively, noisy crowd was pouring through the entrance at arena level and circling up and on to the wooden benches. Adrianus Maximus put his arm protectively round Bron so that she should not be jostled, as they negotiated their way past knots of excited people who were clamouring to place bets with bookmakers. They found space to sit half way up the terrace.

To her left at ground level was a semicircular niche lined with flints where stood a statue of the good luck goddess, Fortuna. In a similar niche opposite strutted Mars, the soldiers' god, and above him sat the president of the games with his female companion.

The first spectacle in the arena, to settle the spectators, was a match between individual pairs of wrestlers, wearing little more than loin cloths and wrist bands. Bron was shocked to see that two of them were women.

When the crowd grew tired of them, they booed them off, and on came the gladiators, who marched with arrogance through their entrance to her right, which her father told her was called the Gate of Life.

Defending their bodies with shields, they attacked each other with the gladius, the Roman short sword, its double-edged blade two inches wide, but deliberately blunted. No longer fighting to the death, as in the old days, they could still inflict some nasty wounds. Those who finished with their opponents stretched full length on the sand received winners' medals from the president.

The crowd grew tired of them, too, and shouted for the animals. Slaves pushed in four cages with bears inside. Bron squealed with excitement. She had never seen a bear before. The slaves on top of the cages pulled up the barred doors.

Two of the great furry brown creatures shuffled out and lolloped around the arena, blinking in the sunshine, snuffling the air. The other two retreated to the back walls of their cages and the slaves had to clamber down on to the sand and try to poke and prod them out with long poles. The crowd roared its approval. When the bears got angry and rushed at them, the men ran out of their way and clambered up on the roofs of the cages again, much to the delight and laughter of the raucous crowd.

The bears did not want to fight and as the gladiators in pairs taunted them and pricked them from a distance with their javelins, they roared their terror and pain, sometimes standing up on hind legs and pawing the air, sometimes trying to find refuge in their cages, but by now the doors had been lowered and there was no escape.

One by one they staggered round the arena, trailing blood. Then the gladiators yelled as they hurled their javelins at them and soon all four were dead or nearly so and were dragged away by their hind legs to be skinned and butchered. The cages were pushed off and the sand raked.

"Not much of a fight," remarked Adrianus Maximus. "They were old and had had their teeth and claws pulled out. The young virile ones are probably too expensive for the provinces." Bron sat quietly.

Next came the bulls, running in by themselves. There was already blood on their flanks. The gladiators were waiting for them. The crowd was roaring again.

Adrianus Maximus must have suddenly realised that Bron was making no sound. He looked down at his daughter and gently brushed away the tears running down her cheeks.

"Bron, my dear, what's the matter? Don't you feel well?"

Bron shook her head, still crying.

"Do you want to leave?"

"Yes, please," she answered in such a tiny voice that he couldn't hear her in the hubbub of the crowd, but her distress was obvious to him.

Apologising for the disturbance, they sidled along the row of spectators. He held her hand as they walked down the wooden steps then left the amphitheatre the same way as they had entered.

"Something's upset you, Bron. What is it? You can tell me."

"It's those poor animals," she said. "They didn't want to fight and they didn't stand a chance."

Her father looked surprised, as if he had never given any consideration to the notion that animals had any feelings or rights.

"I'm so sorry," he apologised, confused and contrite. "I shouldn't have taken you in your condition."

Bron wailed, "And when that big bear fell, I felt the baby move!"

CHAPTER LVI (56)

Next morning, time for Bron's departure, her father sat with her as they waited for the wagon to arrive at Chrystella's door.

"I don't want to leave you," she confided, with tears in her eyes again.

He put his arm round her and kissed her curls. "And I don't want you to go, sweetheart, but you have people who love you waiting for you, and so do I." He had already told her that she had a half-sister and five nieces and nephews. "I'll be leaving myself tomorrow, for Eboracum."

"Will I ever see you again?" she asked, looking up into his face.

"I don't think so," he said, then added, "Bron, take care of your mother. She is very dear to me – you both are."

Because this was her last opportunity, she was emboldened to ask, "Did you *really* love her, you know, when –"

"Yes, I did, really – I still do. You were a love child."

"She loves you, I know, but she will never leave Father – my real father – I mean –" She stopped, confused.

He laughed. "It's all right, Daughter. Hestig *is* your real father. He is a good man. I would never have let her go to him if I had thought for one moment that he wouldn't care for you both." He sighed. "Perhaps in another life –"

"Chrystella says we only have one earthly life, and it's important to get it right, as it's the only chance we get."

"Chrystella's a wise woman. She probably knows."

Just then the wagon arrived, with Asher already seated at the side of the driver. Adrianus Maximus called to Chrystella, who had discreetly left them alone together for their goodbyes, then led Bron outside and lifted her into the wagon.

"Goodbye, dear," said Chrystella, reaching up and clasping Bron's hand between hers. "I hope we meet again."

"Thank you for having me," said Bron politely. "Goodbye, Father. I've had the most wonderful time. I'll never forget you."

"Goodbye, my dear, and good luck with the baby."

"I hate the baby!" said Bron. "He just makes me feel ill and stops me doing things."

He kissed her on the cheek and the tears started in her eyes again. She didn't know that he was keeping a tight rein on his own.

He and Chrystella were still waving when the wagon turned the corner.

The carrier and Asher tried to raise Bron's spirits by asking her riddles, but she would not be distracted until the great walls of the town had disappeared behind the rolling hills. Then she seemed to brighten a little and Asher clambered back and sat beside her.

They began to talk quietly together and soon Bron was telling him everything that had happened to her since his last visit to Byden – Iraina's disappearance and the cancelled Midsummer ritual, so that Bron had been able to avoid taking part, which Veneta had described as "a miracle" (Asher smiled at this), the strange way the settlement's money had been found so that Hestig had been released from prison, the fire at their house, the potency of the amber and pearl necklace, Vortin's attack on her, the attempted abortion, her marriage and meeting her Roman father. The pilgrim listened with sympathy, a frown frequently on his face.

Bron asked him about the cross on the altar in the Christian church.

"It reminds us that Jesus was crucified," he explained, "but we Christians believe that he rose physically from the dead on the third day, before he finally went home to Heaven."

Bron's thoughts wandered to her friends' graves in the wood. She had not visited them since leaving the Temple, although Pulcher had often laid bunches of flowers there for her. Now she asked Asher if he would visit them with Pulcher and say a blessing over them.

"Gladly," he replied, and added, "Where do you think they are now, your friends?"

"I'm not sure," answered Bron slowly, "but wherever they are, Sorin told me she will always be singing for me."

They crossed the last hill and Byden came into view. Soranus was looking out for them and, as soon as he saw the wagon, ran to meet her. For the past two days, Bron had almost forgotten that she was married.

"Bron, I'm so pleased to see you! I've missed you!" he exclaimed, holding her hand and running alongside the wheels.

"I've had such adventures!" she told him and, with words falling over each other, described all she had seen and experienced – all, that is, except for meeting the young legionary, Aurelius Catus.

When they reached the market place, she and Asher alighted. He went to find accommodation at the inn and she walked over to the house of Campania, her mother-in-law.

Soranus ran to tell her parents that she was back and soon the whole family, with Selena and Pulcher, came to welcome her home.

At the first opportunity, as he had promised, with Pulcher acting as his guide, Asher visited the graves of Sorin, Naila, Edreda and baby Aelia in the wood.

The dwarf watched as Asher prayed his quiet blessing, with face and hands uplifted. He was surprised at the simple informality of the intercessions and lack of sacrifice; neither were there ritual sentences nor elaborate protracted bowing.

After that, Asher was a frequent visitor to the graves, but not on his own. Pulcher ran messages between him and Veneta, and when the weather was dry, pilgrim and priestess met secretly, sometimes accompanied by Selvid when he would not be missed from the Temple. Pulcher sat on guard at a distance, straining his ears to hear and his mind to comprehend all that was being questioned and discussed. He knew that Veneta was sharing her new knowledge with Bron whenever they met. This was very often, because Vortin had instructed his priestess to keep him abreast of news concerning mother and baby.

Veneta always said in later years that the secret meetings in the wood were the beginning of the Christian church in Byden.

Soranus was working hard at the forge, under the direction of Attryde. Together they cleared up the rubbish from over three years of non-use, they cleaned the tools, and ordered charcoal from burners who worked in nearby woods, as well as supplies of pig iron.

The day arrived to light the fire and many of the village folk, as well as Bron and the family, came to support the young blacksmith. She felt very proud of her young husband as he stood confidently by the side of the forge, wearing a new cowhide apron that reached to his ankles, his open-toed sandals protected by cowhide coverings. Attryde stood at his elbow.

There was a hush as he struck flint against iron, one, two, three times, and long sighs of "Aaa-hhhh" as a spark flashed in the compacted sawdust. When well alight, wood was laid on top, then charcoal, piled high.

It didn't take long for the flames to spread in the charcoal, encouraged by a pair of old pig's-bladder bellows enthusiastically pumped, at one end of an air tube, by some of the village children, obeying or ignoring the comments and suggestions of those watching.

At last Attryde pronounced that the fire at the centre of the forge was at the correct temperature, burning orange-red. A length of smelted iron was placed in it, and soon Soranus began hammering under her direction, his left hand rolling the iron rod on the anvil towards himself while his right hand hammered out the thickness and shape required, constantly returning the rod to the fire for re-heating.

It was obvious from his lack of hammer rhythm and the final shape of the blade he had forged that he needed a lot of practice, but everyone cheered and clapped him on the back and wished him well, until his face burned as brightly as the fire.

Attryde was regarding him with misty eyes, knowing that the end of her employment at the inn was in sight.

Newly confident, Soranus decided it was now time Bron and he moved into a home of their own. Campania said she was delighted at this decision, but knew she would be lonely in her house without them. However, that problem was solved when her mother-in-law, Selena, suggested moving in with her when the young couple left.

Soranus chose a house that had been vacant since its owners died of the plague four years ago. He thought that this was a good arrangement as it was near Pulcher's home and their friend would be able to keep an eye on Bron when he was out.

It was a round house like most of the others in the settlement, with space enough for a pigsty, chicken coop, dovecote and lamb or calf pen, with a lynchet for growing vegetables and fruit. It had a curved, walled pathway approach to prevent cold winds from blowing directly through the front door, a stone wall base surmounted by turf interwoven through branches, and was topped by a thatched roof. On the beaten earth in the living room was a central hearth, and a raised platform provided room for their mattress bed, with another bedroom and the kitchen adjoining.

Soranus bought, repaired, then modestly furnished the property, using gold coins that had been a gift to him from Vortin on his wedding morning, and the young couple moved in. Pulcher was delighted to have them living so near and was available whenever they needed him.

So Selena went to stay with Campania, occupying her third home in ten months. After the disastrous fire that had robbed Bron's family of their house, she had abandoned hers to give them a home and had gone to live with Louca and Hoad. However, Louca had recently revealed that she also was expecting another baby.

She confided to Campania, "I can't say I'm sorry that your mother-in-law is leaving, she has become so difficult lately. She says one thing one moment and contradicts herself the next, and is often so irritable that she is causing trouble between Hoad and me."

"That's not like Selena," commented Campania.

Only a few weeks after her mother-in-law came to stay, Campania began to regret the arrangement, as Selena was so moody and sometimes could not be bothered to speak at all. However, Campania could see that she wasn't well.

"I seem to have lost all feeling in my hands," Selena complained one day. "See how limp they are."

Campania went to see their doctor, Kendrus, who looked worried when she explained Selena's symptoms, and asked questions about mood swings, internal pains and mental confusion.

"I've seen this many times before," he told Campania when he came to visit Selena and had made an examination. "She has a blue-black line at the base of her gums, and is complaining of a bad taste in her mouth. Have you noticed that her breath smells metallic?" Campania nodded agreement.

"There is no cure that I know," he said, "but we can only do our best. Give her olive oil when the pain is bad, and raw eggs beaten up in milk, or cream and flour beaten up together – and don't let her fall into a stupor."

"But what has caused it?" Campania asked.

"A natural poison, I think, but no one knows what," he admitted.

On a frosty afternoon two months later, Campania found Selena lying on the floor. She was in a coma, from which she could not be awakened, and died on her mattress in the arms of her daughter-in-law later that evening.

Having laid out and perfumed the body, using a recipe of salt, honey, myrrh, balsam and cedar oil, Campania walked alongside the litter as Selena was carried to the sacred pits. With her walked Trifena, Soranus and Bron, heavily pregnant, and other members of the family, friends and the choir from the Temple. There Selena was buried by the priestesses in accordance with the customary ancient ritual. Alongside her body, they laid materials and threads and craft tools, so that she could earn a living in the next life.

"My grandmother was special," said Soranus.

"And a dear friend," added Trifena.

Asher felt it was time to move on, and came to see Bron before he left to travel further north. "But I'll be back," he promised her.

Epilogue

AD 398 – A February Afternoon

Trifena lifted the hem of her thick woollen cloak away from the oozing mud as she squelched along the woodland path on Byden's eastern border. She jumped from patches of grass to narrow strips of dry islands where farm carts had ridged the soft earth – needlessly, because her stockings and leather shoes were already saturated. Intrusive drops of February rain slid along bare branches and dribbled down her neck, making her shiver.

She couldn't explain, even to herself, why she felt so restless, and now that she was out in the wood, why so nervous? Ashuba was smiling down on them. Even the wickerwork god posed no threat any more. The reason, of course, was her daughter's pregnancy. She knew that no harm would come to the family while Bron carried Vortin's baby. There was no need of any lucky charms or incantations.

The path to Shubinata's small temple branched off to the right. Trifena sniffed. There was a faint malodour among the misty trees. Puzzled, she tried to recall where she had encountered that smell before. It was not until she sensed movement among the tangle of undergrowth and raised her eyes from the mud that she remembered.

"Umbella?"

The hag materialised through the grey veil that hung between the trees and stood as she had, thirteen years ago, blocking the path. As always, she was swathed shapelessly in black, only her piercing dark eyes visible, but they were penetrating Trifena's soul.

"So, Trifena, our paths cross yet again," she croaked. "How is Bron?"

"She's well – no thanks to you!" Trifena accused her.

"I did what you asked, but there was a power greater than mine at work that day," countered the hag. "Didn't you feel it?"

"All I felt was the pain you caused my daughter by your clumsy attempt at abortion!"

"I wasn't the cause, as you well know. It was Vortin's lust and Vortin's pain. Of course, she has no choice." Umbella cackled at the inevitability. "Our venerated High Priest wants Bron, and Ashuba wants that baby, Vortin's heir. She might as well get used to the idea."

"Bron's married now."

"I know. But do you think that will make any difference?"

Trifena was nonplussed. "You told me once –"

" 'Sword, fire and total destruction' – I remember. What of it?"

"Your prophecy hasn't come true."

"How impatient you are for catastrophe! My prophecy *will* be fulfilled, make no mistake – but not yet. There are other fires to burn first."

"What other fires?" Trifena asked.

"Fires will rage where they should never have been lit. Your daughter –"

"Bron?"

"You have two daughters," Umbella reminded her.

"Trifosa is still only a child."

"Children grow up. You should inflict more discipline on that one. And what flames burn in your heart, my fine lady?"

Trifena's cheeks flared. "They are quenched!"

"Spent fires can be rekindled," Umbella cackled with relish, now in full flow. "Soranus, your son-in-law –"

"What about him? He's a good boy."

"When Bron burns, he will light more than one fire at Attryde's forge."

"You speak nonsense. You talk in riddles. I'm going home."

"Go – but you will have cause to remember that old Umbella isn't as crazy as you'd like to believe. Go, Trifena, go, and enjoy your peace while it lasts because there is coming a time when you will burn… all of you… burn… burn…"

The old woman's insane cackling reverberated round and round inside Trifena's head, making her so dizzy that the dark grey clouds caught in the top branches of the trees spun in circles above her.

She turned from Umbella and fled.

To be continued…

Author's Notes

- *Two spurs, which were fixed to the legs of fighting cockerels, have been found.* **p26**

- *Skeletons of babies are being found all over the site. Some will have resulted from miscarriages, others from still births, some newly born. Only one adult skeleton has been discovered – an elderly male lying in a crouched position in a shallow grave.* **p68**

- *Part of a rim of a cream-coloured jug, with the head of a goddess beneath it, was a surface find.* **p93**

- *There was a total eclipse of the sun on 20th November, AD 393. Totality lasted for two minutes – 9.46 to 9.48 a.m.* **p175**

- *Dog bones were found at the bottom of a pit. A copper-alloy ring was found on the spoil heap among material that had been excavated from a pit. The raised bezel was oval, sitting at right angles to the hoop. The decayed glass setting, imitating a sardonyx gemstone, fell out after discovery. Plain stones were frequently used to ornament rings in the third and fourth centuries.* **p249**

- *Lead was the then-unknown poison from which Selena died.* **p316**

Author's contact: iris.lloyd@virgin.net
www.irislloyd.co.uk